"I WANT YOU, KENDALL."

Jason's voice was low, thick. "I've wanted you from the moment I saw you stand up to that old bitch at the funeral."

For an instant, she felt a surge of satisfaction. Then caution rose in her. He'd thought she was Aaron's mistress. She didn't know if he still believed it, but if so, this could be some twisted way to strike at his dead father.

"A-Aaron," she stammered, "you think I—"

He hushed her with a finger to her lips. "I know better now. And Aaron has nothing to do with this. Nothing to do with us."

He gave her plenty of time to move, to dodge away, but she knew she would do neither. Nothing in her life had made her feel the way Jason's kiss had. The moment his mouth came down on hers, heat leapt in her so quickly it would have taken her breath away had not the feel of his lips against hers already done it. She felt the strong, gentle touch of his hands at the back of her neck as he threaded his fingers through her hair. She let her head loll back, feeling unable to do anything else. He deepened the kiss, his mouth moving coaxingly on hers.

But she didn't need coaxing. . . .

Wild Hawk

Justine Dare

A TOPAZ BOOK

TOPAZ
Published by the Penguin Group
Penguin Books USA Inc., 375 Hudson Street,
New York, New York 10014, U.S.A.
Penguin Books Ltd, 27 Wrights Lane,
London W8 5TZ, England
Penguin Books Australia Ltd, Ringwood,
Victoria, Australia
Penguin Books Canada Ltd, 10 Alcorn Avenue,
Toronto, Ontario, Canada M4V 3B2
Penguin Books (N.Z.) Ltd, 182–190 Wairau Road,
Auckland 10, New Zealand

Penguin Books Ltd, Registered Offices:
Harmondsworth, Middlesex, England

First published by Topaz, an imprint of Dutton Signet,
a division of Penguin Books USA Inc.

First Printing, March, 1996
10 9 8 7 6 5 4 3 2 1

REGISTERED TRADEMARK—MARCA REGISTRADA

Printed in the United States of America

PUBLISHER'S NOTE
This is a work of fiction. Names, characters, places, and incidents either are
the product of the author's imagination or are used fictitiously, and any
resemblance to actual persons, living or dead, events, or locales is entirely
coincidental.

BOOKS ARE AVAILABLE AT QUANTITY DISCOUNTS WHEN USED TO PROMOTE
PRODUCTS OR SERVICES. FOR INFORMATION PLEASE WRITE TO PREMIUM
MARKETING DIVISION, PENGUIN BOOKS USA INC., 375 HUDSON STREET, NEW
YORK, NEW YORK 10014.

For the people whose encouragement kept this idea alive.

But most of all for Hal Ketchum,
whose words and music gave me the key. Again.

Thanks, Heck.

Chapter One

❦

It snowed in Sunridge for the first time in twenty years the day they put the old man in the ground, and Jason West knew damned well the bastard had summoned it up himself.

He wondered what they would do, these people in their somber dark dresses and respectable suits and ties and coats, if he gave in to the urge to spit on the old man's grave. They were already staring at his jeans and boots, noses up, as if only good manners prevented them from sniffing disdainfully.

Or maybe it was just him they were staring at; he knew from a youthful photograph he'd seen of Aaron Hawk in a business magazine—accompanying one of those stories in which the old man had boasted of the Hawks' extraordinary history—that he bore a strong resemblance to the man who had fathered him. He'd resented it then, but he was enjoying it now. He liked knowing that everyone was wondering who he was, and that those who knew or guessed were wondering why he was here.

He lifted his head to look at them all, barely stifling a smile as he thought of their expressions if he were to follow through on the impulse to spit.

Or maybe not; there wasn't a single one of them who looked like they were here because they wanted to be. They might have come, but it wasn't to say a sorrowful good-bye. Good riddance, maybe. The smile threatened again. Then he wondered why he was bothering to restrain it, and let the smile loose. And savored the shocked looks he got.

Icy water from the rare snow, caught and melting in his hair, trickled down his neck. Yes, the old man had probably made a deal with the devil already, he thought as he tugged the collar of his dark, heavy coat up around his neck. But then, that shouldn't surprise him; Hawks had been making deals with the devil for centuries. By all accounts, the old man had been proud of it; if the stories were to be believed, they'd even sometimes beaten the devil at his own game. Jason had often suspected there were things in the Hawk history that were better left unexamined.

But no more. That history would come to an end. His plans were being buried along with that old man today, but he could still see to the end of it all. He'd made his own deal, not with the devil but with life—if there was any difference, Jason thought sourly—long ago. On the day he'd buried his far too young mother and sworn that someday his father would regret what he'd done.

But he'd left it too late. He'd been planning for that day of atonement for twenty years, and now it would never happen. He'd barely made it to the cemetery in time for the end of the funeral service. And the unexpected snowstorm that had hit the little town in the western foothills of the Sierra Nevadas. He wasn't sure which was colder.

He watched as the old woman standing closest to the edge of the grave stepped forward. She wasn't weeping. Her face was stiff beneath the wide brim of the black hat that accented the somber elegance of her dress. A dress that probably had cost enough money to feed a family for a month, he thought, recognizing a public declaration of wealth when he saw it.

And the lack of grief when he saw it. It didn't surprise him; he doubted that Alice Hawk had a tear in her. She wore the expression of a woman who'd lost the capacity for any soft feeling long ago. The only thing that showed in her face was hatred. And she looked as if she'd be very, very good at it. Better, perhaps, than anyone, except maybe the man in that hole. And, he thought with grim satisfaction, his son.

The thin, straight woman lifted a hand clad in a black

glove. Jason's eyes narrowed when he saw what she held: a single yellow rose. She tossed it into the open grave. He heard the faint sound as it hit the polished cherry-wood surface of the coffin. He looked at her face, in time to see the flash of rage that, for a brief moment, distorted her features.

And then he did the unforgivable.

Jason West laughed out loud.

Alice Hawk's head whipped around. She stared at him. The hand that had tossed the rose came up in a sweeping movement, tearing off the hat as if the wide brim blocked her vision, or she couldn't believe what she was seeing. He saw heads turning, felt the puzzled looks, but he never took his eyes off the old woman's face as she came toward him in a rigid-backed walk.

"You bastard," she hissed.

"Exactly," he agreed mildly. The epithet had lost its power over him years ago, when he'd come to terms with who—and what—he was.

"How dare you come here?"

He laughed again, finding her fury very satisfying. Her face reddened even more, and the hand that had held the rose came up as if to slap him.

"I wouldn't," he whispered, just loudly enough for her to hear and doing nothing to leash the menace in his low tone. "You just might wind up in that hole with him."

She cursed, a low, graphic obscenity that seemed out of place with her elegant appearance, yet fit utterly with her obvious rage.

"Yellow roses were my mother's favorite," he said softly, again just loud enough for her to hear. "How many do you suppose he bought her in all those years?"

"You bastard," she spat out again.

"I thought we'd covered that already. Surely you can come up with something better to call me. Son, perhaps?" he suggested in a tone that did little to conceal his laughter.

For an instant he wondered if he'd pushed too far, if his threatening words might come true. The woman's face grew redder as he stared levelly back at her, and the not-too-upsetting thought of an impending heart attack or stroke crossed his mind. What irony, he thought, should Alice Hawk actually topple over into the yawning hole that held her bastard—in the finest figurative sense—of a husband.

"Alice, please. Calm down."

The woman whirled on the source of the soft, quiet voice, none of her fury abated. The other woman—girl? Jason wondered, eyeing the slight figure he hadn't noticed before—didn't even flinch as Alice snarled at her.

"Calm down? Look at him! It's obvious who he is. He dares to show up here, now, and you have the nerve to tell me to calm down?"

The shorter woman never moved, nor did she raise her low, pleasant voice. Impressed with anyone who could face down Alice Hawk so coolly, Jason looked at her with a bit more interest than before, trying to see past the shadowy black veil that hid her face. He really hadn't seen her amid the small gathering, and wondered where she'd been; it wasn't like him to overlook any details. Even small ones like this petite woman.

"It's not worth making yourself ill," she said.

"As if you care. You probably had something to do with this outrage."

"Of course I care," the woman said, ignoring the accusation. And it was a woman, Jason decided; that voice was too low and rich. And no mere girl would have the nerve to stand up to the old battle-ax like this.

"Then go get Carver to throw him out. I will not have him here!"

"Why don't I just handle it?" the younger woman suggested coaxingly.

"I know what you're up to, and it won't work." Jason wasn't sure who the ominous words were directed at, himself or the woman who was handling the older woman's venom so calmly. "Just get him out of here."

Jason stood motionless as his father's widow stalked away. Then, as the smaller woman turned and began to come toward him, he crossed his arms over his chest, tilted his head, and watched her approach with interest. She was even smaller than he'd thought; of course, at six-two, many women seemed small to him. And as he

saw the way she moved, he wondered how he'd thought
for even a moment that she was just a girl. No, this was
definitely a woman. Definitely.

And you'll find me a bit harder to face down than
Alice Hawk, he promised her silently as she came to a
halt before him. She pulled back the veil that had hidden
her face, looked up at him with a pair of huge, sad gray
eyes beneath a fringe of dark bangs. There was no mistaking the grief there. Here, then, was at least one person
who genuinely mourned the passing of Aaron Hawk.
That it would be this somewhat fragile-looking woman
surprised him.

And then this woman he'd never seen before spoke,
and proceeded to startle him into a moment of uncon-
cealed surprised reaction.

"I'm sorry, Jason. She's very upset. But I'm glad
you're here. I'm Kendall Chase. We've been looking for
you for a very long time."

Kendall watched his eyes, in the way Aaron had taught
her. Eyes that were so much like the old photos she'd
seen of Aaron; eyes that gave the lie to anyone who
would challenge this man's parentage. Eyes that were
like his father's in another way as well; they held as much
cold harshness as those of the man who had bequeathed
them. Perhaps more.

But for a moment they had held surprise. At least
she thought so; the impression had been so fleeting, she
couldn't be sure. He couldn't think he wouldn't be recognized, not when, except for the nose, which in Aaron's
face had been much more prominent than his son's nicely
chiseled feature, he was the living image of a young
Aaron Hawk. So it must have been something else she'd
said. Perhaps he hadn't expected her to know his name?
Perhaps he hadn't expected to be approached at all, not
here, not now. Or perhaps, she thought, she was wrong
and he hadn't really been surprised at all.

"It is Jason, isn't it?"

"And just how," he said, his voice ominously tight,
"do you know that?"

Kendall smothered a sigh. She'd known this wouldn't

be easy, but now, as she stood looking up at eyes that were also as brightly, piercingly blue as his father's, as she stood looking up into a face that was set in lines of cold hatred, she began to see just how big a task Aaron had left her.

"I told you, we've been looking for you for a long time. Will you walk with me, please?" She gestured toward a narrow path that wound between the headstones and markers.

"So you can keep me from causing a scene on the old bastard's final day?"

"Partly," she admitted. "It won't accomplish anything."

"You don't know the first thing about what I want to accomplish." His voice was calm now, whatever other emotion she'd stirred vanished now behind that cool expression.

Kendall sighed aloud this time. "You're very angry, aren't you?"

"No."

The denial was abrupt, and too sharp for Kendall to believe it was true. She studied his face for a moment. She'd developed a knack for interpreting expressions, but this man's face was unreadable, as if he'd had as much practice as Aaron at hiding himself from others, despite the fact that he was so much younger.

She wondered what had happened to Jason in the almost thirty years since Aaron had lost track of his son. Whatever the course of his life had been, there had been some hard stretches, to put that kind of harshness in his eyes, Kendall thought. That kind of coldness wasn't inherited, it was learned. In unpleasant ways.

After a moment she began to move away, in the direction she had indicated. Jason waited, watching, and when she looked back at him he stayed motionless, long enough for her to understand he was telling her she couldn't assume he would do anything she asked.

"This isn't some power play, Mr. Hawk," she said, retreating into formality, hoping it would convince him even as she acknowledged the oddity of addressing anyone other than Aaron by that name. His reaction was immediate.

"My name isn't Hawk. It's West."

He didn't raise his voice, but there was no mistaking the biting undertone. West. So he had been using his mother's name, Kendall thought. Aaron had said his son had carried the Hawk name, at least until they left Sunridge, and had even sadly admitted it had probably been an attempt to force him to acknowledge the boy. She wondered if changing it to West had been his own choice, or his mother's. Knowing it for sure would have sped up the search, but they hadn't known which name he'd be using now, and so had had to check both. But she didn't comment, sensing he was in no mood to discuss his name. Or his father's. She went on as if he hadn't spoken.

"It's a simple request. I'd rather not talk to you with an audience."

He glanced at the several people who, although the service was over, had lingered, watching him, some curiously, some with open shock on their faces. After a moment he followed her.

As if the interruption had never occurred, Kendall went on speaking in a speculative tone. "I think I understand. Admitting that you're angry would give him far too much power over you, wouldn't it?"

Aaron had always called the accuracy of her intuitive guesses uncanny; she'd always laughingly said she just put together clues that were there for anyone to see. But clearly she had startled Jason Hawk; this time he couldn't hide his surprise before she was certain of it. Jason West, she corrected herself; she didn't want to offend him before she had a chance to complete her task.

"That old man," he said, his voice flat, "never had any power over me. None. Not when he was alive, and sure as hell not now."

Kendall shook her head, but said merely, "Then why did you come?"

He gave her a level look that warned her she was about to hear a truth he thought she wouldn't like.

"To spit on his grave."

Yet again he looked surprised when she wasn't

shocked. She simply nodded. "Aaron expected that. He'd be pleased to know he was right."

This man who looked so much like the man they'd just buried stopped in his tracks. His dark brows had furrowed at her use of his father's first name, but he only asked, "He'd be pleased that I came to spit on his grave?"

Kendall nodded, her mouth curving into a slight smile. "It means he mattered to you. One way or another."

"He mattered, all right. I've hated him all my life."

She was surprised he had admitted that, and he didn't look very happy about having done it either, so Kendall was careful not to let her expression change. Nor did she point out that his words gave the lie to his claim that his father had held no power over him.

"Aaron could always appreciate a healthy hatred. And he'd be the first to admit he'd given you ample cause."

Jason made an inelegant snorting sound. He backed up a step, and looked her up and down. For a moment Kendall felt as she did after walking into a high-level meeting, when the people present watched with careful nonexpressions as she took a seat at Aaron's right hand rather than starting to pour coffee or sharpen pencils. But she forced herself not to flinch or draw back from his intent study of her.

"Who are you, Kendall Chase?" he asked at last.

"Your father's executive assistant."

"Executive assistant?" The words were followed by a disbelieving laugh. "You're all of . . . what, twenty-five?"

"I'm thirty-three," she said carefully. "I've had the job since I got out of college."

Something flickered in his eyes, but she couldn't tell if it was surprise or amusement.

"And just what exactly did you do as his . . . executive assistant?"

She lifted a brow at him. "I think the title is self-explanatory."

He laughed again. "Oh, it's self-explanatory all right. I'll bet you were . . . indispensable."

She drew herself up to her full five-foot-two. She knew her size and gender sometimes made people—especially men—tend to belittle both her position and her intellect. She resented it, but hadn't yet found a way around it other than working harder to prove herself. And occasionally slicing the hapless offender to ribbons with what Aaron had called a whiplash tongue commanded by a razor wit.

"I was your father's executive assistant for ten years, Mr. . . . West. There wasn't a move made in or by Hawk Industries that I didn't know about," she said. "Aaron trusted me completely."

"Went a long way with pillow talk, did he?"

For a moment Kendall didn't understand. When his inference registered, she felt herself pale, then redden as anger flooded her. With an effort, she fought it down, drawing on the control she'd learned in the early years of dealing with Aaron Hawk, who back then could have given even this arrogant son of his lessons in rudeness.

"Now that was an interesting parade of expressions." Jason sounded mildly amused. "Can't decide between righteous indignation and insulted fury?"

"What I can't decide right now," Kendall said, proud that her voice was steady, "is whether you're worth all the effort Aaron put into looking for you."

His amusement vanished. "That's the third time you've said something like that."

"Pardon me, but it's at the forefront of my mind, after spending all these months watching Aaron so desperately trying to find you."

She'd thought his eyes hard before; but they'd been warm in comparison to the icy blue she saw now. "To find me?"

"Yes."

"Why?" he said, in a tone that told her clearly he didn't believe a word of what she'd said.

"You're his son," she said simply.

"And you expect me to believe he gave a damn about that?"

Kendall had to remind herself of her purpose here in order to bite back a sharp reply. She managed an even tone when she said, "I can show you the bills from the investigator he hired, if you like."

"Oh, I don't doubt you can. You don't look stupid enough to say that if you couldn't back it up."

She wasn't quite as successful this time in keeping the snap out of her voice. "Why, thank you. You certainly are a flatterer, aren't you?"

His mouth quirked. "I'm sure you didn't reach your position as—what was it again, executive assistant?—by being stupid." He looked her up and down in an assessing manner that was cool enough to be insulting. "Despite your obvious qualifications."

"This is about your father and you, Mr. Haw—West," Kendall said tightly, his exaggerated drawl of her title rating on her, "I would appreciate it if you would keep your assumptions about me out of it."

"And what makes you think I care one bit about what you would appreciate, Ms. Chase? I'm not the sucker for a pretty face that my *father* apparently was."

She drew in a breath. *Forgive me, Aaron,* she thought, *but this is really too much.*

"So that's all your mother was? A pretty face?"

He drew back sharply. He stared at her for a long moment. His face held no expression she could read, but his eyes held more than she could interpret.

"Touché, Ms. Chase," he said at last. "I think I begin to see why the old bastard kept you around." Something must have shown in her expression, because he added quickly, "In whatever capacity."

She wondered why he bothered to ameliorate it, but decided not to pursue it; her feelings were hardly the issue here. Aaron's final wishes were.

"No matter what you think, Aaron did try to find you. He'd been trying for months."

"I repeat, why?"

"I told you—"

"And I told you that I don't believe a word of it. If you're going to try and convince me that old man had some kind of late in life change of heart, you can forget it. He didn't even *have* a heart."

With an effort, Kendall smothered a small sigh. "So most people think."

Jason laughed harshly. "I noticed." He gestured

toward the milling people around the graveside. "Every one of them is here because they have to be, probably because that old battle-ax ordered them to come. You can see it in their eyes. There's not a one who really mourns him."

Kendall had no answer; it was true and she knew it. She stood staring at the gathered group, knowing each of them probably felt relief if not actual joy that the old man who had ruled their lives mostly by intimidation was dead.

"Except you," Jason added after a moment.

"Yes," she said softly. "I do mourn him. I knew an Aaron Hawk most people here would deny existed."

"I'll bet you did."

Her head snapped around; his tone made the inference unmistakable. He obviously hadn't abandoned his theory of who and what she had been to his father. And she'd had enough of it. More than enough.

"Do you insult any woman in a position of some power, or am I just lucky?"

"I never insult a woman who's earned a position of power, because I know she probably had to work twice as hard as any man to get there."

"I see. Insinuating, I presume, that I haven't *earned* my position?"

"Oh, I'm sure you have. One way or another."

She was known at Hawk Industries for her level head and her even disposition, both having been necessities for dealing with the irascible Aaron Hawk. She'd thought herself prepared for this encounter. But while she'd expected Jason to be difficult, she hadn't expected him to be worse than his father. And she was rapidly losing her grip on her temper.

"I will say this once, Mr. . . . West"—she drew the name out in the same exaggerated way he had said "executive assistant"—"I worked for your father. My duties were varied and extensive. But at no time did they ever include anything of a sexual nature. Your father loved only one woman in his life. And that woman was your mother."

A chill swept her at the look that came over his face

then; had Aaron still been alive, even he would have shivered, Kendall thought. She had never in her life seen a man look so grim.

"You may be beautiful, Ms. Chase, but you are also either a fool or a liar. And I don't suffer either gracefully."

He turned on his heel then, and never looked back as he walked away.

Chapter Two

❧

"He's been using the name West as you suspected. That should help. All of the other information is the same. And he's here, now."

"What?"

The startled query from the private detective Aaron had hired echoed in Kendall's ear. She understood his surprise. Despite what had seemed to be a genuine effort on her part to remain hidden, and the extreme coldness of the trail, George Alton had managed to methodically trace Elizabeth West's movements with her son up until her death in a traffic accident in Seattle twenty years ago, news that had devastated Aaron.

And he had discovered that after her dreary, meager funeral, her sixteen-year-old son had literally disappeared. When the county child services agency had gone to their small apartment to pick up the boy, he'd been nowhere to be found. No one had seen him since. He had, quite simply, vanished.

Alton had been unable to find even a thread to follow; he'd had to resort to simply searching out men of the right age, going on the assumption that the boy had stayed in the Seattle area. He had found a couple of Jason Hawks, whom he'd soon eliminated as possibilities, and far too many Jason Wests to check out easily or quickly. He'd kept trying, but had honestly told Aaron success was unlikely for a long time. Time Aaron hadn't had.

"He's here," Kendall repeated. "In Sunridge. He showed up at the funeral."

There was a pause. "If you know where he is, why do you need me?"

"First, I need to know where he's staying. And then, I want to know who he is."

Another pause. Kendall waited; Alton, a one time homicide investigator, was usually a very perceptive man. She knew he had understood her request when he didn't ask her to explain what she'd meant.

"Where he's staying should be easy enough to find out, especially if it's in Sunridge. Who he is could take some time. I'll get on it. Do you know how he got here? Or where from?"

"Afraid not. But he left the funeral in a dark gray coupe. It looked like a rental from the sticker on the bumper, but I couldn't see what company."

"What kind of coupe?"

She thought for a moment, trying to remember. She'd watched Jason West pull off his dark, heavy coat, revealing a black sweater over black jeans and boots, toss the coat into the back seat, and fold his tall, lean frame into the car. She'd been so intent on him, more than a little fascinated by the fluid grace with which he moved, that she hadn't really noticed the car.

"I'm not sure," she said at last, regretfully. "Something racy, though."

"Not a bottom of the rental scale compact, then."

"No," she said, "definitely not."

"Interesting."

She supposed it was, but she wasn't exactly sure why at the moment. "Maybe he's just too big for a compact. He's over six feet tall, I'd say." And nicely built, she added silently, with that kind of rangy muscularity that had always appealed to her.

"Maybe. Can you give me more of a description, now that you've seen him? It might help."

She laughed. "Use any picture of Aaron from thirty years ago, pare down the nose to a nice size and shape, and you've got it."

"That much of a resemblance?"

"Yes. There's no mistaking him."

"I'll get to work on it. I assume now that Aaron is gone, you'll be wanting the report?"

There was nothing in the man's tone except polite inquiry, but Kendall found herself a bit touchy lately, for reasons she hadn't yet had time to explore. She had a feeling it was more than simple uncertainty about her position now that Aaron was dead. She felt a jab of pain as she thought the word. *Dead.* That final, irrevocable, and last word. It put an edge in her voice.

"Is there a problem with that, Mr. Alton?"

"Not at all," the man said easily. "Aaron told me at the beginning that if it came from you, it came from him. I was just checking."

"Oh." Kendall felt a bit deflated, and more than a little silly for her reaction. "Thank you. Yes, I want whatever you find out. And I need to know where he's staying right away. I don't want him to leave before I have the chance to talk to him again."

"Again? You've already talked to him?"

"Yes. Briefly, at the funeral."

"But he didn't tell you where he was staying?"

"Jason West," Kendall said dryly, "stopped just short of telling me to go straight to hell."

She heard a chuckle, and could picture the expression she imagined was on Alton's face. The silver-haired, rather rotund ex-cop looked like everybody's ideal grandfather, a fact she suspected he used to wheedle information out of people who instinctively trusted his benign face and jovial personality.

"Like father, like son, is that it?"

"Precisely," Kendall agreed, although she wasn't sure if the son wasn't worse than the father had been.

"Usually people cheer up at the mention of that much money."

"We never got that far."

"Really? I find that surprising. You could charm a vulture out of his feathers."

Kendall laughed; Alton was given to absurd flattery couched in down-home observations that invariably made her smile. He was also very observant, and she

supposed he had sensed her tension earlier and was trying to ease it.

"Well, that sounds like a very useful knack," she said.
"But Jason West would have to improve his disposition
a bit before I'd lump him with the vultures."

"That bad?"

"Worse," she said ruefully. "You'd swear Aaron raised
him, and then he went bad."

Alton, who had dealt with Aaron by simply ignoring
his explosions of temper, letting the old man run down
before he went on as if it had never happened, laughed.

"Well, if anyone can get through to him, you can. You
had that old curmudgeon wrapped around your little
finger."

"No one," she retorted, "ever had Aaron Hawk
wrapped around their little finger. I just knew him better
than most people."

And it hadn't been easy, she thought as she hung up
the phone. The man who had been a powerful, charismatic figure as he'd built his fortune had become a set-
in-his-ways despot as he'd aged. It had been a long, difficult trek to get from the somewhat starry-eyed girl she'd
been, thrilled to get a high-level job right out of college
at a place the size of Hawk Industries, to the coolheaded,
unflappable woman who took Aaron Hawk's temper in
stride and got results when everyone else had given up
on making the old man see reason.

The question was, was she cool-headed and unflappable enough to deal with Aaron Hawk's son?

She didn't know. Her complex relationship with Aaron
had been built over ten years; she had only a very short
time to convince Jason West to listen to her. And he
didn't seem to be in a very receptive mood. He'd
laughed, hadn't he? At a funeral. Out loud, and in front
of the entire gathering. Not the act of a man who was
sorry or grief-stricken. But then, why would he be? He'd
never known Aaron. Had never known even the gruff,
quarrelsome man the rest of the world knew, let alone
the gentler man she had known, or the man who had
become nothing less than repentant in those final
months.

Jason West had never seen the softer Aaron, the man who had given an inexperienced girl the chance of a lifetime, the man who had taught her more than all her years of college ever had, the man who had spent hours in the evenings telling her incredible tales, legends of magic and the Hawks through the years, as if the two were inextricably and forever linked. Fanciful legends of his ancestors, and wizards and magic books, that she was half convinced the old man truly believed.

With a sigh, she went back to work. Her desk was cluttered with files, and papers buried her computer keyboard. She felt as if she were swimming madly through a sea infested with unknown threats. And one very large, very well known shark. Aaron had warned her she'd have to move fast, because it wouldn't take long for Alice to begin circling.

"She won't even wait until I'm cold, girl, so don't you either," he'd said the day he'd begun to dictate to her the lengthy and involved list of things he wanted her to do when the inevitable happened.

By that time she knew he was truly dying, and hadn't wasted any breath on efforts to deny it. And if he suspected that at night she wept in her room, he never let on. She knew he wouldn't have welcomed her tears. Aaron Hawk had never had time for such soft emotions as grief and pain—or love—in his life. Except for once, years ago, in the affair that had resulted in his son.

She brushed at her eyes; crying was not going to get all of this done. But she found she missed the temperamental old man more than she would have thought possible. Aaron might have been considered a bullheaded, intractable tyrant by many, but he'd always been fair to her. More than fair on occasion, she thought. There had been times when Aaron had been nothing less than kind and generous to her, although few would believe it.

Especially Jason West.

He would never believe the Aaron she'd known, the Aaron who had one day called her into his office, telling her to put on the voice mail and close the door after her. She'd known he hadn't been feeling well, knew he'd been seeing several doctors in the past few months, fear-ing a recurrence of the cancer that had cost him a lung two decades ago, so she'd been appalled but not shocked by his first announcement.

"I'm dying," he'd said in his typical blunt manner. Then, before she could even react, he had gone on to add the words that had startled her into not being able to react at all. "I only have a few months. I have to find my son before then."

She'd gaped at him. "Your son? You have a son?"

He'd given her the patented Hawk glare, which had lost its power to intimidate her the day she'd discovered the softness at the core of this ill-tempered man who had become so much more to her than a boss.

"You don't know everything there is to know about me, girl, even though you think you do. This goes at the top of that list I gave you. Nothing else matters as much as finding that boy. Nothing."

She had stared at him for a long moment, her only coherent thought being that he'd done it this way on purpose, delivered the news of his impending death quickly, then followed it up with what he knew would be a shock that would take her mind off of that news before she could react with any kind of unwelcome emotion.

Then a series of things had clicked in her mind, like the last number of a combination causing the lock's tumblers to fall into place. All the times when she'd come upon him sitting silently in his office long after the rest of the staff had gone home, looking at a photograph he always hid the moment she came in, all the times when she'd seen him searching crowds with eyes that had lost none of their quickness with age, when she'd seen him look sharply at a blond woman on the street, or in a restaurant, or a hotel ... and what she had finally realized was a ritual on October twenty-seventh every year.

"The yellow roses," she had whispered.

Aaron had stared at her as if stunned. "I swear, girl," he'd muttered at last, "you're as fey as that crazy grandmother of mine was."

She wished it were true, she thought now. She could use some supernatural foresight. Or maybe a little magi-

cal help, out of one of Aaron's Hawk family legends.
Help to get this list of Aaron's completed. To keep Alice
at bay until she did. To figure out what she was going
to do with her life now that Aaron was gone.

But she had a feeling she was going to need magic the
most to deal with Aaron's son.

"He's here."

"Who's here?"

Idiots, Alice Hawk thought. She was surrounded by
them. And this lawyer was no different. "Aaron's bastard," she snapped.

"Oh."

Alice's grip tightened on the telephone receiver. She
was paying Whitewood obscene amounts of money, and
all she got was "Oh?" She reined in her fury; the man
was the best she could do on such short notice.

"You're certain it's him?"

"Certain? Of course I'm certain. It was like looking at
a young Aaron all over again. The eyes, the hair, the
jaw, everything but the nose was Aaron—"

She broke off abruptly, hating herself for the pain that
had crept into her voice. She steadied herself and went
on.

"We have to move now, quickly."

"Move? We have the will, and the—"

"I'm not talking about that, you fool. I want him followed. I want to know where he goes, what he does, why
he's here."

"Wasn't he here for the funeral?" Whitewood asked,
sounding puzzled.

The man was a bigger idiot than she'd thought. "For
a man he hasn't seen in thirty years? If you think he
doesn't have more than that in mind, you're a fool."

"You think he's after something?"

"I know he is. Especially after he talked to that bitch
of Aaron's."

"Kendall?"

"Yes, *Kendall,*" Alice spat out, sick of the effect that
woman seemed to have on men even as stupid as
Whitewood.

"Do you think she told him?"

"I don't know. They didn't speak long. But I can't take any chances. There is far too much at stake."

There was a pause before the man said hesitantly, "What do you want me to do?"

"I want you to use those contacts you're always bragging about. Find someone to follow him. I want to know where he is at all times, in case we have to take action."

Another pause before a nervous query. "Take action?"

"Yes," she said, her tone biting. "A concept you're no doubt unfamiliar with."

"Well, I—"

"Never mind that. Just do it."

"Why don't you just hire someone to—"

"I have. You."

"I meant—"

"I know what you meant. And I don't care to discuss it. You're being well paid, now earn it."

Slamming down the receiver did little to ease her rage. The man was too dense to realize she couldn't hire someone who might be compelled to reveal her involvement later, or be tempted to blackmail her. She couldn't allow herself to be connected to this in any way. She shouldn't have lost her temper with the bastard at the funeral, but she'd been so startled—and outraged—at his unexpected appearance that she had, for one of the few times in her life, reacted impulsively.

But now she was back to her cool, far-sighted self. She would be prepared for anything, and she would deal with this as she dealt with every roadblock. Swiftly. And if necessary, permanently. Aaron's bastard had made a big mistake, coming here. He should have stayed away, stayed out of her life.

But then, he also should never have been born. And she just might have to see that he paid for that mistake, as well.

Jason didn't know why he was hanging around. He should have gone straight back to the motel after the funeral, packed his things, and headed straight for the airport. Instead, he'd found himself driving around the small town, up and down streets he hadn't seen since he was five years old. Not surprisingly, nothing looked familiar; even if the town hadn't changed, the perspectives of a five-year-old and a thirty-six-year-old were very different.

And he wasn't scared now.

It hit him strangely, that sudden gut-level realization. He didn't know where it had come from. But he knew it was true, knew that the five-year-old he'd been when he'd left Sunridge had been frightened. Very frightened.

Why?

He sat at the stop sign he'd halted for, turning the sudden insight over in his mind dispassionately. He felt no particular empathy for that child, felt nothing but a scornful disdain for his foolishness and naiveté. His vague curiosity was as much about what had brought on the revelation as to the cause of that long-ago fear.

He lifted his foot from the brake and let the car begin to roll forward so he could see past the bus stop on his right. The street he was at was a small, narrow one, and he didn't expect much in the way of cross traffic, but—

Gray Street.

The name fairly leapt off the street sign at him, triggering a surge of memories. Down two blocks to Simpson, just past the brick hardware store building and the chain-link fence that held back Monty, the German shepherd that had—

The German shepherd that had no doubt been dead for decades, Jason thought wryly, shaking his head to clear away the unexpected rush of remembered images. One of his earliest memories was toddling over to that fence, fascinated by the big black dog he'd seen romping with the owner of the building, tongue lolling joyously. He'd been lured by the sense of fun, a rare occurrence in his young life. But his adventure had taken a nasty turn when as he rattled the fence to get the dog's attention, the animal charged him, barely missing his outstretched fingers with snapping teeth.

His mother had explained carefully that the dog was a guard dog, and that he hadn't understood Jason had meant to be friendly, but it was a lesson that had stayed with him a long time: beware of smiling creatures of any kind. He'd encountered many friendlier dogs since then—more dogs than people—but the wariness remained. He figured it a blessing that he'd learned so early what many learned in a much harder way later in life, in a lesson that usually chewed them to bits.

And some, he thought as he made the turn, never learned at all. Some went through life trusting, giving, loving, never giving up even when it was all thrown back in their faces.

He hadn't meant to do this, hadn't meant to make this turn, hadn't made a conscious decision to follow this old route. But now that he had, he kept going. He kept going, remembering the day his mother had been so furious with him because he'd slipped away from old Mrs. Brooks, who watched him during the day, and had gone down to meet her at the bus stop. The bus stop he'd just driven past. It had only been three blocks from their apartment, but she'd been alarmed when she'd seen him there. He'd been very proud of himself, until he realized that he'd somehow badly frightened her. Or something had.

And she'd been frightened from then on.

He wasn't sure how he knew that, he'd been too young to really understand, but he didn't doubt it. It made too much sense. It must have been her fear he'd been feeding on; at barely five, he hadn't known enough to be afraid of anything except Monty. And the nights when he heard his mother crying in the dark.

The hardware store was still there, and a dog that could be Monty's twin, and probably was a descendant, raced along the fence line, barking at him warningly as the gray coupe he'd rented at the airport slowed to make the turn onto Simpson Avenue. He suppressed an instinctive shiver that made his lip curl in self-disgust, and kept going. He pulled to a halt in front of the small, four-unit apartment building on the corner, and for a time just sat there, staring. The building was obviously old, the yellowing stucco that had once been pristine white was laced with cracks like meandering lines on a road map, and the narrow walkway that led around the corner to the tiny back unit where they'd lived was broken and overgrown with weeds.

It had been shortly after the day he'd sneaked out to the bus stop that they had left Sunridge. It had been a rushed episode, carried out in the night, when he was too sleepy to even respond to his mother's attempts to make a game out of it. But even then he had sensed her fear, her desperation as she told him he had to be very quiet, because no one must know they were leaving. And her fear had transmitted itself to him, scaring him as only a child realizing an all-powerful parent is frightened can be scared.

He had his hand on the door lever, in his mind already out of the car and walking up to the building, before he realized what he was doing and slumped back in the seat.

"Jesus, West, you've really lost it," he muttered under his breath.

Going to indulge in a little sentimental nostalgia after thirty years? Maybe go knock on the door and do one of those emotional little displays human interest reporters loved?

"Hi, I used to live here, do you mind if I look around?"

Hell, anybody who opened their door to that line deserved what they got, which was more often than not a burglary later on.

Shaking his head in disgust at this unusual bout of reminiscence, he made himself look at the dreary little building clearly. It *was* dreary, old and run-down. It hadn't been new when he'd lived here; now it was a ramshackle structure that looked on the verge of collapse. And his mother had worked herself ragged to pay the rent for this place.

While his father had lived in the huge, expensive house on the hill, with the big circular driveway, servants to cater to his every whim, a fancy car to drive . . . and Alice Hawk to come home to.

Jason chuckled in savage satisfaction. Perhaps the old man had paid after all, he thought, remembering the furious, embittered woman who had confronted him at the cemetery. She was a forceful old broad, he admitted. She had to be—what, seventy something? Aaron had been sixty-eight, the newspaper had said, and he knew she was older. But she was as arrogant as her husband had been. More, even, judging from the imperious way she had ordered him thrown out. He hoped the old bitch had made Aaron Hawk miserable every day of his life.

And he wished he hadn't left his own little piece of retribution until it was too late.

Chapter Three

～

"How dare you?" Alice Hawk said imperiously. Kendall's jaw tightened as she stared at the woman glaring at her. It was all she could do not to turn her back and walk out, but she knew she couldn't. She had to see this through. It was going to be ugly, she could sense that. Long and ugly. But she had to do it. For Aaron. No matter what it took.

"How dare *you*!" she retorted. She gestured at the sheaf of papers the older woman held. "This is a lie, and you know it!"

A smooth masculine voice interrupted. "I beg your pardon, Miss Chase, but—"

"As well you should," Kendall snapped, wheeling on the polished, good-looking man. He was sitting to the right of Alice Hawk, who had wasted no time in moving herself into Aaron's seat at the mahogany table in the formal dining room of the big house. "Are you a party to this?"

"Perhaps you should explain," the man said, carefully shooting the cuffs of his white shirt out from the sleeves of his blue silk suit coat, so the heavy gold cuff links were more visible, "what you mean by 'this,' Miss Chase."

Kendall suppressed a grimace. Darren Whitewood reminded her of Mrs. McCurdy, the woman she'd lived with during her high school years. Not because of any physical resemblance, but because the gruff but kindhearted woman had always judged people by a simple rule: if their eyes were too close together, she didn't trust them. She never would have trusted Darren Whitewood.

"You know exactly what I mean, Mr. Whitewood. You are not Aaron Hawk's attorney, and this will does not represent Aaron's final wishes."

"But of course it does," Whitewood said smoothly. "It's in the correct format for the state of California; it's been signed, witnessed, and properly filed. And I've been appointed executor."

"Aaron wouldn't appoint you to clean his windows." Kendall eyed the man disdainfully. "Charles Wellford was Aaron's attorney for years. He is the executor of Aaron's estate."

Flushing at the insult, Whitewood glared at her. She smiled sweetly back at him. So much for the halfhearted pass he'd made at her when Alice had first brought him to the house, supposedly to deal with a little "personal problem." Personal indeed, Kendall thought.

"He *was* the executor," Whitewood said with exaggerated dignity. "I'm in charge now, at Mrs. Hawk's request. And it is now my duty to see this will executed properly. When Mr. Hawk passed on, Mr. Wellford wasn't available. He's in Europe on an extended trip." His lip curled. "But I'm sure you know that. Mrs. Hawk has told me repeatedly how ... efficient you are."

"Thank you. How sweet of you to notice," Kendall made her response intentionally effusive; she knew his words had been meant as an insult to her femininity—Whitewood appeared to be the type of man who thought femininity and any kind of competence were mutually exclusive—but she refused to rise to the bait.

And she found herself thinking of Jason West. *I never insult a woman who's earned a position of power, because I know she probably had to work twice as hard as any man to get there.*

Although he'd followed those words up with more of his distasteful insinuations, she found Jason's assumptions, rising out of his anger and his hatred for his father, and his not knowing anything about her, easier to stomach than Whitewood's view of women in general.

"I also know," she said, "that Aaron made an addendum to his will, negating several clauses and adding a new one, just three weeks ago."

"Oh, really?"

Kendall turned slowly. She recognized Alice's tone; she'd heard it before when the woman had succeeded in backing some hapless victim into an inescapable corner. It made the skin on her arms crawl to hear it directed at her.

"Yes," she said carefully. "I wrote it at his dictation, and witnessed it."

And she had been absurdly pleased that Aaron, even at his late date, had seen fit to acknowledge and bequeath a more than sizable piece of his personal fortune to his son.

"Did you?" Alice asked.

Kendall stared at Aaron's widow; the woman's eyes were dark and cold and radiated a force that made Kendall shiver. Evil, she thought, then laughed inwardly at her own fancy.

"Yes, I did," she said determinedly. If this was to be the first of her battles to carry out Aaron's wishes, then she wasn't about to start out faltering.

"Produce it."

"Mr. Wellford is Aaron's attorney. And his executor. The codicil to the will was sent to his office to be filed. So this will just have to wait until he can be reached in Europe."

"Do you, by chance, mean this?"

Kendall's breath caught as Alice lifted something from beneath the stack of papers before her. It was the brightly colored pasteboard envelope of the express delivery service she had used to send the signed and notarized codicil to Charles Wellford's office. She leaned closer and saw that the address label was the one she'd hastily handwritten before the courier had arrived to pick it up.

Her gaze went to Alice Hawk's face. The moment she looked into those eyes she lost all doubt that the woman had indeed intercepted the document; too much gloating triumph gleamed there for her to be bluffing. Kendall's hands curled into fists. She'd never trusted Alice, had always been wary of the bitter enmity she sensed every time she felt the woman watching her, but she hadn't thought she'd go this far.

"If you think that's the only copy, you're underestimating Aaron," she said.

"In forty-two years, I've never underestimated my fool of a husband," Alice said, not bothering to hide the acid in her tone. "But he often made the mistake of underestimating me. As have you, Miss Chase. You have the stock Aaron left you, and that trust fund he set up. Yes," the woman said as Kendall blinked, "I know about it. And what you no doubt did to get it."

She wasn't surprised that they knew of the fund Aaron had established, over her protests, but Alice's accusation startled her. God, Kendall thought, her, too? She'd always known the woman didn't like her, but she'd never suspected it was at least in part because Alice thought she was sleeping with her husband.

Kendall's stomach churned. Was there no one who could believe the kind of relationship they had really had? That it had been one based on mutual respect? That if anything personal had ever entered into it, it had been as much father to daughter as anything? She wanted to sink down onto the chair beside her, but fought the urge; she could not give Alice any sign of weakness.

"If you're after more—"

Kendall cut her off. "The only thing I'm after is seeing that Aaron's final wishes are carried out."

"I'd advise you not to waste your time contesting," Whitewood put in. "This will is unbreakable."

She gave the snake-smooth attorney a withering look. "I don't have to break it. The codicil Aaron added supersedes it."

"What codicil?" Alice interjected, her voice sounding as her face looked, triumphantly gloating. Kendall turned back to her, reading what was coming in the woman's eyes before she said it. "I think you'll discover that no such thing exists, Miss Chase."

Kendall watched the woman silently, her mind racing. Aaron had anticipated something like this, had told her to make copies of the codicil, to hide them—

Alice's laugh cut off her thoughts; it was a pernicious sound that made her skin creep again.

"If you're thinking of Aaron's little hiding places, be assured, I know them all. The compartment in his desk, the wall safe, all of them. I've known for years, but I'm not the fool he thought me. I waited until it was worthwhile to use what I knew."

Kendall schooled her face to impassivity. There was one thing the woman couldn't know, had no way of knowing, and no way of getting to even if she did. But if Alice were to even suspect there was still another copy—

"And even if you were able to produce a copy of this supposed addendum," Whitewood put in smugly, "I promise you you would never be able to prove its validity."

"I witnessed it myself," Kendall said, "as did Mr. Carver."

"Carver," Alice said, with a thoughtfulness too studied to be genuine. "Oh, I remember. He used to be our driver."

Kendall was very still. "Used to be?"

"Yes. Wonderful that he came into all that money, wasn't it? Now he'll be able to open his own mechanic's garage, as he's always wanted."

Kendall stared at Alice, unable to believe what the woman had admitted so easily. She had to be very, very sure she was going to win. Perhaps, Kendall thought grimly, with reason.

"You paid Carver? To deny that he witnessed Aaron's will?"

"Not at all. Although I'm sure he's grateful for the money, and wouldn't want to see any harm come to his benefactor."

Kendall took a deep breath. She knew they would have an answer for what she was about to say, but she had no choice. "You're forgetting one little detail," she pointed out. "I witnessed that document, too."

"Well, now," Whitewood said, again adjusting his cuffs, "I don't think that will be a problem. It is, after all, a forgery."

Kendall whirled on the man. "What?"

He gestured at the pasteboard envelope Alice held. "I can produce several expert witnesses to testify that that isn't Aaron Hawk's signature, but a forgery. A good one, but a forgery."

Kendall suppressed a shiver; Aaron *had* underestimated his wife's viciousness. She wanted to run, to race out the big front doors and into the fresh air, away from the miasma that permeated this room. But she couldn't. She had to stay, she repeated silently, and see this through.

She drew in a breath. She put her hands on the back of one of the heavy mahogany chairs, trying not to grip it so hard that it would betray her anxiety as she met Whitewood's smug gaze.

"But I know it's not," she repeated firmly.

"The court," Alice interjected, "is not likely to believe someone who's already been paid to produce this forged document."

Kendall froze, then relinquished her grip on the chair as she slowly turned to face the woman who had made her uneasy from the day she had moved into the guest wing of this house at Aaron's behest. Alice Hawk was laughing, that chilling, malignant sound again. The woman leaned back in her chair, confident, smiling.

"What," Kendall said carefully, "are you talking about?"

"Why, I'm talking about the fifty thousand dollars that was deposited in your bank account this morning, dear."

She didn't bother to question it; she knew that if she checked her account, the money would be there. Alice was, again, far too gloatingly triumphant to be bluffing.

"Deposited . . . by whom?"

"The one person who stands to gain from this forgery, of course."

Kendall let out a long exhalation. She should have known. "Of course. Aaron's son."

"His bastard," Alice corrected coldly.

Exactly.

Jason West's quiet, unperturbed reply to Alice's declaration of that same fact at the funeral echoed in her mind. She felt an unexpected stab of sympathy for the man who would no doubt scorn the emotion just as his father had.

"That hardly matters," Kendall said. "Legitimate or not, he would still have a legal claim. Anyone looking at him would know he was Aaron's son, but there are tests that will prove—"

"He'll forfeit any legal claim," Whitewood interjected smoothly, "when it's revealed he attempted to perpetrate a forgery for financial gain."

Kendall backed up a step, looking from the attorney to Alice Hawk. "Do you really think anyone will believe this? There's been no contact between them for over thirty years."

"I made certain of that." Alice's words seemed to hiss out. "And I will make certain that that tramp's son never sees a dime of my money."

Kendall's eyes widened. She'd made certain there was no contact? Had she known where Jason was? And somehow kept Aaron from finding out? This was something they had never considered. It was a moment before she could go on.

"What, exactly, do you expect me to do?"

"Why, Miss Chase," Whitewood said cheerfully, "we expect you to enjoy yourself. Fifty thousand dollars in accessible cash should keep you nicely until you're able to find work. As a bonus, we won't contest the trust fund Mr. Hawk set up for you."

"So I'm fired?"

"Yes," Alice said with great emphasis.

"Now, now, let's not look at it that way," Whitewood cautioned; Kendall wasn't sure if the caution was meant for her or Alice. "You were Mr. Hawk's assistant, and now that he's gone, you are, naturally, no longer needed."

"I see. And if I refuse your ... generous offer?"

"Then we'll see you in court," Whitewood said, with the first hint of ultimatum she'd heard from him. "With evidence that you were paid that fifty thousand to both produce this forgery and perjure yourself as to its validity."

She didn't doubt for a minute that they'd do it.

"And are you going to try and pay Jason West off as well?"

"He'll get nothing from me," Alice spat out. "Ever. We'll prove he paid you that money, that he committed a felony for personal gain. It will be his word, a bastard who doesn't even carry his father's name and is obviously out to get rich quick, against mine. And believe me, there's not a court in this county that will believe him. He'll go to jail, and you along with him."

Kendall didn't doubt that was true, either. Alice Hawk was a power in the county, and despite the supposed fairness of the American judicial system, she'd seen it go wrong too many times not to believe that the woman's influence couldn't do exactly as she said it would.

"You don't even know this man, but you'd send him to jail?" Kendall asked, shaking her head incredulously.

"He should never have been born!"

It had been a foolish question anyway, Kendall realized. If Alice had no qualms about falsely accusing her, after ten years of utter and complete loyalty to Hawk Industries, of aiding in a fraud, she would hardly hesitate to do the same to Jason West, a man Alice felt she had every right to hate.

She turned, ready at last to make her escape, knowing there was nothing further she could do. She took three steps toward the door, then stopped as an image of Jason from the funeral this morning, his eyes as fierce as his father's, his jaw as stubborn, his expression as forbidding, came to her. Perhaps Aaron had underestimated his wife. But Kendall couldn't help thinking that, just perhaps, Alice was also underestimating Aaron's son.

She looked back at Whitewood. "Just how do you plan to prove that Aaron's son could even put his hands on that kind of cash?"

Whitewood shrugged, and Kendall wondered how much that nonchalance in the face of extortion was costing Alice per hour.

"I have contacts," Whitewood said smugly. "Including someone who will testify he loaned him the money with the expectation of a large return out of what he would gain from this . . . crime."

Kendall shook her head in wonder. "You've covered it all, haven't you? You knew you couldn't deny he's Aaron's son. Even if there wasn't the resemblance, it's easy to prove with blood and DNA tests. So you set up this frame. Very slick."

"Thank you." Whitewood's tone was just short of smug.

"And if we have to," Alice said coldly, "we'll prove Aaron was of diminished capacity. With all that spouting off he used to do, telling those crazy stories about wizards and magic, it wouldn't be hard to do. To hear him tell it you'd think the Hawks had descended straight from Merlin."

Kendall turned her gaze on Alice, suppressing a shiver. All those lovely, wonderful stories Aaron had told her in those last months, Kendall thought. Those magical tales that made her long for the family she'd never had. Tales that had made her feel like she had as a child, when she'd read a particularly moving story that she wished with all her heart would be true. And this woman would use them to destroy Aaron's dream.

"You were right. Aaron did underestimate you."

"He *always* underestimated me." The woman gave her a baleful look. "Don't you make the same mistake."

Kendall stood quietly for a moment. She felt oddly detached, as if the shock of this afternoon's revelations had numbed her somehow. It enabled her to ask, with the appearance of only mild curiosity, "Do you really believe I was sleeping with Aaron? A man old enough to be my grandfather?"

"I knew my husband," Alice said icily. "He was a man of . . . carnal appetites. He could no more resist a pretty young face at sixty than he could at twenty-five."

"And of course it was impossible that a woman could ever resist him," Kendall retorted with some acidity.

For an instant, the barest fraction of time, surprise flashed in Alice Hawk's eyes. Surprise Kendall knew instinctively was at the mere suggestion that a woman, any woman, could have resisted Aaron Hawk. And Kendall realized, with some shock, that Alice had loved Aaron.

As much as she was capable of loving anyone other than herself, the woman had loved Aaron.

And he had despised her.

Unbidden and unwelcome, a pang of sympathy stirred in her. Sympathy for Alice Hawk, who had been married to a man she loved for forty-two years, and he'd never loved her back. And within a year of their marriage, he'd begun an affair that had lasted seven years. An affair, he had told Kendall, with the only woman he'd ever really loved.

And suddenly Alice Hawk's venom was pitiable.

Or would be, she thought, if it weren't for the fact that it could very well ruin two innocent lives: her own, and that of Aaron's son. Again that image flashed in her mind, of a face younger than Aaron Hawk's, yet with eyes no less fierce with intelligence, no less hard with implacability.

"And what if Aaron's son decides on his own to sue for a piece of Aaron's estate?"

Whitewood looked uncomfortable. Kendall watched as his gaze flicked to Alice, then away. He shifted in his chair and shot his cuffs yet again. Then it came to her. She looked at Alice.

"You didn't expect him, did you?" she said. "You were as surprised as anyone else when he showed up at the funeral."

"Who would have thought he would have the gall to show his face back in Sunridge?" Alice snapped.

Kendall glanced at Whitewood with a new kind of twisted respect. "You pulled all this together in one afternoon? Perhaps you're smarter than Aaron thought."

He called her a name under his breath, a crudity she decided to ignore.

"So you haven't had time to work that out yet?" she asked. "What you'll do if Jason decides to take you on himself?"

"Jason?" Alice sneered. "You're on a first-name basis already? Perhaps you've already decided to throw your lot in with him. If you have, I warn you, you've made a serious mistake."

Kendall's lips curved sightly, into what Aaron had al-

ways called her "decision" smile, because, he'd told her,
it usually meant she'd made up her mind and the devil
take the hindmost.

And Aaron's words were in her mind when she said
softly, "In this case, I think it's better the devil I don't
know than the ones I've just met here."

She turned her back on them and started toward the
door.

"I won't have it," Alice called out after her angrily.
"He will never see a penny of Hawk money. I'm warning
you. If you value your miserable life, stay out of this."

Kendall stopped then. She turned slowly back, giving
Alice a level look. "Are you threatening my life, my
health, or merely my freedom, Mrs. Hawk?"

"Just be warned. I'm not as gullible as my husband
was. I know what you want. You got more than you
should have, and if you're smart, you'll settle for that
and get out."

"Mrs. Hawk," Kendall said softly, "you don't know
the first thing about what I want."

And it wasn't until she was out of the room that she
realized she had virtually echoed Jason West.

Chapter Four

~

Alice Hawk sat in silence for several minutes after Kendall walked out. She took a few deep breaths, knowing she must control her anger. Her heart was pounding in her chest, and she felt the heat of rage flushing her face. Her doctor's warnings rang in her mind, and she made an effort to slow her racing pulse.

"She could be a problem," Darren Whitewood said.

She glanced at the attorney. He was a preening, conceited fop, she thought, with his silk suit and ostentatious gold jewelry, and could be trusted only to look out for himself, but he had one great advantage over Charles Wellford; he could be bought.

"She always has been," Alice said.

An understatement, she thought as she gathered up the papers from the table. Her feelings about Kendall Chase had always been somewhat confused. When she'd first come to work for Hawk Industries, Alice had recognized a keen intelligence, akin to her own. Kendall's seeming innocence and apparent naiveté had made Alice consider the possibility of using her herself, as a conduit to Aaron, who had, infuriatingly, closed himself off to her more and more over the years. But the girl's loyalty to the man who had hired her for a position far above her qualifications was unswerving, and Alice's early attempts at subverting her had only turned the annoyingly honest young woman against her.

So Alice had been relegated to watching Aaron lavish time and attention on the girl, teaching her, training her, treating her as if she were nothing less than his heir apparent. As if she were the child Alice had never been able to give him.

An old, familiar pain jabbed at her. It was, she supposed, the true source of her ambivalence about Kendall Chase. She had seen the gradual softening in Aaron, seen the gentleness with which he had treated the girl, a tender regard she herself had never known from her husband. It had enraged her, and no matter how many times she told herself she was a fool to be jealous of a mere child, she knew she was.

She had never really believed Kendall and Aaron had been involved sexually, but it was easier to believe in a replay of that kind of betrayal than in the idea that Aaron was capable of simply loving the girl for herself. That was an emotion she didn't want to believe him capable of, because it made the knowledge that he had never loved her even harder to accept. And made the relationship between Aaron and Elizabeth West too painful to even contemplate.

She knew Aaron had married her for money. Forty-three years ago Hawk Manufacturing, the foundation company that had grown into the conglomerate known now as Hawk Industries, had been in severe financial trouble. It was her father who, with the unerring eye that had rarely failed him, had picked twenty-five-year-old Aaron Hawk as a minnow that would one day become a shark.

But it was then that Alice Caruthers had done the one unforgivably stupid thing she had ever done in her life; at age thirty she had, with all the intensity of an infatuated teenager, fallen in love with the dynamic, darkly handsome, young Aaron Hawk. She had picked him as the only man she wanted, and had set her powerful father to the task of doing whatever it took to get him for her.

Once he'd gotten over his surprise that she was interested at all in a man, Harold Caruthers had energetically set about doing as she wanted, pleased in a manner that was hardly flattering that his plain, sometimes unpleasant daughter might be taken off his hands long after he'd given up hope of her ever marrying. Alice knew this, she'd heard him say it often enough, but she was so blindly enamored of Aaron Hawk that she hadn't cared. Nor had she cared what it took to get him.

"You've got a vicious tongue, Alice," her father had told her more than once during the delicate negotiations. "Curb it, or this will all be for nothing."

And she had. She'd become what she despised: a simpering, awestruck female. She even went out of her way to try to appear attractive, something she'd never cared about before. She had masked her true nature and become quiet and submissive, to convince Aaron that the money he needed would not come with a price tag too high.

And she had won. She suspected her father had done some underhanded manipulating beyond the open money negotiations, even, perhaps, managed to make Aaron's financial problems more urgent, but she didn't care. All that had mattered then was that Aaron was hers. It had never occurred to her that the price she would pay might be too high.

She had thought Aaron could learn to care for her, if not love her, and that it would be enough. But then she had learned of his affair with Elizabeth West, and knew it wouldn't happen. She thought then that if she could give him a child, it would be enough. But after years of trying, of going through every kind of painful procedure developed, she had failed. Then she had learned Aaron's mistress had borne him a son, and she had known that nothing would ever be enough.

And Kendall Chase had driven the truth of her failure home to Alice every day of the last ten years. The girl's presence, and Aaron's response to her, proved to Alice that had she been able to produce a child, her own position would have changed. That as the mother of a child Aaron loved, she, too, would have received some of that love. Love that had been given instead to the slut who had become his mistress. And then to the girl who had become his surrogate child. But never, ever, to Alice.

The only thing that could have been worse would have been the presence of Elizabeth West's bastard. Aaron's son. The blood child she had never been able to give him. The son who was a living, breathing symbol of Aaron's unfaithfulness. The personification of his hatred for the woman he'd married and his love for the woman he'd taken as his mistress. The son Alice Hawk hated with a passion that sometimes threatened to overwhelm all else in her life.

The son who was here now.

"You'll never see a dime of my money," she muttered fiercely.

"Ma'am?"

Darren Whitewood's voice had taken on that lubricated tone that he used when he was trying to calm her down. She hated it; it reminded her too much of her father's condescension. But it was her father, she reminded herself, who had enabled her to keep Aaron under control all these years, by legally tangling up the money he'd funneled into Aaron's business so completely that while it might be in Aaron's name, the reins were in Alice's hands.

"I said that bastard will never see a dime of my money," she repeated, in a voice so savage Whitewood looked at her warily. "I'll see him dead first."

Jason picked up his leather carry-on bag from the motel-room floor, then yawned yet again as he put the bag down on the edge of the bed. He'd only gotten four hours of sleep last night, between the late-night flight from Seattle and the funeral, and he probably shouldn't be driving even the few miles from here to the small airport. But he didn't want to stay one more night in this town, either.

Then why the hell did you spend all afternoon driving around in it?

The question had rung in his mind with annoying frequency ever since he'd pulled into the parking lot of the motel shortly after dark. And that frequency had increased while, fighting off yawns, he pondered whether or not to throw the few things he'd brought into his bag and get out of this place right now.

He yawned again. He didn't understand it. He'd gone longer than this without sleep, had done it often, and hadn't felt this tired. And he hadn't changed time zones, so that wasn't the reason. Yet there was no denying the fact that he felt enervated, utterly drained. And he'd never experienced such an odd heaviness in his legs and arms, as if there were some unseen force pressing down on him. As if he were moving underwater. Dazed. Almost drugged.

He glanced up at the vent for the room's heating and air-conditioning, idly wondering if there'd been some malfunction that was slowly poisoning him with some invisible, deadly combination of gases. He'd heard about such things often enough. But there was no rush of air from the unit, no sign that the heat was even turned on, despite the unusual chill outside. He yawned again. Then he turned around and sat on the edge of the bed beside his bag, even knowing it was a mistake, that he'd probably fall asleep sitting up. Resting his elbows on his knees, he lifted his hands to rub at his weary eyes, then let his head rest against his palms as he yawned yet again.

He didn't know how long he'd been sitting there when at last he lifted his head again. And immediately saw something he hadn't noticed before, something he couldn't remember even unpacking. The book that lay on the dresser. He stood up and took a step forward. And stopped dead.

He hadn't brought a book with him.

And he was certain it hadn't been there when he'd come into the room.

His gaze shot back to the vent he'd been studying. It was as unhelpful as before.

Had he actually dozed off while he'd sat there with his head down? Without realizing it? Long enough and soundly enough for someone to come in and leave the book on the dresser without him knowing it?

"Not likely," he muttered under his breath. He slept lightly, a legacy from years of sleeping with one ear open, in places where menace was the norm, not the exception.

Only then did he realize the odd lethargy was gone; vanquished by a surge of adrenaline at the thought that somebody had been in here without him being aware of it. It was impossible, yes, but that hadn't stopped his body from preparing for the threat in a rush, throwing off that overpowering sleepiness and kicking sluggish muscles back to life.

But how had the book gotten here?

He turned on his heel and strode swiftly toward the door, yanking it open to stare out into the chill night. There was no one in sight, no doors just closing, no cars just now pulling out of the lot. No sign that anyone had just been here and was leaving in a hurry.

The snow hadn't lasted, there were only traces of it left in the cold night shadows of the trees and buildings, and on the occasional car coming down from a higher elevation with a thin layer of snow still coating its roof. And not a soul was outside moving on this chilly night. Out on the main road, cars whirred by, but within his immediate field of vision, nothing moved.

The cold air from outside washed over his face, chasing away, for the moment, even the natural weariness of lack of sleep. His mouth quirked. Maybe he was just so tired he was hallucinating. He glanced back over his shoulder.

The book was still there.

He backed up into the room and examined the door's lock. Both it and the dead bolt looked intact and undamaged. He shut the door against the cold, and with a wry expression locked it. Again. He turned and walked back to stand before the dresser.

There was nothing uncommon about it, it was the same as thousands of other pieces of furniture in thousands of hotel and motel rooms around the world. Bland and unremarkable. Except for the fact that between the television and the tray that held an empty ice bucket and two glasses was a book that couldn't possibly be there.

He had to have blacked out. It was the only explanation. He would have thought perhaps he had in fact been drugged, except for the fact that he hadn't eaten or drunk anything since the rather minuscule breakfast on the plane. Maybe that was it, he thought. Maybe he'd been too out for it from lack of both sleep and food.

Maybe.

But he couldn't deny what he was looking at. And if he was a little hesitant to add the evidence of touch, it was only because he was being cautious. This was obviously meant as some kind of a message, and the fact that it had appeared here, now, under circumstances he couldn't explain, was more of a coincidence than he was willing to accept. He didn't like things he couldn't explain.

He stood staring at it for a long time. From all sides. It appeared to be an ordinary book, although it looked very old. It was, in fact, rather beautiful. It was bound with what looked like real leather, deep, rich, and dark blue. The pages looked thick and heavy, and were gilt-edged in a way he thought was rarely done anymore. And, oddly, there was no sign of a title, or an author, on the cover or the spine.

But most importantly, he thought wryly, there was no sign of any wires or other devices to indicate the thing might be more than just a simple book. Lethally more. He reached out and nudged the book a fraction of an inch. Nothing happened. And it wasn't any heavier than he would have guessed.

God, you're a suspicious son of a bitch, aren't you?

He laughed silently at himself. *Stir up a few old memories, and you're looking for trouble behind every door. Bombs in every book.*

You're not on the street, dodging stray gunfire or the cops anymore, West. Give it a rest.

But he wasn't a fool, either. True, he just might have dozed off—even sitting up—long enough for someone to sneak this book in here. But how had they gotten in in the first place? He knew he'd locked the door when he closed it; he always did, it was a habit learned long ago. There were no signs of damage to the door, and the window to the outside was still tightly shut and wedged with the burglar bar.

A key. It had to have been somebody with a key. Perhaps it had been a helpful motel employee; perhaps someone had left the book at his door and they'd moved it inside.

That made sense, he thought. A helpful employee with a key. His tension eased slightly. It was hard for him to believe he'd slipped that quickly—and sitting upright, yet—into a heavy enough sleep not to hear the turning of a key in a lock. Hard for him to believe he hadn't sensed the presence of a person in the room, or that person leaving. Hard to believe it had all been done without saying a word to him.

But it was impossible for him to believe any of the alternatives.

He'd analyzed it enough, he decided abruptly. At this point it didn't matter how it had gotten here. What mattered was whatever message was being sent. Maybe it wasn't even directed at him. Maybe the whole thing was a mistake. His mouth quirked at the idea of whoever had gone to all this trouble to stealthily deliver it getting it in the wrong room. He reached out and picked up the book.

And nearly dropped it.

It felt ... odd. For an instant it had felt as if he'd touched a person, some living being, instead of an inanimate object. As if he'd just shaken hands with someone he knew and trusted, few though they were in the world. He dismissed that nonsense immediately, but the feel of the book as it lay in his hand wasn't quite so easily ignored.

It was . . . warm. Well, not exactly warm. It wasn't really any warmer to the touch than the temperature of the room, but somehow, holding it, *he* felt warmer. And he couldn't define the strange sense of peace that seemed to have overtaken him. Peace was a state he'd had little experience with in his life, inwardly or otherwise. He'd always thought it overrated, the first step toward complacency, to be followed rapidly by failure through softness.

But he couldn't deny this sensation was alluring, this gentle easing of tension and strain, this feeling that perhaps he wasn't as alone as he sometimes felt—

"Damn," he muttered. "Where the hell did all that come from?"

He almost slammed the book back down atop the dresser; only the realization that to do so would give too much reality to his unexpected and inexplicable reaction stopped him. He was just tired, that's all. It was exhaustion that was making him feel so strange, nothing more.

Determinedly he switched the book to his left hand and opened the cover with his right.

The pages were, as he'd thought, of an unusually

heavyweight paper, with almost a parchment feel to them, paper made heavier and stiffer by the gilt of the edges. The inside of the cover was lined with an even heavier paper that also made up the first page, a paper marbled with an unusual design in shades of blue that blended with the color of the cover. A design that seemed to change as he looked at it, to flow and fluctuate, until he almost thought he was seeing something more than a random design, thought he was seeing images there, shadowy figures of people, seeming to move as he looked. He felt an odd light-headedness, shook his head sharply, and the pattern settled down into a merely intriguing flow of lines and ripples.

"You," he pronounced to the empty room, "have got to get some sleep."

He flipped the heavy inner page over and found a blank sheet of the heavy, gilt-edged paper. He turned it as well, looking for the title page. Or what should have been the title page. Instead he found a picture of a couple, dressed in costumes of some kind, clothing that made him think of misty forests, castles, and high stone walls, for a reason he couldn't fathom. The man had long, dark hair and a strong face marked with a thin but very visible scar that ran from his right temple down to his jaw; the woman had even longer, but lighter hair, a wealth of it, and eyes that he instinctively knew, despite the fact that the picture was in black and white, were blue. Vivid blue.

It made no sense to him that he knew that. He stared at the picture, only now realizing that what he'd at first thought to be an old photograph was instead a drawing, a drawing so finely done and so incredibly detailed that it seemed impossible that it had been done by human hands.

A computer, he thought suddenly. That must be it. It was some kind of computer-enhanced image, taking an old drawing and augmenting the image until it looked almost like a photograph. It was effective, he had to admit, especially bound as it was in this ornate, antique-looking book.

But that still didn't explain why he was so certain the woman's eyes were blue, when the image before him was not in color. He stared at her, barely noticing the petite size of her next to the man, who appeared to be at least a foot taller than she, with shoulders to match his height, and a look in his eyes that didn't bode well for whoever had given him that scar on his face. He vaguely noticed as well the length and sheen of the woman's hair—red, perhaps?—and the shape of the slender body beneath the vaguely familiar layers of some kind of flowing gown, but he couldn't look away from her eyes. Wide and bright beneath arched brows, they were fringed with thick, soft lashes, and looked strangely familiar. It was like looking at a picture of something seen so often it didn't register anymore.

Then it hit him. It was like looking into a mirror. And seeing his own eyes look back at him.

He nearly slammed the book shut. He needed to get out of here. To get away from this place; it was playing tricks on his mind. He had never in his life been given to the idiot flights of fancy he'd been experiencing since he'd arrived here. The tangible evidence of his senses, purified in the exacting filter of his brain, had been all he'd ever trusted, all he would ever trust. He had survived when many hadn't because of it; it had gotten him where he was; he wasn't about to change now.

It's a picture, West. A damned picture, that's all. What the hell is wrong with you?

He set his jaw as he moved his fingers, aware even as he did so that it shouldn't take this much determination to simply turn a page in a book. In his haste, he instead turned several pages at once.

He felt better as soon as the picture was hidden. But his forehead creased as he looked at the page he'd wound up on. It took a split second for him to realize what the intricate network of lines and blurred names and dates, printed at odd angles, were. He turned the book sideways and the names came into focus, confirming his guess. It was a family tree.

The Hawk family tree.

Fury welled up in him. He slapped the book shut with a sharp, jerky motion. He flung it across the room fiercely, feeling a grim satisfaction as it hit the far wall with a heavy thud and fell to the floor.

He should have known. He should have known the old man wouldn't be able to resist one last jab, one more twist of the knife in the back of the son he'd never known, never acknowledged. He didn't know how his father had pulled it off, didn't have to know; he knew all he needed to know. Aaron Hawk had sent his final message.

These are the real Hawks. You're not one, you never were, and you never will be.

"You made a mistake, old man," Jason muttered, the words coming out loud in spite of himself. "You thought I wanted to be a Hawk, when I'd slit my own throat before I'd let anyone hang that name on me."

He stood motionless, looking at the book on the floor for a long, silent moment, fighting the rage that he hated himself for feeling.

Admitting that you're angry would give him far too much power over you, wouldn't it?

Kendall Chase's words echoed in his mind, taunting him with their truth. The man was dead, so his son's anger couldn't reach him now. Not that it would have, even had Hawk still been alive; he'd meant nothing to his father. Less than nothing.

And he'd be damned if he'd spend another night in this town that the Hawks owned. He whirled around and began to move with swift purpose. He'd be out of here and back home before morning.

Kendall saw the brightly lit windows and neon sign first, then spotted George Alton's small white truck backed into a space in the parking lot of the convenience store across the street from the Sunridge Motel. When Alton had called her with the information on where Jason West was staying—a simple matter of calling in some favors owed him by the few motel owners in town, favors earned by his discretion in his years on the small local police force—she had gotten here as soon as she could, but there had been some necessary delays.

"Is he still here?" she asked as she pulled into the

space beside him, thankful that the man had arranged his car so they would be facing opposite directions, enabling them to talk without having to step out into the chilly night air. A cop thing, she supposed.

Alton nodded. "Room nine."

Kendall breathed a sigh of relief; she'd been afraid she would miss him, but she'd had to pack up the things in her room at the house that were indispensable to her; she didn't trust Alice not to toss them out or lock them up now that she'd so gleefully given Kendall her walking papers. And she'd had to stop by Aaron's office at Hawk Manufacturing and gather some essential items from there; it was only a matter of time, she knew, before Alice realized some key things were not in Aaron's big mahogany desk in his study at home. Then she'd go looking, and the office was the first place she'd think of. Especially since she no doubt now had Aaron's keys.

"Leaving town yourself?" Alton asked, eyeing the boxes and luggage piled in the back seat.

"Not yet," she said. "But I think it's only fair to tell you, Mr. Alton, I no longer work for Hawk Industries."

Alton merely lifted a shoulder negligently. "Hawk Industries didn't hire me. Aaron Hawk did. And he made it clear from the beginning that this was purely personal, and had nothing to do with the business. And," he added, " 'Mr. Alton' is my father."

"All right." She smiled. "George."

It seemed Aaron had, as always, chosen well. She remembered when she first realized that half the reason Aaron was so rough on the people who worked for him was to see which ones would stand up to him and which ones wouldn't. The ones who did were the ones who rose up the ranks; the others were either intimidated into quitting or remained in their low-profile positions, praying not to draw the attention of the big boss. George Alton didn't seem the type to be intimidated by much of anything, despite his easygoing demeanor.

And while he had a demeanor that was anything but easygoing, neither did Jason West. She turned her head to look across the street at the motel. She could see the racy gray coupe parked in front of a room with the lights on. A room separated from the next obviously occupied one by several dark and apparently vacant rooms in between. She wondered if it was by chance or Jason West's choice.

"I found out from my airport source that he came in on a flight from San Jose," Alton said, "connecting from Seattle."

Kendall looked back at him. "So he does still live there?"

Alton shrugged. "Can't be sure yet, but it's a good possibility."

"We had several Jason Wests on the list from that area, didn't we?"

Alton nodded. "I called an old buddy of mine who has an agency in Tacoma, after I found out they were living up there when his mother was killed. I faxed him the list, and what little we knew about the kid. Now that we've got more to go on, we'll find out who he is and where he's been." He grimaced. "Too bad we didn't get through the list before Aaron died."

Kendall didn't think her expression changed, but Alton gave her a kindly look of sympathy.

"You have someplace to go?" The man gestured at her baggage. "I know you were living up at the house, so you're not just out of a job, you're out of a roof, too."

Kendall smiled, touched by the man's concern. "I'll be fine." Her smile turned wry. "If all else fails," she added, pointing across the street, "it seems they have plenty of rooms."

Alton frowned. "That might be all right for a while, but not long-term. If it's money, with Aaron dying—"

"Really, I'll be fine, Mr. . . . George. Aaron paid me very well, and his investment counselors have given me some good advice over the last ten years."

It was true; if she was careful, she could live nicely for years on what she had. After that there was the trust fund, if she needed it. But unemployed idleness was not a goal she aspired to. She needed to work. She had to work. She'd find something, somewhere. Someplace without an Alice Hawk to deal with.

At the ugly reminder, she pondered telling Alton the

whole story, of the codicil and the threat of a criminal frame that was hanging over her head. It seemed wise to have someone else know, but she wasn't certain she should make that decision alone. Jason was involved in this as well, although he didn't know it yet. He had a right to decide what should be done. She would wait, she thought, for now.

Besides, she had other things to attend to first. Like living up to the trust Aaron had placed in her. She looked over at the motel again.

"You want me to stick around while you talk to him?" Alton asked.

She glanced back at him. "I don't think that will be necessary."

Alton didn't look very happy. "I heard he got kind of ugly at the funeral."

Kendall sighed. No uglier than the widow, she thought. "Can you blame him?" she asked aloud.

Alton shrugged. "I suppose not. But that doesn't mean you should try and deal with him on your own."

Kendall, again touched by the man's concern, considered his words. "He's very angry. And bitter. He hated Aaron, and he had every right to. But I don't think he's violent."

"If you're wrong, you could be sorry. In a way, you still represent Aaron Hawk, and he might decide to take it out on you."

"That's just a chance I'll have to take." She turned her gaze back across the street.

The lights in room nine went out.

Seconds later, the door opened, and she saw a tall man in a dark coat step out, carrying a small black leather bag. She couldn't see his face from here, but she knew it was Jason West; she recognized the easy grace of his stride.

"I'd better go if I'm going to catch him," she said hastily.

Alton only nodded. But Kendall had a feeling that, despite her assurances, the man wouldn't move a foot from his present position until he was certain she hadn't been wrong. Until he was sure the man who had apparently inherited his father's temperament wasn't prone to violence after all.

Chapter Five

~

Jason unlocked the door of his rental car, tossed his bag on the passenger seat, then threw his coat in on top of it. The brisk air was reviving, although he hadn't really yawned again since he had started to pack. In fact, he hadn't felt at all tired since he'd tossed that damned book across the room.

His mind shied away from that topic; he still had no explanation of how the book had gotten into his room, at least none that didn't involve accepting that he'd been so out of it he hadn't seen or heard someone come in. He might be a long way from the streets he'd once fought to survive on, but he didn't think he'd gone that soft. Nor did he have any explanation for the puzzling lethargy that had overtaken him in the room; a call to the desk had resulted in an insistent reassurance that nothing at all was wrong with the heating system.

And he was gaining nothing by wondering about it. The message had been sent and received. That was all that really mattered.

He glanced over at the motel office and adjoining coffee shop about fifty yards away. He decided to walk; it would finish the job of waking him up for the drive to the airport.

He shoved his hands into the pockets of his jeans as he started walking. Coming here had been a really stupid idea in the first place, he thought. He had work he should have been doing, instead of haring off on this futile trip. He didn't know what had possessed him to do it.

Maybe he'd just needed to see for himself that he'd

left it too late. Maybe he'd needed to see the old man buried, before he could really believe it was over, that now he'd never have the chance to make Aaron Hawk pay for what he'd done. Somebody long ago had said revenge was a dish best eaten cold, but he'd let it chill too long. Somehow he'd never expected the old man to die. Everything he'd ever read about the man had emphasized his seemingly unceasing vitality. Aaron Hawk was too damn mean and stubborn to die.

But he had. And now that his target was dead, Jason didn't quite know what to do with the festering hatred that had propelled him through most of his life.

He settled his bill, paying for the extra day without comment, although he wondered why the clerk was looking at him so oddly. And why he was looking at his credit card like he'd never seen one before. But the man suddenly seemed to realize he was acting strangely, and became briskly efficient.

Jason stepped back outside and started to walk back toward his car. He shrugged, as if that would rid him of the odd prickling sensation that had begun as he'd walked to the office and now had settled between his shoulder blades. Although it had been a long time, he recognized the feeling, that awareness of something not quite right. It was a sensation he hadn't experienced in a long time, and no matter how he told himself it was just this place, stirring up old memories, it wouldn't go away. He hadn't lived here long enough to pile up enough memories to cause this, he thought, so why was it happening, this extra hum of awareness that had him looking over his shoulder?

When he looked forward again, he thought he saw the reason for it.

His steps slowed when he saw the second car, a dark-colored expensive-looking European sedan parked at an odd angle, close behind his rental car in a way that would prevent his leaving. He felt tension snake through him, and the hair on the back of his neck stood up in primitive reaction.

Then he saw a movement next to his car, a small, slender shadow, and a completely different kind of tension spiraled through him, accompanied by an unexpected heat. He ignored it, thinking he also had his answer now to how the book had so mysteriously appeared in his room.

He knew it was Kendall Chase. He didn't know how he knew from this distance, any more than he knew why he had been so certain the eyes of the woman in that book had been blue. And in fact, it was the same kind of certainty, deeper than gut level, and beyond explanation. And he still didn't like things he couldn't explain.

He started walking faster.

As if she'd heard his steps, she turned her head to look in his direction. The glow from the amber lights that lit the parking lot poured over her, giving her slender body an oddly ethereal look. Above her shoulders, all he could see was the satiny gleam of her hair, still pulled back in the demure bun that had restrained it at the funeral, the pert tilt of her nose, and the soft, inviting shape of her mouth.

Inviting?

Oh, yes, he murmured inwardly. Definitely inviting. Not only inviting the kind of kisses that inevitably led to other things, but inviting other carnal explorations that were still illegal in some states.

He knew it hadn't suddenly warmed up, he could still see his breath when he exhaled into the chilly air. But the sweater that had seemed barely enough when he'd stepped outside now seemed too heavy, and his body too warm beneath it.

He had better, he thought with a detachment he had to work far too hard to achieve, attend to his libido when he got home; he'd obviously ignored it for too long. He'd find some willing lady who didn't look upon a mutually pleasing romp as a down payment on a lifetime, and that would solve that.

But first he had to get Kendall Chase out of his way.

She was standing beside the driver's door as he came to a halt, her hands tucked into the pockets of some sort of heavy, sheepskin-lined leather coat. Beneath it was a light-colored sweater that rose in a soft, loose turtleneck above the collar of the coat. She wore dark-colored leggings that emphasized the slender curves of her legs. Not that he needed reminding of their shape. He remembered all too well the feminine calves, narrowing to slender, delicate ankles that had been nearly all of her he had seen beneath the bulky dress coat she'd worn this morning. She'd worn heels then, but moderate ones, just enough to curve her legs deliciously.

And he, he thought wryly, had better get out of this town *fast,* if he was now reduced to standing here cataloging the undeniably attractive attributes of his father's mistress. Or executive assistant. Or whatever she really was. He didn't know. He didn't care. It meant nothing to him. Nothing. Except to prove that the old man had good taste. Kendall Chase was a beautiful woman.

So that's all your mother was? A pretty face?

Her words came back to him so clearly that for a moment he thought she'd spoken them again. But he knew she hadn't, she'd only been staring at him determinedly, her delicate-looking jaw set firmly, since he'd stopped in front of her.

And something about the way she was looking at him made him even more uncomfortable about the distinctly sexual turn his thoughts had taken when he'd seen her beside his car. He didn't like the feeling. He didn't like a lot of things he'd been feeling since he'd made the mistake of coming here. But most of all he didn't like being taken for a fool.

"You didn't need to come out here to make sure. I got the message," he said abruptly.

She blinked. "Message?"

Oh, she was good. If he didn't know that she had to be the one behind planting that book in his room, he'd almost believe she didn't know what he was talking about. But obviously she wasn't about to admit it, and he'd never been one to waste his time or his breath on lost causes.

"Never mind. You're in my way, Ms. Chase," he pointed out unnecessarily. "I'm on my way to the airport. To get out of Sunridge. Since that's what the Hawks want from me, I'm sure you'll be glad to move your car."

She ignored his tone. And when she spoke, it was with a soft earnestness that sounded so genuine it shook him.

"There are only two Hawks left. One in name only. And one by blood. You."

She didn't sound like a woman who had just delivered Aaron's final renunciation. She sounded as if she believed what she was saying. That she thought of him as a Hawk, more of one even than his father's bitter widow.

And she sounded like a woman who could have charmed even an old bastard like Aaron Hawk. And apparently had. He laughed harshly, his momentary softness forgotten.

"You're barking up the wrong tree, Ms. Chase. If you think I'm going to come begging now for the acknowledgment my father never gave me when he was alive, you can forget it. The name Hawk means nothing to me. I wouldn't take it if you offered it up to me on a platter."

She studied him for a moment. "And if that platter was literally silver?"

"Not even if it was pure gold, and you brought it to me naked." He thought he heard her breath catch, and he looked her blatantly up and down before he added in an exaggerated drawl, "Although I admit, I might let you try to convince me before I tossed you out on your cute little butt."

"If you're trying to embarrass me, you can stop. It's been tried by experts."

"Meaning my father?"

"Your father never purposely embarrassed me. Or anyone else, for that matter. Not that he was above letting people embarrass themselves, and he used to say they did that often enough he never had to bother."

He stiffened. *Just let them run, and sooner or later they'll trip themselves up. They always do.* His own words, eerily similar and spoken so often in a conference room in Seattle, rang in his mind. The unwanted coincidence put an edge in his voice.

"Right. A genuine saint, he was."

"No. He was a dynamic, charismatic man who became a short-tempered tyrant as he got older. As his time grew shorter, so did his patience. Your father was many things, but he was not a saint. Nor would he have wanted to be."

Jason did not want to hear any more about the man who had been such a force in his life despite never having been there physically.

"Is there a point to your being here?"

"I need to talk to you."

"You have. I don't believe a word of it. We have nothing more to discuss."

She tilted her head and looked at him with every evidence of nothing more than curiosity. "Have you always been like this?"

"Like what?" he retorted impatiently.

"Curt. Blunt. Arbitrary."

"Thank you," he said, making it sound as if she'd just given him the greatest of compliments. His faintly veiled sarcasm didn't faze her.

"I just wondered if you'd learned it or inherited it."

His jaw tightened at the inference. "Get to the point, Ms. Chase. Or get out of my way."

"Will you listen to me?"

He gestured toward her car. "It appears, unless I want to walk to the airport, and pay for the rental company to come out here and pick up this car, I don't have much choice. So talk. But make it fast."

"I'd rather not do it here."

"Well, then," he drawled again, expansively, waving in a vaguely southerly direction, "perhaps we could fly someplace nice and warm, like Tahiti, and have our little friendly chat over a couple of pink drinks with umbrellas in them. Then you could offer me that silver platter. Or forget the platter. Just you, naked, will do."

Suddenly, unexpectedly, she smiled. Instead of being intimidated or mortified, she smiled. It was like the sun rising over that island he'd joked about, and he almost smiled back before he realized what he was doing.

"If you only knew," she said, chuckling, "how much you look and sound like Aaron. That arrogant tone, the exaggerated drawl, the grand, waving gesture. He'd be proud."

His hand curled into a fist and slammed down hard on

the roof of the car beside her head. She jumped at the sudden, loud bang. He leaned toward her, surmising what his expression must be from the way she drew hastily back, pressing herself against the side of the car in an effort to get away from him. Yet he saw no fear in her eyes, only caution. Her steady nerve made him feel a reluctant spark of admiration.

"Did you have some crazy idea that that would please me? Or that I give a damn what Aaron Hawk would think of me?"

"He was your father—"

"He was an arrogant bastard who deserved to die a hell of a lot sooner than he did!"

"He may have been—"

"I hope he died hard. Real hard. I hope he had a damned lot of pain, and time to think about what he'd done to people, innocent people, and people who had done nothing to him except—"

Love him.

For a moment, as they resounded in his head, he thought the words had slipped out. The instant he realized they hadn't, he turned away from her to assure they wouldn't. He wasn't about to tell that particular truth to anyone, especially this woman. It hurt enough to admit to himself that his mother had never stopped loving the man who had abandoned her the moment he'd found out she was pregnant with him.

"He did." Kendall's voice came softly, so softly it was as if she'd heard the words he'd barely managed to bite back. "He died hard. Very hard. In a lot of pain. And he had a lot of time to think about his life and the wrongs he'd done. And to regret them."

"Regret?" He whirled back on her. "He plays his little games with people's lives for decades, but when he finds out he's dying he gets scared and says he regrets it all, and that makes it *all right*?"

"Of course not. Please, can we go inside somewhere? It's cold."

It was time to put an end to this, right now. "Sorry, I've already checked out. But if you're that determined to ... talk to me, I could get another room." He lifted a hand and with his index finger traced the line of her lower lip none too gently. She looked startled, but not afraid. "Just how badly do you want to talk to me, lady?"

Her chin came up, and she gave him a level lóok. He should have realized that anyone who could deal with Aaron Hawk wouldn't be easily intimidated. That admiration sparked through him again, but in his anger he ignored it.

"You're not going to drive me away with sexual threats, Mr. West. Nor can you embarrass or humiliate me into leaving. I have a job to do, and I'm going to do it."

"A job?"

"Yes. To carry out Aaron's last wishes. And if I have to dog you all the way to Seattle to do it, I will."

Seattle? He drew back then, eyes narrowing. "Been checking me out, Ms. Chase?"

She let out a sigh. "What did you expect? I told you, Aaron spent months of precious time and thousands of dollars looking for you. Then you suddenly show up, and you think I could let you just disappear again, without a clue about where to find you?"

"I'm not hard to find. I haven't been hiding." Not for a long time, anyway, he amended silently.

Kendall's mouth twisted. "Do you have any idea how many Jason Wests there are in this country? For that matter, how many of them there are in the greater Seattle area alone? And how long checking them out one at a time takes? Aaron died waiting, praying that the next one would be you."

"If you expect me to feel sorry for him, you're once more barking up the wrong tree, Ms. Chase."

"Aaron would scorn your pity."

He shrugged. "I'm surprised. Having people feel sorry for you is a powerful tool."

"Is that how you see pity? As a tool to be used?"

"That's how I see everything, Ms. Chase."

"Then you truly are your father's son."

His stomach knotted this time at the unwanted comparison. It was time for this farce to end.

"Your personal car?" he asked shortly, gesturing toward the dark blue sedan.

"Yes," she answered, looking puzzled.

"My insurance company will be in touch," he said. Then he moved around her, resenting even as he did it the fact that he was being very careful not to touch her as he reached for the door of the rental coupe.

"Go ahead," she said before he could get in, "but smashing up my car won't stop me, either."

She was quick on the uptake, he had to give her that. He turned around, leaned back against the roof of the car, and wearily asked, "What will, Ms. Chase? What will it take to get you to leave me alone?"

"Simple, Mr. West." She said it with a slight emphasis, as if to point out she knew very well his constant formal use of her name was one of those tools they'd spoken of, to keep her at arm's length. "It will take you listening to what I have to say."

"And why should I?"

"Many reasons. Curiosity. Anger. The possibility that there's really something in it for you. Maybe a search for more of those tools to be used. Perhaps even to feed your hatred of Aaron, if that's what you need."

He didn't like her inference, that he needed ... anything, but couldn't completely deny it, either. Nor, he thought a little uneasily, could he deny that she had just enumerated with uncanny accuracy most of the reasons he would even consider listening to whatever laughable story she had to tell.

And then she smiled, that quick, unexpected curving of her lips that made him automatically want to smile back. He barely stopped himself yet again.

"But probably most of all," she said, the smile almost becoming a grin, "because I'll haunt you until you do listen. I promise you that."

For a split second before he quashed it, he had the thought that that might not be a punishment too harsh to bear. *You* are *tired,* he muttered inwardly. But even tired, there was one thing he was sure of, with an instinct he'd learned the hard way; she meant what she said. She wouldn't give up until he listened to whatever far-fetched story she had to tell. What her real purpose was, he couldn't guess. Yet. But he knew it wasn't anything as simple as carrying out some last wish of Aaron Hawk's. She had some private agenda; everyone did. She just hid hers better than most people.

He stared at her. She met his gaze unflinchingly. She was facing him down, in a way no one had done for years. He, who was used to intimidating people who had considerably more power and stature than Kendall Chase with a glance, seemed incapable of making this one petite woman back off.

As if she'd once more read his thoughts with uncanny accuracy, she smiled again. "I can be very, very persistent. And inventive, if need be."

Images of a different kind of inventiveness, a kind that would use that lovely body to great advantage, leapt into his mind. But he'd learned that sexual innuendo failed to daunt her, so he didn't bother trying it again. But he wasn't sure what to do next.

Jason realized with no small amount of shock that she had him completely off balance. Reluctant admiration made his mouth twist wryly, even as he made an effort to regain the control he wasn't quite sure how he'd lost.

"All right," he said suddenly. "My plane leaves in an hour. You've got twenty minutes."

She hesitated, then said, "I suppose that's enough to make a start."

It better be enough to finish this, he thought. He couldn't wait to get out of this town; even the air seemed oppressive to him, as if Aaron Hawk had owned it as well, and resented his son breathing it. And he doubted very much if anything Kendall Chase had to say would change that feeling.

Alice Hawk paced the elegant, pale mauve and blue sitting room with a speed and urgency that belied her seventy-four years. And without even a glance spared for the perfect loveliness of the room around her. She had ordered it up out of a designer's sketch book, complete, to make the proper impression on those she wished to impress, and it had no more to do with her personally than did the cold, conspicuous diamonds she wore for the same reason.

She cared little for her surroundings, and scorned the kind of women who spent their time on such frivolous pastimes, although she admitted a certain grudging respect for the decorator who had gotten away with charging her such an exhorbitant fee. She herself had no time for such useless things; she was a power to be reckoned with in this community, not some brainless socialite who spent her time on club luncheons and garden parties.

Nor was she the perfect corporate wife anymore. She was through with that forever. She'd had, by necessity of Aaron's position, to do her share of the social niceties, but she'd despised every minute of it, every minute of being talked down to as Aaron's wife, as if she had no existence outside of her connection to him. As if she weren't really the controlling force behind Hawk Industries.

And she'd heard the whispers. Enough of them so that she had once resorted to setting up a concealed tape recorder, then directed several of the corporate wives there to freshen up after cocktails and before dinner. She'd learned then that Aaron's affair with Elizabeth West was common knowledge among them all, and that the wives perversely sympathized with Aaron, calling her a cold, cold fish. Worse than that, they commiserated with Aaron's mistress, pointing out how much nicer she was than Aaron's arrogant wife.

And at the same time they laughed at her. There, in her own house, while accepting her hospitality, guests at her own party, they laughed at her. Joked about her trying to keep a man like Aaron on a short leash. Once even the old rumor that her father had bought Aaron for her surfaced, although she'd thought it long quashed. The women had laughed again, this time at the idea Aaron could be bought. Little did they know, she'd thought as she listened to the tape, her fury growing every second that the laughter went on.

But that had been nothing compared to the fury of learning Aaron had fathered a son with Elizabeth West.

"Damn you," she whispered harshly, not clear in her

mind whether the curse was aimed at Aaron or his son. And not certain there was any difference to her any longer.

She tried to fight off the sense of foreboding that had enveloped her since the moment she'd heard that laugh at the cemetery, and had looked up to see the living image of Aaron as she'd first seen him. It had come on her after the initial shock had faded, this sensation of unease, of being threatened, and she didn't like it.

And as much as she hated to admit it, it was her own fault. Her fault, for being too soft, all these years. The moment she'd found out about the existence of Aaron's son, she'd wanted him dead. But foolishly, she'd let the child live, settling for merely ordering him and his mother out of her—and Aaron's—life. And then he'd dropped so completely out of sight after that slut died that she hadn't been able to find him. Only the fact that the boy never appeared to lay claim to his family connection had kept her from pouring great effort into the search; simply interfering with Aaron's hunt for his son had been a drain on her time, money, and energy for far too long.

When the phone rang, she went for it with the haste of someone badly needing a distraction.

"Mrs. Hawk? Sorry to call so late—"

"Never mind," she said, cutting Whitewood off sharply. "What is it?"

"You said to keep you informed, and I thought you'd want to know this right away—"

"What?" she snapped, irritated by his self-aggrandizing tone.

"The man I hired found him. He's staying at the Sunridge Motel."

"I could have found that out myself," she said coldly. "There are only three motels in town. I hope that's not all you have."

"No, of course not." He sounded so smug she wished he were present so she could slap the expression off his face. "She's with him."

She didn't have to ask who he meant. She bit back an oath, and with a great effort simply waited.

"They're having quite a talk," Whitewood said. "My man's watching them."

"Damn her." It escaped this time despite her efforts to stop it.

"She must be telling him about the will. Maybe even the money in her account. Now what?"

Of course she was telling him, Alice thought. It was exactly what she would expect of Kendall Chase. Aaron had been many things, but a fool in choosing the people who worked for him wasn't one of them.

"You want my man to keep watching?" Whitewood asked.

"Yes," she said.

"What if they split up? Who do you want him to follow?"

"Stay with him," Alice said. "The girl is predictable enough. She'll stay in town."

"I'll tell him."

"I want to know every move West makes," she ordered the lawyer. "And continue with our other plans. I want to be ready to move at a moment's notice."

She hung up abruptly; she had no time for the niceties now. She had to think. She knew, had expected all along that Kendall would try and do as Aaron had wanted. It was Aaron's bastard who was the wild card. She'd hoped, after all these years, that he'd accepted his fate, that he'd seen the wisdom in not crossing her. It was why she'd left him alone, even though it went against her every instinct. But his showing up here, now, ruined that hope, proved that she should have followed her instincts and rid herself of the problem long ago.

She wasn't quite sure what to do about it. It had been a while since she'd had to deal with a situation like this. She'd had things under control for a very long time.

And she wasn't going to let that change now. She would do what she had to do. She had before, and she would now. Even if she had to resort to extreme measures again.

Extreme measures.

She sank down on the chair beside the phone, her mind racing.

Extreme measures.

She had thought that part of her life long over. But the arrival of Aaron's bastard changed everything. She had to protect what was hers, and if anyone thought she wouldn't—or worse, thought her too old to do it—she would prove them wrong.

And if that meant calling the man who had helped her before, if it meant using the beast she'd once created, then she would do it. She would do whatever it took.

She went to her desk and began to look for the phone number she'd thought never to call again.

Chapter Six

~

Neither Jason nor Kendall spoke until they were inside the comfortably warm coffee shop. She gratefully ordered a hot chocolate, anticipating the pleasure of curling her cold fingers around the warm jug. Jason ordered black coffee, asking the waitress for the strongest she had. The tall, statuesque woman, who had been looking decidedly bored when they'd come in, looked him up and down, then glanced at Kendall, as if trying to assess their relationship.

The tension between them must be obvious, Kendall thought, and had her guess confirmed when the woman set her mug of chocolate down without comment, then slowly poured Jason's coffee and asked, in a suggestive voice, if there was anything else he wanted, anything at all.

Jason gave the woman a sideways look and a crooked smile. "I'll let you know," he said.

The woman smiled invitingly before turning to go, but Kendall barely noticed. She was too busy watching Jason, aware that everything depended on her being able to judge him. And right now, she was evaluating Jason's reaction to the waitress's obvious come-on. It had been easy, and smooth, suggesting long practice. She wasn't surprised at that; a man with Jason West's dark good looks must deal with that kind of thing regularly.

But she'd also sensed something else in that response, more in the sideways look than the casual words, an assessment of sorts, as if he were judging whether even this woman in a lonely motel coffee shop could somehow be useful to him. It was automatic, she realized, that assessment of everything and everyone he met, of what value they might have to him. What kind of possible tool they might be.

That's how I see everything, Ms. Chase.

It hadn't been said for effect, or to discourage her, it had been, quite simply, the truth. And for the first time she began to wonder if that hardness in his eyes was matched by a hardness in his soul that was beyond redemption. Had Aaron truly left it too long, was there nothing left in his son to be reached?

Kendall took a deep breath. She'd been over this again and again, trying to decide where to start. The amount of money Aaron had left to his estranged son was, she had thought, enough to get anyone's undivided attention. But now she wasn't so sure. It seemed to her that Jason hated his father enough to refuse to take anything that had anything to do with the Hawks. And she wouldn't be surprised in the least that when she told him what Aaron had left him, he would laugh in her face for thinking he would ever touch Hawk money, even this much. But that was only an impression; how could she gamble Aaron's last wishes on it?

She took a careful swallow of her very hot chocolate, still pondering. Aaron had always told her to trust her perceptions, and now, when she was trying so hard to carry out his wishes, didn't seem to be the time to abandon the tactic that had worked so well all these years. Even if it made her job more difficult, she thought, as she looked at the man across the table from her.

Already Jason West's powerful personality was making her see the differences as well as the similarities between him and his father. The old man had been stubborn, aggressive, sometimes belligerent. He had also been dynamic, brilliant, and shrewd, living by his own inflexible code that had been, if nothing else, consistent. And to her, perhaps to her alone, he had been kind. And except for the kindness, she was willing to bet Jason was the same kind of man.

Jason would never believe that Aaron had been as sincere in his desire to find his son as he had ever been about anything in his life. He was too bitter, too angry, too set in his view of his father, and she couldn't blame him for that. So if she couldn't begin with money, or with Aaron's feelings about his son, what was left?

Too set in his view of his father.

Living by his own inflexible code.

Her thought about Aaron flashed through her mind again as she thought about Jason's feelings about his father. Were they more alike than she had even realized?

Aaron's code had had many facets, and one of the most basic had been that no one cheated him and got away with it. They had disagreed over his tactics for enforcing that more than once, because Aaron's reaction to being cheated was usually a fury so great he lost sight of anything except retribution, and sometimes innocent people got hurt in the process, something Kendall had never been able to write off as simply "the cost of doing business," as Aaron had.

If Jason was like his father in so many other ways, perhaps they were alike in this as well, she thought. Perhaps Hawk pride ran as strongly in his veins as it had in Aaron's. It was as good a place to start as any. And she was still furious enough herself that she didn't mince any words.

"Alice Hawk is trying to cheat you, Jason."

She didn't know what he'd been expecting to hear, but she could tell from the look that flashed across his face that it hadn't been what she'd said.

He looked at her for a long, silent moment, eyes narrowed. She could almost feel his mind racing, assessing, and knew she hadn't underestimated the intelligence here. When he finally spoke, she was surprised; he asked the last thing she'd expected.

"What happened to 'Mr. West'?"

She hesitated, trying to guess why he'd asked that particular question. No logical reason came to her, so she gave him the simple truth.

"I've always thought of you as Jason Hawk. It's hard for me not to call you that, but it obviously upsets you. So I thought I'd compromise. But if that upsets you as well, I suppose I'll just have to stick to 'Mr. West.' "

He gave her a level look. "The name Hawk doesn't upset me. Offend me, yes. I don't like it, and like even less it being hung on me. Jason will do."

She didn't argue with him on this relatively pointless issue. "Fine. So will Kendall. I find you have a knack of saying 'Ms. Chase' as if you'd bitten into a lemon. If I have to feel the bite, I'd prefer it to at least be my first name."

"Think that will make it sweeter?"

"No. Just easier to ignore."

He lifted a dark brow at her, and something flashed in his eyes that was almost a salute. But he said only, "All right . . . Kendall. You're running out of time."

"Which, I'm sure, was your intent," she said, only realizing it now. He merely looked at her. She sighed. "Don't you care that someone is trying to cheat you out of what's rightfully yours?"

"I don't want anything from the Hawks. Why are you telling me this? You work for the Hawks."

"Not any longer. And I never worked for Alice."

Both dark brows rose this time. "I wondered why your car looked like you'd taken up living on the road. Or were going to check in here."

"I probably will," she said dryly.

"Get fired?"

She didn't bother to deny it. "Yes. I've been living at the house since Aaron got sick. I had to pack my things in a hurry."

"I'll bet." He leaned back against the cushion of the coffee-shop booth, raising one arm to rest it along the back of the seat. "So your job died along with the meal ticket, huh?"

"I no longer work for Hawk," she said carefully, "because I refused to go along with Alice on this. That's why she fired me."

His eyes shifted then, downward, to stare into his now half-empty cup. When he looked back up at her, she heard him let out a compressed breath.

"All right, Ms. . . . Kendall. Let's get this over with. But make it fast."

He wanted it fast? Fine, Kendall thought. And delivered it with rapid precision.

"Two weeks before he died, Aaron added a codicil to his will, leaving you a sizable bequest. Alice found out. She located or intercepted all but one copy of that codicil. She plans to deny its existence and file Aaron's original will as the official one. She swears you'll never see any of Aaron's money."

She could have just conversationally mentioned that it was cold out, for all the reaction she got. And she had the sudden feeling that nothing, not the air, not even the lingering pockets of snow outside, was as cold as this man was capable of being.

"Is that it?" His voice was as cool as the things she'd just been thinking about.

"Not quite."

"Finish it."

"They've set me up. And you." She related the story quickly, in brusque, businesslike terms, ending with Whitewood's promise to provide the necessary witnesses.

"Convenient," Jason said.

He seemed completely calm, utterly uninvolved. She envied him his control; just thinking about Alice made her furious.

He gave her a look she couldn't read. "Why didn't you just take the money and shut up?"

She looked at him over the rim of her mug. If she were the kind of woman he seemed to think her, that would no doubt be exactly what she would do. She wished he would see that, but she didn't hold out much hope.

"A very good question. Why do you suppose?"

He seemed to consider that for a moment, and she shrugged. "Maybe you figure you'll get more in the long run out of me than you will out of my father's widow. I don't imagine she feels particularly munificent to her late husband's—"

"Tell me something," she began, stopping him before he again repeated his assessment of her relationship to Aaron, "do you always make assumptions about people without knowing the first thing about them?"

He never blinked at the interruption. "I assume my father was a cold, ruthless bastard who wouldn't marry my mother or acknowledge his own son. And that his widow is equally coldhearted and would perjure herself to keep me from seeing a dime from my father. And that the Hawks use crooked lawyers or whatever is necessary to make sure things go their way. Anything you'd like to deny so far?"

She sighed. "No."

"So I'm batting a thousand. Why the hell should I believe I'm wrong about you?"

"It doesn't matter," she said wearily. She could live with his assumptions, she thought, if he'd just listen. "What matters is that Alice is trying to steal what's rightfully yours, what your father wanted you to have. And she's willing to send us both to jail to do it, if she has to."

He laughed. "She's too late. I've already been to jail."

Kendall blinked in surprise. "You have? For what?"

"A youthful indiscretion, isn't that what they say? I borrowed a car. Except I forgot to ask permission. Hey, it wasn't my fault, I was a victim of my rotten childhood." His mouth quirked sardonically. "I didn't say that, the county shrink did."

"Was it rotten? Your childhood?"

He shrugged. "No worse than a lot of others."

"So why did you borrow the car?"

He gave her a look she could only describe as wary. She wondered if it was because he'd already told her more than he'd intended to. It seemed Aaron had been right in his fears; Jason had apparently not done much with his life, if he'd already been in jail even before adulthood.

"You're about out of time. You sure you want to waste it discussing my misspent youth?"

Reluctantly, although she wasn't sure why she felt that way, she agreed. "What are you going to do about the will? You can't let her get away with this."

"Why not?"

She gaped at him; she couldn't help it. "Jason, we're talking about a huge sum of money—"

"I figured that. If they're willing to sacrifice fifty thousand to keep it, it can't be pocket change, even for the Hawks."

"Try a hundred times that."

"Sounds about right."

My God, Kendall thought, *could nothing shake this man's cool?* She threw out a number like five million dollars, that would make most people gasp, and he didn't turn a hair. He just sat there nodding, as if it were nothing more complex than a simple multiplication problem.

"So what did my charming father leave you, Kendall?"

She shivered when he said her name. And she resented the fact that she had. *Wonderful,* she muttered silently, chastising herself. *He doesn't even blink at the mention of five million, and you get chills at the sound of your own name. Or him saying it. You're supposed to be the cool one, the level head, why are you letting him get to you?*

"Your father paid well and advised me on some investments. He didn't need to leave me anything."

"But he did, didn't he?"

"What makes you say that?"

"I get the feeling you use words very precisely, Ms. . . . Kendall. You didn't say he didn't leave you anything, just that he didn't need to."

For a moment she was back in front of Aaron, when she'd first come to work for him. "Say what you mean and mean what you say, girl. Save the obfuscation for when I tell you it's necessary." He'd taught her so much, given her so much, and denied it every time she tried to thank him—

"Kendall?"

Her gaze shot to Jason's face, and only when she saw his image was a bit blurry did she realize her eyes had begun to brim with tears. She looked away, swiping at them hastily.

"Damn." She heard Jason swear quietly, but couldn't meet his eyes. "You really loved that old man, didn't you?"

She did look at him then; she wouldn't deny Aaron, not now, not to his own son.

"Not in the way I'm sure you'll assume, but yes, I

loved him. He gave me my first job, when I hadn't an ounce of experience to justify his faith. He challenged me at every turn, forced me to grow, to find my full potential. And in the end he trusted me with his soul."

Jason stared at her for a long, silent moment. "You think he had a soul?"

"I know he did. Because I know it was a tortured one, at the end. When he learned your mother had been killed, even though it was twenty years ago, it nearly destroyed him." She took a deep breath to steady her voice. "Your father was everything you've said, Jason. But he was so much more, besides. There was a part of him he never let the world see, a gentler side, a side that laughed, and was generous, and told wonderful stories ..."

Her words faded away, and because she couldn't stop herself, she gathered her nerve to ask him something, more in the hopes of making him think than actually expecting an answer.

"Was your mother the kind of woman who would fall in love with an awful man, and stay with him for seven years? Despite the fact that he wouldn't get a divorce, would never marry her?"

For the first time she saw his jaw tighten. Perhaps Jason West wasn't frozen solid, not quite.

"My mother," he said tightly, "was a ... kind, gentle woman. She worked harder to take care of me than anyone should have to. All because she was foolish enough to *love* Aaron Hawk."

He nearly spat out the word, as if it were something so unpalatable he hated the taste of it.

"You wanted to know why I took that car?" he went on, his voice suddenly fierce. "It was our neighbor's. I took it one day when it was so cold the rain had turned to sleet, and I knew she was walking home from work in it. Because our car was broken down, and she couldn't afford to fix it. And she shouldn't have been out anyway, she was sick, but she had to pay the rent on that dive we lived in. And my *father* never gave a damn."

Kendall felt a choking tightness in her throat. She wanted to explain, to say that Aaron had tried, but her instincts told her Jason was in no mood to hear it. It was a moment before she was able to say quietly, "But she loved him."

"Yes." Jason's tone was almost acid. "She did. She never, ever said a word against him. Never once did she blame him. She said he never lied to her. Like that makes it all right."

Kendall looked at him for a long moment. "Who are you angry at, Jason? Aaron? Or your mother?"

"What's that supposed to mean?"

"Just that it must have been hard, for you to hate him so much when your mother never stopped loving him. You must have been ... upset with her, that she still cared."

"It wasn't her fault. She was a smart woman. She just had this ... blind spot."

"About Aaron?"

His mouth twisted. He sipped the last of his coffee, set down the cup, and stared into it. "And about love. She believed in it. I think she believed up until she died that someday he'd come for her. Falling in love was the only foolish thing she ever did." He let out a breath. "Except maybe for having me."

Kendall nearly gasped at this betrayal of pained emotion in a man she would never have expected it from. Anger, yes, but never this kind of pain. Her voice was barely above a whisper when she finally managed to speak.

"You don't really think she regretted that, do you?"

His head came up abruptly. He glared at her, looking as furious now as he ever had, when just moments ago she had thought she was really making progress with him.

"Damn, you are good, aren't you? Maybe you really were what you said you were. Did the old man teach you that?"

"Teach me ... what?" she asked carefully.

"How to find the weak spot and go for it. How to lull with those big eyes, coax people into spilling their guts for you—"

"All I did was listen, Jason. If that's all it took, then perhaps you needed to ... spill your guts, as you so charmingly put it. Although if it's any comfort, you didn't let slip much I hadn't already guessed."

It didn't seem to comfort him. The silence spun out, strained and somehow bleak.

"More coffee?"

The waitress's chipper voice increased the tension between them rather than breaking it.

"No," Jason said flatly. "I'm leaving."

He ignored the woman's rather blatant pout as she walked away, and stood up. He pulled a crumpled bill out of his pocket and tossed it on the table.

"Jason, please—"

"I should let you pay for it," he said, his voice as cool as if that momentary break in his composure had never occurred. "But I don't want a damn thing from the Hawks. Not five dollars, not five million. Now are you going to move that fancy car of yours, or do I move it myself?"

He missed his plane. Not only that, but the reservations clerk had practically broken down in tears when he'd snapped at her because the soonest she could manage to get him back to Seattle was for him to take the last small commuter flight to L.A., which didn't leave for another hour and a half, and then he'd have to literally run for a connecting flight that left there for SeaTac twenty minutes later.

He'd tried to apologize, but he was reasonably sure he'd only made things worse. So he'd accepted the ticket she'd handed him with unsteady hands in silence, then felt like a complete ass when he overheard the older woman who relieved her at the desk tell her to hurry home to her sick daughter.

He walked over to an isolated pair of seats near the boarding gate, dropped his coat and bag on one, and sat heavily down in the other.

Great, West, he muttered to himself. *You miss your plane, make a woman with a sick kid cry, and now you get to spend an hour and a half sitting here doing nothing.*

Nothing except what he'd been doing ever since he'd

left the motel, after Kendall Chase had moved her car, saying nothing more to him, as if she'd finally given up.

Nothing except thinking of question after question that he wanted to ask her, even though he resented his own curiosity. Questions like did she really believe Alice Hawk would go to such lengths to make sure her husband's illegitimate son never saw a penny of Hawk's money? And just what exactly did this supposed codicil say? And where was the one copy she'd said Alice hadn't found?

But even those were questions he could live with. He could understand why his mind kept turning to them. They didn't matter, because he didn't really believe the whole preposterous story in the first place. It was the other persistent questions that really bothered him. The things he shouldn't even be wondering about at all. Things like why she really hadn't taken the fifty thousand and just gone on her merry—and considerably richer—way? What had Aaron Hawk really left her? And what had her relationship with the old man really been? What had she seen in him that no one else had?

If, of course, any of it was true.

Even if it was, what was her real motive? He couldn't believe it was simply to carry out an old man's last wish; he didn't even believe this was the old man's last wish. No, there was something else going on here, something he couldn't see yet.

But he would. Nobody went to all this trouble for nothing. Perhaps she got a bonus or something if she pulled this off. But that would have to mean that Aaron really had left him something, which was even harder to believe; the man hadn't given a damn about him or his mother for thirty years, there was no reason to believe he'd changed simply because he'd run out of time.

And if his suspicions were correct, and it was all a scam of some kind, what did she get out of it? Maybe the alleged codicil really was a forgery, and she figured he'd pay her a bigger chunk to help him pass it than the widow would to stop her. Now that made sense. If she could convince him to fight the will, and the forgery was good enough to stand up in court, then she might figure she was in for at least another zero tacked onto the end of that tidy little deposit. Ten percent of five million was a nice round figure.

He yawned widely, wondering if the useless cycle of conflicting questions was tiring him out, or if it was the prospect of a long, not particularly comfortable journey home. He leaned back in the chair, which squeaked noisily with the sound of denim rubbing on vinyl. He yawned again.

Maybe he'd go for another cup of coffee. He wouldn't be able to sleep on the little prop jet plane he'd be getting on anyway. He looked around the nearly empty terminal and at the small cafeteria across from the second gate down. He glanced at his bag, wondering if it would be safe here or if he should take it with him, not that there was anything of much value—

He went rigidly still. His heart seemed to stop for an instant, then began to slam in his chest.

Sticking out of the side pocket of the leather bag was the book.

Chapter Seven

~

He was glad it was cold. It explained why he was shivering. And he'd had more than enough of things he couldn't explain since he'd arrived here. He pounded on the motel-room door again.

She had to be here. Her car was here, still full of boxes and bags, and it was parked right in front of the only room with a light still on. Apparently, as he'd hoped, she hadn't been kidding about checking in here. Or about moving out of the Hawk mansion.

He knew he was doing it on purpose, concentrating on the mundane, the normal, so he didn't have to think about the rest. He was going to have his answers about that soon. Very soon. As soon as Kendall Chase opened her damn door.

He lifted his hand to knock again, ready to use his fist this time. He stopped himself midmotion when the door swung open before he connected.

"I thought you were on a plane."

"I . . . missed it."

He swallowed, annoyed at the catch in his voice. But he hadn't expected her to come to the door like this, in a robe that enveloped her in peach-colored satin yet somehow emphasized her feminine shape, with her hair down and flowing over her shoulders in a dark, thick, smooth mass that made his fingers curl with the need to touch it, to see if it could possibly feel as silky as it looked. This was a far cry from the formal, poised woman he'd seen at the funeral, and the slightly less formal but equally poised woman he'd sat across from in the coffee shop.

She let out a tiny sigh. "I'm sorry. That wasn't my intent."

He had to concentrate to keep himself from once more letting his gaze slide over her, lingering on the unexpectedly lush curves of hip and breasts, and that he had to make the effort irritated him. That, and the feel of the book in his left hand, brought his sense of purpose raging back.

"Then tell me just what your intent is with this."

He held the book up in front of her. She looked at it blankly. "I don't understand."

"Don't play dumb, Kendall. Surprisingly enough, it doesn't suit you."

"And surprisingly enough, constant insults don't suit you. If that's what you came back for, you can just leave."

This time he let his gaze drift over her slowly, enjoying the view. He lingered for a moment on the curve of her breasts, wondering if perhaps her nipples, peaked now from the cold air that had reached her from outside as she stood in the doorway, matched the soft peach color of the robe.

"And if I came back for something else?" he said, his mocking tone leaving her no doubt as to what he meant.

"Then I'll slap you and you can just leave."

Her retort was so quick he grinned before he could stop himself. Her eyes narrowed, and for an instant he thought he'd finally rattled her. But when his gaze went back to her face, he knew he was wrong. She was looking at him as if she were mightily tired of this whole thing.

"You would, too, wouldn't you?"

"Slap you? Yes." Her mouth quirked. "But don't take my word for it, any more than you have for anything else. Make the wrong move and let me prove it."

He was almost tempted to try. He had a feeling many people had underestimated this woman. And he had a suspicion he might just be one of them. But he wasn't going to do it now. Not before he got some answers. A lot of them.

"Later," he said. "Right now what I want is an explanation."

Her glance flicked to the book as he gestured at her with it. Then she looked back at his face.

"Of what? That book? What do I have to do with it?"

"I know you planted it in my room, and then somehow slipped it into my bag. What I want to know is why? What's the point?"

"The point is," she said, her voice sounding as frosty as the air was becoming as it neared midnight, "that I'm getting very tired of being accused of doing things I've never done."

She moved as if to shut the door. Jason moved faster, planting his booted foot across the sill, preventing her from closing him out.

"You were outside my room right after it appeared. And you were the only one around before it showed up at the airport."

She went very still. "Appeared?"

His mouth twisted ruefully; he hadn't meant to phrase it like that. "Never mind. Just answer the question. I already know I'm not a Hawk, and never will be. So what's the point? Why the family history to remind me?"

Her eyes widened. In shock. Unmistakable shock. Her gaze flicked to the book he held.

"Family history?" she whispered.

"I suppose you're going to tell me you don't know anything about this?"

Even as he said it, he would have staked his life that her shock was real. Then he gave himself a mental shake; he'd never been fooled by a pretty face, and he wasn't about to start now.

Her gaze came back to his face. Her expression was one of pure awe now. "It came? It really did? The Hawk family book?"

He stared at her. She spoke as if it were a royal title. And with such reverence that she could have been speaking of . . . he wasn't sure what. He couldn't think of anything that would make him feel the way she sounded. And that made him even more wary.

"It's real?" she asked, a little breathlessly.

"What is that supposed to mean?"

"Aaron told me about it, often, but ... I thought it was just one of his stories."

"Stories?"

"One of the Hawk legends."

Jason snorted inelegantly. "You mean one of Aaron Hawk's grand visions of himself."

"Not Aaron. The Hawk family."

"Same thing."

"No. It's not. And that's what Aaron finally realized. That there was much more to it than just him."

She glanced at the book, still looking a little awed. Jason had to force himself not to follow her glance, and the effort, oddly, made him shiver. She seemed to notice it, because she stepped back, making room for him to pass her and step into the room if he wished.

"It's very cold. If you'll come in, I'll ... try to explain."

He hesitated. He told himself it was because he didn't want to hear any more of her tales of his father's supposed deathbed change of heart. And when he changed his mind and decided to cross the threshold, he told himself it was because he was going to pry the truth out of her, make her admit she'd planted the book both times he'd encountered it. And he refused to consider that either his hesitation or his decision to accept her offer had anything at all to do with the effect the sight of her in that swath of peach satin had on him.

The moment he was inside the room that was a tan and blue twin to the one he'd had, and had closed the door behind him, cutting off that blast of cold air, she disappeared into the bathroom. He stared at the closed bathroom door for a moment, brows furrowed, wondering what had made her dodge out of sight like that. Could she somehow have sensed his sensual reaction to her? Or had she taken his earlier mocking threat seriously?

A bare two minutes later she emerged, clad in a pair of faded blue jeans and what appeared to be the same sweater she'd had on before, that he could now see was a pale gray-blue. He barely had time to notice that before irritation kicked through him. What the hell did she think he was, some kid who was ruled by his hormones?

"You didn't have to do that," he said, his voice clipped. It didn't help anyway, he thought, looking at the way the soft, worn denim clung faithfully to her curves, and how the soft sweater made her seem so eminently touchable.

She gave him a long, steady look. "Maybe I wanted you to know I felt like I had to."

Startled, he stared at her. Yet again he had the feeling that he had underestimated this woman. And again, unwillingly, he found himself acknowledging it.

"Touché again," he said, touching a finger to his temple. "I had that coming."

She looked startled in turn, as if surprised he'd said it. He was a little surprised himself, something that had happened all too often since he'd been here. And that irritating knowledge put an edge in his voice as he tossed the book down on the bed.

"Are you going to explain this, or are we going to play games awhile longer?"

She sat down on the bed, crossing her legs in front of her. Her feet were bare, he saw. They were also small, gracefully arched, making him wonder if she was sensitive in that finely boned curve. He thought of all the ways to find out, and suppressed a shudder at the resulting wave of heat.

But she wasn't paying any attention to his steady regard this time. She was completely focused on the book before her, staring at it. After a moment she reached out, touching the cover with a tentative finger, like a person who isn't quite sure what they were reaching for wouldn't vanish, like a dream figure who faded when wakefulness returned. Slowly, with exquisite care, she lifted the cover of the book. He watched, not the book but her face, her eyes, wondering if the flowing design on the inner flyleaf would have the same effect on her as it had had on him. When her fingers moved, tracing the curving lines, his stomach knotted oddly, but when she lifted her head to look at him he saw nothing of puzzlement or surprise or even fear in her expression.

Instead there was a strangely awed look in her wide gray eyes.

"It is real," she whispered. "All this time I thought it was just a story, but it's real. And it came to you. Just like he said it would."

Impatience gripped him again. "I've had enough of these cryptic statements. I want an explanation. And I want it now."

"Jason," she began, then stopped. She looked at him as if she were debating whether to go on. Then, gently, she asked, "Your mother never ... told you The Hawk stories?"

"She didn't have time to waste on fairy tales."

She looked about to say something, then obviously changed her mind. Instead she asked, "Have you looked at the book?"

"Enough to know it's full of my father's crazy idea of a family history. The old man must have been loony to have gone to all this trouble to preserve a fantasy."

"Aaron," she said, her tone level, "never saw this book. It never came to him. But he knew about it."

He let out a compressed breath, trying to rein in his irritation. And for God's sake, he was pacing. He never paced. But he'd never encountered anyone like Kendall Chase before. How could a woman who was so obviously intelligent continue to spout ridiculous lies and expect him to believe her?

"I know," she said, as if he'd spoken his thoughts. "You don't understand. How could you? You don't know the legend."

"And I don't want to," he snapped as he turned at the far wall and started back. "I just want to know what the point of this is." He jabbed a finger in the direction of the book she was still touching, wonderingly, as if she still couldn't believe it was real. "And why you're so determined I take it with me."

"I had nothing to do—" She broke off when he opened his mouth, holding up a hand as if to fend off his words. "Never mind. That doesn't matter. What does matter is that Aaron was right, that the book came to you, just like the legend says."

"You keep saying that. That the book came to me. If you're trying to convince me you didn't put it there—"

"You came here for answers. I'm trying to give them to you."

"You're trying to give me fairy tales."

She gave him a level look. "All right. I don't blame you for thinking that. I did, too, when Aaron told me. But this"—she ran a finger along the gilt edges of the heavy pages in a way that made his stomach knot again— "this is real. And it's here. And I can't explain how any other way."

"I can," he said coldly.

"Yes, I know. You think I did it." She didn't bother to deny it, as if she'd given up trying to convince him of anything about herself. "Why?"

"Because it's the only logical explanation."

"And of course, you must have a logical explanation. For everything."

"What's that supposed to mean?"

She looked at him steadily for a long moment, with such sadness in her eyes it made him uncomfortable. "You gave up on the magic of life very early, didn't you?"

"Magic?" He gave her the scornful look that deserved. "Magic is for people who can't deal with reality."

"Too bad," she said softly. "I think it's the people who can and do deal with reality who need the magic the most. Reality can be pretty ugly sometimes."

"Life is ugly. Most of the time."

She looked away then. She was still touching the book, stroking the gilt edges, tracing the flowing lines that apparently looked perfectly normal to her. He watched her long, tapered fingers move, but jerked his gaze away when he realized it was making him feel as light-headed as staring at that flowing pattern had. He spun on his heel and started back across the small room.

His sudden movement seemed to decide her. "You've missed your plane. You're stuck for a while. Can it hurt to listen?"

He stopped pacing abruptly. He turned, and stood for a long moment, simply looking at her. She met his stare without flinching, and he couldn't help thinking of how rare that simple act was. He'd once been told that if the eyes were the mirror of the soul, his soul had obviously turned to stone. That had been a woman, who had been crying when she'd said it, and he'd walked out then, knowing he'd stayed too long. But he'd heard it from men over the years as well, in cruder terms, but the sentiment was the same: Jason West was one tough, cold-hearted bastard. He'd worked hard at making the adjectives as true as the noun was.

And it was rare enough that anyone faced him down this steadily that he made a sudden decision. He yanked off his coat, tossed it on the bed behind her, pulled a chair out from the small table beside the window, and sat down, swinging his booted feet up to rest on the bed.

"All right, Mother Goose. Tell me the tale."

Her mouth twisted. "Actually, I'm feeling rather Grimm at the moment."

He grinned at the awful pun; he couldn't seem to help it. He heard an odd sound, as if she had taken a quick, deep breath. Or had lost one. He leaned back in the chair, raising his arms to clasp his hands behind his head.

"A fairy tale by any other name," he said. "Now's your chance. Go for it."

She looked at him silently for a moment, clearly taking in his casual posture, his insouciant expression. Her gaze shifted to the book then, as if it could tell her how to begin. She caught one side of her lower lip between her teeth and worried it gently. Jason watched her for a moment, feeling that odd sense of light-headedness again. He'd meant to make it as hard as he could for her, but it was becoming harder on him. He spoke hastily.

"Go on."

"And of course you'll listen with an open mind," she said dryly.

"And deprive you of the challenge of convincing me? I wouldn't dream of it."

She gave him a rather sour look, but he knew she was going to try. He settled back to listen, thinking that if nothing else, he could watch her as she spun the silly tale. That alone would be worth it.

                    *   *   *

It had been easy, after all, Alice thought. She'd been afraid after all these years that he might have changed his methods, or his line of work, or perhaps even finally met his match and be in prison. Or dead. But the cryptic message she'd left on the answering machine that now answered the old phone number had worked. And he'd called her back with a promptness that would have been flattering in anyone else, but from him only succeeded in making her edgy.

When he suggested they skip the formalities, being as they were very old friends, she was quick to agree.

"You are still . . . working?" she asked.

"What can I say?" His voice, a voice that seemed familiar despite the years since she'd heard it, echoed with blithe cheer. "I love what I do."

"I need something done."

"I assumed that, but I'm afraid I'm very busy right at the moment—"

"Too busy for me?" she interrupted. "The person who gave you your start?" He obviously needed some reminding about who was in charge, Alice, irritated at his cavalier tone, thought. And about who he owed.

"Well, there is that," the breezy voice conceded. "I guess, in a way, I do owe you."

"Yes, in a way, you do." She'd begun him on a career she knew, if what he'd charged her was any indication, had to be very profitable.

"I suppose I can rearrange my schedule. If the problem is serious enough, of course."

She knew what he was asking, knew what her answer would tell him. He was a man who didn't deal in petty problems. But she didn't hesitate.

"It is. Very serious."

"All right. I'll be on my way as soon as I can. I'll contact you when I arrive."

He hung up without further ceremony. While she was not used to being dispensed with so abruptly, Alice consoled herself with the knowledge that the solution to her problem—one that would be very final if she ordered it so—was forthcoming.

She'd had enough of waiting for something to happen. For too long she had had to settle for being the power behind the scenes, manipulating instead of ordering, and she was tired of it. Now she would make it happen, and she would make it happen her way.

Ever since the day she'd found out Aaron was dying, and she had realized this was her chance to finally have the public power and authority she'd always craved, she'd been planning for this. Before that, even, for that matter. She supposed, in some way, she'd been planning for this since the day she'd finally had to admit that her husband didn't—and never would—love her. He'd wasted what capacity he had for that emotion on that slut, who had thought she could force his hand by giving him a child. And on Kendall Chase, who would soon learn Alice Hawk wasn't to be trifled with.

A lesson Aaron had learned the hard way.

Seized with a sudden restlessness, she began to pace. But soon that wasn't enough to ease her tension. She glanced at her diamond watch. Although it was late, she knew she was far too restless to sleep. But there was nothing more she could do, not tonight. She'd begun her extreme measures. She should be satisfied, knowing she had the power to unleash such a fate. But she wasn't. She was in no mood to feel satisfied. She was in no mood to sit back and wait. And she was certainly in no mood to sleep. She was far too angry.

And there wasn't anyone to vent her anger at.

But she could appease the need for some kind of action. When she'd been searching Aaron's office, car, and safe here for the copies of the codicil, she'd found the keys to his office at Hawk Manufacturing. She'd been infuriated when he'd had the locks changed and refused to give her a set of those keys, fobbing her off with some feeble excuse about plant security after a break-in. Especially since it hadn't been a break-in at all; she had been the late-night visitor who had gone through the files. She had every right to that information whether Aaron saw it that way or not.

And she had every right to go there now. She needed to see those files; they would help her marshal her forces, plan her strategy. Knowledge was power, and she needed what Aaron had kept from her. She had to move quickly, solidify her position, take over so swiftly and thoroughly that the thought of questioning her right to it could never be reached.

She snatched up the keys and her coat and left the house. Resentment built inside her as she drove through the night toward Hawk Manufacturing. She shouldn't have to be going through this at all. She'd put up with Aaron and his faults and unfaithfulness for all these years, and now that everything was in her hands, as it should be, she was going to have to fight yet again to keep it. And that she was going to have to fight the likes of Kendall Chase and Aaron's bastard only made it worse. The girl was merely a nuisance, but the boy . . .

She would teach them both a lesson they would never forget. And if the lesson had to be a final one, then so be it. In the end, all that mattered was that she keep what was hers. She'd worked too hard, endured too much, and she would not see it lost now. She had a lot of years left to her, and she intended to live them as she wished, as she was meant to.

Even if it meant stealing a lot of years from the two who would dare to try to stand in her way.

"Let me get this right," Jason drawled. "The family legend says that some prehistoric Hawk saved the life of some wizard, is that right?"

Kendall sighed. He knew she was tired, he could see it, but the whole thing was so absurd he had to make her go through it again.

"Back then, any . . . questionable arts were construed as magic," she said.

"Right. And in gratitude, the man promised that the Hawk name would never die out."

"And created the means by which the promise was kept. A book that appears when it's needed."

Jason's mouth quirked. "You say that like it materializes out of thin air."

"For all I know, it does."

"Kendall," he began, but stopped when she lifted a hand.

"All I can tell you is what Aaron told me. According to the legend this book has been in the Hawk family for centuries."

"Centuries? It's old, but not that old."

Kendall sighed. "If you're going to question everything I say, this is going to take all night."

Her words sent another burst of heat through him as he thought of ways he'd like to spend all night with this woman. His voice was husky when he said, "I missed my plane, remember? I've got all night."

Color stained her cheeks, as if she knew what he'd been thinking. But he guessed she wouldn't say anything about it; his words had been, after all, perfectly innocent and true. Only that annoying break in his control of his tone had made them anything other than that.

After a moment her blush faded, and she picked up the book. For the first time she opened it past the patterned flyleaf page. She paused at the drawing that was so like a photograph, then glanced up at him. He waited, wondering as he had with the flyleaf if she would notice anything out of the ordinary. She turned her gaze back to the book, and turned another page. And then another.

And she began to smile, a gentle curving of her lips that was touched with wonder.

"It's just like he said," she whispered, turning the book slightly to read the family tree that stretched on unbroken through generations. "From the beginning, centuries ago. All the Hawks. All those years."

He stayed silent, watching. It wasn't the family tree that concerned him; there was nothing unusual about it, other than perhaps the uninterrupted length of it. It was what came in between, at various points in the genealogy, that had him unwillingly curious: why were one or two Hawks every century not just listed on the tree but pictured, along with what seemed to be a detailed account of their lives, ending with a story of the way those Hawks had found the women they eventually married?

He'd reached that realization when he'd gotten to the third photograph and accompanying tale. It had made his lip curl with aversion; he had little time or patience with people fool enough to believe in love, the biggest fairy tale of them all.

Kendall turned another page, coming to another of the unusual pictures. Jason saw her eyes widen, flick to his face, then back to the picture. He knew what she was thinking. He'd thought it himself. At the airport he'd gone through the book from picture to picture, reluctant to admit what he was seeing. She did as he had, jumped forward through the pages to the next picture. Again she looked at him. Then she repeated the action, and again stopped, reading for a moment the story accompanying this picture, then lifting her head to stare at Jason again.

"It's you," she said. "The last Hawks ... they all look like you. Or you look like them. Even more than you look like Aaron. This man could be your twin brother."

"I noticed," he said, his voice tight. "Now will you explain what the hell you mean by this 'last Hawk' stuff?"

"That's when the book appears. The only time it appears. When the line has dwindled to one surviving Hawk." She looked over at him again. "You."

"I'm not a Hawk." He sounded dogged even to himself.

Kendall sighed. "You can deny it all you want, but that doesn't change the fact that you're a Hawk. The legend says the book follows the blood, legitimate or not, recognized or not."

She gestured at the picture before her, of the man who looked enough like him to be a twin, and a tall, willowy woman who might be considered plain if not for the spirit, life, and pure joy that glowed in her eyes. They were dressed in what appeared to be clothing of the post Civil War era, the man in a dark coat and pants, the woman in a pale gown trimmed with lace. A wedding gown, Jason had belatedly realized after staring in shock at his mirror image for several minutes.

"Joshua Hawk," Kendall read aloud. "He was the last Hawk, then. Look at when he was born. He must have been too young to fight in the Civil War. But his family wasn't. They were all killed, except for his grandfather. Leaving him as the last."

"So what's the point?"

God, he thought, he was treating this like it was for real, like it made any kind of sense. He must be losing it. But Kendall answered him as if the question had been genuine.

"The point is the promise that the Hawk name would never die out."

"So you said." Damn, this was crazy. And what was craziest is that she seemed to believe it all. Maybe she wasn't as smart as he'd thought. "Pretty sexist, isn't it? The patriarchal tradition of having a son to carry on the family name?"

She smiled, a sudden flashing smile that made him wonder if this room, too, had some kind of problem with its air system; it seemed suddenly in short supply.

"It would be," she agreed, "if the starting point of the legend wasn't that the first Hawk, the one who started it all, was a woman."

The first picture, he thought instantly. The woman with the intense, vivid eyes he'd been so impossibly certain were blue. She'd certainly looked capable of starting a legend that would last for centuries. And for a moment he couldn't summon up his sarcastic doubts.

"She passed on the name?"

Kendall nodded. "Back in a time and place where written history didn't exist or was lost in some kind of vague mist, she was responsible for a large clan of people who were in danger. She couldn't save them alone, so she found a champion, a warrior with no name . . . and in the end he took hers."

An image of the man beside the woman in the drawing flashed through his mind. A warrior. The appellation didn't seem nearly as fanciful as it should have.

"It was the foundation of the Hawk dynasty. Your ancestors."

His rationality returned in a rush at her words. "Nice bit of make-believe," he said. "You tell it well."

She shook her head. "Those were Aaron's words, not mine. He told me the stories." He gave a disbelieving snort. "I know," she said. "But it's true. He used to talk for hours, toward the end." She stopped, took a deep breath, and lifted the book from the bed. "He said to tell you to read this. And believe. That it was the legacy you should have had from the beginning."

"You're telling me he never saw this book, but he told you to tell me to read it? Why?"

She gave him a steady look that made him shift his feet uncomfortably. "Do you always look for an ulterior motive?"

"Only because I always find them," he said. "So I repeat, what's the point? What does this"—he jabbed a finger at the book she was holding—"have to do with anything?"

Without answering immediately, she turned to the back part of the book, where he'd noticed the blank pages before. He watched as she riffled the pages, back to where the filled pages came to an end. Then she turned the next blank page. Oddly, the text began again after that skipped page, as if leaving room for something before it began again.

Silently she turned the book so he could read the page where the text resumed. As with all the other sections of the book where individual stories began, this part began with a name recorded in an elegant brush script. But here it was followed by what appeared to be a list of dates rather than story. And he knew this hadn't been there before; when he'd looked at the last page in the airport, the family tree had ended at his father's name. And Kendall hadn't had time to do it herself; he'd been face-to-face with her most of the time the book had been out of his sight.

So he had no explanation for it. But he also couldn't deny it. He could only stare at the scripted name.

Jason Hawk.

Chapter Eight

~

"What do you think she'll do?"

Alice glared at Whitewood, weary of his incessant questions. She wasn't paying him this exorbitant amount of money to have to deal with stupid questions; he should just do what he was told and keep quiet.

"She'll do," she ground out, "whatever will cause me the most trouble."

She tried to control her annoyance. She knew she was tired, she needed sleep after last night, but instead she was here, pacing the floor, wondering if everything she'd worked so hard for was in danger, if all the humiliation she'd put up with in her life had been for nothing.

She'd never been under any illusion about why Aaron had married her. Her father had made it quite clear, telling her if Hawk Manufacturing had been even a month further away from bankruptcy, he wouldn't have had the leverage to force Aaron to agree to his terms. But she had been much more foolish then. She'd thought she could make him care, that if she was amiable enough, loving enough, he would look at her differently. It was a mistake she had never made again.

"Do you really think she was sleeping with him?"

She turned to look at Whitewood. He was patting his hair once more, a familiar gesture, but there was a lascivious glint in his eyes that turned her glare icy.

"I fail to see how that is any concern of yours."

Whitewood shrugged. "I was merely curious."

"If you're thinking of seducing her, I suggest you think again. You'd never succeed."

"Oh?" He sounded a bit offended at her assessment.

"She's impossibly loyal. And her loyalty is to Aaron. The fact that he's dead won't alter that."

The attorney's brows lowered. "You sound as if you admire her."

"I despise her." She meant it. Kendall Chase had gotten everything from Aaron that he had refused to give to his wife: time, attention, caring. But she had learned long ago not to let useless emotions interfere with her judgment. "But I'm not blind. I've watched her for ten years, and I know her. She won't betray Aaron's wishes."

"Then why did you even try to buy her?"

Alice wasn't sure she knew the answer to that herself. She didn't know what had compelled her to try, when she'd known the girl would throw the offer back in her face. That certainty alone added to her antipathy toward Kendall; she hated to admit there was anyone money couldn't buy. Money was power, and power the only thing worth having in this world. The only thing that made people treat you with respect. People who didn't play by that rule made her nervous.

"It was an alternative that had to be explored," she said flatly.

"Do you think she'll keep her mouth shut?"

Alice gave him a withering look. He was pretty, but he was a fool. And had absolutely no talent for judging people. No wonder he'd failed as a defense lawyer and turned to probate jobs. And no wonder he'd been willing to go along with her plan, once she'd made it sufficiently worth his while.

"Ms. Chase has a foolishly strong streak of rectitude. Aaron obviously counted on that. That's why he entrusted her with this absurd codicil. He knew she would do everything possible to carry out his wishes."

She knew she was right. What she didn't know was how Aaron had managed to inspire such loyalty. At best he was gruff and impatient; at his worst he'd been unbearably arrogant.

She was aware of Whitewood giving her a guarded

look. "Maybe you should have tried to string her along a little longer. Stall her. We could have accepted the codicil, then told her we were going to have its validity verified by an expert. We could have had a few days, at least."

"Pointless," Alice snapped. "She has her own agenda. She's an orphan, and has some kind of fixation on family. She has always had it. It even began to affect Aaron, before he died. She planted a lot of idiotic ideas in his head. I'm sure she was behind this determination Aaron developed to find that bastard of his." Alice gave a disgusted snort. "She doesn't know how lucky she is. Family ties are more nuisance than benefit."

"So you think that's that what she was doing with him, telling him about the codicil? And that we . . . er, confiscated it?"

"I would wager the five million dollars my dolt of a husband tried to give away that that is exactly what she was doing."

Whitewood opened his mouth, then shut it again as she glowered at him. She didn't like this young shyster criticizing her tactics. She'd been controlling her powerful, arrogant husband for years by controlling the purse strings, and she'd done well enough. She'd made him pay every day of his life for cheating her; she'd made him pay a high price for whatever satisfaction he'd found in the arms of his mistress. And she'd made his life pure hell at every opportunity since the day she'd found out that mistress had borne him a son, announcing to the world that Alice, not Aaron, was the reason the Hawks were childless.

When Whitewood spoke again, he had obviously decided discretion was wiser than criticism.

"Perhaps we should keep close tabs on Ms. Chase, as well," he said neutrally. "I can have my man hire some help—"

Alice almost smiled. "Don't bother. And tell your man to keep on through tonight, but he'll no longer be needed after tomorrow. I have a man coming in the morning. He's handled some . . . delicate matters for me before. He'll handle this, as well."

Whitewood looked wary. "He knows ... what your plans are? You trust him?"

He knows more than you do, you ninny, Alice thought. *And he knows that I know enough to hang him.*

"Yes, I trust him. It would be ... most stupid of him to cross me." She gave Whitewood a look that made it clear that warning was meant for him, as well. "And he knows it."

"What is he going to do?"

"Whatever I tell him to do," Alice told the lawyer pointedly.

Whatever is necessary, she added to herself. *By any means necessary. It wouldn't be the first time.*

She left the lawyer stuffing papers into his briefcase and made her way slowly upstairs. It was becoming more difficult every day, and her breathing more laborious when she finally made it to her room. She hated the encroachment of age, hated the betrayal of her body when her mind was as sharp as it had ever been. But the satisfaction of remembering her past success did much to alleviate her sour mood.

No, it wouldn't be the first time she had resorted to extreme measures to hold what was hers. And if this was to be the last time, she would at least have the pleasure of knowing that it was to thwart the final wishes of the man who had never loved her. And that the son who should never have been born would pay the price.

"Aaron used to say the Hawks were either blessed or cursed, depending on who you asked," Kendall said quietly. "In the old days, people said there was a special god who looked out for them. Some said it was something closer to the devil."

She looked, as she had been doing periodically for the past hour, at Jason. He didn't react. He just sat there, staring at the book in his lap, not reading, just staring.

He'd begun with his name, and read until he'd reached the blank pages after the list of dates that followed that script entry. He'd muttered under his breath several times while reading, and twice had looked away from the book, his hands tensing as if he were about to slam it shut. But each time, looking like a man drawn utterly against his will, he had resumed reading that list. Intently, so intently that she doubted he was even aware of his surroundings or her presence.

Then he at last actually had slammed the book shut. But he hadn't said anything, he'd just continued to sit there, staring, his breathing strangely audible, as if he'd been running. It was after several long, silent minutes of this that she had finally begun to speak to him, in a soft, quiet tone that she hoped was soothing. She wasn't sure it had worked; his hands had tightened around the leather-bound volume. And he looked no less tense than he had before.

She tried again, her voice even softer this time.

"Aaron said most Hawks had only heard of the book, that many thought it didn't really exist. Hawks tend to be . . . logical. Pragmatic. They don't deal well with unexplainable things."

His grip on the book tightened visibly. He had beautiful hands, she thought irrelevantly. Long, agile fingers, tendons that stood out, defining the strong, masculine structure. The thin white line of a scar marked the top of his left hand, curving down from his wrist, across the back and fading away just above his ring finger. The mark only emphasized the strength there, and she wondered what it would be like to be touched by him, to know that strength was harnessed into gentleness for her.

She nearly gasped aloud at the unexpected thought; what on earth had come over her? She never indulged in silly fantasizing. Never. Not even about men as strikingly handsome as Jason West.

It must be the oddness of the whole situation, she told herself. The appearance of the book that, despite Aaron's insistence, she had doubted really existed. The impossibility of the whole thing was affecting her. Along with, she supposed ruefully, the suggestive remarks Jason West had made. But she'd never been one to fall prey to that kind of thing. Especially when she knew perfectly well those remarks had been made mainly to intimidate her, not out of any genuine desire or attraction to her. Men like Jason didn't pursue small, quiet women like her; tall, leggy, dramatic females were undoubtedly more his speed.

Hastily she got to her feet, turning away from him as she went on, afraid he was going to look up at any moment and catch her gaping at him, afraid he would read the knowledge of her wayward thoughts in her face. She resumed her explanation.

"Aaron was like that. He liked the heroic aspect of the Hawk legends, but he hated the magical parts. He used to scoff at them even as he told them to me. He'd laugh about it, and people who tagged anything they didn't understand as magic."

She turned back in time to see Jason's hands move, as if testing the book to be sure it was still real and solid beneath his fingers. As if he were looking for some way to deny its existence. Its presence. Its appearance. Its magic.

Kendall went on, knowing he was listening, and afraid she might never get another chance to convince this man that his father truly had changed before he'd died. She stood facing him, putting every bit of earnestness she could manage into her voice.

"But when he was so ill . . . he didn't laugh anymore. He said he'd come to believe in the book, and that it only appears when the last Hawk is in danger of becoming just that, the last."

She hesitated, watching him, but he still didn't move, didn't look at her.

"Like you," she said.

He flinched, as if she'd struck him, but he didn't speak. And still he didn't look at her. He just stared at the leather-bound book. She took a step toward him.

"I know this all sounds crazy," she said, her voice even quieter now, "and impossible—"

"What's impossible," he said, speaking for the first time since he'd seen his name inscribed on that gilt-edged page, "is what's in this book."

His voice was tight, tense, like a wire pulled to the point of snapping. Kendall sat down on the edge of the bed, near Jason's feet. He hadn't changed his position, but the air of insouciance had vanished. His body was rigid, his jaw clenched.

"Jason," she began, but stopped when, at last, his head came up and she saw his eyes. They had been either glacial or hot with anger since she'd met him, but nothing like they were at this moment. She'd seen Aaron in a rage over a threatened hostile takeover of Hawk Industries, and had thought then she never had and never would see a fiercer gaze. She had now.

"There are things in here that no one knows. *No one.*" His voice dropped on the words, but they were no less harsh because of it. "Things about me. About my mother. Things I never knew about her. Things I never told her, or anyone else, about me."

"So it is . . . magic," she said, thinking it ridiculous even as she said it, knowing that it was only some childishly hopeful part of her that wanted to believe.

"Don't be ridiculous," he snapped. He gave her a look that was half scorn, half disbelief. "You want me to believe that you helped run Hawk Industries, but your best explanation of this is magic? That's crap, and you know it. Or should."

She didn't react to his tone, and she had no way to answer what were soundly logical points. "Then what's your explanation?"

He grimaced. "I don't have one. Yet."

The last word was ominous and, coupled with the look he gave her, almost threatening. And it poked at a sore spot within her that had had more than enough prodding since Jason West had come to Sunridge. Her chin came up.

"If you think I managed to sneak that into your room, while you were inside, then right under your nose sneak it into your suitcase, and somehow in between, also right under your nose, add an entire section of hand calligraphy to it, then perhaps it's *your* theory that needs rethinking."

He glanced at the book he still held. She saw his jaw tense, and knew he'd already, however reluctantly, realized the truth of what she'd said. She hastened to pound home the point.

"It seems you have two possibilities. One you can physically disprove, and one you can't. Perhaps I could have waltzed the book right past you into your room, but there's no way I could have gotten it into your bag, because it was already in your car when I got here."

"You could have followed me to the airport."

"And put the book in your suitcase without you seeing me? And got back here before you? You don't give yourself much credit, do you?"

He shifted uncomfortably, and she knew that she'd struck home. He wasn't the kind of man who missed things. Like Aaron, she suspected his son missed very little of what went on around him. Under any circumstances.

"Even if that were true," she said, "there's certainly no way I could have added that new section. That would take time. The book wasn't out of your sight long enough. You *know* that."

His hands clenched around the book, so tightly she could hear the faint sound of his fingers moving on the leather. His booted feet came off the bed and hit the floor. He stood up. With a wild movement, he flung it across the room. It bounced off of the wall with a heavy thud, barely missing the mirror over the dresser. It dropped to the polished surface of the dresser, then slid across it to fall with a more muffled thud to the floor.

"There's another option," he muttered. "I'm losing my mind."

"No, Jason. You're not going crazy." She paused, then added softly, "Don't try and resolve everything now. Right now you need to concentrate on Alice."

He grimaced. "Ah, yes. The charming widow."

"There's no excuse for what she's trying to do." Kendall took a deep breath. "But I think I . . . understand her a little better now. She's very bitter. As bitter as you are. And for the same reasons, I think."

Jason turned on his heel to glare are her. "What's that supposed to mean?"

"Aaron never loved her. She was married to him for over forty years, she loved him as much as she could ever love anyone, and he never loved her back."

Jason's mouth twisted. "Is that what you think this is about? That my father never *loved* me?" He nearly spat out the word. "Grow up, Kendall. Only a fool twists himself up into knots over what passes for love in this world."

"Then why are you so angry?"

"I'm angry," he bit out, "because I don't like being played for a fool. I'm angry because whatever crazy game you're up to, you think I'm going to buy it. I'm angry because whoever did this"—he kicked at the book, lying on the floor near his feet—"has been prying into things that are no one's business but mine. You told me whoever Aaron hired hadn't found me yet. If I'm supposed to believe that, then explain to me how things no one else knows got into that book."

"The same way the book got here in the first place."

"Are we back to that? Magic?" He shook his head scornfully. "You really believe it, don't you? How did you last as long as you did with that bastard? From everything I've read, he was the most hard-nosed, skeptical son of a bitch in the world."

"He was," Kendall agreed. "And that part of him fought with the Hawk heritage every day. I think that's what drove him to tell me the stories. He wanted someone else to find them as absurd as he wanted to."

"He wanted to find them absurd?"

She nodded slowly. "I think so. He couldn't deal with that part of it. Any more than you can."

His eyes narrowed as he looked at her. "But you can? You didn't find them . . . absurd?"

She sighed, knowing there was no way to explain without telling this man things she didn't want to tell him. If she could explain even then; she wasn't sure she understood herself. But she also sensed that if she didn't, his willingness to listen would evaporate. If it took baring her soul to a man who would no doubt laugh to get the job done, then she would do it. She would just be prepared for the ridicule when it came, she told herself.

"Maybe I didn't want to find them absurd," she said slowly.

"You wanted to believe in stories about magic books?"

She nearly changed her mind then, but made herself go on. She had to, she told herself. For Aaron's sake. She was his voice now, his only chance to reach out to the son he'd never known.

"It isn't the book or the idea of magic. Not really. It was the idea of the Hawks, a family that continued uninterrupted, over centuries, that appealed to me. I think it's wonderful."

"Wonderful?" He nudged the book with his toe, none too gently. "This thing is some kind of bad cosmic joke, and you think it's wonderful?"

"I never knew about my family, never knew where I came from. My parents died before they could tell me. Maybe that's why . . ."

Her words trailed off as he gave her a look rife with suspicion, a look she read easily.

"No, this isn't a ploy to try and gain your sympathy." He looked startled, and she chuckled wryly. "You looked at me just like Aaron looked at anyone he thought was trying to manipulate him. Sorry," she added hastily when he stiffened, "I know you don't like being compared to him, but it's really amazing."

He glanced at the book on the floor, and she somehow knew what he was thinking.

"But not as amazing as the resemblance between you and Joshua Hawk, is it? What does the tree say? Is he your . . . that'd be what, half a dozen or so greats before the grandfather?"

"I don't know," he said as he stood there, staring down at the book, and there was something in his voice that hadn't been there before, some catch, some tightness. She couldn't put a name to it, but it made him seem vulnerable somehow. It didn't seem possible, but it was an impression that wouldn't go away. And Aaron had taught her to trust her impressions.

"You didn't look?" she said, making her voice matter-of-fact with an effort. She leaned over to pick up the book.

"No," he said. That odd tone was still there.

"Well, let's see then," she said, trying to sound no more concerned than if she were simply looking something up in a dictionary. She found the page, stared again for a moment at the uncanny resemblance between Jason and the man in the picture. She wished she could read the whole story, she wanted to know about this man, and the woman beside him. But now was not the time. She turned past the picture and the story to the page where the family tree began again. She turned the book sideways and lifted a finger to begin tracing the intricate trail that began anew with the five children born to Joshua and Kathleen Hawk. A trail whose first line belonged to their firstborn son.

Jason Hawk.

Chapter Nine

He didn't know where he was going. He only knew he had to get out of here. He had to get away from this room. Away from that damned book. And away from Kendall.

He'd again thrown the book across the room, realizing the absurdity of reacting so strongly even as he did it. Just as he realized the absurdity of the fact that he was running, actually running, as if to escape some fate too horrible to be met head-on. Running in a way he hadn't run since he'd been that scared kid living by his wits on the streets of Seattle.

The whole thing was nonsense, but he was reacting as if it were real. As if Kendall's ridiculous tales were real.

He jammed his hands into his pockets as he slowed to a walk, wishing he'd grabbed his coat. Wishing he'd been rational enough to take the car, if not rational enough to stop himself from taking off at all, into the middle of the night.

And, he thought wryly, rational enough not to go charging down the main highway, where even at this late hour cars at high speed claimed the right of way and pedestrians were, if not actually targets, at least fair game. That white sedan had nearly taken him out.

He should go back. Or at least get off this road, he thought as he heard the squeal of tires as a car made a sharp turn.

What you should do is get the hell out of town, he told himself. *Get yourself back home, where the only mystery you have to deal with is when and where are the salmon*

*going to run, and why won't that diesel on McKenna's
old trawler smooth out. Real things. Not fantasies. Not
legends made up by a dying old man. Not books that
materialized out of thin air and haunted you.*

And sent you running away like a scared kid.

He lifted his head and looked around. If he hadn't
already known from the fresh, crisp breeze, here flowing
down from the higher elevations of the Sierras unim-
peded by buildings, carrying the scent of pine and fir and
the coldness of snow, the gravel shoulder he stood on
told him he was outside the city limits. Sunridge preferred landscaped highways, and with the Hawks as part
of their tax base, they could afford it.

He sighed. If he went back, Kendall would . . . He
wasn't sure what she would do. She hadn't tried to stop
him from leaving. She hadn't said a word, even when
he'd slammed the book she seemed so enamored of
against the wall.

He took a couple of steps back from the road and sat
on the metal guardrail. It was cold and bit into the backs
of his thighs. He thought he'd long been past this feeling
of not being sure what to do, and he didn't like revisiting
it. And now that the initial reaction to the impossibility
he'd just confronted had ebbed a little, he was feeling a
little foolish. And he didn't like that either.

He didn't know how long he'd been sitting there in
the dark when it registered, that itchy feeling at the back
of his neck, the same kind of prickly feeling he'd had
coming out of the motel office. His head came up sharply
and he looked around, wondering what was causing it
this time. The only thing he noticed was a white sedan
pulled over to the side across the road, its driver sitting
motionless, appearing to be staring at something over
Jason's left shoulder.

A white sedan. Very much like the one that had nearly
hit him minutes ago. The sound of those screeching tires
seemed to echo in his head. And there was nothing but
a stand of trees over his left shoulder. Especially nothing
that could be seen in the dark of night.

He went very still, then grimaced. There were a million
cars like that on the road. And it was unlikely that the

driver of this one had made a screeching U-turn just to sit across the road and pretend not to be watching him.

It's that damn book, he thought with biting acidity. *It's put your imagination into overdrive.*

He stood up swiftly, shoved his hands back in his pockets, and started walking again. Only once did he glance back, laughing at himself when he saw the white car still sitting there, clearly uninterested in his departure.

He went slowly, uncertain if he wanted to go farther, but certain he didn't want to go back. Even though he was tired. Too tired. He hadn't slept in what seemed like forever, and he'd lost perspective on this whole thing, that was all. He was off balance, that was why he was thinking this way. Why he was imagining people following him. Why he was reacting like this to the book. And to Kendall. All he needed was some sleep, and things would slide back into place. Hell, maybe he hadn't really seen what he thought he'd seen in the damn book. Maybe it was just too many memories stirring in his exhausted mind.

Every step made him feel more the fool. By the time he finally reached the mileage sign that told him the small airport was five miles away, it was almost overwhelming. He didn't even have the energy to straighten his shoulders when he realized he was hunching them; he felt like he had in those wild years on the street, when he'd spent so much time trying to fade into the background, to make himself inconspicuous.

When another car whizzed by at close range, he thought again about turning back. He didn't know where the hell he was going, anyway. Or what the point of this was.

And the farther you go, the longer it's going to take you to get back, he thought wryly. *Even if it's just to jump in the car and get the hell out of Dodge.*

Another car went by, slower this time. White again. His head came up sharply; the same car?

Before he could decide, he caught a glimpse of another car out of the corner of his eye. Blue, it looked like, although it was hard to tell in the faint light. He turned to see Kendall's coupe approaching. He stopped walking, and she pulled to a halt beside him. The passenger window went down. She leaned over to look at him.

"It's late. And it's going to be a long walk back."

"In more ways than one," he muttered.

"Finding any answers out here?"

"No."

"Might as well get in, then."

He had a feeling that was a sure way not to find answers, but to further confuse the issue; Kendall Chase had a strange effect on his thinking process. When he was with her, she even managed to have him taking that silly book half seriously. But he still found himself reaching for the door handle.

He didn't say anything, just pulled the door shut and sat looking rather doggedly forward. To his surprise, she didn't head back for the motel. Instead she took a side road he didn't recognize, and that wasn't marked except with a county road sign. In what seemed like moments the busy highway was out of sight. And out of hearing; the buffer of hills and trees made it seem as if they'd crossed over into another world.

He gave her a sideways glance. Although she didn't look at him, she seemed to sense his scrutiny.

"I thought you might want to go someplace ... conducive to heavy thinking," she said calmly, as if he hadn't taken off like a seal spooked by a pod of orcas.

He didn't say anything, just turned his attention back to the passing scene, trees and brush looking ghostly in the darkness. They climbed a little farther, then she turned off onto a narrow, unpaved track that wound through a thick stand of Douglas fir. The familiar trees, which grew in profusion at home, were an unexpectedly comforting sight. And smell; he rolled down the window and breathed deeply.

A few minutes later he caught a glimpse of water between the needled branches of the evergreens. He heard the crunch of dry needles and the sound of soft dirt beneath the tires as she turned off the unpaved road. She stopped the car a few yards farther on, near a break in the trees that led down to the edge of a pond large enough to be called a small lake. When she turned the car off, the quiet rolled in almost palpably, the only sounds the occasional stirring of branches and the rustle of some night creature not still confused by the unexpected snow.

A peaceful place. Conducive, as she'd said, to heavy thinking.

He leaned his head back on the headrest. He moved his hand to the seat to shift to a more comfortable position, and his fingers brushed a solid object. He smothered a sigh. He didn't have to look to know it was the book; he'd gotten that same odd rush of warmth and comfort he got every time he touched the thing. It figured that she would bring it along. And right now he was too tired to care.

Silence spun out between them, but it wasn't filled with the tension he'd come to expect. And when, after what seemed like a long time, he spoke, he was able to do it with some semblance of rational calm.

"I never told anybody where I'd gone when I ran away."

She didn't seem surprised that he'd picked up where they'd left off when he'd flung the book aside. She merely flipped on an interior car light and reached for the book.

"You mean when you were twelve?"

He nodded without looking at her. "No one ever knew I came back here. I didn't see anyone, talk to anyone, and nobody saw me. The cops found me on a bus back to L.A., and I never told them that I'd come here. Or my mother. She would have been ..."

He stopped, unable to find the words for how upset he knew his mother would have been had she ever known he'd come back here, how hurt she would have been if she'd known he'd come to try to find out something about his father. He'd wondered, later, if she'd guessed, if that's why she had packed them up and moved to Seattle a month later, to put more distance between him and the man he was so angrily curious about.

"But it's there," Kendall said. "Listed with the date you left and were found."

"No one knew," he insisted. "There's no way that could be listed there."

Jason looked at Kendall then, with eyes that felt dry and gritty from lack of sleep. He locked his hands together, resisting the urge to rub at his eyes, knowing it would only exacerbate the sandy feeling to a burning that would be even worse. She looked at the book, her expression pensive.

"I never told anyone about that knife fight, either," he added.

He saw her gaze flick from the book to his left hand, and realized he'd been unconsciously running his fingers along the scar. He made himself stop. His mouth twisted. "And I learned to fight a lot better, after that. With or without a knife."

Or with or without a gun, or damn near any other weapon you could find on the street, Jason added silently, catching himself rubbing at the old scar again and yanking his hands apart in irritation.

"The point is," he said, "there's no way in hell anybody could have found out all this. So how the hell did it end up here? And why—how—is it changing? First it was just a list of dates and events, now it's becoming a story in places, written like some damn family saga, like the rest of this thing is."

Kendall hesitated. He didn't blame her. She kept coming up with the same answer, and he kept throwing it back at her. It was pointless. She glanced down at the book, then reached to open it to the section that began with his name. It didn't bother him much that she'd probably read it; there didn't seem to be much point. This whole thing was becoming too weird to worry about someone discovering secrets he'd kept for years. Especially when they'd apparently already been discovered.

She turned in the driver's seat to face him. "Is the rest ... true, too?"

He shrugged wearily. There didn't seem to be any point in denying the truth, either.

"The timing fits. I don't know if the exact dates are right. What happened to me is ... accurate. And the facts about my mother are right, I think. What I remember, anyway. The rest, about the old man, I don't know. My mother never talked about him."

"I didn't mean the part about Aaron. I know that's true. He told me how he met your mother, when she came to work for him. He said he knew the first time he saw her that she was the one, but he was already married to Alice."

"Love at first sight?" His tone was bitter.

"He loved her, Jason."

"Right," he muttered. "If that book is right, then no matter what his reputation, he was a spineless, gutless coward. First he let that woman buy him, then walk all over him."

"Alice had him over a barrel," Kendall said, "thanks to her father tying up what he'd loaned Aaron with stock and options. The only peace he found in his life was with your mother. But he couldn't divorce Alice and marry her."

He lifted a brow. "So you don't think he should give up his empire for love? And here I thought you were a romantic."

He heard her breath catch, but Jason had the oddest feeling it wasn't because of what he'd said. At least not in the way he'd meant it. She as looking at him as if she were afraid he could read her mind.

"What I think he should or shouldn't have done doesn't matter," she said. "Even Hawks have their weak spots, and perhaps Aaron's was not having the courage to give it all up and go to the woman he loved."

" 'Even Hawks'? Is that him talking, or you?"

"That doesn't matter either. What matters is that he couldn't walk away. Hawk Industries was Aaron's life. He'd fought for years to build it, and then fought to keep it."

"Sold himself, you mean. Body and soul."

"Yes," she said, surprising him with her easy agreement. She leaned forward. "He did. And he knew it. Alice made certain of that. But I swear, Jason, he never knew how vicious she really was. He never would have stayed if he had."

"I doubt that."

"You wouldn't, if you'd seen the life he lived with Alice. The longer he lived with her, the worse he got. And the worse she got. She made him pay every day of his life."

"As my mother paid every day of hers," he said coldly. "I heard her crying at night, when she thought I was asleep. I saw her get old before her time, never smiling, never laughing. So much for love."

"He did love her," Kendall insisted.

"Then why the hell did he send her away?"

She looked at him in surprise. "What?"

His mouth twisted. "Never mind. I know. Because of me. Because after years of being his quiet, obedient mistress, she had the bad judgment to get pregnant. So he fired her. Then he dumped her."

"That's not true." Kendall sounded so indignant it startled him. "Aaron never sent her away. She quit, after she told him she was pregnant but he told her he still couldn't divorce Alice, because he'd lose everything. That's when she left him." Her arched brows furrowed as she looked at him. "Did she actually tell you Aaron abandoned her?"

Jason tried, but remembering that far back was difficult with a brain that was groggy from lack of sleep. "I . . . don't remember. I just always knew."

"It doesn't make sense, Jason. If Aaron had truly done that, why would your mother have stayed here until you were nearly five?" She lifted the book. "Besides, you read it, you know why she left. You know it was because of Alice, and her threats."

"She left because Aaron Hawk didn't want her anymore," he answered automatically. "And he sure as hell didn't want me." His brows lowered as the rest of what she'd said registered in his foggy mind at last. "I did read it. There wasn't anything in there about Alice threatening my mother."

Kendall blinked. She glanced down at the book, still open to the last page of precise, elegant script. Then she lifted her head to look at him again.

"It's right here. After the list of just dates, in this part written like a story. Where it says you left Sunridge, and why."

"Why?" he asked, his voice tight.

She looked at him curiously, but went on explaining without comment. "Yes. You know, about how Alice found out about you, and threatened your mother, and you, if she didn't take you and leave Sunridge. That's what I meant about Alice being so vicious. When she found out you'd been born, she seemed to lose control."

Jason shook his head sharply, his gaze flicking from the book to her face. "What are you talking about?"

"Did you miss this part?" She pointed at the last page of writing. "Here, where it says your mother found you outside the apartment one day, and there was a man watching you, a man she'd seen with Alice before."

"The bus stop," he murmured, stunned as she mentioned the day he had remembered so vividly ... was it just today? Yesterday, he thought vaguely. It had to be after midnight. God, he couldn't think. "There was a man there ..."

"Yes, it says so, right here." She gestured at the page again.

He stared at the book. Then he looked at her face. There was no sign she was lying, no sign that she was anything but puzzled by his reaction. Jason's heart began to slam in his chest.

"What else does it say?" His voice was taut and hoarse.

She looked mystified, but after a moment glanced down and said, "Just that she was frightened, frightened that Alice truly would harm you. So she took you and left for Los Angeles that same week." Her head came up again. "Jason, are you all right?"

He ignored her concern, not wanting to hear about what must be showing in his face. He reached for the book.

"Let me see it."

His voice was still harsh, and she surrendered it to him without protest.

"What's wrong?" she asked. "You look ... pale."

He stared down at the stylized writing. It was there, amid the simple timetable of events that no one should have been able to put together. It was just as she'd said. The story of Alice's threats, of his mother's fear, and their late-night escape from Sunridge. Just as it had happened. Even the explanation of how Alice had discovered in one her spying forays into Aaron's personal papers that five years prior he had paid the hospital bills for one Elizabeth West, who delivered a baby boy on October twenty-seventh. It was all there.

"My God, Jason, what is it?"

Kendall sounded distressed. And when at last he managed to look up at her, he saw that she looked more than concerned, she looked alarmed. Twice he tried to speak and failed. When he finally got the words out, they came brokenly, an echo of what he was feeling.

"I . . . this wasn't there . . . when I read it. It only showed . . . the dates we moved. It never said why . . ."

Kendall stared at him. And he suddenly understood what it had been like for her to go up in the face of his disbelief. She looked at the book, then back at his face. He turned the book around and jabbed a desperate finger at the last page.

"Kendall," he said urgently. "It wasn't there. None of this was there. None of this stuff about Alice."

"Are you saying," she asked slowly, "that when you read this back in the room, these words weren't there? That it ended"—she reached out and flipped a page backward—"back here?"

He nodded, feeling an odd numbness overtaking him as he stared at the page her finger rested upon. He couldn't believe she'd done it. She hadn't had time. But it was there. And she looked as bewildered as he felt.

"It was blank," he whispered. "Right after that line. I swear it."

Kendall stared at him, her eyes wide with wonder. "I believe you," she said softly.

He dropped the book, heedless of how it fell to the floor, as if it had burned his fingers. He stared at it, very much afraid it had seared his soul.

"It's cold out here," the man with the barren eyes and wispy, pale blond hair complained as he sat on the handi-

est gravestone. He looked down at one sleeve of his dark
jacket, frowned, and plucked at something. "And why
did we have to meet so damned early in the morning?
It's barely after dawn."

"I'm almost twice your age," Alice Hawk said unsym-
pathetically. "If I can stand it, you can."

It gave her a perverse sort of pleasure to do this here,
beside Aaron's fresh grave. This was the final payback,
and it was fitting that it should be arranged here.

It was a gloomy, dismal day, a major snowstorm was
in the forecast for the coming week, and the wind that
blew up the small valley to whirl around the cemetery
seemed exceptionally chilly today. It bit into her bones
despite her heavy coat, but she hid all signs of discomfort, knowing with some primal instinct she didn't question that to show weakness to this man could be
dangerous.

The man held up what appeared to be a pale blond
hair from his sleeve, apparently one of his own, and
frowned again. He flicked his fingers to discard it, then
looked at her assessingly. He grinned, a mirthless contor-
tion of his thin mouth that spoke more of cruelty than
pleasure. Or of a man who got the latter out of the
former.

"You always were a tough old bat," he said with an
admiration that could have been real.

"I still am," Alice answered, the faintest hint of warning in her voice.

He had been a twenty-year-old punk, cocky and arrogant, when she'd first met him. She'd overheard him
mentioned then as a ruthless kid who didn't much care
how he earned his money as long as it was enough to
keep him in the lifestyle he aspired to. It had been ludi-
crously easy for her to convince him her plan would be
mutually beneficial to them both, and he'd had the
shrewdness to take her money—and her assurance of
retribution if he ever talked—very seriously. He'd done
the job neatly, without incriminating evidence left behind, and had kept his mouth shut as promised. For
twenty years.

She'd had someone watch him, for a while, long

enough to satisfy herself that he wouldn't be foolish enough to attempt some kind of blackmail. But instead, he'd used her money and the little task he'd done for her to build a profitable career out of handling messy little problems for people who needed the guarantee of discretion.

In a way, she really was responsible for him, she thought, with a twisted sort of pride. Whether that actually had anything to do with his quick response when she had contacted him after this time, she didn't know. It didn't matter. He was here, that was what counted, and if necessary he would do what had to be done, when it had to be done. She could relax; everything would be all right, as long as she had this last line of defense. And in the meantime, he would be useful in hurrying things along.

She studied him for a moment. In the twenty years since she'd first used him, he'd changed very little. He was a bit heavier, and his hair was thinning, but his eyes were still the barren, lifeless things they'd been at twenty.

And he was still the only person she'd ever met who made her genuinely, thoroughly nervous. He was worse than a restless tiger on a thin leash, he was that tiger with that leash already chewed halfway through. She would use his nerveless, emotionless expertise, but she would never, ever turn her back on him.

He was exactly what she needed now.

"It's been a long time," he said.

"Yes."

"Things have been going pretty smoothly for you since I took care of that little problem," he asserted.

Smoothly. She quashed an acid retort. Smooth was hardly the word she would use for her life in the past twenty years. She had had to fight every day of that time. She had known the gamble she was taking when she'd hired him the first time. She had known that were Aaron to find out, it could well be the last straw, the one thing that would break her hold on him. She'd lived in fear of that for years. But he hadn't found out.

And she'd had the pleasure of knowing she'd taken

the heart out of the man who had refused to give it to her.

"So," he said, "what is it this time?"

"The end," she said flatly.

"The end?"

"Of something that never should have happened. That should have ended a long time ago."

He looked at her with those inert eyes that had at first made her think he wasn't very bright, but that she had soon learned were merely the outward sign of his inward amoral nature. He was ruled by no law but his own unyielding, egocentric one. It was what made him good at what he did. And unswayable in intent; right and wrong were merely words to him, and his targets just that and nothing more, rousing no more emotion in him than any inanimate object.

Suddenly he grinned at her again, that same twisting of his lips as before. "Something that should have ended twenty years ago, maybe?" he suggested.

She hesitated, then decided it would be wise to give him his due.

"Exactly," she said. She reached into her bag and pulled out a manila envelope. "Here are photographs of the two people I'm concerned about. And what information I have."

He took it without looking at the contents, without ever looking away from her face. He waited, silently. She wondered if the silence was some kind of power play, the kind she had learned early on from watching her father, then Aaron over the years. For a moment she weighed the possible cost of giving in to him, the chances he would think her afraid to play the game with him.

She smiled at him, a chilly, superior smile that told him she knew exactly what he was doing, and that she was willing to concede on this small point because she was still, ultimately, in charge. She'd come to enjoy this kind of encounter, she realized. Having a dangerous man like this at her beck and call was simply another form of exercising her power. The more powerful the man who had to come to heel at her command, the greater her enjoyment.

She had never quite managed to bring Aaron completely to heel. But she would settle for destroying his son.

"Are you ready for your instructions?" she asked.

He smiled back at her, allowing her the superiority as she had allowed him the power play. They understood each other, Alice thought.

Yes, he was just what she needed.

Chapter Ten

~

The tap on the door brought Kendall out of a light doze. She felt disoriented, looking around the motel room groggily. The grayish light of early morning was seeping in from behind the customary blackout curtains. She moved gingerly, stiff from having fallen asleep in the chair, her head on the table, pillowed by her arms.

She shook her head to clear it. And became instantly aware of the sound of Jason West's steady breathing. She glanced at the bed, able to make out only the long, lean shape of him in the dim light.

He'd looked so worn out last night, and she could guess the kind of emotional toll the past few hours must have taken on him, even if he refused to acknowledge it. When they'd at last come back here, and he'd finally admitted how long he'd been up, with only four hours of sleep, she'd made him lie down. Or rather, she suspected, he'd let her convince him, no doubt only because he was too exhausted to argue. And despite the mystery, despite the unanswered questions, he'd tugged off his sweater and boots, toppled over, and gone quickly, if restlessly, to sleep.

The tap on the door came again, and her head cleared a little more. She got up from the chair and went to peer through the peephole. The sight of George Alton's round, comfortably familiar face, made rounder by the fish-eye effect of the peephole, eased her nerves a little. As quietly as she could, she unlatched the locks on the door and edged it open enough so she could slip outside without waking Jason.

"Are you all right?" Alton said, glancing into the room in the moment before she closed the door, stopping just short of the lock snapping so she could get back in.

"I'm fine."

"I swung by here on my way to the office and saw that car here, next to yours. It looked like the one West had rented, so I stopped. It is the same car. The plate matches."

She nodded. "He came back late last night. He missed his plane."

Alton swore softly. "Damn it. I should have stuck with him. I followed him out to the airport, watched him check in his car and go into the terminal. I figured he was on his way, so I came back to town. He must have walked right back out and gotten the same car back."

"It's all right, George."

"Why didn't he just take another flight last night? Why did he come back here? Why didn't he stay out near the airport, for a flight this morning? Did he bother you? Is he in the next room or—"

She held up her hand to stop the flow of questions. She could answer them all, but she knew that for all his amiable disposition, Alton was a man very much grounded in reality. He'd be no more likely to believe in the appearance of the Hawk family history than Jason had, and she didn't have the energy to go through that again.

"He didn't bother me, George."

At least not the way you mean, she amended silently, and somewhat embarrassedly; she figured bother was a good enough word for the strange effect Jason had on her.

"And he's not next door," she added, nodding at the door behind her. "He's in there."

"What?" Alton said, clearly startled.

"Asleep. He was exhausted," she explained. "He'd been up for nearly forty hours, and only slept here for four hours before the funeral. I couldn't very well kick him out when he was dead on his feet, practically falling over."

Alton didn't look happy. "I'll stay until he wakes up, then. And gets out of here."

Kendall shook her head. "That's not necessary."

Alton looked at her much as Aaron sometimes had, when she'd come in the morning after one of her rare dates. Since her father had died when she was so young, it had taken her a long time to recognize it as a sort of fatherly concern. It touched her, but still she stifled a sigh. She was thirty-three years old, yet so many men seemed to feel compelled to treat her as if she were a child who needed protection, simply because she was small and looked younger than her age.

Stop it, she chastised herself inwardly. *You should be glad someone cares at all.* She smiled, reaching out to pat Alton's arm appreciatively, tried to reassure him.

"Thank you, George. But really, believe me, he has a lot more on his mind than . . . bothering me. It would be better if you left. We made some progress last night, and I don't want to lose that."

"He actually listened to you?"

"A little," she said carefully, knowing full well it had been the mysterious book that had gotten Jason's attention so undividedly, not any power of persuasion on her part. "I think he'll really listen today, after he's had some sleep. I'll be fine."

Alton didn't look happy, but he finally agreed. And again Kendall was touched by his obvious concern; it was something she'd had little of in her life. She knew Alton had grown children of his own, and she felt a pang she hadn't experienced in a long time, a wish that she had had her own father a little longer. He would have been an honest, caring man like this, she thought. She knew he would have.

"If you're sure," he said doubtfully.

She nodded. "I think he'll listen," she repeated.

She was certain he would; he'd been too agitated over the extraordinary happenings with the book not to. Not that he didn't have reason to be agitated, what with the contents changing practically before their eyes—

"George, wait," she said in the instant he turned to go. He stopped and turned back to her.

She had earlier decided not to do this, not without consulting Jason, but what had appeared in the book last night had changed her mind. If the events detailed there were true, and Alice had threatened Jason's mother, if she had stooped so low as to threaten a small child, then her threat to frame Jason and herself was just the latest in a pattern. A pattern someone else should know about.

Quickly she told the detective what had happened in her meeting with Alice and Darren Whitewood. When she'd finished, he whistled, long and low.

"She's going for all the marbles, isn't she?"

Kendall nodded. "I just wanted someone else to know." She didn't say "just in case," but she knew Alton knew it as well as she did.

"You want me to talk to some people on the force?"

Kendall shook her head. "Not yet. She hasn't really done anything, just . . . threatened."

"And bought a lawyer. You want me to start looking into it? Maybe check out this Whitewood character, see who these contacts he's bragging about might be?"

She thought about it for a moment, then shook her head. "Keep going on doing what you're doing. I don't think they'll do anything until they know for sure they have to. And I need to know about Jason first. How to get him to accede to what Aaron wanted."

"You think he will?"

"I don't know. I only know I have to try."

"And if he won't?"

"Then I'll do it myself." She reached for the door, which seemed to have slipped open a little.

"And bring Alice down on you? She'll carry out that threat, you know."

"I have no choice," she said simply. "It's Aaron's last wish that Jason have this inheritance."

"You know he never would have wanted you to risk going to jail."

She smiled wryly. "I'm under no illusions about Aaron, George. No, he wouldn't have wanted me in jail, but he wanted this more. Jason is his son."

"I think you underestimate Aaron's feelings for you." Alton jerked a thumb toward the door. "That may be his son in there, but you were practically a daughter to him. I knew Aaron for a long time, and he never worried about anyone the way he did about you."

"Especially not his son."

Kendall smothered a startled yelp and spun around at the sound of the deep, sleep-husky voice from behind and above her. The door obviously hadn't slipped open by itself, and she tried to remember when she'd noticed it, how much Jason might have heard. And tried not to think about the havoc that throaty voice had caused in her.

"So," Alton said, looking Jason up and down, "you're the young Hawk."

Kendall darted a glance at Alton, thinking she'd have to appease Jason, knowing how he reacted to being called by his father's name. But when she looked back at Jason, and really saw him this time, her breath caught in her throat and all words escaped her.

He looked just like he had sounded: slightly rumpled and tousle-haired, and sleepily sexy. His shirt buttons had worked loose in his restless slumber, and the fabric was gaping open, baring an unsettling amount of muscular chest and belly to her. She had to force herself to look away, to raise her eyes to his face.

There was nothing sleepily sexy about his eyes. They were fixed on George Alton, and they were as coolly assessing as Kendall had ever seen them. But to her surprise, he didn't react to Alton's use of the name. Nor to Alton's obvious knowledge of who he was.

"So," he said, mimicking Alton's tone perfectly, "who—and what—are you?"

Kendall tensed, but Alton handled it smoothly.

"I'm a friend of Kendall's. I saw her car here and stopped to see if she was all right." His eyes flicked over Jason once more, seeming to linger for a moment on the unbuttoned shirt. "I didn't expect to find you here."

Jason's mouth quirked. "Worried about her virtue?"

"Not unless you're a lot dumber than you look."

Jason didn't react at all to the jab. He just stood there, watching Alton steadily, unflinching. After a moment the older man chuckled.

"Damn. You really are a chip off the old block of ice, aren't you?"

"So I've been told."

Jason's tone was dry rather than sharp, and Kendall wondered if it was a sign he was perhaps beginning to accept his heritage. More likely, she told herself firmly, it just meant he still hadn't had enough sleep.

Alton gave Kendall a final glance before saying, "I'll be on my way, then."

Kendall nodded, reassuring the man without speaking that she was in no danger from Jason. At least, not the kind of danger he was thinking of. The only danger she was in when it came to Jason West seemed to stem from her own seemingly irrepressible imagination.

She wondered, as she watched Alton give them a final glance before driving away, if the strangeness of this whole thing with the mysterious Hawk book was affecting her, making her react in a way her unruffled composure and level head never would have allowed before.

"Who is he really?"

She turned back at Jason's words, to see him leaning with one shoulder propped against the doorjamb, his arms crossed in front of him. His stance thankfully hid that heart-accelerating view of his chest, and the ridged, flat abdomen that made her want to touch to see if it was truly as solidly muscled as it appeared, but somehow he was having the same effect on her as before. The same effect he'd had on her when she'd sat in the chair he'd been using, watching him sleep. Watching the dark, thick semicircles of his lashes, so long they rested against his cheeks, watching the slight relaxation of his mouth, allowing her for the first time to recognize the sensual fullness of his lips.

She had wanted to lie down beside him, to soothe away the lines of strain from his brow, to simply hold him until he slept quietly, without that restive tossing and turning. She had wanted to smooth his hair back from his forehead, to run her fingers through the dark thickness of it. She had wanted to kiss his temple, his cheek, his mouth.

She had wanted to do things that utterly astonished

her with both their unexpectedness and their unfamiliarity. Things that made her blood heat and her heart pound even now, when he was looking at her with that cool detachment she'd come to know so well.

With an effort—enough of an effort to embarrass her with her own foolishness—she made herself remember what he'd asked her.

"George Alton is ... what he said. A friend."

It was true. More than she'd realized until the past couple of days. It just wasn't all of the truth.

Jason just looked at her. The way Aaron looked at someone he didn't believe. The way Jason had been looking at her since she'd first seen him at the cemetery.

And she'd had enough. She straightened her shoulders and said with dignity, "He was a friend of Aaron's for years. And now he seems to be looking out for me."

"Did the old man ask him to?"

Startled by the idea, she considered it. "I . . . don't know. I never ... why would he?"

"Seems logical," Jason said. He gestured in the direction Alton had gone. "According to him, you were practically the old man's daughter."

A fierce, swamping emotion flooded her, one she'd been experiencing off and on since the day Aaron had first told her he had a son he'd never known. It was guilt, that most crippling of emotions, and no matter how often she told herself it wasn't her fault, that she had had nothing to do with Aaron's choices, she still felt it.

"I'm so sorry, Jason," she whispered.

He blinked, apparently startled. Then, as usual, his expression settled into one of wary suspicion. "Sorry about what?"

"That I was here, and you weren't. That I had Aaron's help and support when you didn't. That he spent so much time, gave me so many chances, and that he ... cared for me, when it should have all gone to you."

For an instant she saw something flicker in his eyes, some hesitation that she'd never seen there before. But it was gone before she could put a name to it, to be replaced with his usual mocking flippancy.

"Very nice, Kendall. Touching. Generous. If I were

even the tiniest bit of a fool, I might buy it. But I assure you, I'm not."

"No," she said on an exhalation, weary of the fight, "I'm sure you're not. You're too much your father's son for that."

She pushed past him back into the room, wishing right now for nothing more than that he would go away and let her sleep for about a week. Hopefully she would then wake up recovered from whatever lunacy had seized her, making her look at him as she had while he slept, imagining a softness that wasn't there, a need for comfort he would scorn, and a pain he would no doubt deny to the death. But the memory of his face when he'd talked of his mother, about stealing a car to save her a long walk in freezing rain, had settled somewhere in a corner of her mind and refused to leave.

She went into the bathroom. She looked at the louvered window above the counter, considering opening it to let in a blast of cold air from outside. But instead she turned on the tap marked C, and splashed water liberally onto her face. It was chillier than usual now due to the abnormally cold weather, and was reviving, clearing away some the weariness, although doing nothing to help her mixed emotions.

With some idea it might help further, she reached for her toothbrush in the travel bag that sat on the sink. Maybe she'd even take a shower, wash her hair; it would feel good after a night spent in her clothes. She reached back into the bag and pulled out her shampoo.

"Not planning on staying long enough to unpack?" Jason said from the doorway, gesturing at the boxes and bags she'd brought in from her car but left untouched.

She gave him a wary look over her shoulder as she fished out the brush, then picked up the tube of toothpaste. She was using the supplies she kept ready for traveling, never having known when Aaron might decide at the last minute to jump on a plane to just about anywhere. Up until his last illness, he had had the energy and stamina of a man half his age, and Kendall had more than once had to plead her own exhaustion to get him to rest at all.

"I'm used to living out of a suitcase when necessary."

"This is a big change from that fancy house. Quite a comedown."

She turned to face him then, her fingers tightening around the thin plastic handle of the toothbrush. "I lived in seven different foster homes from the time I was eight years old. I've shared rooms with three other kids, five cats, an incontinent dog, and the occasional cockroach. I've slept in an attic, a laundry room, and a garage." She gestured at the motel room with a sweeping motion driven by anger. "This is paradise. So for once in your life, why don't you just shut up about things you know nothing about?"

"Well, well, well," Jason said, brows raised as he grinned at her. "The lady has teeth."

Kendall gave him an acid look. "And I'm going to brush them. In private."

With great satisfaction, she slammed the door in his face. And locked it.

Jason was still chuckling as he pulled open the rental car's door and slid into the driver's seat. He had finally stirred her to outright anger, had gotten her mad enough that she didn't try to hide it, or rein it in because it would interfere with whatever her purpose was.

He started the engine, then sat there for a moment, considering. He needed to make a phone call, and he needed to do it in private. Or someplace so public he wouldn't be noticed. Or recognized; his resemblance to his father was apparently more striking than he'd realized before coming back here to Sunridge. The solution came to him, and he turned right out of the parking lot and headed toward the airport. He nearly laughed out loud when he caught himself looking for a white sedan like the one he'd seen last night.

"You're paranoid," he muttered ruefully.

Unless, of course, the sedan that had been behind him since the city limits really was the same one, having been painted brown overnight. He grinned at himself, and shook his head when the brown car pulled into the airport lot, parked a couple of rows away, and the driver,

a man with blond hair that was almost white, got out
with a briefcase.

Still chuckling at himself, Jason strode across the parking lot. He found a bank of five phones just inside the
door of the small terminal, and made his call. The deep
voice he'd expected answered the private number.

"Mike?" he asked.

"Who else? You still goofing off, boy?"

He smiled at Mike McKenna's gruffness, which he
knew masked a caring heart the man took great pains
to hide.

"Yeah. Just lazing around," he said.

"Hmpf. Figures."

Jason's smile widened; he knew McKenna knew that
lazing around wasn't in his vocabulary. "What's going on
there? Things holding together?"

"Hmpf," McKenna repeated. "You may think you're
indispensable, boy, but you ain't. We're all just fine."

Jason laughed then. "I know you're worth ten of me.
But humor me. What's going on?"

The man gave him a rundown that proved what he'd
said had been true; they weren't missing him at all at
home. Not yet, anyway. As he listened, he caught a
glimpse of the man with the briefcase, standing at the
ticket counter a few yards away, and smiled wryly again
at his own paranoia.

"Okay, I believe you. I'm expendable," Jason said
when McKenna finally ran down. He paused, wondering
how to phrase the next question so as not to worry the
man. "Anything else I should know about?"

"Nah. Things are purring like a well-tuned diesel. Oh,
there was some guy who called, talked to Donna in the
office. He was asking about you."

Jason's grip tightened on the receiver. "Asking what?"

McKenna's tone was the equivalent of a shrug. "Just
general stuff. Where you were from, that kind of thing.
Said he was looking for somebody for a class reunion."
McKenna chuckled. "Donna told him he was looking for
the wrong guy."

As he hung up a few moments later, Jason acknowledged that he wasn't surprised someone had still been

nosing around, asking questions about the origins of Jason West. He hadn't expected it to stop just because he'd shown up here. For now they'd been stalled, but Jason knew the reprieve would only be temporary; sooner or later somebody was going to put the pieces together.

What he didn't know, he thought as he walked back to his car, was whether that particular somebody was working for Alice Hawk or Kendall.

Kendall.

He smiled again as he started the car and pulled out onto the highway, remembering Kendall's flash of temper. It was nice to know that she was capable of erupting if pushed hard enough. People who had too much control made him nervous. He preferred those you could prod to erupt the way you wanted.

The way you wanted.

A sudden image of Kendall Chase out of control in an entirely different manner shot through his mind. Naked. Writhing. Wanting. Reaching for him. Clawing at him. He tried to fight it off, making himself remember how angry she'd been at him when she'd slammed that door. But that only brought on a flood of images as hot and steamy as the water that was no doubt pouring over Kendall's naked body right now. Visions swept over him, images of her silken skin glistening, her curves providing intriguing paths for rivulets of water, her nipples tightening as they were caressed by the stream of—

Need hit him like a blow to the belly, exploding in a burst of heat and sensation that nearly doubled him over. His body clenched fiercely, and he nearly swerved off the road onto the shoulder.

He took in a deep breath. Or tried to; no matter how much air he tried to pull in, it didn't seem to be enough. He'd never felt anything like this sudden, raw, pure need in his life, and he didn't like it. Sexual desire was like any other itch, you attended to it if you could, with a willing woman who played by the same rules, and if not you ignored it. That's the way it had always been, and that's the way he liked it. Either way, it eventually went away.

It didn't hit you like a runaway boom on a sailboat.

So why was he sitting here like this, barely able to drive because his body was cramping with a hunger beyond any he'd ever known, for a gray-eyed, barefoot waif in a pair of worn-out jeans? A woman who, at least in her present mood, would probably slap him silly if he tried anything? A woman whose motives he hadn't figured out yet, but whom he didn't trust any more he ever trusted anyone?

A woman who had quite possibly been his own father's mistress?

What air he'd managed to suck in left him in a rush. The image that went through his mind then nearly doubled him over again. Kendall and his father? Nausea welled up in him, a reaction that stunned him even as it made him furious. Shaken, he pulled to the side of the road.

What the hell was wrong with him? When had these sloppy feelings gotten such a grip on him? He never reacted emotionally to such things. He assessed them, examined them, determined if they could be of any use to him. He'd done it with this, in the beginning, assessing the relationship he presumed had existed between this woman and his father, analyzing the possibility that it might be a tool for him, the knowledge that Kendall had been sleeping with Aaron Hawk.

No.

His mind screamed it as his body shivered with rejection. He didn't believe it. He couldn't believe it. Not anymore.

And that shook him more than the image of Kendall and Aaron together had.

His jaw clenched, he fought for some semblance of his normal control, his usual calm. Even anger would do, he thought. Anything to shake this sudden inexplicable desire to believe that Kendall was just what she appeared to be, a loyal, courageous woman who would risk everything to carry out a dying man's final wishes. He closed his eyes, willing himself to picture again Kendall and Aaron together, intimately. What came instead was that other vision, of himself with her, vivid and hot and painfully arousing.

You damn stupid fool, he swore inwardly, slamming his fist against the steering wheel, hoping the impact would vent some of these asinine feelings and jar his brain back into working again. It didn't work. He leaned back in the driver's seat, rubbing his hands over his face, then letting them fall to his sides in weary frustration.

His knuckles brushed something warm and solid. His eyes snapped open. Impossibly, the book lay open and facedown across the console between the seats, just beside his right hand. His instinct was to jerk his hand away, but the connection was somehow reassuring. As if an old friend had his arm around his shoulders comfortingly. It reminded him of the feeling he'd had when he'd first picked up the book, that feeling of unexpected peace. Experiencing it now, when just seconds ago he had been in a near frenzy, should have made him uneasy, but he couldn't seem to summon up the feeling. Nor could he summon up that sense of panic at the impossibility of the book having appeared here when he knew damn well he hadn't taken it from the room, and that he'd locked the car while he'd gone into the terminal. Instead, he reached for it, turning it over, wondering what part of the story it was rewriting now.

He sat staring at it for a long, silent moment. It was open at the first picture, opposite the first page of the graceful writing. He looked at her again, this woman with the incredible eyes, this woman of legend, who had lived in a time so old even the date of her birth was unknown, this woman who had found a miracle for her people in the man who stood beside her. Jenna Hawk, he read. The first of the recorded Hawks. And together she and her warrior had begun a dynasty that would last for centuries.

And they had earned the promise that it would always be so. Given by a man apparently with the power to keep that promise.

Jason shook his head, trying to fight off the compelling urge that seemed to be overtaking him as he read. The urge to believe in this nonsense, to believe that some-

where back before recorded time a woman had saved
the life of a wizard, and had thereby won eternal life for
her bloodline. The urge to believe in the impossibility of
this book. The urge to read every story here, to study
every branch of the intricate family tree, to know of each
Hawk who had come before. And most ridiculous of all,
the urge to believe himself part of it. To have a connection to them all.

He flipped the book closed. Or tried to. The cover
seemed oddly stiff, and he only succeeded in making a
few pages turn. He found himself staring down at another of the impossibly detailed pictures, of a man whose
resemblance to himself could not be denied; Hawk blood,
it seemed, ran very true and very strong. Matthew Hawk,
this one was, according to the header that began his
story. The first Hawk to come to America. Whose family
had died on the long journey, leaving him as the last
surviving Hawk, and thereby to be visited by the book.

Only when a truck rumbled loudly by did he realize
how long he'd been sitting here, reading story after story.
Each similar, in that they were tales of the last bearer
of the Hawk name, yet each different because each was
his own man, strong in character and personality. And
each of them, he noted wryly, had fought believing in
the magic of the book, as he was fighting it now.

And it had, if the book were to be believed, done
them no good at all.

He looked back at the page the book was now open
to, the steady if irregular sound of passing traffic providing an oddly comfortable normalcy to the hallucination
he seemed to be living in at the moment. He stared at the
picture of Joshua Hawk, still more than a little stunned; it
was like looking at a recent photograph of himself.

And he felt an unexpected kinship with this man, not
only because of the startling resemblance, but because
this man had, of all the Hawks he'd read about, resisted
the entire ridiculous process longer and harder than anyone. Jason could relate to this man; Joshua had been a
tough, practical-minded cynic, a rather grim realist who
had survived on his wits and the speed of his reflexes in

a time when that was enough to build you a reputation you could never quite leave behind.

It was rather entertaining to think that he had an apparently celebrated gunfighter as an ancestor. Assuming, of course, that any of this stuff was for real.

But his own story was real enough. Accurate enough. His mouth tightened. *Impossible enough, you mean,* he muttered to himself.

He tried to shut the book again. And again it seemed to resist. He released it, letting it fall back onto the console. Pages riffled. And stopped, on the last page of the graceful writing, the page that marked the end of his own entry.

He looked away. He couldn't read it, couldn't make himself go over yet again what seemed to be an ever-growing chronology of his life, with dates, times, and now written pieces of his history that no one should know. Things that couldn't be here, yet were, just bits and pieces appearing seemingly at random. He couldn't read it again; it would only make him crazier. He'd given up wondering how she was doing it, how she was making the changes without his knowledge, even given up wondering how she'd found out the things that kept appearing here. What he couldn't quite give up was wondering what Kendall was really up to, what she hoped to gain.

He reached to close the book again, determined this time. But the last entry caught his eye, for it was yesterday's date. As if the book had finally caught up with him. He stifled a shiver at the absurd idea. But he couldn't stop himself from looking.

He sat staring at the words on the page before him.

Words he'd never seen before.

Words that had not been there last night.

And then, as he read the last entry, he was suddenly sure for the first time what Kendall was really after. An unexpected sense of disappointment filled him, and either possible cause, that he had hoped either Kendall or the book was for real, was unacceptable to him.

He started the car, turning the key with much more force that was necessary. The tires barked a protest as he sent the car darting back out into traffic. He was back at the motel in much less time than he'd taken leaving. The door was as he'd left it, closed but unlocked. When he went inside, the bedroom was empty, the bathroom door still closed, even though he'd been gone for more than an hour. As if she'd wanted to be sure he was gone before she came out.

And now he thought he knew why.

When she did come out, dressed in a trim, charcoal-gray jumpsuit that darkened her eyes to the color of Puget Sound on a rainy day, he was sitting at the table. The book lay beside him, still open to the page that had made everything so very clear to him.

He watched as she retrieved a pair of black pumps from her open suitcase in the closet alcove and set them on the floor. She began pulling her hair back, and tying it with a silk scarf in several shades of gray as she walked back into the room. She came to a halt when she saw him. Her gaze flicked to the book, then back to his face.

He leaned back in the chair, swung his feet up onto the bed, and clasped his hands behind his head, in a purposeful return to his earlier nonchalant manner. He kept his eyes on her steadily.

"I know it's a lot of money," he said easily, "but don't you think marrying me to get it is a bit extreme?"

Chapter Eleven

❧

"I don't believe it."

"You're the one who's been doing the hard sell on this thing," Jason said, nudging the book with one hand. "Now are you saying it's a fake?"

Kendall shook her head, knowing she was staring at him with what had to be an utterly astonished expression. "No. I just ... it can't really say that."

"Sorry, honey. Just like all these other poor souls whose stories are in here, it seems I've met my match." He turned the book to face her. "Read it and weep. We're destined, beautiful."

His tone had gone beyond sarcastic; it was pure acid, beyond anything she'd ever heard from him. She glanced at the last entry in the book, read it quickly, and relief flooded her.

"It only says you met the woman you'll marry," she said. "It doesn't mention me at all."

"And who else do you think it means?" he asked, his tone no lighter. "The merry widow, perhaps?"

"I was thinking more along the lines of that waitress," Kendall said, some bite of her own coming into her voice.

The instant of puzzlement on his face was, somehow, reassuring; it seemed he had put the woman who'd been so obviously interested in him out of his mind. She could almost see him assessing the possibility, then discarding it.

"No," he said. "You're the one with the motive, Ms. Chase."

Kendall stared at him. "Motive? What motive?"

"Five million of them," he drawled.

"You think I'd try to marry you? For Aaron's money?"

"Well, I sure as hell don't think you'd do it for love, sweetheart." He smiled, a coldly mirthless curving of his lips. "Did you and Aaron plan this out? Is this his way of seeing that you're taken care of, now that he's dead? Oh, it's clever, I'll give you that. The lure of all that money, and of your admittedly lovely self, all wrapped up with a little magic and dangled in front of the poor bastard son . . ."

Absurdly, all Kendall could focus on for the moment was the fact that he'd called her lovely. Then the full meaning of his words registered, that he suspected her of somehow engineering this whole thing. Kendall supposed she should be angry, but somehow all she could do was laugh.

"I'm surprised you're having such trouble believing the Hawk legends. You obviously have a much wilder imagination than I do."

"Do I? It makes perfect sense. If five hundred thousand dollars is better than fifty thousand, then access to the whole five mil is better yet, isn't it?"

She straightened, wishing she were taller; even when he was sitting down it was hard to glare down her nose at him.

"I don't need anyone to *take care* of me. And I don't need your money. But even if I did, five million wouldn't be enough to put up with your condescending, insulting behavior. And if you really believe this nonsense about some kind of plan Aaron and I cooked up, then I was obviously wrong about you. You're not nearly as smart as I thought you were."

"That's nonsense, but this"—he slammed the cover of the book shut—"isn't?"

"Tell me, Mr. West, just how do you think I've managed this sleight of hand? And why? Especially the way that's coming out, piece by piece? Why not just tell the story, in order, if it's all a lie anyway? Why make it more confusing?"

"I haven't figured that out yet. But I will."

"Then tell me why I would come to you, tell you what Alice was trying to do, when I could end up in jail for it."

"With me in the next cell, don't forget," Jason said, his tone dry. "Or was that part of the story just insurance, to make sure I kept my mouth shut if your little plan didn't work?"

"What plan?" Kendall exclaimed in exasperation.

Jason gestured at the book. "I guess I'm supposed to ... what? Be gratified that the old man willed you to me along with all that money?"

Kendall rarely swore, but she barely bit back an oath now. "I have nothing to do with this. *You're* the one who's reading me into that book."

"So how is it supposed to work? You just present me with the idea, and overwhelmed by your beauty—and all that cash—I meekly fall into line?"

Spinning on her stockinged heel and striding away from him, she let out a strangled sound of frustration. "God, you're as stubborn as Aaron!"

"What if I already have a wife?"

Kendall stopped, her anger dampened abruptly by that unexpected question. Not that it mattered to her if he had a wife, she told herself. It made no difference to what she had to do. So she didn't understand why she couldn't stop herself from turning back to him and asking, "Do you?"

Jason smiled, a twisted lift of one corner of his mouth that spoke of cynical satisfaction more than anything else.

"That would put a kink in your plan, now wouldn't it?"

"If any such plan existed, I suppose it would," Kendall said, surprised at her own distraction at the idea that he might be married. "But since it doesn't—"

"You mean since you already know I don't have a wife? I'm sure your detective told you that. Have you known where I was all along, when you and the old man planned this?"

Kendall walked back across the room. Reining in her irritation with an effort she couldn't ever recall having to make so often before, even with Aaron at his worst, she spoke evenly.

"That plan exists only in your head. I told you, the detective Aaron hired hadn't been able to find you yet. He was still searching, but you dropped out of sight very efficiently, after your mother was killed."

"Thank you," he said caustically. "You can run far and fast when you've got the prospect of winding up in some foster home hovering over you."

"They're not always so bad," Kendall said neutrally.

He had the grace to look discomfited, as if he had just recalled what she'd told him about her own life in foster care.

"Maybe," he said after a moment. "But I wouldn't have made it in that system."

"It would only have been until you were eighteen."

His mouth twisted. "At sixteen, two years is an eternity."

She couldn't argue with that. "You could have . . . gone to Aaron."

He laughed, loud and harsh. "Right. Like he wanted me. Besides, I'd promised my mother a thousand times I never would, no matter what."

If she could get him talking, she thought, maybe she could get past this unexpected snag the book had thrown at her. And if she could just stop wondering why, when the book had told him he'd met the woman he would marry, he had assumed it was her.

"So what did you do?"

"I got by. For a year or so. Then I got tired of dodging the juvie authorities, so I left Seattle."

"Where did you go?"

"Alaska. I worked on a fishing boat for a few seasons."

"But what about school?"

"Fish don't care if you've got a diploma or not."

"But—"

"Forget it, Kendall. Changing the subject isn't going to work. I want to know how you planned to carry this off."

"I didn't—"

She broke off, irritated by his single-mindedness, and the fact that she hadn't been trying to change the subject at all, that she had genuinely wanted to know what had happened to him after his mother had been brutally run down on a Seattle street.

"Were you figuring to buy me the way Alice bought my father? Did Aaron tie all this together somehow, so that I only get the money if you come with it? Is that how you get your share? Because I'm his son, it's less likely to be invalidated than if he left it to you outright?"

"I told you, I have all the money I need—"

"I'm supposed to believe you'd turn down five million?"

"Why not?" she snapped, feeling provoked. "You did."

He blinked. Then his face took on an unreadable expression. "Touché yet again," he said softly.

Her irritation faded at his tone. "Why are you so determined to think I have some hidden agenda here?"

"Because everybody does, whether they admit it or not."

She shook her head slowly. "It must be awful, never to trust anyone."

He shrugged. "I trust people, sometimes. Once I know what their agenda is, and can predict how they'll react, what they'll do. No surprises."

"And you call that trust?"

"What would you call it?"

"I'd call it an awfully cold, calculating way of living."

"And I suppose you prefer trusting blindly and having that trust betrayed?"

"It's better than never trusting at all."

"Is it? My mother trusted Aaron Hawk. If she hadn't, it would have saved her a lot of crying."

"And what would she have lost? If you never taste the tears, you never taste the joy, either."

"Joy," he retorted, "is overrated."

"And if she had never loved Aaron," Kendall pointed out, ignoring his comment, "you wouldn't be here."

She saw his jaw tighten, his eyes narrow, but he didn't answer. Something he'd said before rang in her head as clearly as if he'd just spoken the words again. *Falling in love was the only foolish thing she ever did. Except maybe for having me.*

She suppressed a sigh. Despite the string of foster homes she'd lived in after her parents had been killed when she was seven, she had never had to fight that particular battle. Her memories were hazy, but warm and comforting, she had been loved, and wanted. There had been no ambivalence about her birth.

She had no answer for this. She stood looking at him for a long, silent moment. It seemed pointless to argue with a man who was already so convinced he was right. Even though she understood why he was reacting this way, even though the thought of the kind of life he'd had, that had left him with so little faith in anyone other than himself, made her heart ache for him, his suspicions still hurt.

Not because he didn't trust her, she told herself firmly, but because it was making it so hard to do as Aaron had made her promise with almost his last breath. She was beginning to suspect she would have to do this herself; it seemed she would get little help from the man whose birthright she was fighting for.

"Let me see if I understand," she said carefully. "You think that I was Aaron's mistress, that Aaron and I knew where you were all along, and that we planned this all out, a package deal, an inheritance that includes me as your wife, since obviously I need a keeper. And that somehow I've managed to manipulate that book and its contents in a way that would have made that original wizard proud. And did we concoct the story of what Alice is trying to do as well? Ah, yes, I recall, it was insurance, isn't that what you said? So that you keep quiet if by chance you don't go along with our little scheme. Have I got it right?"

"Close enough."

"That," she said with sour emphasis, "is more absurd than believing that book was handed straight down from Merlin."

But a lot easier, she thought suddenly. For a man like Jason, it would be much easier to believe that people were behaving as he seemed to expect, out of pure, greedy self-interest, than to believe that magic had truly touched his life. No matter how complex the explanation, no matter how unlikely, any answer based in reality, his cold-blooded, analytical reality, would always win out with Jason West. There was no point in arguing with this man. Just as there had been no point in arguing with Aaron.

Aaron.

That's who she should have been thinking of. She'd taken the wrong track altogether. Jason didn't respond to emotional appeals any more than his father had. While Jason's emotions seemed a bit closer to the surface than Aaron's had ever been, they were still buried deep, and she didn't have time to try to reach them. Not when Alice would be making her move right away.

She drew herself up to her full height. She stepped into her pumps, which would give her another two inches she felt she needed right now. Then she turned to Jason once more.

"What do you plan to do?" she said, in her most brusque, businesslike voice. She would keep her feelings out of this, no matter what he said, she vowed silently.

"If you're waiting for me to go down on one knee and propose, don't hold your breath, sweetheart."

She ignored his jab and his tone, although his words made it hard to breathe for a moment. "I mean about the will."

"You mean, assuming I believe any of what you've told me about this supposed plot?"

"It's the truth. You can believe it or not, as you wish. I just want to know if you intend to contest the will."

His brows lowered slightly, as if he didn't quite understand her change in tone and demeanor. She waited, silently. When she didn't go on, he shrugged.

"All right. For the moment, let's assume it is all true. Fight it how?" Then, as if it had just come back to him, he added, "Ah. I forgot. You have the one remaining copy of this alleged codicil, don't you? How convenient."

Again she ignored the sarcasm. And kept her voice carefully even. "Aaron made me get a safe deposit box in my name, and put a copy in it, along with some other things. He didn't trust Alice. He was right. Will you fight her?" she asked again.

"Aren't you forgetting something? Trust me, you wouldn't like jail."

"I like the idea of her getting away with this less," Kendall said flatly. "Besides, you're assuming we'd lose."

"I'm just the poor, illegitimate son, remember?" he said. There was an odd glint in his eyes, a glint that made her think of his bloodline namesake, circling with deceptively lazy grace before focusing those piercing eyes on a target and diving in with talons outstretched for the kill. "Go up against the Hawk Widow? With her resources? In a court in a county she probably owns most of?"

"You have a right to this, and a legal claim. That has to count for something."

"I'm sure it will make a big difference," Jason said dryly, "when they drag out your little bank book and prove I put you up to this."

"Then you won't contest?"

For a moment he turned that piercing stare on her. She felt oddly pinned, and more than a little uneasy, but she forced herself to meet his eyes. Silence spun out between them, taut, wire-drawn. Finally something in his steady gaze changed, as if he'd backed off. He nodded slightly, as if in salute.

"I think," he said slowly, "I should be asking you what you intend to do if I don't."

Kendall took a deep breath. "If you don't, then I'll fight her myself."

"That would be very foolish, Kendall. What's to stop me from leaving you holding the bag? I could opt out of the whole deal, maybe go to the merry widow and offer to sign away any claim in return for that fifty thousand she gave you."

"You wouldn't get it. She'd never agree. Not with you."

He was silent for a moment. Then, "She hates me that much?"

Kendall nodded. He didn't look hurt, or angry, or even upset, merely thoughtful. And, she realized, he was responding as if he did, indeed, believe this was true. Was he just humoring her, or had she somehow convinced him?

"Since she doesn't know me well enough to know how truly disagreeable I can be," he said, without a hint of humor or even sarcasm, "I assume it's because of who I am."

Again Kendall nodded. "I believe you're a symbol to her. Of what she never had from her husband. And she blames your mother for Aaron never having loved her."

"Pardon me if I don't bleed," he said. "My mother never had much to show for loving Aaron Hawk. And she's been dead for twenty years. That's a hell of a long time to carry a grudge."

"Yes. It is."

She said no more, and there was no particular inflection in her voice, but his eyes narrowed as if she'd gone on to point out the obvious; he'd carried a grudge against Aaron for longer than that. Again she waited, silently, until he spoke again.

"Then I guess I'll just have to tell her to keep her money. That I'm out of it. Out of her way, out of her life. That ought to make her happy."

"I doubt," Kendall said, "that Alice knows how to be happy."

He gave her a considering look. "Then she should be really ticked if you insist pursuing this."

"Yes."

He let out a compressed breath. "I don't want any part of this. You're on your own."

She'd been half expecting that. "All right. That's what I needed to know."

She turned and walked over to the dresser, picked up her purse, and reached for her car keys. She sensed rather than saw him get to his feet.

"You're still going to do this?"

"Yes."

"I don't get it. I told you, I don't want anything my father might have left me to ease his guilt. I don't want anything from the Hawks. Not money, not the name, nothing."

"I know."

"Then why?"

She turned to face him. Despite the two inches she'd gained in her pumps, he was still so much taller than she that she was more aware than ever of her lack of stature.

"Partly just because it's right. Because it's only fair that you get what Aaron wanted you to have. Because you should have had him in your life, but didn't."

"I didn't want or need that old man in my life. And nobody would risk jail for reasons like that."

Kendall didn't try to tell him he was wrong. "I said partly. The main reason is much simpler. I promised Aaron I would see this done."

"He's dead."

"That doesn't change anything. I promised him as he died." His mouth twisted at her words, making her add, "With your mother's name on his lips."

She brushed past him and headed for the door. She was a little surprised when he followed her outside.

"Is that supposed to make me feel for him?"

She'd known the moment she'd said it that she would regret wavering from her vow to keep this conversation purely business.

"No," she said, unlocking her car door. "I doubt if anything could change how you feel about Aaron."

He gave her a speculative look. "And you? Could anything change the way you feel about him?"

She returned his steady gaze for a long moment, thinking. She didn't believe anything she said would change his feelings. Neither had Aaron. He'd assumed the son he'd never known wouldn't harbor any tender feelings for his absent father, no matter the reason. But perhaps she could make Jason understand. She reached down and released the door locks.

"Come with me," she said. "I'm going to his office."

He drew back a little, dark brows swiftly lowering; he clearly wasn't impressed by either the offer or the destination.

"Aren't you even a little curious?"

Still he hesitated. But after a moment he nodded. She

went back and locked the room door, and by the time she got back to the car he was already inside.

She waited until they were on the road to speak. "I met Aaron when I was nineteen. I was in my second year of college."

She heard him move, but didn't look. "You said you'd worked for him since you got *out* of college."

"Yes. But I met him three years earlier. I was driving home from work late one night, and I found Aaron staggering along the road. He'd been attacked, and his car stolen. There was a hospital just down the road, so I took him there."

"Dangerous, for a woman alone late at night."

"He was hurt. And alone."

"It could have been a setup."

She gave him a sideways glance, then sighed. "I suppose it could have been. But it wasn't." She noticed him glancing behind them, but he said nothing and she went on. "I stayed with him until the police and doctors were done and released him."

"Why?"

"I told you, he was alone."

His mouth quirked, and she waited for some sarcastic observation, but he only asked, "What happened?"

She smiled in rueful memory. "I didn't know who he was. I just knew the robbers had taken his wallet, so he had no money or identification. So I offered to help him pay the hospital bill, and he could pay me back later."

"You offered to pay Aaron Hawk's bill?"

He sounded so amused she couldn't help looking at him. "Even if I'd heard his name, I wouldn't have known it. I didn't have time to keep up with the who's who of the business world."

"I'll bet he got a laugh out of that."

"No. He never laughed at all. He thanked me. And started asking me questions."

He looked through the rear window again. "Questions?"

"About school. What I was taking, what my plans were, when I would graduate, that kind of thing. We talked for hours."

He looked back at her. "And you never knew he owned one of the bigger conglomerates in the state?"

"No," Kendall said. "My first clue was when a private limo arrived to pick him up. I was pretty embarrassed."

"I'll bet."

For once, there was no sarcasm in his tone, only what sounded like genuine amusement. It was amazing, what a difference it made, to hear his voice without that underlying cynicism that she'd begun to think was always there.

"He told me when I graduated to come see him."

Jason rolled his eyes. As quickly as that the scoffing tone was back, along with the cynical glint in his eyes. "Don't tell me. You graduated, appeared on his doorstep, and he took you in."

"No."

"Well, that's a relief. I thought this was going to be a bad movie." He looked behind them again, his forehead creasing, and continued to look out the rear window as he asked, "You mean he didn't generously put you through school?"

"I put myself through school. It took me five and a half years to get my degree, because I was working the whole time. And I . . . got sick one year, and lost some time. And more paying the bills."

"Sick?"

"It doesn't matter now. But when—"

"Sick with what?"

She studied him for a moment, wondering why he was persisting, why he wanted to know. "Nothing that's still contagious," she said dryly. "You're safe."

She nearly jumped when he chuckled; it sounded almost as genuine as his earlier amusement had. It changed his entire appearance, and made her very wary for a reason she didn't quite understand. And when he repeated his question, again the caustic undertone was missing.

"Sick with what?"

"I . . . the hospital said it was exhaustion and dehydration."

He stared at her. "Hospital? You were pushing that hard?"

"I didn't want to spend my life in some dead-end job, with no hope of really making something of myself. Like the other kids I saw growing up."

"Other foster kids?" His tone was, amazingly, almost gentle.

She nodded. "So many of them wound up that way. With no hope. I thought school was the way out."

"And it was?" He glanced in the mirror again, then back at her. "With some help from the illustrious Aaron Hawk, after your Good Samaritan act?"

She nodded. "Now will you tell me what you keep looking for?"

He seemed embarrassed. "I . . . Nothing."

Her mouth quirked. "I think you have a reason for everything. Even looking over your shoulder every mile."

"Never mind," he said. "Tell me what happened when you graduated."

"Aaron showed up. Offering me the kind of job you only dream about right out of college."

"Where was he when *your* hospital bill needed paying?" Amazingly, he sounded almost angry.

"Watching," she said.

Jason blinked. "What?"

"Watching. To see what I'd do, if I really had the gumption to keep going, to not give up."

He raised a brow at her. "Kind of cold-blooded, wasn't it?"

"I know you think I'm some kind of naive fool, but I assure you, Jason, I knew exactly what kind of man your father was. There wasn't an ounce of pity or sympathy in him. He neither gave nor accepted either, right up to the end. He was a Hawk, and Hawks aren't soft, he used to say."

She looked at him then. "And apparently," she said, looking at him steadily, "Hawks also breed true."

As with Alton, he again didn't react to the comparison. When he spoke, his voice was quiet, but somehow more ominous because of it.

"Are they gullible, Kendall?"

She thought of the book and knew what he meant. She really hadn't made any progress at all, she thought tiredly. He didn't believe any of it. She turned her eyes back to the road.

"No," she finally answered. "But Aaron grew up with centuries of family history. Stories told by his father, his grandfather, and his great-grandfather."

"And he believed them."

"I don't know if he really did, or if at the end it was just hope."

"But you believe it."

"Who was it who said that once you've eliminated the impossible, what remains is the truth, no matter how improbable it might be?"

"More fairy tales," Jason said with a grimace. "Well, I haven't eliminated anything yet. But I'm about to. That book is a joke, doling out little scraps of supposed fact in whatever order suits the purpose. A little here, a little there, just to nudge me in the right direction, because that's what it's all about, isn't it? And there's going to be a way to prove it. And trust me, Kendall, I'll find that way."

She slowed the car and pulled over to the curb. Jason looked at her, then out the window. "I have to go to the bank," she said, a little abruptly. "And maybe it's not such a good idea that you go to Aaron's office. You're still too angry."

He didn't deny it. "I don't know what the truth is here, yet. Whether you're in cahoots with the old lady, figuring you'll scare me off with that threat of jail, whether you really think you can get your hands on that five million through me, or whether you're up to something else. But I'll find out."

"You left out a possibility. That I'm telling the truth."

He laughed. "Lady, that's so far down on the possibility scale it doesn't even register."

"Thank you," she said sarcastically, beyond hiding her weary annoyance now. "I appreciate your faith and trust."

"You want something to appreciate? How about a little advice?" He lifted the book again. "If you plan on trying to make this little fabrication about our future together come true, you might want to change your approach."

"My approach?"

"You would have gotten a lot farther in that direction if you'd joined me last night."

Joined him? It hit her then. Joined him in bed, he meant. For the first time in a long time, Kendall had to fight very hard to keep from blushing. The images that flashed through her mind astonished her. Her experience was, at best, limited, but somehow she was picturing things she'd never thought of doing, let alone ever done. And at a time when she should be angry, not having lewd fantasies about a man who was making her life so difficult. Her effort at control made her voice very cool as she gathered her scattered poise around her and made herself meet his eyes.

"If that's all it would take to change your mind, then perhaps I was hasty in saying Hawks breed true," she said. "I doubt if there's ever been one who was controlled by his libido."

"Well," he said, his voice silky soft, "if you want to talk about control . . ."

He leaned over to her, not suddenly but so unexpectedly she didn't have time to react. And the moment he touched her, his fingers sliding around to the back of her neck, she wasn't sure she could have. For an instant, one terrifying instant as she looked up into his eyes, she wondered if she'd been wrong—lethally wrong—about his potential for violence. But then his thumbs came up under her chin to tilt her head back, and she realized the storm she'd seen in the blue depths had an entirely different source.

His mouth came down on hers, hard and fierce. She put her hands up to push against his chest, but after the first effort suppressed the attempt to struggle. He was so much bigger, so much stronger than she, that she knew it was useless. The best she could do was give him no reaction at all.

She managed it, until suddenly his lips gentled on hers, until he turned from aggression to urging, from fierceness to suggestiveness, from overpowering to invitation. She didn't know why he'd changed, knew only that she was responding before she could help herself, that her resistance turned to surprise, then shock as heat rippled through her as he moved his mouth coaxingly on hers. Her eyes closed seemingly of their own will, as if her body wanted to concentrate solely on the new, amazing things it was feeling. He was kissing her like the man she'd had glimpses of just now, the man who had laughed genuinely, the man who had gently prompted her to continue her story.

His fingers threaded through her hair, tugging it free from the scarf. She felt the faint brush of his tongue over her lips, tempting, luring. Through the odd haze that seemed to be enveloping her, she knew she should pull away, but instead she found herself parting her lips for him, accepting the stroking caress. Welcoming it. And, with a bit of boldness that astounded her even as she did it, returning the caress, meeting his tongue with her own, craving the contact in a way that she'd never craved anything before.

She heard a sound from him, a low groan that held a note of protest, as if he were fighting some battle of his own. It sent a shiver through her, one she couldn't suppress, and she heard him make the sound again. Again she shivered, this time in reaction to the thrill that raced through her, especially when he pulled her closer with a jerky motion she sensed was rife with that same inner protest. Gone was the feeling of being overwhelmed, her sense of the sheer power inherent in his size and strength. Left behind was the echo of that low sound, that protest she had wrenched from him, as if it were she who had the power, and it could bring him to his knees.

He wrenched his mouth away. Kendall heard a tiny sound, and realized it had come from her, that bereft little moan of loss. When she opened her eyes to look up at him, there was an instant when she thought she saw confusion in his face. But it was quickly gone, and she focused on his eyes in time to see the heat that had burned there fading, in time to see the satisfied glint that replaced it, and she knew that whatever sense of power she'd had had been an illusion. A fanciful delusion she should have known better than to succumb to.

He released her and sat back, appearing completely calm and at ease, in stark contrast to her own heart-hammering dishevelment.

"Care to discuss control some more?" he drawled.

She grabbed her keys, her purse, and the scarf that had slid down to the now tangled ends of her hair. It took every bit of self-command she had learned at Aaron's side, but she managed to give him a level look.

"You don't *discuss* anything. You assume, you arbitrarily decide, and you ignore the truth when it's in front of you." She shoved open the car door, then looked back at him. He looked insufferably smug as he sat there, arms crossed, leaning against the other door nonchalantly. "And," she added, "apparently you enjoy kissing unwilling women."

"Unwilling?" he asked softly.

She couldn't stop the blush this time. And she could think of nothing to say. They both knew that however it had started, she had become an enthusiastic participant before the kiss had ended. She got out of the car, slamming the door shut with a fierceness that betrayed her agitation. She heard the passenger door open, and knew he was getting out as well. She didn't look at him, even when she heard the other door close, much more gently than her own.

"Kendall?"

She stopped, knowing he was going to make it worse, knowing he was going to taunt her with her own response to his unexpected kiss. She couldn't look at him.

"What?" she muttered, her fingers tightening around her keys until they dug into her flesh.

"Don't start anything."

Astonishment flooded her, and her head snapped around. She stared at him across the roof of the car. "Start anything? Me? You're the one who swooped down on me like your feathered namesake, Jason *Hawk*."

His eyes widened, as if she had surprised him. Then

his mouth quirked, and she sensed he was suppressing an amused smile.

"I meant about the will."

It was her turn to be surprised. And chagrined. She should have known that the kiss that had shaken her to her soul had had little effect on him.

"Oh," she said, feeling more awkward—and foolish— than she could ever remember. Then, suspiciously, "Why? You don't even believe me about it."

He shrugged. "Let's just say I like to keep my options open, at least for the moment. That's hard to do from a jail cell."

"Fine." The word was short, clipped. She didn't care.

"I'll see you later. I think I'll . . . take a walk."

"Fine," she repeated. She started toward the heavy wooden front doors of the bank, then turned back once more. "Jason?"

He lifted a brow in query.

"Make it a hike," she said.

She closed the bank door on his laughter. And tried to ignore the strange feeling she had, a prickling at the back of her neck, as if she were being watched.

She mocked herself as the sensation lingered as she kept going. Jason might be intimidating, he might be full of surprises, he might have rattled her more with that unexpected—and unexpectedly arousing—kiss than she'd ever been rattled in her life, but he couldn't be watching her.

Even Hawks couldn't see through walls.

Chapter Twelve

~

Jason laughed inwardly at the irony of it, him, in the Aaron Hawk wing of the Sunridge library, searching out information to prove Aaron Hawk was crazy.

Not that it was going to take much. It was obvious that the old man hadn't just been interested in his family history, he'd been obsessed by it; the size of the collection of donated books here, taking up nearly an entire set of four-foot-wide shelves, was proof of that. The presence of the Hawks in Sunridge was chronicled continuously, going back nearly a hundred years. If there was even the slightest mention of a Hawk anywhere, the document was here.

It had been a long time since he'd been in a library. Odd, he supposed, considering he had practically lived in them as a kid. For years he'd almost daily spent the hours between the end of school and his mother's arrival home from work amid bookshelves very much like these. He'd started going there because it seemed safe, there were people around, and he'd liked it better than the lonely, echoing apartments they had lived in. But soon he'd become fascinated by what he discovered there, other places, other people, other worlds.

At first he had just read magazines, about boats, cars, fishing, whatever caught his eye. But he'd soon worked through all those, and begun on the books. And later, he'd had another cause, a reason to track down everything he could find on a particular subject. By the time he was fifteen he'd read more than he could keep track of.

A good thing, he thought as he picked up one more

book to add to his stack, since by the time he was sixteen
he'd been on the run, with no time for reading or anything else except staying alive and one step ahead of the
authorities who were determined to slap him in a house
with strangers who got paid by the state to take care
of him.

They're not always so bad.

Kendall's words came back to him, but he quashed
them determinedly. He wasn't going to let an obviously
practiced ploy for sympathy get to him. He wasn't going
to let her get to him. No matter how good she was at
pulling strings he'd never even known he had.

He set the pile of books on a table and pulled back
the nearest chair.

*I lived in seven different foster homes from the time I
was eight years old. I shared a room with three other kids,
five cats, an incontinent dog, and the occasional cockroach. I've slept in an attic, a laundry room, and a garage.*

Was it true? Had that really been her life? And had
she come out of that with enough determination to get
herself through college, on her own? So much drive that
she had landed herself in the hospital?

No, he told himself. *It's all part of the game, part of
the con, you know that.*

*So for once in your life, why don't you just shut up
about things you know nothing about?*

Damn that woman! Why did everything she'd ever said
to him keep running through his mind like an endless
loop? And what the hell had happened today? He'd
meant to show her how wrong she was. That he wasn't
some idiot adolescent at the mercy of his hormones. He
wasn't controlled by whoever made his body come to
attention.

And she'd certainly done that.

Heat shot through him at the memory of how swiftly
he'd reacted to her. Something low and deep inside him
tightened again, with an erotic fierceness. He nearly
groaned aloud at the strength of it. He didn't know what
had happened to him when he'd kissed her, what had
made him lose track of his intentions. It wasn't her expertise; if anything, she'd been tentative, unpracticed.

She hadn't even seemed to realize the effect she'd had on him. All she would have had to do was glance down and she would have known his nonchalance was nothing but a very shaky pretense; he'd been hard as an Elliott Bay fireboat hose at full pressure.

But she hadn't looked. She hadn't been able to even look at his face, let alone anything else.

But her seemingly natural response had set him on fire. And the memory of it now threatened to send him racing back to her like the kind of boy he'd just sworn he wasn't. Racing back to take up where he'd left off, with another hot, searing kiss, and go from there. Go a long way from there, for a very long time, until they were both exhausted.

He battled it, trying to summon up that image of Kendall with his father that had turned him so cold before. But somehow he couldn't do it. He couldn't picture it, couldn't quite believe it anymore. He'd been wrong about that. What that meant in relation to everything else she'd told him, he didn't know. And didn't want to think about, not now.

With an effort he resented even as he made it, he shoved her out of his mind. He had work to do, and there was every chance it would resolve the problem of Kendall Chase as well as the book he couldn't seem to rid himself of.

He grabbed the first Hawk reference book on the stack and flipped it open. He was startled for a moment; he'd known Hawks had been in Sunridge forever, but he hadn't known they'd actually founded the town itself. Maybe Aaron really had owned the town, literally. He began to scan the pages.

Hours later he sat there, stunned, a huge stack of books beside him, and an impossibility in front of him in the notes that filled several pages of the notepad he'd bought at the convenience store across from the motel.

Everything matched.

He'd checked every recorded date, every event that had been listed in that damned book that seemed to be haunting him. He'd checked the microfilm copies of the local newspaper back to the turn of the century, and found independent verification of the historical occurrences. He'd found records of births and deaths that exactly matched the intricate family tree. He'd used every resource the surprisingly well equipped little library had, and hadn't been able to find one variation except a disparity of two days on the recording of the deed that had begun the town of Sunridge.

He'd verified that most of the material had been compiled by separate researchers and scholars, only a few of whom had been commissioned by the Hawks themselves, and only one by Aaron. He'd even checked the data against other outside sources, encyclopedias, other history books, old magazines, anything he could find here.

Of course, he told himself. They would use this material to put the book together in the first place. No wonder it matched. This wasn't some slipshod plan, they would be very careful. He hadn't gained anything by this, except to fall further behind back home. He usually worked on Saturdays, catching up on all he hadn't been able to get to during the week. Now he'd have that to do, plus Friday's work, when he got back.

Irritated at himself, he began to put the books back on the shelves. A slim volume with gold lettering on the spine fell over as he replaced the last book, and he reached to set it back. *Hawks at War,* it read. He picked it up, intrigued by the rather militant title.

It was just what the title suggested, a compendium of Hawks who had fought or served in various wars throughout documented history. Compiled by a history professor Jason suspected had been bankrolled with Hawk money, it began with a foreword that suggested they'd been fighters and warriors long before documented history as well. The picture of Jenna Hawk and her warrior, Kane, flashed into his mind. Now there was a pair you could be proud to claim as ancestors, he thought. Tough as they had to be, yet still able to look as if the world began and ended with each other.

His mouth twisted at the fanciful thought. But they were a striking pair, he had to admit that. They stood out. Like Joshua Hawk and his Kathleen. At that thought, he flipped the pages, wondering. Stopping at the section on the Civil War, his eyes widened at the number of names, at the Hawks who had died, on both sides. Fathers, sons, brothers, cousins. And at the end was a footnote, indicating that the only Hawk survivors, Edgar and his very young grandson Joshua, headed west after the war, as many others had.

Jason glanced over his shoulder at the baffling volume that still sat on the table. If it were to be believed, Joshua Hawk had become the man known simply as The Hawk, a notorious figure in his time, a gun for hire who had lived the kind of life legends were made of.

And who had, of course, Jason thought cynically, been changed by the love of a good woman.

He slapped the book shut and shoved it back on the shelf with a rather fierce motion. The Hawks, he muttered inwardly, spent far too much energy on love. The most vastly overrated emotion on earth. Love made you weak. It made you soft. His mother had been living proof of that; she'd been a strong, determined woman, a woman to be admired for what she'd done against very difficult odds. But she'd had that weak spot. That one vulnerability. She loved a Hawk.

Two of them, he supposed. For he couldn't deny any longer who he was.

And only now did he think of what it must have done to his mother to look at him and see the image of the man who had fathered him. Every day she had had to confront the evidence of what her folly had cost her. Yet never had her love for him wavered, never had he been made to feel culpable for their situation.

He felt his throat tighten. She had been so strong, but her weakness had been Aaron Hawk. Just as Aaron had been Kendall Chase's weakness, her blind spot. What the hell was it about that old man that had made two strong, bright, beautiful women look past his arrogance and see . . . what? What had they found beneath the surface that had made them stay? That had made them both insist there was so much more to the man than the imperious front he presented to the world?

Wearily he sat back down in the chair. For a long time he just sat there, staring at the book with the gilded pages, thinking. He could understand his simple curiosity; he'd spent a lot of time growing up wondering about his history, about the family he'd never known. His mother had had no family except an older brother with whom she'd had no contact; Jason had been nearly fifteen before he'd discovered it was because of him, because the straight-laced uncle he'd never met had disowned his mother for having a child out of wedlock. So, not having had any real family other than his mother, a certain amount of curiosity was natural, he told himself.

What he couldn't understand was this odd sense of connection he was feeling, this sense of a link between him and the Hawks who had gone before. They seemed to call to him, from Jenna Hawk and her warrior on down through time. And especially those who had been the last of the Hawks, those who, like him, had been blessed—or cursed, Joshua Hawk had observed wryly— with the appearance of the book.

Jason again felt that special affinity for Joshua. A tough man who'd had a hard, lonely life, he had, judging from the story Jason had read, fought believing in the magic of the book to the very end.

But in the end, it seemed, he had believed. Because of the woman he'd found. And it had changed his life. Forever.

"Listen to you," Jason muttered under his breath. "You're sounding like you believe in this farce."

He resisted reaching for the book, resisted it until he realized what he was doing and why, that he was afraid to look at it. Because this time there would be no explanation for any changes, no time spent asleep, no time with the book out of his sight.

He was being sandbagged by a book. By a damned book.

His mouth twisted as the thought occurred to him that perhaps his adjective had been disturbingly accurate. Perhaps that was it, perhaps the devil had finally arrived to collect his due from the last of the Hawks. Perhaps it would be Jason who paid the price for Aaron's princely little power structure here in Sunridge. Perhaps that was

Aaron's final bit of malice toward the son he'd never wanted.

Jason shook his head sharply. He was losing it. He'd never spent so much time wallowing in utter absurdity in his life. There must be something about the air in this town that gave rise to such idiocy.

And the biggest idiocy of all was this thing, he thought, grabbing the book and pulling it across the table toward him. Determinedly he opened it. There would be no addition this time, no further chapter in his own story, simply because there couldn't be.

He reached to flip the pages. His hand jerked back when they seemed to turn on their own, coming to a halt at a left-hand page of the elegant lettering that faced a blank page. He stared at it, trying to deny what he knew was true, that it had changed yet again. That when he'd left the motel, the writing had ended at the bottom of the previous page. It had ended with yesterday's date and the announcement that once again the last Hawk had met the woman he would marry, and with whom he would continue the Hawk bloodline.

Now it documented the very thing he'd done today. The hours he'd spent pouring over Hawk history, looking for anything that would prove what he knew, that this whole thing was impossible. It even called him a typical last Hawk, fiercely resisting the inevitable.

He barely had time to resent the characterization, because the next entry, also dated today, referred back to the woman he supposedly would marry. And ended with the statement that he would soon learn that that woman is in danger.

He slammed the book shut. She'd gone too far, this time. If there was anything he hated, it was being manipulated. He didn't know how she was doing it, the mechanics of it, but that didn't really matter now. What mattered was that she apparently thought he was a fool. That he could be controlled by the pushing of some insultingly simple emotional buttons.

He got up and shoved the chair back under the table. For a moment he stood there, staring at the book that had become a symbol of this whole absurd situation.

Then, his jaw set with determination, he picked it up, walked back to the bookshelves, and shoved it with emphasis between the history of Sunridge and *Hawks at War*. Nodding with finality, he turned his back and walked away.

Kendall glanced in the rearview mirror again, wondering where this idiot behind her thought she was supposed to go. There was no place for her to pull over and let the big brown sedan pass, and she was already uncomfortable with how fast she was going. This narrow, winding road, with its steep drop-offs, wasn't anything to fool around with; every year it seemed·at least one reckless teenager found that out the hard—and frequently fatal—way.

She probably shouldn't have come out here anyway. She hadn't accomplished much of anything except reddening her eyes. And Aaron certainly wouldn't have appreciated her maudlin show of sentimentality, sitting beside his grave as she poured out the story of the snarl things seemed to be in. All she'd ever wanted to do was what Aaron had wanted, yet it seemed that she was being thwarted from all sides. Alice threatening her, Jason refusing to believe anything she said . . .

She'd begun to cry, there beside the grave with its newly rolled sod. But after a few minutes she could almost hear Aaron's gruff voice berating her.

Knock off that foolishness, girl. Tears accomplish nothing. Get moving.

"Fine," she had muttered, "what do you suggest I do?"

You don't quit until you've fired your last round.

She'd always called that his circle the wagons mentality, but for the first time she began to see the point. She didn't have much left in the arsenal, but it wasn't quite empty yet. She'd picked up what little remained this morning. She didn't think showing it to Jason would make a difference, but at least she would know she had tried everything. And she couldn't give up until she had.

She had scrambled to her feet then, determined to make one last try to convince Jason.

If, she thought now, glancing apprehensively to her rearview mirror again, squinting as sunlight glared off the windshield of the sedan that was far too close, she ever got off this road alive.

The man was crazy. That had to be the explanation for this guy. He was so close he was practically knocking bumpers with her.

And then he was, she felt the small tap, and her heart leapt into her throat. It came again, harder. She tightened her grip on the steering wheel. They were coming up on the big, sweeping curve that was the last before the road dropped down to the valley floor again. The big curve that had claimed two young lives just last summer. The big curve delineated by the metal guardrail that didn't seem nearly as substantial to her now as it once had.

The big brown car edged up once more, this time to her left side. She saw the grill on the brown car, gleaming like the silver teeth of some monstrous, mythic creature, as the vehicle swung out from behind her. Surely he wasn't going to try to pass on this curve? On this road?

He was. He was pulling up even now, driving on the wrong side, in the oncoming lane, his front bumper even with her left rear wheel. She took her foot off the gas, and made herself not hit the brakes in this precarious place. The brown sedan gained on her.

And then it hit her.

In her mirror she'd seen the sharp movement of the driver's hands in the instant before the impact. She'd seen the intent in the set of his shoulders, his head.

Then she saw nothing but a spinning mosaic of colors as she skidded toward the drop.

Chapter Thirteen

❧

He was pacing again.

Jason shook his head in disgust. He didn't even know why he was here, why he just hadn't gone straight back to the airport and caught a plane for home. It was over, all his plans useless, all his years of preparation for nothing. The old man was dead, and beyond his reach.

But instead he was here, in the parking lot of this motel, waiting for the woman who had already taken up far too much of his time and energy. He resented the fact even as he admitted the reason he hadn't taken that plane: he wanted to see her again. Just, he assured himself, to see how far she was willing to take this.

His pacing steps faltered as hot, vivid memories of that kiss hit him with the force of a blow to the gut, followed by images of pursuing the heat that had exploded between them to its natural conclusion. Would she go that far to sell him her bill of goods?

Reaction shivered through him, an odd combination of heat and chill that seemed as confused as he felt. He'd always kept sex a simple thing, a straightforward approach to easing a basic need. He'd likened it to a craving for a particular food; once it was satisfied, the craving went away for a while. But this, this was different. Mixed up. Complex.

"Only because you're making it that way," he muttered as he turned and began to pace back the other way.

Where the hell was she? After catching a cab back here to get the car, he'd gone by Hawk Manufacturing, thinking she might be there; a sign informed him they were closed due to Aaron's death. He'd even driven by the big house, thinking it would explain much if she was there, meeting with her cohorts in this scam. But there had been no sign of her car, only a large white limousine in front of the grand entry, parked across the curving driveway that led in from the street. He supposed her car could be in the garage, out of sight, but not if that limo had been there when she'd arrived; it effectively blocked any car trying to get past it.

So he'd come back here, figuring she'd show up eventually. Perhaps she was out looking for a place to live, although why anyone would stay in this town after being fired by the Hawks was beyond him.

If, indeed, she really had been fired.

He stopped his pacing to lean against the fender of his rental car. He hadn't had the time or the inclination to shave since he'd arrived, and now he rubbed a hand over his stubbled face wearily. He didn't know what he believed anymore. His brain was telling him her entire story was a load of crap, but he kept catching himself thinking and reacting as if it were true.

There were so many possibilities, and combinations from those possibilities, that his head was spinning. He knew he hadn't had enough sleep, but it was more than that. Something else, or a combination of things, was at work here, and it was draining him. It was that feeling he couldn't shake that someone was watching. It was the mystery of the book, and how she was managing the changes in it. And it was that unsettling and peculiar feeling he got when he touched the thing, that feeling of comfort when he should have been shaken, or anxious, or scared.

Or angry.

Yes, that's what he should be feeling. Angry at this whole thing, at whatever scheming plot was at the center of all this, because whatever it was, it was obviously aimed at him. And they thought him stupid enough to buy it. So where was the anger that had overtaken him in the library? Where was all that righteous fury?

His hand slipped up and around the back of his neck,

massaging tight, knotted muscles. He let his head loll back, closed his eyes, and reluctantly admitted he was too damned tired and distracted to maintain anything as focused as anger right now.

Maybe he'd get a room here again and just sleep for a few hours. Kendall would turn up sooner or later. She had to, all her stuff was here. And if he just waited, she would come to him. He wasn't sure how he knew that, or why he was so certain she wasn't through with him yet. He just knew, on some instinctive level he'd learned over the years not to question, that there was no quit in this woman. She'd said she'd haunt him, and she meant it.

Too bad all that drive and energy and determination was aimed in the wrong direction, he thought, smothering a yawn. She could be hell on wheels under the right circumstances. Maybe she really had been the old man's right hand. She sure had the nerve for it. Maybe she—

The sound of a car approaching made him open his eyes. When he saw it was a police car pulling into the parking lot, he straightened up slowly. When he saw it was headed toward him, he pushed away from his car and stood ready on the balls of his feet. It was an old reaction, one he thought he was long past, but nothing that had happened here was quite ordinary, and he was more than a little edgy.

It was only when the black and white unit drove past him and pulled to a halt on the other side of his car, in front of Kendall's room, that he realized there was a passenger. In the front seat, not the caged rear used for prisoners.

Kendall.

He walked around the front of his car, toward the marked unit, his gaze fastened on her through the windshield. Her head was bowed, her dark hair loose now and falling forward, masking her face from him. She didn't look up as he approached. The officer who was driving got out, gave him that curious, speculative look that cops everywhere seemed to give everyone unknown to them, glanced at Jason's car, then walked around to the other side of the unit and opened the door. He leaned over and offered his passenger his arm.

How gallant, Jason thought dryly.

No, he thought again, it wasn't gallant. It was necessary. Kendall was moving stiffly, gingerly, as if every motion hurt. Or as if she expected to be thrown down at any moment.

As she straightened beside the police car, the thick mass of her hair slid back from her face. Jason's eyes narrowed as he saw the thick bandage on her forehead midway above her right eye and temple.

She is in danger.

The book's words came back at him like a slap.

"What happened?" he asked sharply.

Kendall didn't react, but the officer's head snapped around. He eyed Jason warily as he crossed the four feet between them in one stride.

"Traffic accident," the smartly uniformed young man said, then turned back to Kendall, clearly indicating that any more information was none of this apparent stranger's business.

"Give me your room key, Kendall. Then I'll get the things we retrieved inside for you," the officer said with courtly politeness. "You just lie down and rest."

"How badly is she hurt?"

The officer looked at him again, obviously reassessing his initial dismissal of Jason as merely a curious bystander. Jason returned his gaze levelly, noticing the small gold name tag above his right breast pocket. S. Browning. He looked young, Jason thought, maybe twenty-five. Or maybe that was just because he was so tired he was feeling damned old right now.

"Excuse me, sir," the officer said, "but I'm afraid that's really not your business."

The politeness was still there, but there was no sign of the gentle concern that had marked his words to Kendall. Jason's gaze flicked to her face. She was frighteningly pale, her skin almost translucent beside the darkness of her hair. There was another smaller, unbandaged cut on her cheek, and a third on her chin. As if sensing his scrutiny, she lifted her head to look back at him, then looked tiredly away, as if she didn't have the strength to deal with him right now. And Jason knew with gut-level certainty that this was no act.

"Kendall," he began, but she ignored him, looking down and searching in her purse with hands that were shaking. He shifted his gaze to the officer. "I'll take care of her."

Jason froze as he heard his own words, wondering what had possessed him to say them.

"I don't need taking care of."

The tremor in her voice belied her words, and Jason suppressed the urge to reach for her. That he even had to do it irritated him, and he purposely drew back, as if distance could alleviate whatever was making him react this way.

"Is this a friend of yours?" Browning asked her, his gaze flicking from Kendall to Jason suspiciously.

"No," Kendall said, pulling out her room key at last.

"No?" Jason said, recovered enough to assume a mockingly hurt tone. "How can you say that, after the night we spent together?"

Her head came up, but she said nothing. She barely reacted at all. Jason had figured she'd come up fighting at that one, and the fact that she didn't worried him. What the hell had happened to shake her so? She didn't seem the type to be so upset by a simple traffic accident.

So maybe it hadn't been a simple one.

She is in danger.

"Kendall," he said softly, "what happened?"

She ignored him, looking at the officer. "I'd like to go inside, please. I need to sit down."

Browning nodded, and gently took the key from her. He opened the door for her and held it while she stepped inside. Jason started to follow, but found his way blocked by the man in uniform.

"I don't believe the lady wants company."

"That's for her to say, isn't it?"

"I think she just did."

He looked over the man's shoulder to where Kendall was now sitting on the edge of the bed. She didn't look up.

Browning motioned him away from the door. Jason backed up, and the officer kept an eye on him as he went back to the police car and opened the back door.

"What happened?" Jason asked again.

For a moment Browning ignored him as he leaned inside the police car and picked up a small box that appeared to contain some papers and envelopes, then straightened and gave Jason an assessing look. After a moment, as if he'd reached a decision, he said, "Some reckless driver almost ran her off Laurel Road."

Jason drew back, tension spiking through him. "The cemetery road? The big curve?"

The officer's eyes narrowed. "How do you know that? Do you know something about this?"

God, how many times as a kid had he looked up into the face of a man wearing a badge and tried to answer that same question without seeming too scared, when inside he'd been scared to death they were going to somehow know he was a runaway. The panic response was instinctive, the knotting of his stomach, the sudden sweat, the tension of muscles getting ready to run.

If not for the shock of what the man had said, he would have laughed out loud at himself; he had four inches and ten years on this kid, yet he was reacting as if he were sixteen again, and on the run, when in reality he was farther from that scared kid than he'd ever dared hope to be.

"No," he said, "I don't know anything about it. Did you catch him?"

"Not yet." Browning shifted the box he held to his left hip, not coincidentally, Jason knew, freeing his gun hand. "But we will. She gave us a good description of the car."

"What kind of car?"

The officer shook his head. "Sorry. That would be compromising an ongoing investigation, to give that out before it was okayed for public release."

Jason's lips tightened. "What about the driver?"

Browning's eyes narrowed again. "How long have you been here?"

Jason smiled slightly despite his unease. "A couple of hours. Want to check my car?"

Browning returned the slight smile. "I already did."

"Good," Jason said, meaning it.

Something flickered in the officer's eyes, and Jason sensed he was once more being reassessed. "May I ask your name?"

Jason wondered if the politeness was ingrained, or if they were training them in it these days. "Jason West."

"And your business here in Sunridge?"

Jason didn't bother to question the man's assumption that he was only visiting; there didn't seem to be any point. But neither did he see any point in announcing he'd been here for Aaron Hawk's funeral, because the old man had been his father.

"It's personal." He could see his answer hadn't satisfied the man, so he added, "I used to live here, a long time ago. That's how I know about the road."

After a moment Browning nodded, as if in acceptance. Jason looked over his shoulder once more, to where Kendall still sat, unmoving.

"She looks pretty shaken," he said. "She shouldn't be alone."

"She didn't seem to want you around," Browning said.

"I know. She's . . . angry with me. Maybe with reason. But I wouldn't . . . I'm not . . ."

He stopped and took a breath, wondering what the hell he was doing and why it was so difficult. What did he care if Kendall Chase just sat there, dazed? She'd tried to con him, for God's sake, tried to manipulate him, and thought he was stupid enough to fail for some crazy tale about an ancient magician and a magic book. And a prediction about his future that would set her up for life.

"Never mind," he said. "Just forget it."

He turned on his heel, and walked back toward his car. He heard Browning, who had set the box down on the table just inside the door, ask Kendall if she needed anything more. Jason couldn't hear her answer, but Browning came out and pulled the room door shut behind him.

"You leaving town?" he called out.

Jason's patience snapped; he was tired, his nerves were drawn wire-tight, and he was feeling a little ragged around the edges. And right now he wanted nothing more than to do exactly that; get out of this place.

"You have a problem with that?"

The officer lifted a brow at him. "Not as long as I can find you if I need to."

Jason grimaced. "Ask Ms. Chase. I'm sure she can tell you anything you want to know about me."

He unlocked the car door and yanked it open. Then he slid into the driver's seat. Browning watched him for a moment, but then walked back to his unit and got in. He picked up the radio microphone and spoke into it, listened for a moment, glanced at Jason, then spoke again before hanging the mike in its rack and driving out of the motel lot rather quickly.

Jason sat there, staring at the logo embossed in silver on the steering wheel of the rental car. He felt slightly rudderless, like a man who had spent his life heading for a certain destination only to arrive and find out it didn't exist any longer. There was nothing left for him to do here. There was no reason for him not to do exactly what he wanted to do, just drive out of here to the airport and never look back. No reason at all.

Except for the image lingering in his mind of Kendall huddled on the edge of the bed he'd slept on last night, her hands clasped between her knees as if that were the only way she could stop them from shaking.

Some reckless driver almost ran her off Laurel Road. She is in danger.

He shook his head vehemently and jammed the key into the ignition. He started the car, revving it unnecessarily. And still he sat there, that image of an uncharacteristically distraught Kendall haunting him.

"Damn."

Irritation rang in the short oath. Determinedly he released the parking brake. He reached for the gearshift lever, thumbed down the button, and yanked it into reverse. He turned the wheel sharply, looking over his shoulder, ready to back out of the parking spot and head for the driveway.

He didn't even realize he'd hit the brakes until the car halted with a little jolt. He looked back at the closed door of Kendall's room, his jaw rigid. Uttering a string of self-condemning curses he hadn't used in years, he slammed the gear lever back into park, stomped the parking brake pedal down once more, and shut the car off.

He shoved the car door open so hard it creaked as the hinges protested. He got out and slammed it shut just as hard. Damning himself every step of the way, he strode toward that closed door. Only the memory of how shaken she had been enabled him to knock instead of pound on the door. He ended up pounding anyway, when he stood there for several minutes and nothing happened.

Maybe he should head for the office, he thought. Make up some story about being worried about her health after the accident and get the manager to unlock the door. It wasn't even a lie, not really. Not the accident part, anyway; he wasn't really worried about her.

Then why are you here?

He ignored the nagging little echo in his head and pounded once more. He was about to turn and follow through on his idea when, at last, the door swung open.

She said nothing. She just stood there, staring up at him with eyes he could only describe as hollow. Although she was barefoot, she was still wearing the gray jumpsuit she'd had on this morning, but it was torn in a couple of places and stained in an oddly splattered pattern on the right shoulder.

Blood.

His gaze flicked to the heavy bandage at her temple, and he wondered how many stitches were beneath it. He opened his mouth to speak, but couldn't think of anything to say. Instead, driven by an urge he didn't understand, he took a step forward and gently put his arms around her.

Kendall stiffened and tried to pull free. Firmly, but also with a gentleness he didn't quite recognize in himself, he held her fast. After a moment she seemed to give in. He moved one hand up and down her back in a soothing motion, much as his mother had soothed him as a child when he'd had a particularly ugly day. Slowly her head lowered, until she was resting it against his chest. He continued to stroke her, lightly, carefully.

"Don't worry about it now, Kendall," he said. "Any of it. It can all wait."

Amazingly he found that he meant it. He, who never trusted anyone until he was certain what their angle was, couldn't find it in him to believe that she had done this on purpose, gotten herself hurt like this, that this was part of whatever elaborate plan she and Aaron or Alice, or she alone, had concocted. Right now, he was having trouble believing anything except that this soft, trembling woman was exactly what she appeared to be.

"You just need to rest," he said, still holding her with great care.

Her head came up off his chest, and he half expected some biting comment that that was what she'd been trying to do when he'd come pounding on her door. But no words came, and she lowered her head again without even looking at him.

"Come on," he said softly, urging her back inside. She went without protest, moving slowly, as if she were still dazed. He shut the door behind them and, without taking his eyes off her, flipped the lock. He led her over to the side of the bed. When he released her, she simply stood there, as if not certain what she was supposed to do.

"Are you sure you don't have a concussion?" he asked, looking at her eyes. He'd had one once, when he'd fallen off that scaffold at old man McKenna's diesel repair shop, and he'd felt exactly like she was acting. When she didn't answer, he lifted her chin with a gentle finger. "Kendall?"

She seemed to focus then. "What? Uh . . . no. No concussion. They checked."

"Did they give you something? Medication or something?"

"I . . . yes. I took some a little while ago."

He saw a shiver wash through her. "You'd better sit down before you fall down."

Her gaze shifted downward, as if she were only now

realizing she was still dressed, and she lifted a hand to touch the stained shoulder of her jumpsuit with one trembling finger.

"I . . . I need to change."

"Okay."

She just stood there, staring at the grim pattern of drops left by the blood that had dripped from her forehead onto her shoulder. Jason smothered a harassed sounding sigh. What was he supposed to do, strip her himself? Not that the idea didn't have great appeal, but not under the current circumstances. He'd been told he didn't have a romantic bone in his body, and he didn't doubt the assessment, but he wasn't quite cold enough to take advantage of a dazed, injured woman.

"Kendall, are you going to change, or sleep in your clothes?" he asked, hoping she would move herself.

She did. Or she tried. Her hands moved to unfasten the buttons of her jumpsuit, as if he weren't even there. But it didn't matter; she was shaking so badly she couldn't manage the buttons. He reached out and grabbed her hands. She looked at their hands, then, slowly, up to his face.

"Kendall, what's wrong? What really happened out there?"

"I . . . I'm all right. The railing held. Just enough. The back wheels caught . . ."

A chill began in Jason's stomach. His hands tightened over hers. "Caught? You mean you were just . . . hanging there? Over that drop?"

"It took them so long to get out there . . ."

He could just imagine. The nearest fire station was a good ten minutes away, down that winding road. Ten minutes that must have seemed like an eternity. That drop-off had to be a good seventy-five feet. The chill spread, sending an involuntary shiver through him.

"No wonder you're so shook up," he said.

"No."

"What?"

"That's not . . . why."

"It's enough," Jason said grimly. "But what, then?"

She looked at him for a moment, with an expression

he couldn't read. Then she sighed and, lowering her gaze, shook her head. And pulled her hands free of his.

"You won't believe me. You never do. Even the police don't believe me, not really."

"What don't they believe?" When she didn't answer, he lifted her chin once more, but she avoided his eyes. "What, Kendall?"

She let out a long breath. "It wasn't an accident."

The chill blossomed, and he shivered again.

In danger.

"What," he said carefully, "do you mean? The cop said it was a reckless driver."

"I told you they didn't believe me. He wasn't reckless. He knew exactly what he was doing."

"Kendall—"

"I know. I'm hysterical. Wrought-up. And all those other labels men like to hang on agitated women. I've heard them all this afternoon. Well I'm not. I'm scared. But I'm not hysterical."

Some of the life was coming back into her voice, but it felt wrong to him, like the last fierce glow of a light before it burnt out.

"I was only going to ask why you're so sure," he said quietly.

"He tailgated me all the way from the cemetery. When we got close to the curve, he nudged my rear bumper. When we reached the curve, he pulled out from behind me, and then swerved. To hit me. Deliberately. I saw his hands move on the wheel."

Jason was silent for a long moment. There was no way she could have planned this, he thought. No matter how much the scam was worth, no one would take a chance of going over that drop, not when a much safer accident could easily be arranged. But if she was telling the truth . . .

"Why?" he finally asked. "Who?"

"I couldn't see the driver, because of the sun, the glare."

"What kind of a car?"

"I'm not sure. Brown, and big. That's all I can be certain of."

An image of the brown car he'd seen at the airport flashed through his mind. He tried to dismiss it, but it wouldn't budge. But he didn't want to frighten her, not now, she was already shaken enough.

"That's the who," he said. "So, why?"

"I . . ." Her voice trailed away, but he'd seen the flicker of suspicion in her eyes.

"You suspect somebody," he said. "Who's behind this?"

"Alice," she said flatly. "She told me if I valued my life I'd leave this alone."

Jason's brows lowered. "She threatened you? Physically? You didn't tell me that."

She met his gaze then. "Nothing else I said seemed to make any difference to you. Why should that?"

He couldn't answer that, because he didn't know why it made a difference, only that it did. Then, as he'd feared, the brief burst of animation faded. She sagged, her normally straight posture vanishing. She swayed on her feet, and his hands shot out to catch her shoulders.

She was about to collapse, he thought. Her eyes were closed, she had lost what little color had remained in her face, and she seemed unaware of his presence.

This was ridiculous. He wasn't a nursemaid. He didn't know the first thing about taking care of people like this. He'd made some pitiful efforts as a child, on the rare occasions when his mother had admitted to being too sick to go to work, but other than that, he'd rarely dealt with ailments of any kind, he never got sick himself, and hadn't really been seriously hurt in years.

But he had to do something. He couldn't just leave her like this. Feeling a little like a character in a bad movie, he methodically unbuttoned her jumpsuit and tugged it down and off her legs. She never protested, just let him do it, her eyes still closed, her body still slack, barely standing.

A part of his mind that he'd been trying to keep under stern wraps noticed the lovely contours of her body, the narrow waist, and the gentle, feminine curves of hips and breasts. Too curved for modern fashion, he supposed, but he liked a woman who could never be mistaken, even from a distance, for a boy. And his body certainly liked this one. He tightened the controls another notch, reining in the response, and after a moment was pleased to find that he was able to look at her dispassionately. Well, dispassionately enough to get through this, anyway.

Plain, functional underwear, he thought. Cotton, in a pale blue, with just the barest touch of lace on the high-cut panties and the bra. His control slipped for a moment as he remembered when he'd wondered if her nipples matched the soft peach color of her robe. He clamped down on the urge to find out the answer. He gritted his teeth and reached past her to flip back the covers. He lowered her to the bed.

She relaxed with a tiny murmur, and he let out a breath of relief. Then he sucked it back in again as she moved, turning on her side, emphasizing the womanly curve of her hip as one leg moved forward, and the soft fullness of her breasts as they were pressed together by her arms.

With a grated curse, he pulled the covers up over her. It was going to be, he thought, a very long afternoon.

Kendall woke slowly, feeling disoriented and oddly groggy. She lay quietly for a moment, fighting the muddled fog that seemed to have enveloped her. Where was she? Why did she feel this way, almost drugged, as if—

Her breath caught as a vivid image flashed through her mind, her car careening as she fought the wheel, the sound of rubber squealing on asphalt, the hideous thump and vertigo-inducing lurch of her car over the railing, leaving her staring down over a drop that seemed endless.

All grogginess vanished. She jerked upright. Strained muscles protested, and she winced. The movement pulled at the extremely tender spot on her forehead, and she remembered the three stitches the doctor in the emergency room had used to close the cut. Instinctively she lifted a hand to touch the bandage.

"You should leave that alone."

Kendall smothered a startled cry. She turned sharply, wincing again as a sharp pain shot through her shoulders.

Jason sat in the chair he'd been in before, the chair she had used while he'd slept. The book sat once more on the table next to him, open to a page she couldn't see from here. His feet were raised, resting on the end of the bed again, but there was nothing of insouciance in his manner this time, or in his face. His expression was utterly unreadable as he watched her steadily.

Under his scrutiny her awareness of various aches in her head and body faded, and she suddenly realized she was clad in only her underwear. And that her swift movement had sent the covers falling to her waist. Reflexively she grabbed at the sheet and pulled it up in front of her. Jason's eyes seemed to follow the movement. Another image came back to her, of Jason carefully unbuttoning her jumpsuit ...

Her gaze shot to his face. There was still nothing she could read there, nothing her years of practice enabled her to see, to understand his mood. His expression seemed emotionless, yet there was an odd tension about him, not in his body but in the sheer unwavering steadiness of his gaze, as if he were concentrating so intently that any movement would be a distraction. And the longer she looked at his eyes, the less concerned she became about her state of undress.

"Jason?" she asked softly.

He didn't answer her. She glanced at the open book again, then back at his face.

"Is it the book again?"

He glanced at it almost with disinterest. "I left it this afternoon," he said. "At the library in town."

She didn't ask what he'd been doing there, she thought she could guess. "But now it's here."

He nodded.

She took a deep breath. "Jason, I didn't—"

"I know. You were out like a light. It wasn't here when I ... put the covers over you. But when I turned around ..."

Her brow furrowed, but she quickly stopped the instinctive motion when it tugged painfully at the stitches again.

"The legend says ... it won't be left behind. That it

can't be destroyed. That it will always reappear." She expected his usual scoffing comment, but nothing came. After a moment, she asked, "Has it . . . changed? Again?"

"Yes."

She was afraid to ask. He sounded so strange. She hadn't realized how much inflection there usually was in his voice, until now, when it was utterly flat.

"What is it, Jason?"

He still didn't look at her. "Do you believe this book is for real? That the things in it are authentic?"

She noticed that he was no longer accusing her of being behind it, but she didn't think commenting on that would be wise right now. "I can't be positive. Only you would know."

"But you believe in it. The . . . legend, I mean."

"My mind doesn't. My heart . . ." She shrugged, even though he wasn't looking at her. It didn't hurt to move quite as much this time. "I'd like to believe it. Yes, it's foolish, but I think it's . . . wonderful, as well. And when it comes right down to it, I have no other explanation for what's happened."

"Neither do I," Jason said, still in that flat, inflectionless voice. "But if it's true . . . if it's right . . ."

"What?" she asked yet again when he trailed off.

"If it's right . . ." he said again, finally lifting his head to look at her; his eyes were as opaquely expressionless as his voice. "If it's right . . . Alice Hawk murdered my mother. And probably meant to kill me along with her."

Chapter Fourteen

~

"I didn't want her dead," Alice snapped. "I just wanted her warned."

"She's not dead."

"She could have been. That drop is—"

"She was never in any danger of going all the way over. I'm very good at what I do, Alice. That's why you hired me, remember?"

Alice felt a spurt of irritation at his use of her first name, but this was hardly the kind of man you demanded respect from. She turned and walked to the head of the grave. She stopped, staring down at the stone that had been installed just this morning.

It was inscribed simply with Aaron's name and the dates of his birth and death. They had tried to sell her something more elaborate, something with some loving sentiment inscribed, but she had refused. She had humbled herself to Aaron, declaring her love, too often in his life; she wouldn't do it yet again now that he was dead.

"You wanted her to know you were serious about what would happen to her." The voice came from very close behind her and she barely managed not to jump; she hadn't heard him move at all. "You wanted her scared. Well, she's scared. Trust me, she is scared."

"But is she scared enough to back off?" Alice muttered, not looking at him, still staring down at the headstone.

"You'd know that better than I." Those barren eyes looked at her, not even a hint of curiosity in them.

He didn't care, Alice realized. He'd done his job, accomplished his objective, and that was all that mattered to him. And, she realized with a little thrill of fear she quickly quashed, he would have been just as detached, just as uncaring, if her orders had been to make sure Kendall Chase had gone over that deadly drop. She shivered, certain it was the chill of the early evening air and nothing more.

But had what he already done accomplished the objective? Alice didn't know, and she didn't like the feeling of uncertainty.

"She's a tough one, for all that sweet, big-eyed exterior," she said, more to herself than out of any illusion that the man cared one way or the other; a large part of his reputation had been built on the certainty that nothing would sway him from his purpose, even—some said particularly—a pretty face.

He plucked a pale blond hair from the sleeve of his jacket, held it up, frowned at it, flicked it away, then went on. "She seemed pretty cool when I picked her up this morning in front of the bank over on California Street."

Alice's head came up then, quickly. "The bank?"

The man shrugged. "That's where I first saw her. I was on my way to your old man's office, like you said, to wait for her to show up, when I saw her car. I parked and waited, and she walked out of the bank right in front of me, pretty as you please. So I followed her here."

Alice grimaced. He had told her of Kendall's visit here to Aaron's grave, had told her that the girl had sat here for a very long time, crying. He'd related the incident coldly, unimpressed by either the sentimental visit or the tears. His lack of solicitude had soothed her displeasure at this further evidence that there had been a genuine bond between her husband and this young woman.

The bank, she thought, going back to what had caught her attention in the first place. What had she been doing at the bank? There were only two banks in town, and the one she'd been at was the one Kendall's personal account was in. The account that Alice had had the money deposited in.

Had Kendall decided to take the money? Had this afternoon's exercise in coercion been unnecessary?

With a smothered exclamation she turned and strode back to the waiting car. She didn't drive much anymore, but she had done so today, needing to maintain anonymity. It wasn't that she couldn't drive anymore—hardly, she was as alert and quick as she'd ever been, she told herself firmly—it was that she preferred the luxury and convenience of the limo and a driver. She deserved it. But she hadn't yet found someone to replace Mr. Carver; she would have to see to that.

Sitting in the driver's seat of the Mercedes, she turned on the car phone, and in a few moments had the number for the bank Kendall had been at. She dialed, and demanded to speak to Brad Simms, the bank's manager, immediately. Her name had the usual effect, and she was quickly put through. It didn't take much persuasion to get the information she wanted, but she hadn't expected it to; the Hawk name was at the top of the list of the bank's board of directors, and on a large chunk of shares of the bank's stock.

"Damn that little bitch," she said moments later as she turned off the phone.

"Oh?"

Alice looked up at the man who had followed her to the car. "She pulled the money from her account. In cash. And put it straight into a safe deposit box. With dated and timed records. In front of the bank staff."

The man lifted a pale blonde brow. "So she can show she never touched it?"

"It won't stand up in court," Alice declared. "And I can make sure that the staff swears they never saw a thing."

The man shrugged. "Still, it could be a problem. Reasonable doubt, and all that. Clever girl."

"Too clever. She always was." Alice tapped her fingers on the steering wheel, beating out a rapid little tattoo of irritation. "And she's had the box for a while. No doubt she had a copy of that codicil stashed there, too. She must have it with her now. So she's decided to fight me."

"Maybe she's changed her mind after this afternoon."

He inspected his jacket sleeve, as if searching for more blond hairs. "A lot of people don't respond to threats until they've been forced to look the consequences in the face."

"Maybe."

Alice wasn't convinced. She'd watched Kendall for ten years, watched her take on more and more, watched her grow, watched her meet every challenge Aaron had thrown at her. And she had watched the girl manage Aaron in a way she'd never been able to herself, never arguing with him, merely planting suggestions and re-treating until Aaron, after much blustering and posturing, reached the conclusion she had wanted him to.

Kendall hadn't seemed to mind never getting the credit for having had the idea in the first place, an attitude Alice had never been able to understand. But even she had had to admit that the girl's instincts were good; she had even, reluctantly, admitted that some of her ideas had been very beneficial to Hawk Industries.

It was too bad the girl was so damned virtuous.

"You want me to make another move on her? Scare her some more?"

Alice thought for a moment. "Not yet. Not until we know what's she's going to do. But be ready."

"Want me to keep following her?"

"Yes. I want to know where she goes and who she sees."

He nodded. "What about the guy?"

Alice's lips thinned out in distaste. "Don't do anything. Yet. I don't want him spooked into running. I want to be able to get my hands on him."

The man's mouth quirked. "I get the feeling you have some very unpleasant plans for him."

"That," Alice said, fighting the rage that always filled her at the thought of Aaron's illegitimate son, "is my business."

"For now," he said agreeably.

"Aaron did send your mother money," Kendall said. "Just like it says he did."

Jason's head came up at that. He was sitting in the

same chair as before, his feet on the floor now, his elbows resting on his knees as he stared at the floor between his feet. What he'd told her was so grim that she'd stayed away from the subject, staying with something relatively simple and less painful.

"I can prove that," she added. "Right now. It's one of the things I did today, before . . ."

She suppressed a shiver; what had happened since she'd awakened in the motel bed early this evening had done much to distract her from the horror of her own afternoon, but the memory still had the power to shake her. To cover her reaction, she stood up—a little gingerly, favoring stiff muscles that had made getting dressed in her jeans and sweater again a slow process—to dig into the box Officer Browning had brought inside for her. She took out a small stack of envelopes and held them out to Jason.

He made no move to take them, until she tilted them so he could read the name and address on the top one. She saw his eyes narrow and then, slowly, he reached out for the small bundle. She watched as he flicked through the first few envelopes.

"They're all to her," she said. "She wouldn't meet him, not after he'd told her he still couldn't leave Alice. She wouldn't let him see you, either. He started writing when she refused to even talk to him on the phone. He sent her money. She sent it all back. When she left for L.A., he found her and went after you both. She sent him away."

He didn't look at her, he just stared at the stack of unopened envelopes. "He . . . kept these?"

"He had them hidden at the house for a while. But when he got sick this last time, he gave them to me, to put in my safe deposit box. He thought I might need them to convince you."

"Convince me?"

"That he never abandoned you."

"He just gave up looking."

Kendall's brow furrowed. "Yes, he did. And I don't know why. Aaron never gave up on something he wanted. But he gave up on finding you. When I asked, he would only say he'd had to stop."

He grimaced. "Just wait. It'll show up in that damned book."

Kendall gaped at him. Was he really joking? Even wryly? She couldn't quite believe it. She took a breath. Now or never, she thought.

"Does it really say . . . Alice had something to do with your mother's death? I thought it was an accident."

His head came up then, and she nearly shivered again under the fierceness of his gaze. "That's what they said. A hit-and-run. Someone ran her off the road."

Kendall's breath caught in her throat. "Off the road?"

"Sounds familiar, doesn't it?"

Her knees suddenly unable to support her, Kendall sank down to sit on the edge of the bed. "What . . . what does the book say?"

"That Alice arranged it. Hired the driver that did it."

"And . . . you?" She didn't want to hear it, but needed to know.

"I should have been with her. Would have been. She usually picked me up at the diesel repair shop I worked at after school. But old man McKenna closed down early and gave me a ride. I'd left her a note, and she was on her way home when . . . he came out of nowhere. Pushed her off a bridge into the Duwamish River."

Kendall shivered violently this time. It was so eerily similar to what had happened to her, and some gut-level instinct told her both incidents had the same source. Alice Hawk.

Jason made a low sound that could have meant anything. Then he shoved the book at her. "Everything matches. Even why I wasn't in the car. It's all there. Places. Dates. All of it."

She didn't want to, but she couldn't stop herself. She forgot her own aches as she read; the account of Beth West's death was no less grim for having happened twenty years ago. She had to blink and look away from the tragic narrative. When she looked back again, her eyes still slightly blurry, something else entirely seemed to leap out at her. She stared at the juxtaposition of dates, the comparison she'd never made before.

He just gave up looking.

Yes, he did. And I don't know why.

The exchange echoed in her head. As did Jason's later words.

It's all there. Places. Dates.

And then it was Aaron's words, ringing with fury and frustration, telling her he'd been forced to stop looking for his son, but refusing to explain why.

"My God." She sat staring down at the book on her knees. "I think I see what happened twenty years ago. And earlier, when you were little. It all fits the pattern."

"What are you talking about?"

"Don't you see?" She looked up at him. "It makes perfect sense. When Aaron was diagnosed with lung cancer twenty years ago, he was afraid he was going to die, so he started again to try to find you. And within a month ... your mother was dead."

He was watching her intently, and she kept going.

"It's just like before, when Alice found out about you from the old hospital bills. She threatened your mother. And you. So your mother took you away, for your own safety. Alice must have threatened Aaron, too, when he kept trying to see you, after you'd gone. She must have told him that she'd ... do something drastic if he didn't give you and your mother up. So he did. And he only began searching again, all those years later, when he knew he was dying. It's the only thing that makes sense."

She saw his brows lower, saw his eyes change, sharpen somehow, and she knew the intelligence she'd sensed early on had kicked into high gear.

"Canada," he said, his voice barely above a murmur.

"What?"

"She used to talk about how close Seattle was to Canada. That we could make it in a day, if we had to. I always wondered why we would ever have to, but if I asked, she just told me not to worry about it." He'd said it without looking at her, but the moment the last words were out, his head came up and that predatory gaze fastened on her. "Are you saying my mother was killed just because the old man started looking for us again?"

"I know it sounds . . . incredibly sinister, but think about it. If Alice also thought Aaron was going to die twenty years ago, and knew he was looking for you again, she must have suspected he wanted to . . . make amends, to provide for you and your mother. And she wasn't about to let that happen."

"You're forgetting one little detail," he pointed out. "How did she find us?"

Kendall shook her head. "Maybe she didn't have to. Maybe she knew. Maybe she had you tracked from the time you left L.A."

"You're saying she knew where we were, but the old man couldn't find us?"

"Maybe she was why Aaron hadn't been able to find you. I wouldn't put it past her to have paid off the investigator he hired." Realization struck her. "That's why he hired . . . a friend this time. Someone he knew he could trust. He must have suspected she'd done something like that before."

"So she . . . what? Kept tabs on us for years? And did nothing?"

"As long as your mother did as Alice told her, there was no reason for her to do anything. But when Aaron began to search again, there was always the chance he might find you."

"So she hired a killer?" He shook his head. "I don't know if that boat's going to float, Kendall. That's presupposing a lot of craziness."

"Don't underestimate her, Jason." Her mouth twisted sourly as she flexed muscles that were still tight with strain. "Not like I did."

"You really think she's capable of trying to murder you?"

A chill swept through her at his words, but after a moment Kendall shook her head. "The day she told me what they'd done about the will, she was so smug, so . . . contemptuous . . . but I don't think she intended that. She just wanted to scare me. To show me that she . . . meant what she'd said."

"I'd say hanging by your back wheels over a seventy-five-foot drop is more than just a warning," he said, his mouth twisting downward at one corner.

"I just can't believe . . . Alice is a very calculating person. She'll do what she thinks is necessary, but only that. Otherwise, she would have—"

She broke off, suddenly aware of the insensitivity of what she'd been about to say.

"Otherwise she would have killed my mother when she first found out about her," he finished for her. His tone was blunt, unemotional. As if he were talking about somebody else.

"Yes," she said simply.

He lapsed into silence then, and she couldn't begin to guess what he was thinking. Her knack of reading people had never been as erratic as it was with Jason. Sometimes she looked at him and knew exactly what he was thinking, other times he was an enigma that seemed beyond her comprehension. And sitting here staring at him was not helping her resolve that particular dilemma. All it was doing was making her too aware of the unexpectedly soft, thick fringe of his lashes, the lean strength of his body . . . and the remembered heat of his mouth.

She forced herself to think about something else, anything else. To think about what else was in that box, and to ponder the wisdom of showing him now or waiting until he was more apt to listen to her.

In spite of it all, she nearly laughed at the idea of waiting until Jason was in a more receptive mood. He'd been about as receptive as a cornered porcupine ever since she'd met him. Decided now, she got up once more and took the single step to the table that held the box containing the things the police had retrieved from her wrecked car.

She took out a heavy manila envelope and held it out to Jason. It was a moment before he looked up; he was still staring at the small stack of letters he held. She wondered if he would ever read them. At last he put them down on the table and shifted his gaze to the big envelope she was holding.

"What's this?"

"The codicil to Aaron's will. The only copy Alice hasn't gotten her hands on."

His expression was unreadable as he took it. "It was in your safe deposit box, too, I presume?"

"Yes. I took it and the letters out when I—"

"When you what?" he prodded when she stopped.

"It doesn't matter. I just—"

"Right now, everything matters, Kendall. What else did you do at the bank?"

He had the right to know, she supposed. After all, if Alice went through with her nasty little plan, he'd be implicated as much as she would. With a sigh, she told him what she'd done with the fifty thousand dollars Alice had had put in her account. And to her amazement, he smiled.

"You walked across the bank lobby carrying fifty thousand in cash, and just plopped it into your deposit box?"

She nodded. "I had the notary who works in the bank witness that I went in with the money and came out without it. And when."

"How long after the time on the withdrawal record?"

"Two minutes."

He shook his head, still smiling. "Nice work."

Her mouth quirked. "I know a good lawyer would tear it to bits, but it was all I could think of on short notice. And I'd be a lot more confident if the Hawks didn't own half the bank, and Alice didn't sit on the board."

His smile faded. "And have the bank's staff in her hip pocket?"

"Probably," she agreed reluctantly. "But I couldn't risk taking it somewhere else. Too much time delay for them to use against me. I wanted it out of the account and into the box as fast as possible, and some kind of record of it."

"Then she could know what you did. That it means you plan to fight her. And if they called her, she knew where you were."

A new, frightening edginess filled her, and Kendall began to pace. "You think they did?"

He answered her with a question she knew she should have thought of already. "Either that or you're being followed. How else did the guy who rammed you know where to find you?"

"I can't believe she'd really hire somebody to ... kill me."

"Why not? Hell, maybe it's even the same guy from twenty years ago. He did a damn good job then."

She stopped pacing. He sounded bitter—rightfully so, she thought—and only half joking. For a long, strained moment she looked at him. Then, quietly, she asked, "Then you believe it?"

"That the merry widow had my mother killed?" Kendall saw his jaw tighten. "I don't know. But I know how to find out."

"How?"

"Simple," he said, standing up. "I'm going to ask her."

Chapter Fifteen

~

The minute Alice Hawk had walked into the room, the hair on the back of Jason's neck stood up in primitive, gut-level reaction. And he knew what Kendall had said, in her effort to talk him out of this, was true; this woman had the capacity for genuine viciousness.

Kendall had nearly begged him not to confront her, but he'd only become more determined. He couldn't face down the old man, but he could do the next best thing. And whether she wanted to or not Alice Hawk would tell him, one way or another, the truth.

"How dare you come here?"

The old woman's voice rang with outrage. Jason, who had been lolling with intentionally insulting casualness on the expensive sofa, his booted feet impudently on the even more expensive marble coffee table, controlled his instinctive reaction and looked up at the woman glaring down at him. She was even thinner than he'd thought, and no less rigidly straight and furiously angry than she'd been at the funeral. Definitely a tough old bird, he thought. A vulture, given the chance. But he'd turned the tables on more than one scavenger in his life; it was a lesson he'd learned years ago.

"Come now," he drawled, "I'm sure that's not why you let me in here. If you just wanted the pleasure of throwing me out, you would have had that bouncer at your front door do it already."

"I may still do just that."

She was really playing the grande dame, he thought.

And she looked the part, dressed even at this hour in a businesslike dark silk dress, her silver hair swept up into a regal style atop her head. A large solitaire diamond graced the ring finger of her left hand, surrounded by the glitter of several smaller stones. A small fortune on that one finger, Jason thought. He wondered if Aaron had bought it for her, or if she'd bought the ring for herself along with the husband.

"No, you won't throw me out," he said, grinning at her. "You're too curious."

Something flickered in her dark, narrowed eyes. It was the same sort of look Kendall gave him right before she told him he'd done something that reminded her of Aaron. Except in this woman the look was somehow malevolent, especially compared to Kendall's amused wonder.

"Perhaps I am," Alice said. "Curious about where you got the gall to show your face here, in my home."

"From what I've heard, I'd say the gall came straight from my father."

As he'd intended, she reacted to the last two words as if he'd slapped her. She went rigid, but before she could speak, he went on.

"But I'm happy to say I inherited my mother's spine. You won't control me by controlling the purse strings, like you did my father." He used the words again purposely, knowing it rankled her. "I don't want a damn cent from the Hawks."

And as quickly as he spoke the words, her expression changed. Calculating, Kendall had called her. It showed right now. Clearly.

"That's very good," Alice said with cool contempt, "because you'll never get a cent. Never."

"There's only one thing I want from you. An answer."

"I don't answer to anyone, least of all you."

He maintained his casual, careless posture, but kept his gaze riveted on her face, watching her eyes, knowing the reaction he was looking for would be there.

"How about to the police? They may not be quite as impressed with you in Seattle as they are here."

For the first time he saw a hint of caution alter her

expression. But it didn't show in her imperious voice. "Seattle? Why should I care about the police there?"

"I think you know why."

"I don't have the slightest idea what you're talking about. Now leave my house."

"There is no statute of limitations on murder, Alice. Twenty minutes or twenty years after, it's all the same under the law."

For a split second he saw something flicker in her eyes, something beyond wariness but short of fear. "You're impudent. And crazy. Now get out."

"Why did you do it? She did what you told her to. She left. We were out of your way, out of your life. She never even spoke to my father again."

"But he died speaking her name."

Alice's voice quivered with rage, and Jason sensed she had tried very hard to hold back those ill-advised words. And he saw too that she knew very well what was implied by those words. She was quick to try to cover her tracks, and he had to force himself to ignore the realization that Kendall had told the truth about Aaron's last words and concentrate on what Alice was saying.

"I have no idea what you're talking about, and I've had quite enough of you and your wild accusations. You can't prove anything now, and you never will. Get out of my house or I'll have you thrown out."

"Don't bother."

He moved his feet from the table and stood up. Next to his height and bulk she seemed fragile, looked almost brittle with age. But he didn't need Kendall's warning not to underestimate this woman. He'd learned long ago that sometimes the most harmless-looking foes were the most dangerous. They were the ones who carried the knife in their boot or the zip gun in their waistband. And they'd use it from behind more often than not.

"You'll get nothing from me," she repeated loudly as he walked past her toward the door.

He looked back over his shoulder at her. "You're too late," he said, meaning it in more ways than she knew. "I already got what I wanted from you."

He ignored the burly man who had obviously been

lingering outside the library door, awaiting a summons
to bodily throw him out; the man's face wore an expression of disappointment that was almost comical. Purposely Jason grinned at him as he walked past him out
into the night, and began to whistle cheerfully as he
strode out to his car and got in.

He dropped the jovial facade as soon as he closed the
car door. He watched his mirrors carefully as he pulled
away, but there was no sign of a tail. He hoped he'd left
the old woman a little off balance, unsure of what he'd
do now. Uncertain exactly how much he knew. Not realizing that only one thing that he'd discovered tonight
really mattered.

It was the truth. Alice Hawk had murdered his mother
as surely as if she'd been driving the car herself. Rage
boiled up in him. He fought it. It was a dangerous emotion, interfering with clear thinking, and he had too much
to think about.

When he reached the main road he stopped, pondering
for a moment, then he turned the car in the opposite
direction from the motel. He wasn't ready to face Kendall just yet. Not until he'd decided what he was going
to do.

Well, not what he was going to do; he knew that. It
was how he was going to do it that he hadn't decided
yet. He drove through the darkness, thinking.

Alice was guilty as hell, just as the book had said. He
wasn't sure how that made him feel about the book, but
he was sure of one thing. He wasn't through with the
Hawks yet. Not as long as Alice Hawk sat smug and safe
in her mansion, certain of her privileges, exempt, in her
eyes, from the rules that governed others, while his
mother had died far too young, and at this woman's
hands.

She had done it, but she was also right. He couldn't
prove it; he could hardly offer up the book as evidence.
No, he couldn't prove it. But he could make her pay.

She might be more than seventy years old, but a fierce
anger burned in Aaron's widow's dark eyes, and he knew
she would be a formidable adversary. But then, he'd always enjoyed those fights the most, the ones against wor-

thy opponents, because winning meant so much more
then. And he would win this one, too. Alice Hawk didn't
know what she was up against. She didn't know that she
was dealing with a man who had learned to hate at a
very young age, and who had raised it to an art form
when it came to anything and anyone named Hawk.

And that lost, rudderless feeling that had overtaken
him when he'd learned he'd waited too long to take his
revenge on his father had disappeared, vanished before
the growing tide of fury. For now he had a target perhaps
even more deserving than Aaron Hawk. And it was a
target he would enjoy taking as much as the Hawk namesake enjoyed taking an unsuspecting field mouse. And
he would take extra enjoyment in the knowledge that
nothing would enrage Alice Hawk more than to know
that it was he who had brought her world crashing down
around her.

And he knew just who would help him do it.

"You didn't expect her to come out and admit it,
did you?"

Kendall watched Jason from across the table in the
cozily lit restaurant. She'd been startled when he'd suggested they go out for some dinner after his late return
from his meeting with Alice Hawk. But she'd sensed he
was wound up, beyond restless into unsettled, and since
she'd been hungry anyway—she'd been too worried
about what would happen with Alice to eat while he was
gone—she had agreed.

And then she'd been even more startled when he had,
without consulting her, driven straight to Aaron's favorite restaurant in town, the quiet, elegant Gables. She
didn't mention that fact, although it again struck her as
amazing, the seemingly impossible similarities between
the father and son who had never known each other.
Besides, she hardly had to tell him Aaron had come here
often, not when everyone from the maître d' to the head
chef himself approached her to express obsequious sympathy on Aaron's passing. She had smiled graciously;
Jason had ignored them, just as he ignored the startled

looks he'd been garnering since they'd walked in the door.

"No," Jason agreed mildly now. "I didn't expect her to admit to anything. I expected exactly what I got."

He'd told her Alice had been furious that he'd dared to set foot in her house. That she'd threatened to have him thrown out bodily. And that she had denied knowing anything about his mother's death. All of which Kendall would have also expected from Alice. What surprised her was that Jason had left it at that and simply obeyed Alice's orders and apparently walked meekly out. She couldn't see him backing down from anyone, even the redoubtable Alice Hawk.

Besides, she thought, if that was all that had been said, what had taken up the rest of the three hours he'd been gone?

"I was driving around," he said when she finally asked exactly that. "Thinking."

"Thinking . . . about what?"

He lifted his glass of the delicately fragrant wine he'd ordered, a Napa Valley specialty of the house that, ironically, had been one of Aaron's favorites. He looked at her over the rim of the glass, in a way that made her feel like she was being inspected. He took a small sip, then set the wineglass down.

"Let's talk about that later. Things have been a little . . . heavy, and I think we need a break."

And then, quite unexpectedly, he smiled at her. A real, genuine smile. Her breath caught as his entire demeanor changed. For the first time since the time they'd talked about how she'd met Aaron, his bright blue eyes were full of warmth. Gone was the dark, brooding man she'd known, gone was the cool, assessing Jason West, and in his place was a beguiling stranger.

For a moment she wished she hadn't had to say no to the wine, because of the pain medication the hospital had given her; she could have used a drink. But then she thought again; alcohol fogging her brain was the last thing she needed. She was already far too attracted to this man for her own good, and she didn't quite trust this sudden change in attitude.

"And," he said with a touch of ruefulness that was quite winning, "I believe I owe you an apology."

He owed her several, she thought, recovering some of her equilibrium, but said only, "Oh?"

"I made some pretty harsh assumptions about you when we first met. And I underestimated your capabilities and intelligence as well. I'm sorry."

Kendall blinked, taken aback yet again. When the man decided to apologize, he really did it right, she thought, feeling more than a little stunned.

"I . . . thank you."

His mouth curved upward even farther. "Does that mean you accept my apology?"

She struggled to shake off the effects of that dazzling smile. She didn't know where he'd come from, this charming, appealing man, she only knew that Jason West had suddenly become more dangerous to her than ever.

"With reservations," she said, managing to sound skeptical rather than breathless.

The smile became a lopsided grin. The silliness of it, coupled with the unexpected warmth in his eyes and the lock of silky, dark hair that had fallen over his brow, made him look years younger than when she'd first seen him at the funeral, or at any time since.

"As in 'What brought this on?' " he asked, in a tone that matched the grin.

"Exactly," she said, feeling disarmed by his self-deprecating words nearly as much as his amused expression; she barely managed not to respond to the engaging grin by automatically returning it.

He shrugged. "I figured if we're going to work together on this, we'd better clear the air."

"Work together . . . on what?"

He reached into the inside pocket of the coat he'd tossed on the next chair when they'd taken their seats in the quiet back corner of the upscale restaurant. He pulled out the manila envelope she'd given him, the envelope that contained the codicil to Aaron's will. She was surprised he had it; he must have picked it up while she was changing clothes. Then the inference of his action struck her, and her gaze shot back to his face.

"You've decided to fight her?"

There was the slightest of pauses before he said, "She's not going to get away with it."

Kendall had the feeling that he meant much more than what his words appeared to mean on the surface, but she was so relieved that he'd changed his mind that she didn't dwell on it. She hadn't let Aaron down after all.

"Thank you," she said softly.

"Don't thank me," he said, a note of amused warning in his voice. "I'm a tough bastard to work with."

"Good. It's going to take a tough bastard to beat Alice." For the first time since he'd come back from that meeting, she smiled at him.

He went very still, staring at her. She assumed he was startled that she'd so easily tossed the harsh phrase back at him. Suddenly he tossed the envelope back on the chair beside him, atop his coat.

"Later. We're going to take that break. It's been a rough couple of days."

"On both of us," Kendall agreed softly.

Had it really been only two days? she thought in shocked realization. She had expected, if she ever found Aaron's son, that he would take a lot of her time for a while. She hadn't expected him to consume her entire life, to take over every waking and sleeping moment to the exclusion of all else.

It wasn't until their food, a plate of the Gables exquisitely prepared lemon chicken for her and a sizable filet of fresh halibut for him, sat in front of them that he spoke again.

"What happened to your parents?"

The question startled her enough that she stared at him for a long, silent moment before she answered.

"They were killed in a traffic accident when I was seven." Still unable to quite make the mental jump from the suspicious, cold person he'd been to this man showing every evidence of friendly, genuine interest, she added bluntly, "Why?"

He didn't react to her tone. "I just wondered." After she'd taken a bite of her chicken and a sip of water, he asked, "Why foster homes? Wasn't there somebody else to take care of you?"

"No more than there was for you," she said, unable to guess why this topic had suddenly become of interest to him. "I had a grandmother, my father's mother, but she was ill and couldn't deal with a seven-year-old. She died a couple of years later."

"So you were an orphan."

She grimaced. "I hate that word. It sounds so . . . needy."

"I know," he said, in a quiet, gentle tone she'd never heard from him before. It made her feel very strange inside, a softer, less urgent version of what she'd felt when he'd kissed her.

"It wasn't so bad," she hastened to say. "Most of the people I lived with were nice. And Mrs. McCurdy, the lady I lived with in high school, was wonderful. She was a teacher, and she was the one who convinced me I should go to college. She even tutored me so I could improve my grades. I still hear from her."

"She must be proud you turned out so well."

"Yes, she is." She hesitated, then decided to take advantage of this oddly complaisant mood he seemed to be in. "Why did you run away, Jason? After your mother died?"

She expected him to tense up, but he leaned back in his chair and looked thoughtful. "I've been thinking about that. I hated the idea of living with strangers. I must have picked up that feeling from my mother. She always said never to trust strangers. I assumed it was natural maternal caution, but now . . ."

Kendall's eyes widened. "You think she was . . . afraid? That Alice would . . . send somebody after you again?"

"Maybe she knew Alice knew where we were. Maybe she just sensed someone was keeping track of us. I don't know. I just know she was always afraid. I don't remember a time when she wasn't."

"Poor Beth," Kendall murmured. "What a sad way to live."

"Beth?"

Kendall nodded, lost in contemplation of a young woman whose life had revolved around keeping her young son safe from a malevolent woman. "That's what Aaron always called her. His Beth. I got in the habit of thinking of her that way."

The minute the words came out, she snapped out of her reverie, cringing as she braced herself for some kind of biting observation on her continued attempts to convince him Aaron had truly loved his mother. It didn't come. His usually sharp gaze seemed unfocused, and when he spoke, his voice was as softly reflective as Kendall's reverie had been.

"No wonder she hated it when people called her that. She always told people to call her Elizabeth, or Liz, or even Lizzie, just not Beth. It must have . . . hurt too much."

"Oh, Jason," she said softly.

He looked at her then, and for an instant the old Jason seemed to be looking at her, cool and seemingly assessing her reaction. But it was gone so quickly she couldn't be sure, and the engaging smile was back.

"Do you remember your mother, Kendall?"

Disconcerted by the unexpected question, it took her a moment to answer. "Yes. In bits and pieces. And I have pictures, of all of us together. That helps."

They were halfway through the desert Jason had insisted on before she realized she'd spent practically the entire meal talking about herself, her family memories, her time at college, and silly things she knew perfectly well Jason had no interest in. Yet he kept asking, guiding the conversation back to her whenever it strayed, as if finding out about her had become the most important thing in his life. It would have been flattering, had she not had a suspicion that there was some hidden motive to this, some motive she hadn't yet figured out.

Why are you so determined to think I have some hidden agenda here?

Her own words came back to her, mocking her. She had accused Jason of the very thing she was doing now, looking for a hidden motive to everything. And she had nothing more to base her doubts on than a flicker of something in his eyes, something she wasn't even certain she'd really seen.

They rode back to the motel in silence. A comfortable, companionable silence, suited to two people who had just enjoyed a delicious meal and were now pleasantly tired. It wasn't until they pulled into the parking lot that Kendall suddenly wondered where Jason was planning on spending the night.

He'd been so exhausted last night that she'd had little concern about him staying with her. But he wasn't that tired now. And last night had been before he'd kissed her ...

He was around the car and opening the door for her before she could manage to do it herself; she was still feeling the effects of the crash rather strongly. She tried formulating the question in her head a dozen different ways as he walked with her up to the door of her room, but she couldn't think of anything that didn't make her sound like a fool.

"We'll figure out a plan of attack in the morning," he said as she fumbled with her key.

"I ... All right."

This lock hadn't seemed this tricky before, she thought, trying again to insert the uncooperative key. Gently Jason took the key, slid it into the lock, and opened the door for her.

"Good night, Kendall. I'll see you tomorrow."

Her gaze flicked to his face. She didn't think she'd let her thoughts show, but he spoke as if they'd been written across her forehead.

"I got a room when I first got back tonight. I'm next door."

"Oh."

"Not," he said, his voice suddenly husky, "that I'd turn down an invitation to share."

Kendall felt color flood her cheeks. She looked away, but with a gentle touch he held her chin up so she had to look at him. He smiled, an expression that was almost tender on his face.

"I thought it was a bit too soon. But I had to ask."

He lifted one shoulder in an almost sheepish half

shrug, but as he looked down at her, his smile slowly faded, to be replaced by something much more elemental. Heat flared in his eyes as the thumb of the hand that had tilted her head back came up to trace the line of her lower lip.

"Jason." She stopped when she heard the quiver in her voice.

"I want you, Kendall." His voice was low, thick. "I've wanted you from the moment I saw you stand up to that old bitch at the funeral."

For an instant, before heat swamped her from the images those husky words brought on, she felt a surge of satisfaction that he'd said that, rather than some banal comment about her appearance. Then caution rose in her. He'd thought her Aaron's mistress then. She didn't know if he still believed it, but if so, this could be some twisted way to strike at his dead father.

"A-Aaron," she stammered. "You think I—"

He hushed her with a finger to her lips. "I know better now. And Aaron has nothing to do with this. Nothing to do with us."

He gave her plenty of time to move, to dodge away, but she knew she would do neither. Nothing in her life had ever made her feel the way Jason's kiss had, and she had to know if it had been a fluke, an out-of-proportion response engendered by the emptiness of her social life over the past three years.

The moment his mouth came down on hers, she knew it hadn't been. Heat leapt in her so quickly it would have taken her breath away had not the feel of his lips against hers not already done it. She felt the strong, gentle touch of his hands at the back of her neck as he threaded his fingers through her hair. She let her head loll back, feeling unable to do anything else. He deepened the kiss, his mouth moving coaxingly on hers.

She didn't need coaxing. Her pulse began to hammer in hot, heavy beats, spreading the fire, suffusing her with a sensation of rising need and longing she'd never felt in her life. Her hands came up to rest on his chest, but if any part of her mind had thought to push him away, the urge vanished when she felt the slight brush of his tongue over her lips. She parted them for him reflexively, without even thinking about resisting.

He probed forward tentatively, tracing the soft inner surface of her lips, the even ridge of her teeth. When the tip of his tongue, hot, wet, rough velvet, brushed her own, a shiver rippled down her spine and on to her knees, weakening them until she sagged against him.

His hands slid down to her shoulders, both supporting her and pulling her against him at the same time. She barely noticed the stiffness of wrenched muscles now. His mouth never left hers; instead he probed deeper, sending darting little bursts of fire down nerves she'd forgotten existed. If she had ever known them at all. Instinctively, driven by a need she barely recognized, she moved against him, feeling her nipples draw up tight with need against his chest. Echoing darts of fire arrowed downward within her, connecting the aching peaks of her breasts to someplace deep inside her that was turning molten, hot and liquid.

She heard an odd little sound, a breathy moan, and realized it was coming from her. As if in response, Jason's grip tightened. He drew her closer. Then, as if that wasn't enough, his hand slipped down to her waist, his fingers tightened, and he pulled her hard against him. She heard him groan, low and deep in his chest, in the same moment that she felt the insistent press of rigidly aroused male flesh against her belly.

He moved his hips sharply, convulsively, as if he couldn't stop himself. She felt again the prod of his erection, heard him make another low, compressed sound, shorter this time, as if he'd cut off the groan before it could escape.

Then his tongue plunged deep, searching, tasting, urging—no, demanding—a fiercer response from her. She gave it, because she had no choice. Her body had leapt to life at the touch of his mouth, of his hands, at the undeniable knowledge that he was as aroused as she was. It was that knowledge that made the muscles low and deep inside her cramp violently, around a hollow, empty place she'd never known was there before.

This time it was she who moved, shifting her body to

increase the pressure on his, to slowly rub against him.
And this time the groan escaped him, a deep, hoarse
sound that sent a thrill through her. A thrill that intensified when, incredibly, she felt him shudder, felt a sharp
contraction of his fingers, digging into her waist.

Abruptly he backed away, releasing her. The chilly
evening air seemed to rush between them, making her
even more aware of the heat that had risen in her. She
lifted her gaze to his face. Through the haze of lingering
pleasure that enveloped her, she was vaguely aware that
he looked . . . odd. Strained. As if something out of synch
had happened, something unexpected. But as it did so
often with this man who seemed a master at masking
himself, the expression vanished in the next instant.

He lifted one hand and gently brushed her cheek with
the backs of his fingers.

"Good night, Kendall," he said, and she shivered at
the sensual promise in those words, in his voice, heard
as clearly as if he'd said it that he wouldn't be saying
good night to her at her door forever.

And when she at last was able to move, when she
stepped inside and closed the door behind her, when she
should have been feeling relief that things hadn't gotten,
as they so easily could have, out of hand, she ruefully
had to admit that what she was feeling wasn't relief but
disappointment.

And she knew then that she had greatly underestimated just how big a danger Jason was to her. She would
do well to remember that no matter how charming he'd
been tonight, he was still Aaron's son. And Aaron himself had known very well how to use charm when it was
called for.

Maybe Hawks bred true after all.

Chapter Sixteen

~

"You still don't trust me, do you?"

Jason watched as she toyed with one of the foam cups full of coffee he'd brought to her room, along with breakfast rolls and muffins from the bakery down the street, early this morning, as soon as he'd heard her up and moving. The rather vicious mood he'd awakened in had been ameliorated somewhat when he'd seen her tossed, tangled bedcovers; her night, apparently, had been no more restful than his.

"Let's just say I'm as wary of this sudden change as you were of me in the beginning," she said at last.

"I guess I can't blame you for that," he said, leaning back in his chair as he picked idly at the sweet roll he didn't really want. He met her gaze. "Do I need to apologize again for not believing you from the beginning?"

"No."

"I just didn't trust anybody who had anything to do with my father."

"I understand."

"I didn't mean to—"

She held up a slender hand. "Jason, stop. You've apologized. Nicely. I've accepted it. Once is quite enough."

He grinned suddenly. "You sure you don't want to milk this some more?"

He saw her lips quiver, as if she were fighting not to laugh or at least smile back at him. He concealed his satisfaction; he'd used that crooked grin to his advantage before, although not in a long time. It was working on Kendall, as it had worked on countless other women, and that gave him a reassurance he hadn't even been conscious of needing.

"You wanted me to take you on faith," he pointed out after a moment.

"I know." She tapped a finger against the rim of the cup absently. "I guess I didn't realize just how much I was asking for until now."

Until the tables were turned, Jason thought. Ironic, that now it was he himself who was trying to persuade her to trust him. And Kendall Chase was proving to be harder to finesse than he'd guessed. When she'd responded so swiftly last night, he'd thought it would be easy. She'd gone hot and soft in his arms so fast it had made his head spin.

At least that's what he'd finally decided had made his head spin, in the dark hours of the night when he'd lain awake and alone and painfully aroused, aching for the woman who no doubt lay sleeping peacefully on the other side of the wall between them. It had been her unexpected reaction that had thrown him, not the sweetness of her mouth, not the tiny, incredibly erotic sounds of need she'd made, not her tentative caress of his body with her own. He'd been startled, that's all.

What he needed, he thought, was to remember what this was all about. Over and above the unexpected, sizzling fire that leapt between them, he was enjoying himself so much, relishing the quickness of her mind, the easy way she smiled, and how she laughed when she finally began to relax a little, that he had to remind himself regularly that he wasn't doing this just because he wanted to, that there was a reason behind his efforts to charm her. He'd almost forgotten, had lost track of his game plan.

And it was time to get back to that game plan, no matter how wary Kendall was feeling.

"So, tell me about Aaron," he said, able with an effort to get the name he hadn't spoken for years out fairly evenly. "I know he started out with just that little manufacturing company, but how did he get from there to Hawk Industries?"

"By being able to adapt."

"Adapt?"

"That first manufacturing company was geared to post-war defense contracts when Aaron took it over. He soon did well enough to buy several more companies, most along the same lines, each catering to different types of military needs. He consistently delivered high quality for an acceptable price."

"What, no seven-hundred-dollar toilet seats?" Jason asked wryly.

She did smile then, and in that softening of her expression he saw again the tremendous esteem and affection Kendall had had for his father. And again he wondered what it took to inspire such feeling in such a woman. His father had been damned lucky, Jason thought, envying the dead man for a reason he would never have expected: because he'd had the love and respect of Kendall Chase.

Don't be an idiot, he ordered himself silently. That kind of softness was for fools. Tend to business, here.

"No," Kendall answered, "and no thousand-dollar ashtrays, either. That wasn't Aaron's way. He'd squeeze every ounce of profit he could out of a contract, but he never cheated, in billing or on quality."

He'd read somewhere, years ago, he thought, that Aaron Hawk's reputation had been built on a combination of hard-nosed, dogged, aggressive bargaining, and honesty once the bargain was struck. He remembered reading it because he'd spent a long time afterward bitterly wishing his father had wanted his son as badly as he wanted his next business deal.

And he remembered suddenly where he'd read it. In one of the business magazines his mother had had, hidden away in a cupboard. He'd found the small stack one day and had gone through them, puzzled at their presence in the small apartment. There had been several different publications, with no preponderance of any one, and no pattern of dates. He hadn't understood why she had them until, after looking through the first two or three, he had realized that they did have one thing in common: each of them had an article about Aaron Hawk.

He'd been thirteen then, and hungry for knowledge about the man his mother had forbidden him even to mention and never discussed herself, the man whose name wasn't even on his school records, whose name she had somehow even obliterated from his birth certificate. Overwhelmed by his curiosity, he'd read the half-dozen magazines, not just the articles on his father but the rest as well, wanting to know something about this world his father was apparently a sizable fish in.

That had been the beginning of his quest; he'd searched out more, putting his hours in the library to good use. He'd found out a great deal; Aaron's progress was followed closely by those who kept track of the power barons of the business world. And in the process, he'd learned things about that world he hadn't even been aware of learning at the time.

The gradual realization that Kendall was looking at him rather oddly brought him out of his fruitless memories. He spoke hastily, to divert her.

"What did you mean about adapting?"

Kendall shrugged. "Aaron saw the end of the defense dollars coming long before most people. He even predicted the cold war would end and what would happen afterward. So, he diversified. Early on. And had a good head start on most of the rest of the people who had always counted on the Pentagon for their livelihood."

He knew that. In fact, he knew more about his father's work—successes and failures—than Kendall would ever imagine he knew. And for a reason he hoped she would never guess. Aaron might be dead, and Kendall might have no use for his widow, but he doubted she would stand by quietly while he carried out his plans.

"Hawk Manufacturing switched from military components to sports equipment," she explained as if he'd asked. "Hawk Propulsion shifted from jet fighters to public transportation. CeramHawk began to develop their composite materials for commercial rather than military uses."

Jason nodded. He couldn't fault the old man; he'd been ahead of his time, and had reaped the profit for his farsightedness. But then, he'd always known Aaron

Hawk was a hell of a businessman. He was just a lousy father.

He reined in the long-entrenched response to his father, that kind of bitter coldness that had driven him for so many years. He had to keep it under control, or he would never get what he wanted from Kendall.

What he wanted from Kendall.

Fully formed, vivid, hot, and potent enough to slam the air out of his lungs, the memory of last night hit him. Kendall in his arms, her mouth soft and warm beneath his, her body pressed against him so invitingly, until it had been all he could do to wrench himself away from her. If he hadn't been so certain it would have made everything impossibly difficult he never would have stopped last night. He would have pursued that auspicious beginning to its natural, inevitable conclusion, Kendall naked beneath him as he at last assuaged this crazy, raging need he'd suddenly developed.

He sucked in a deep, quick breath, battling for command over a body that had never betrayed him before, but was careening out of control now, responding with wild speed to the images flashing through his mind. Kendall naked beneath him, on top of him, letting him touch her, and touching him, him taking her, and her taking him until they were both mindless with it. His jaw clenched as he fought it; he'd never gotten so damned hard so damned fast, never been unable to contain his responses, but this was killing him.

Too soon, he told himself, it was too soon. He chanted it like mantra, as if it could give him the control he couldn't seem to find anymore.

Kendall was staring at him, wide-eyed and a little pale, as if she could read his every thought. He wasn't surprised. He hadn't had much experience fighting this particular battle; no woman had ever affected him like this. Especially a woman he had other plans for. A woman he needed to reach a goal. A woman he planned to use to reach that goal.

But her expression confirmed his judgment; it was too soon. No matter how receptive she had seemed last night, no matter how eager she had seemed for his kiss, his

touch, Kendall Chase wasn't the kind of woman to fall
into bed with a man she'd kissed twice. The irony of the
fact that he'd once thought her the kind of woman who
would sleep with an old man as a career move didn't
escape him. And it was that irony that finally allowed
him to regain some remnant of control.

He didn't try to deny what he knew she must have
read in his face. He didn't want to deny it; he wanted to
acknowledge it, because he wanted her thinking about it;
he wanted it in her mind, images and visions as clear
and vivid as his had been; he wanted her imagining it,
picturing it in her mind, what it would be like when the
inevitable happened. He wanted her thinking about it so
much that she was as hot as he was, so much that when
the time came she would be begging for it, begging for
an end to the torture of waiting.

So he didn't try to hide the raw desire in his voice
when he spoke.

"I told you I wanted you, Kendall. And I know you
want me back. Did you think it would go away?"

"I . . ."

"We just postponed it, last night," he said. "Because
you weren't ready. Yet."

Her chin came up at that, and despite the fact that he
knew she was going to deny it, that she was going to
fight him, he had to smile; she never gave up.

"Don't feel insulted, Kendall," he said before she
could voice an outraged reply. "You know it's true. You
can't deny what happens between us. What happened
last night."

Color stained her cheeks, standing out against her still
pale skin. But she didn't look away. As usual, she faced
him down. "Just because you've got fire and gasoline
doesn't mean you have to throw them together."

"Ah, but what a waste if you don't. The fire flickers
out, and the gasoline evaporates into nothing."

"But you don't get burned."

"You don't feel the heat, either." He shook his head
as he looked at her. "Aren't you the one who said if you
don't taste the tears, you don't taste the joy, either? Why
are you afraid now?"

"I'm not afraid. I'm ... cautious." She gave him a sideways look. "Besides, you're the one who thinks love is foolish, remember?"

Jason went very still. This was a direction he didn't want her taking. And something he should have anticipated, he thought with chagrin; once he'd realized Kendall hadn't really been Aaron's mistress, that she was the innocent she seemed in that respect, he should have known she was the kind of woman who had to dress up a need as basic as sex, a naive romantic who had to have it prettied up and called love.

Normally he wouldn't care; if a woman was silly enough to mistake lust for love, then that was her problem. He'd never cared before. But for some reason it bothered him now. He wanted this clear between them.

"I'm not talking about love. I'm talking about something much more basic and a lot more necessary. Sex, Kendall. Pure and simple. You and me. Going up in flames."

She went pale again, but her lips parted as if she were having difficulty getting enough air. His voice dropped even lower.

"Do you think I don't know that I wasn't the only one hot for it last night?"

"Jason—"

"You know what I wanted? I wanted you to unzip me, right there, outside the door. I was so hard, just from kissing you, and I wanted your hands on me so badly I didn't care if the whole damned world knew it. Hell, they could have watched, for all I cared."

She made a tiny sound, a strangled gasp. She moved, as if she wanted to rise, but didn't have the strength. He went on determinedly.

"And I wanted my hands on you. I wanted to touch every inch of you. Slowly."

He didn't give her a chance to react, to speak, judging her reaction by the continuing acceleration of the pulse visible at her throat. He wanted her to think of this again and again, until every time her guard was down she pictured them together.

"I wanted it all, Kendall. Right up there against the door, I was that hot."

She was staring at him, her lips parted wider now, breathing in visible gulps. Enough, he thought. He had to stop. He'd meant to get to her, but had wound up driving himself to the brink of insanity instead. He was as hard as he'd been last night, aching, barely able to keep from doubling over in the effort to ease the brutal tightness of his body. With an effort that made his voice sound strained, he softened his tone.

"But I knew that no matter how much you wanted it last night, you'd regret it this morning. And I didn't want that to happen."

As an emotional about-face it was more than effective; Kendall's eyes widened, her expression softened, and the tension in her eased visibly. What amazed Jason was his thought that it was true, that he really wouldn't have wanted her to regret it. When it came right down to it, he liked and admired Kendall. And he really didn't want to hurt her.

Only, he insisted to himself firmly, because it would make his task so much harder. He couldn't get what he needed from her if she was wishing she'd never laid eyes on him. He almost managed to convince himself that was the real reason.

"I'm sorry," he said, managing a suitably contrite tone. "This wasn't the time to discuss this. I promised we'd talk about this." He gestured at the manila envelope that lay on the table between them. "You're sure you want to do this?"

It was a long, very silent moment before she answered, and Jason could only hope she was having as much trouble as he was getting the images he'd invoked out of her mind.

"I . . . yes. It's what Aaron wanted."

She gave her head a slight shake, as if she were trying to physically rid herself of the unsettling thoughts he'd planted. He could almost see her gathering her composure, and this time the sense of admiration was more than a flicker; Kendall Chase was a strong, determined woman.

"Are you sure *you* want to do this?"

He knew this was only the first of his answers that would have to be worded very carefully. She was smart enough and wary enough not to buy into a too complete turnaround on his part. So he chose something as close to the truth as he dared.

"I still don't want Hawk money," he said. "But I want her to have to give it to me."

He watched her eyes as she considered this, and then, finally, she nodded.

"All right."

"I need to know some things, if we're going to beat her at her own game."

She nodded again. "Whatever I can tell you, I will."

He spent the next few hours walking a tightrope, trying to keep her talking, yet keeping her from realizing what he was really after. He listened to more than he ever wanted to about his father, but knew he had to, to get what he needed to know from her.

Much of it was in the way of confirmation; he'd gathered a lot of information over the years, and apparently most of it was fairly accurate. Aaron had owned a little less here, a little more there, and at his death was stretched a little thinner than Jason would have guessed, but that would only make it that much easier. He allowed himself a brief moment of pleasure, contemplating the look on Alice's face when she realized what had happened.

He felt a small qualm when he cloaked his more probing questions about Aaron and his work and holdings in the deceptive guise of an estranged son's reluctant curiosity, and Kendall answered eagerly, as if pleased he was at last interested. And her answers showed him that she indeed knew the inner workings of Hawk intimately, just as she'd always claimed. He'd been very, very wrong about her, and that disturbed him; he wasn't used to being so wrong about people. Perhaps he'd been reacting out of his instant attraction to her, unconsciously trying to quash it by turning her into someone he could despise.

As she talked, he learned a lot. Some things he'd needed to know, some he didn't want to know or care about. Things that shouldn't make any difference to him at all. That there had never been another woman in Aaron's life, after his mother. That no matter how much she insisted it was Aaron's idea, it had really been Kendall, with her fixation on family, who had softened up the old man and made him begin to search for his son once more.

And he'd come face-to-face with the fact that where Kendall's response had been a tremendous effort to preserve the family that had survived for so long, his had been to destroy it utterly. And he didn't know why that thought bothered him.

But he stifled his misgivings by reminding himself of his purpose. It had been at his core, that driving need to prove that Aaron had been the loser for abandoning his only son, for so long, that the loss of it at Aaron's death had sent him reeling. But he had it back now, its focus only slightly changed, and he was more rather than less resolute in his determination. For it wasn't just abandonment and rejection he had to pay back now.

Now it was murder.

Kendall didn't know what had come over him. For hours they had talked—or rather she'd talked; Jason had mostly listened—and he'd been like a different person. He'd been a different person ever since he'd come back from the mansion last night. But it wasn't until Jason had at last gone back to his room saying he needed to make some phone calls that she'd had a chance to think about it.

She sat watching the sunlight fade away as she contemplated the change. When the shadows began to blend together she at last got up; only then, when her muscles protested, realizing that she was paying the price for sitting all day on top of the wrenching her body had taken yesterday.

She stretched gingerly, trying to loosen the battered, knotted muscles. Her back ached, but her shoulders were the worst, especially just below her neck, where they seemed so tight the slightest movement hurt. She began to rotate them, trying to make herself continue her train

of thought, as a distraction. Jason had always been that
to her, she admitted. A very large distraction.

What was strange was not so much that he'd changed,
but the way—or the ways—in which he'd changed. Yes,
he was amusing, friendly, and utterly charming, definitely
a most radical change, she thought wryly, but there were
also moments when she thought she glimpsed something
else in him, just a flash of expression, or a glint in his
eyes, something colder, harsher, and more implacable
than ever before.

She told herself it was only natural, if he'd come to
believe that Alice had been the cause of his mother's
death, but that didn't make it any less frightening.

But she had no qualms about helping him to defeat
Aaron's widow. No matter how cold or calculating Jason
might seem to be about this, nothing could be worse, or
more cold-blooded, than what Alice had done.

Which explained the harshness she'd glimpsed, but not
the sudden excess of amiability. Was this the real Jason?
Had it been hidden by the bitterness he'd felt, by his
suspicions of her? Or was that the real Jason, the man
even colder than his father, and this new, appealing
charmer the facade, constructed for some purpose she
couldn't see?

"God, suspicion must be communicable," she muttered
as she twisted at the waist, trying to loosen up some
more. "It's spreading."

Like fire?

She stopped in midmotion, unable to stop the shudder
that swept through her. Wildfire, maybe.

Yes, there was that to deal with as well. The first time
he'd kissed her, it had been to prove a point, she knew
that. It was what had so confused her, and what had
made her angry when she'd realized that he'd meant only
to use the kiss as a demonstration. And that anger had
enabled her to ignore her response to that kiss.

But last night . . . Last night had been something different. Last night had been . . .

She didn't know what it had been. She didn't know
why he'd done it. She only knew it was insane, the way
she reacted to him. He'd only kissed her. There had been

no reason for her to melt into a puddle over it. Men kissed women good night all the time, and that didn't happen. Men had kissed her good night, and nothing even close to that had happened. Ever.

The only thing that saved her from complete mortification was the knowledge that he'd been as aroused as she had been. There couldn't be, she thought, anything more desolate than knowing you were alone in feeling like this. But he had been right there with her. She knew he had.

Unconsciously, her hand stole down to lay flat over her belly. Heat flooded through her in a rush, flaring up into her cheeks, when she realized she was touching the place where his erect flesh had prodded her. And then his words came back to her, those erotic, seductive words about how much he wanted her, how hard he'd been just from kissing her, and what he'd wanted her to do to him.

She closed her eyes, swaying on her feet as she pictured them, standing alone together in the darkness in front of this room. If she'd been a little bolder, if she'd had a little more experience with this kind of feeling, would she have done it? Could she have?

She imagined it, imagined herself doing as he'd wanted, reaching down and freeing that rigid hardness, caressing it, stroking it. How would he react? Would he groan, make that low, husky sound that had sent such a thrill through her? Would he move like that again, that short, convulsive almost helpless movement of his hips, this time pushing himself harder into her hands?

"Oh, God," she moaned, and her hand pressed down on her belly as those deep muscles rippled again.

A noise spun her around in time to see the door swing open. Jason stepped inside, frowning at the knob.

"You should lock that—"

He broke off at his first glimpse of her face. She could only imagine what she looked like, flushed and aroused by her own silly imaginings. And that she was now face-to-face with the man who'd brought them on only intensified her embarrassment until she thought her face must be literally on fire.

"Are you all right?"

Jason was looking at her in a way that made her think he knew exactly what she'd been doing. She hastened to speak, hoping she could convince him her breathless flush had only been the result of an effort to ease strained muscles.

"I . . . Yes. I'm fine. I was just . . . trying to loosen up a little."

His mouth quirked. "I like the sound of that."

Color flared in her again. And so did irritation; she hated that he did this to her so easily. "I'm a little sore, all right?"

Looking instantly contrite, he shut the door behind him and walked over to her. She watched him warily.

"I'm sorry. I didn't realize. Things knotted up a little?"

"A lot," she retorted, thinking it the understatement of all time.

"I'll bet, after that little ride you took," he said, sounding wholly sympathetic. And then, before she could move, he was behind her, his hands coming up to rest on her shoulders. "Here. Maybe this'll help."

She was ready to protest; most men, she'd found, didn't realize their own strength when it came to kneading aching bodies. But then he began to move, slowly, his strong fingers using just the right amount of pressure, the heat of his hands seeming to gather, then diffuse through her, easing the tightness.

It felt wonderful, and when he gradually increased the pressure she felt no pain, only a growing, spreading warmth and lassitude. He moved to the space between her shoulder blades, rubbing firmly yet gently with his thumbs, until a long, low sigh escaped her.

Her head lolled forward, and she vaguely felt him lift her hair and drape it to one side. She should tell him that was enough, she thought. Except that it wasn't; she wanted this to go on and on.

He began again, this time on her neck, massaging with exquisite care until the tense muscles there relaxed as well. She'd never felt anything like this, not even the time when she'd accompanied Aaron to a business meeting at a spa, and she'd taken advantage of the chance for a professional massage. That had been invigorating, this was ...

She didn't know what it was, only that she never wanted it to stop. The languor spread, until all she was aware of was the heat of his touch and the wish for more.

"Hey," he said softly, so close to her left ear she could feel his breath, "you going to sleep on me?"

Going to sleep on Jason. Now that was a lovely idea, Kendall thought with a languid sigh.

"Hold on to that thought, whatever it was," Jason whispered, pressing his lips to the skin below her ear.

Kendall shivered as an electric sensation feathered along her skin. The tip of his tongue flicked the lobe of her ear, and the sensation spread out in small waves. When he moved slightly and traced the inner curves of her ear, the sensation became a charge rippling through her, making her gasp.

When he stopped, she felt that same chill she'd felt when he had broken the kiss last night. And she couldn't seem to stop herself from feeling the same sense of disappointment she'd felt then. She leaned back against him, still feeling tiny echoes of that current that had undulated through her.

"I think ..." His voice sounded strangely hoarse, and she heard him swallow tightly. "I think if we're going to get that dinner I promised you, we'd better do it now."

Something about the way he sounded made her turn around to look at his face. But the only sign that he was the least bit tense was a slight tautness of his jaw.

"Dinner?" she asked, focusing now.

"I made you eat junk food for breakfast, and lunch. I owe you a decent meal."

"Oh."

To her mortification, the disappointment she'd been feeling a moment ago seemed to echo in her voice. Jason smiled, that same warm, charming smile she'd almost gotten used to since last night. But this time it didn't seem to reach his eyes; they looked as cool and calculating as they ever had. But then he tilted his head to look down at her, the light hit him from a different angle, and she saw that she was wrong. The smile did reach his eyes; they were warm with promise.

"Kendall," he said in a teasingly warning tone, "if we don't get out of here, I won't answer for the consequences. You turn me on too quickly, and that bed is too close."

She felt the heat rising into her cheeks once more. She'd never had a problem with blushing before, and she found it very annoying that she'd developed one now. But she'd never been around a man whose voice, eyes, and virtually every word he said, whose very presence, gave rise to the erotic images Jason West induced in her.

"Dinner," she said firmly. Or tried to; it came out a little unsteadily.

He didn't protest, merely gathered up the papers they'd decided it wasn't safe to leave behind, and the book, then held the doors for her, first the room, then his rental car. She'd thought he meant to go back to the Gables, he even turned into the lot, but pulled out the other side and kept going. She looked at him curiously, but he didn't explain, just kept driving. He seemed very intent, and Kendall's forehead creased.

"We're not stopping?"

He made some noncommittal sound of acknowledgment that she had spoken.

"Where are we going?" she asked.

"I'm not sure," he muttered, still not even glancing at her. Then he made two quick turns, a left, then a right, until they were in a darker residential district. And nowhere near a restaurant of any kind. Kendall sat up straighter in the passenger seat.

Jason drove tensely, and Kendall suppressed the urge to question him further; he was obviously in no mood to answer. He drove down one quiet street of houses, then another, seeming to be looking for something.

Then he suddenly swerved, pulling the car in to a space next to the curb, then backing up so close to the front of a large pickup truck that she could have sworn she felt them touch, although there was plenty of room in front of them. He immediately turned off the headlights, but left the engine running and the steering wheel cranked hard to the left.

"Jason," she began.

"Shh."

There was something in the way he said it that made her subside into silence again. And a moment later she blinked when a pair of headlights flashed at the end of the street, through the windows of the big truck behind them. The truck that practically hid them from behind, she realized suddenly.

"Damn," he said softly.

She didn't like the way he'd said that. Nor what she thought he meant.

"Jason?"

He glanced at her, then confirmed her fear.

"We're being followed."

Chapter Seventeen

~

He must have been watching them at the motel, Jason thought, and pulled out right behind them. He hadn't spotted it until they were almost to the restaurant, but it hadn't taken long for him to be sure.

"It's a dark blue sedan. Four-door. American," he said, without looking at Kendall. "Know it?"

"Me?" She sounded startled. "No."

"Sure?"

"Why would I—"

"I thought it might be your . . . friend, George."

"No. He drives a little pickup. A white one with a red and white shell."

"All right," he said decisively as the sedan crept slowly down the street toward them.

He had to assume whoever it was wasn't friendly. That he was probably even the man who had come so close to nudging Kendall into oblivion. His stomach knotted at the reminder of how close she'd come to death. Not, he insisted, for any reason other than he needed her to get this done, needed what she knew, needed the inside information she had to make sure this went down the right way.

The car came closer, almost even with them now. As he'd hoped, the driver didn't seem to see them, concealed by the shadow of the big truck. As if instinctively, Kendall slunk lower in her seat.

"Now what?" she whispered.

She didn't sound frightened, he thought. In fact, she sounded angry. He glanced at her. She *was* angry, he realized when he saw the tightness of her mouth, the stubborn tilt of her chin. Atta girl, he thought. Then squelched the reaction; he wasn't sure he didn't want her scared, and thus more vulnerable to his tactics. But he'd worry about that later.

"Now what?" he repeated as the sedan, just as he'd hoped, crept past them. Its brake lights came on suddenly, and Jason knew they'd been spotted at last. "Now we get the hell out of here."

He threw the car in gear and flipped on the high-beam lights, sending out a blinding shaft of light, all in one continuous motion. He hit the gas, praying they had enough room. The tires squealed in protest. The gray coupe circled tightly, thanks to his having left the front wheels turned. The front fender cleared the rear of the sedan by an infinitesimal margin. He straightened the wheel and punched it. His last glance in the rearview mirror showed the bigger sedan struggling to get turned around on the narrow street.

He made so many turns so quickly he had only a vague idea of where they were. He didn't care, as long as they were rid of their rear appendage. Eventually he slowed, proceeding at a more decorous pace that wasn't punctuated with the telltale sounds of haste. He stopped periodically, rolling down the window to listen, but heard no sound of a vehicle approaching. There was the occasional car in the distance, but not close enough to make him take off again. He kept driving, turning, heading in a generally northwesterly direction.

Finally, as he pulled up at a stop sign, he gave Kendall a wry, sideways look. "You have any clue where we are?"

He saw her eyes gleam in the darkness as she shifted her gaze from the rear window to him. "You act like you do this all the time."

"Some things are like riding a bicycle. You don't forget."

"You mean driving like a stuntman?"

"I mean running for your life."

She didn't speak for a long moment. When she finally did, it was to say only, "I think if you turn right here, we'll end up on Mission Road. We can take that left, back to the main highway."

He nodded, and made the turn. Then he glanced at her again. She was still peering out the back window, searching for any sign of the dark sedan.

"We can't go back to the motel, you know," he said.

Again she was quiet, then, quite evenly, "No, I suppose we can't."

She was a tough one, all right, he thought, not bothering to stifle his admiration this time. She'd been through a great deal in the past two days, but every time she'd come up fighting. Fighting him, fighting Alice, fighting this unknown, faceless assailant. If she'd been this tough with his father, no wonder the old man had come to rely on her.

"We'll head north, and see what happens," he said.

She nodded, silently. Her guess proved accurate, and they were soon out on the main highway. Twice he pulled off at an exit, waited for a few minutes, and then when no car followed them, got back on the highway.

"Sorry about dinner," he said after the second exit and reentrance.

"I'll survive."

"Yes," he agreed, "you will."

She looked at him, then glanced backward once more. "Do you think we lost him?"

"I think so. But then that's not the problem."

"It's not?"

He shook his head. "Losing him is easy. Staying lost is something else again."

"The voice of experience?"

"Yeah." He checked the mirrors again. "I learned that living on the streets in South Park after my mother was killed." He gave her a sideways look. "They were looking all over for me, and I never went more than ten miles from the old apartment. Even snuck back in once, to get some stuff, before they closed it up and sold everything."

"Is that how you lived? By just . . . staying lost?"

"That's how you survived on the street," he said. "Low profile. I tried to stay out of trouble, but I did a lot of . . . borderline stuff, and worse after I got back from

Alaska. Until I ran into old man McKenna, who owned the diesel shop I used to work in as a kid. He gave me my job back. And let me sleep there at night until I had enough saved to rent a room. Not the greatest neighborhood, but it was a roof."

"That must have been awful," she said quietly.

"It wasn't so bad. You knew what you were dealing with. You knew to always have an escape plan ready, and be a little faster or a little smarter than the other guy."

"And a little suspicious?"

"A *lot* suspicious."

She let out a small sigh. "You certainly haven't forgotten that part."

"No, I haven't. And I've found I'm right more often than wrong."

"Aaron used to say he trusted people. Trusted them to act in their own self-interest."

It was so close to his own outlook that Jason, for the moment at least, gave up denying the similarity. Besides, he was presenting a new image to her, one of reluctant but definite interest in his father. So far it had worked, eliciting several pieces of information he'd promptly put to use in his phone calls this afternoon. He should be satisfied, he thought. But instead he was battling a nagging sense of discomfort whose cause he couldn't pin down at the moment. And the weird sensation of half the time—more than half the time—forgetting that it all wasn't real.

"I'll bet he was rarely wrong," he said at last.

"He was rarely cheated," Kendall conceded, "but who knows how much more he might have achieved if he'd taken the risk of actually trusting people."

"Or how much he might have lost by trusting the wrong one."

She didn't answer, but he thought he heard her let out a short, compressed breath. It hit him then, the irony of it, him defending Aaron Hawk's actions while she criticized them.

They went along in silence, while he contemplated what to do next. He slowed as they neared the Sunridge city limits.

"Any ideas?" he asked at last.

"You seem to be the expert on running."

He flicked a glance at her, wondering just how many levels of meaning there had been in those words. He knew there was more than one; Kendall was too complex for there not to be. But he chose to react only to the surface meaning, at least for now.

"I've got a notion or two." Then, with another glance at her, "Are you all right? Or still sore?"

He heard her breath catch. Good, he thought. She was remembering, thinking of those hot, sensuous moments when they'd nearly careened out of control once more. Or she had, he amended hastily. He'd been in control the whole time.

Sure you were.

Great. He was talking to himself. And sarcastically. Next thing he knew, he'd be doing it out loud. He made himself check his surroundings, and saw the sign he'd been looking for, and slowed even more.

"I . . . I'm fine," she said at last. "It's barely noticeable now. And I took some aspirin a while ago."

"Can you hang on for a while longer? Or do we need to find someplace to stop?"

That idea seemed to frighten her as being followed, possibly by the man who had nearly killed her, hadn't. Jason wasn't sure if he was happy with that response or not.

"I said I'm fine. Do whatever you want." He heard her take in a quick breath. "I mean . . . your idea."

"I didn't think you meant anything else, Kendall," he said softly. He pulled out of the traffic lane and turned into a small parking lot next to a three-story building. He put the car in park, and turned to look at her steadily. "I figure when you're ready, you'll let me know."

He saw her eyes widen, and her lips part for another quick inhalation, as if she were having to remind herself to breathe.

"You'll let me know," he repeated, in a low, husky voice that, oddly, he didn't have to work at all to produce. "You'll look at me with those big eyes of yours, all hot and dark, you'll wet those soft lips for me, and

I'll touch you, everywhere, until you're begging me to stop and go on at the same time. And maybe, maybe if I get really lucky, you'll want to touch me, like you did before, but didn't have the nerve. And I'll end up begging you, like I wanted to last night, but didn't because I was afraid I'd scare you away."

She looked away, quickly. He saw her hands move in her lap, her fingers lacing together as if she were trying to stop them from shaking. Or him from seeing them shake.

"It's going to be ... incredible, you know. You and me. Like nothing either one of us has ever felt before. We're going to fly, Kendall. Right into the sun."

It wasn't until he tried to get out of the car, and found he had to lean against the roof for a moment to steady himself, that he realized that in his effort to seduce her with hot, dark promises, he'd wound up arousing himself once more to the point of pain. And he realized with a sense of uncomfortable shock, that he'd meant every word he'd said.

Kendall didn't care where he was going. All she cared about was that he'd left her alone for the moment. Left her alone, to try to recover some tiny bit of self-possession.

She had never been so off balance in her life. She'd known from the moment she realized her parents were never coming back that above all else she wanted to have something to depend on, something that could never leave her. And she wanted to do it by making something of herself, something that her parents would have been proud of.

She'd spent her life working to make it true. She'd always been so certain, of her goals, her talents, her direction, her sense of right and wrong, herself. She'd been certain enough to deal with Aaron on a level far beyond her years when she'd begun to work for him.

But all that certainty seemed to vanish in the presence of Aaron's son.

As did her common sense, Kendall thought with wry self-deprecation. And as for what vanished when he touched her, when he kissed her ...

She shivered, admitting that it was this, more than anything, that had her so confused. She'd dated, sporadically, over the years since college, but men her own age had seemed far too young, and the older ones all seemed to have their eye on her more as a conduit to Aaron than anything else. Anyone in between didn't seem able to handle her dedication to her work that since Aaron had become ill had overtaken all else.

And none of them had ever made her feel anything like Jason did. None of them had ever set her on fire with a touch, made her want to do things she'd never even thought of, never even heard of. None of them.

God, she'd been so smug. She'd even smiled indulgently when Aaron had told her of the strength of his feelings for his Beth, and how he'd known the minute he'd seen her that she was the woman he'd been meant for. She'd been mildly amused at the thought of the indomitable Aaron Hawk succumbing so completely to anything.

And now here she was, spinning out of control, simply because when Aaron's son touched her, she flared up like one of Hawk Propulsion's jets. And she couldn't fight it anymore. She was tired of fighting it. A crazy recklessness, unlike anything she, who had always been so meticulously careful in her life, had ever felt, welled up inside her. She didn't *want* to fight it anymore.

Smothering a moan that was half pain, half longing, she buried her face in her hands. She was startled to find her cheeks wet; she hadn't realized she was crying. She'd done more than her share of that in the past few weeks. More than she had since the day she'd been told her parents had died.

She felt the cool rush of air and realized Jason was back and had opened her door.

"Kendall? What's wrong?"

She gulped in air, wiping swiftly at her cheeks, but she knew he'd seen. He was crouched beside her, and reached out to take her hands in his. He looked around quickly, as if expecting their grim companion to have somehow found them again.

"What is it?"

"I . . . nothing."

"Nothing? You're crying. You don't cry for nothing."

She supposed, in its way, that was a compliment. She fought for her composure, knowing she could never tell him the truth about what she'd been thinking. She'd seen that glint of ruthlessness too often in his eyes to want to give him that kind of knowledge. He had too much already. So she gave him a partial truth.

"I was just thinking. About Aaron."

"Oh."

"And your mother."

He went very still. "What about my mother?"

"How much he loved her."

She waited, braced for the inevitable denial. It didn't come. No words did. She risked a glance at him, but his face was unreadable in the distorted shadows cast by the interior light of the car and the brighter streetlight behind him. But he hadn't thrown it back at her this time. Was it possible? Had he really begun to . . . perhaps not to believe, but to at least consider the possibility?

"He told me on the day before he died," she said, unable to pass up this chance, "how blind he'd been not to see that the price he would pay for maintaining his world was the only thing in it he loved. And that its loss had made the rest a hollow, desolate thing."

Jason still said nothing, still didn't move, just stayed crouched there beside the car, looking at her.

"You hoped he died hard, Jason. Well, he did. And that was the hardest part. He died knowing he'd thrown away the one thing that would have made all the difference. The one thing that would have made it all worth it. And in the end, he would have given it all away for the chance to tell your mother how sorry he was."

"He was twenty years too late."

Hope soared in Kendall. The words, the first he'd spoken, were typically Jason, harsh, caustic, but his voice hadn't held the bitter tone she'd always heard when he spoke of his father.

"Aaron lost his Beth," Kendall said softly, "and he didn't live long enough to make things right for you. But

I swear to you, Jason, if he had ... if he had lived until we'd found you, he would have—"

"Not now."

"I know you don't want to hear that he—"

"Not now, Kendall. We have a bus to catch."

She blinked, taken completely aback. "What?"

"We have a bus to catch. Grab everything out of the car and come on."

"A ... bus?"

Even as she said it, she heard the familiar sound of a big engine slowing to a stop and caught a whiff of the very recognizable diesel smell. She looked out to the street in time to see the huge vehicle halting at the curb. Automatically she lifted her gaze to the route sign atop the front windows. She blinked again, wondering if somehow Jason's effect on her had slowed her thinking as it had speeded up everything else.

"We're going to the airport?"

"Yes."

"Why?"

"I'm the expert runaway, remember? Just move it, honey."

He stood up then, reaching behind her to grab his coat off the back seat. For a moment Kendall couldn't move, all she could do was think of that endearment, delivered in such a casual tone that she told herself he could just as well have called her any number of other things. Some of them no doubt less than complimentary.

He grabbed her coat, the heavy shearling she'd brought to wear over her jeans and thin silk blouse, and backed away so she could get out of the car. She gave herself a sharp mental shake, picked up the book and the box of papers they had—fortuitously it now seemed—carted along, and got out of the car. And moments later found herself seated on a bus, someplace she hadn't been in ten years.

It brought back memories, lots of them, and she couldn't help smiling a little.

"Something funny?"

"No," she said, "I was just remembering. In college

this was the only way I got around, but I don't think I've been on one since I graduated."

Jason leaned back in his seat. She waited for some biting observation about Aaron seeing to that. She couldn't deny it; Aaron had needed her mobile, he'd told her, and had made a car part of her contract. But nothing came, Jason's new gentleness seemed to hold.

"In Seattle," he said, "you can get just about anywhere by bus, and for not much money. I rode buses a lot, after my mother died. At night, anyway."

At night? Why at night? Kendall wondered. "Buses to where?"

He shrugged. "Anywhere that took an hour or two, and was cheap. Didn't matter. What mattered was that they were heated."

Heated. Kendall felt a sudden tightness in her chest. His mother had been killed in October. A week to the day before his sixteenth birthday. And the beginning of a string of damp, chilly months in the Pacific Northwest.

"I got real good at it," Jason said, as if he were chatting about the weather. As, she supposed, he was, indirectly. "I knew all the routes. I slept a lot of hours on those things."

A sixteen-year-old kid, all alone, stowing away on a bus because it was the only way for him to stay warm. The image tightened her chest even more.

"And nobody ever ... asked what you were doing?"

"I got caught, once. They had an undercover transit guy on the bus, looking for a pickpocket. He noticed I never got off." His brows furrowed. "I had to kick him to get away from him. I didn't dare ride the local runs anymore after that. I figured they'd be looking for me."

"What did you do?"

"I stuck to the ferry boats, when I had the money." She didn't want to think about that, about what he had done to get enough money to survive. She said nothing as he went on. "They were a lot more expensive, and I didn't dare try to sneak on, but ... they were better."

"Better?"

"More comfortable. And if I got on the first boat in the morning, I was set for the day. Then after the last boat of the day, at about one in the morning, I caught a bus for SeaTac.''

"The airport?" she asked, startled.

He nodded. "You can sleep there, and no one bothers you much. Like on the ferries. And people were always leaving food around—"

He stopped suddenly, as if uncomfortable with how much he'd told her. It was just as well, Kendall thought, any more and he'd hear her heart breaking for the scared, lonely kid he'd been. She knew he wouldn't appreciate her sympathy, any more than his father would have. She tried for a lighter tone.

"So you took off for someplace warmer, like Alaska."

He grinned suddenly, that flashing, brilliant grin that made her insides do a kind of silly flip that embarrassed her.

"Hey, that was a great time. Hauling nets that weighed a couple of tons, ripping your hands on fins, slipping on fish guts."

"Gee," she said, grinning back at him this time, unable to help it, "so that's why cruises are so popular."

He laughed, a genuine, lighthearted laugh, and her insides did that little flip again. God, she was acting like a teenager with a crush, and all because this man had kissed her a few times.

And planted some of the most erotic images she could ever dream of in her mind. Don't forget that little detail, she reminded herself in chagrin. And that had been only the beginning. He'd planted the seed with those hot, suggestive words, but she'd nurtured them with her own suddenly fertile imagination, until she was picturing them together, doing those things she'd never done and never thought about doing. Until Jason had turned her life upside down.

She was relieved when they arrived at the airport. Action, any action, was better than sitting there mulling over how confused her life had become. She followed Jason into the small terminal and up to the ticket counter of one of the commuter airlines that ran a shuttle service to Los Angeles, San Jose, and San Francisco. She still had no idea what his plan was, but decided this was not the time or the place to ask again.

The young woman at the counter took one look at Jason and drew back a little.

"It's okay," Jason said to her, his tone rueful. "I'm in a much better mood tonight."

He smiled, a sheepish, boyish smile that Kendall was sure he knew the exact effect of. Unfortunately, so did she.

"And I know," he said to the woman in a tone that matched the smile, "I owe you an apology. I was ... upset, and I took it out on you. Is your little girl all right?"

The change that came over the woman's face as Jason turned on the charm was almost laughable. At least, it would have been if Kendall hadn't been seeing a little too much of herself in the ticket agent's reaction.

"I ... she's much better. Thank you."

"Good. I'm glad to hear it. And I am sorry about the other night."

"That's all right," the woman said, giving him a bright airline smile. Her gaze flicked to Kendall, then back to Jason. "Things ... worked out for you?"

"Oh, yes," Jason said, grinning. "Nicely, thank you."

The woman smiled, this time including them both. Kendall watched in amazement; this Jason was the one who could charm a vulture out of its feathers, she thought, remembering George Alton's picturesque phrase. If he'd turned this charm on her in the beginning ... but he hadn't. She'd seen nothing of this Jason until the past twenty-four hours. And she wasn't sure how that made her feel.

"So, what can I do for you tonight?"

"I need two tickets. One way. One for me, to L.A., one for Ms. Chase here, to San Francisco."

Kendall blinked. San Francisco? She had a sudden vision of her last flight into San Francisco International, coming in over the gray waters of the bay. Why on earth San Francisco? And he was going to L.A.?

"—D-A-L-L." Jason was spelling when she snapped

back to awareness of what was happening. The click of keys on a computer keyboard kept time with each letter.

"Checking baggage?"

"No."

More clicking. Moments later Jason was taking the two ticket folders the woman held out to him. And, Kendall noticed, a silver credit card she hadn't seen him hand over, she'd been so startled by what he was doing. He slipped it quickly into a pocket.

"Gate three for San Francisco, leaving in twenty minutes, gate five, all the way at the end, for Los Angeles, in half an hour," the ticket agent said, smiling.

"Thank you."

Jason gave her that winning grin again, and irritation sparked through Kendall. She waited until they were through the small security check and X-ray machine, not a problem considering they had nothing to put on the conveyor except their coats, her purse, the book, and the small box of documents. She wondered for a brief moment what the book would do under X rays, but the security checker didn't even look twice.

Finally, as Jason urged her toward the waiting gates, she looked up at him.

"What was *that* all about?"

"Several things." He didn't look at her, just kept scanning the terminal, not particularly crowded at this late hour. The small airport closed down to commercial flights at ten; theirs were among the last departures.

"Such as?"

"I did owe her an apology."

Kendall remembered the night he'd gone to the airport and missed his plane—had it only been the night before last?—and could just imagine the mood he'd been in. At least the ticket agent had gotten her apology a lot sooner than she herself had, Kendall thought wryly.

"And?" she prompted.

"I wanted the plane tickets."

"I guessed that." What she couldn't figure out were the destinations, but she'd get to that. "What else?"

He glanced at her then. "I wanted to buy them from somebody who would remember it."

"Oh, she'll remember it, all right," Kendall said, her voice utterly dry.

That grin flashed again. "Jealous?" Then, before she could deny it, "Good. That was one of the reasons, too."

She gaped at him, but they were at her gate before she could respond. He stopped a few feet short of the counter, nodding toward it.

"Check in," he said.

"But we did out front—"

"Do it anyway. Before that group gets here."

She glanced at what appeared to be a family of five heading for the same counter. With a sigh she complied, and the man behind the counter had barely handed back her ticket stub and boarding pass before Jason was beside her again. The agent at the counter didn't notice him; he was already hastening through checking in the family.

"Walk me to my gate," he suggested cheerfully, the strength of his grip on her elbow stopping her observation that her plane was already boarding.

"Will you please explain to me what we're doing? And why I'm going to San Francisco and what I'm supposed to do when I get there? And why you're going to L.A. and what you're going to do when you get there?"

"The key to being a fugitive is taking it one step at a time."

She grimaced at that cryptic nonanswer, and waited as he checked in, and the agent tore down his ticket. Then he led her away from the counter, just as the announcement for final boarding of the San Francisco flight came over the loudspeakers.

"All right," Jason said, "let's go."

"Fine," she muttered. "I'll just fly to San Francisco, for no apparent reason—"

She broke off as she realized Jason was walking, not back toward her gate but toward the escalator that led down to the baggage claim area.

Kendall stopped dead. Jason took her arm, but she refused to move.

"Kendall—"

"No. I'm not taking another step until you tell me what's going on."

"We don't have time for this—"

"Make time."

He glanced around, warily, as if to see if anyone was watching them. "Not here. We can't afford to attract any attention before those planes leave."

She stared at him, not missing the inference that those planes might be leaving, but they weren't.

"It's all a trick, isn't it?" she whispered.

"Let's just call it a diversion. Come on, before somebody notices us enough to remember it later."

She went with him down the escalator this time, silently, and followed him past the baggage carousels and back out into the night.

"Sorry, but I think we'd better walk. The less of a trail we leave now, the better."

Her mouth quirked at one corner. "You're far too good at this, you know."

He looked down at her, and that grin flashed again.

"Nice to know I haven't lost the knack."

"Just where exactly *are* we going?"

His grin widened, but there was something different about it, a warmth that hadn't been there when he'd turned it on that unsuspecting ticket agent. That realization engendered an answering warmth in her, a warmth she couldn't suppress no matter how foolish her mind told her she was being.

"With any luck," he said, his voice vibrant with an undertone that made her think of that moment he'd whispered to her to hold on to whatever thought had made her sigh, "paradise."

Chapter Eighteen

~

He'd half expected her to run. For all her cool poise and quick wit, it was clear to Jason that Kendall was nervous. That was good, he'd wanted her nervous. He'd wanted her edgy, tense, and more than a little itchy.

He'd wanted her as damn hot and ready as he was, he thought, his mouth quirking into a wry grimace.

And she was. He knew she was. Knew she hadn't misinterpreted his teasing but fervent comment at the airport. He'd kept quiet since then, letting her think, hoping she was thinking exactly what he'd been thinking ever since he'd made up his mind the waiting was over.

Kendall had given him a quick, wary glance when he turned and started up the entrance of the large chain hotel that was next to the airport. She hadn't spoken, even when he'd checked them in, asking for only one room. But she'd watched him, he'd felt her eyes on him at every turn, until they had stopped in the small gift shop for some necessities. He'd made a couple of purchases of his own, then walked over to where she was studying a display.

"I suppose you could find a more expensive toothbrush," she was muttering, "but I'm not sure where."

"The airport," Jason suggested.

She gave a little start, as if she hadn't realized he was there. Or as if she was so wound up, him being even this close made her jumpy.

"I . . . suppose you're right," she said, the slight quaver in her voice making him feel like nodding smugly.

It was going well, he observed with a level of calm he had to work a little too hard for. He'd done this before, played this game, drawn a woman into his net for his own purposes, but never had it been so easy. Well, not easy, there was nothing easy about suppressing the driving, aching need he'd unexpectedly developed, but that was something else. That was ... timing. He'd just been too long without. It had nothing to do with Kendall herself.

Right, he thought sarcastically. *Then why do you have to keep reminding yourself that it's not for real, that it's part of the plan?*

But the plan was working, whether he was able to concentrate on it or not. She'd responded better to his lure than he could ever have hoped. A little charm, a little self-effacement, top it off with a sad story of his youth ... it was too easy. He knew as well as he'd ever known anything that she wouldn't resist him tonight. So why wasn't he pleased? He'd done this before, when necessary, with other women.

With women who had had their own reasons for going along. Women who knew how the game was played, who knew what they were—and weren't—getting. Kendall wasn't one of those. He knew that, now. He was even half convinced she was exactly what she'd appeared to be, impossible as that seemed to him. Was that why using her like this had him so unsettled?

Getting soft, West? he muttered inwardly.

Not a chance, he answered himself silently, giving the words a crude spin in his mind in his effort at control. He was hard as that fireboat hose again, he thought as he gauged the tightness of his body, growing rapidly at just the thought of finally having Kendall. It seemed impossible that until three days ago, he hadn't even known she existed. He'd never laid eyes on her, and now he was going out of his mind with the need to touch her, to kiss her, to have her. To take her until she screamed with it, until she was quivering helpless in his arms.

And it hit him again then, as it had before, the unaccustomed, vivid idea of his own desires reversed, of it being him crying out, his quivering under an onslaught of sensation unleased by the gray-eyed woman who had invaded his very being. It had never happened to him before, this need to be taken as well as to take, and it rattled him way down deep. He wanted to run, he wanted time to learn how to deal with this, to learn how to manage it. He just wasn't sure there was enough time in the world. And he had no time at all, now.

He sucked in a breath, realizing Kendall was staring at him.

"Buy the damned toothbrush," he ground out.

They were in the elevator before he trusted himself to speak again. And as it turned out, that was a little soon. His voice was a harsh, desperate thing as he said her name. He reached out and hit the red switch on the control panel. The closed-in car came to a halt.

Kendall pressed herself back as he whirled on her. His arms came up, a hand on either side of her head as he leaned against the wall, trapping her. He stared down at her, aware that he was breathing far too quickly, that he was already far too aroused to be subtle.

"If you don't want this, Kendall, tell me now."

His voice sounded as desperate as it had before, but as she looked up at him with those wide gray eyes, he didn't care. He didn't care about anything except easing this ache, assuaging this raging need. Nothing else mattered, not Aaron, not Alice, not the information he needed from Kendall. Not even the plan he'd spent his life formulating. Somewhere along the way to seducing Kendall Chase he'd been seduced himself. He'd lost control, and he didn't know how to get it back. He didn't want to get it back. Somehow it had all become real, as real as anything had ever been in his life.

"I'm frightened of it," Kendall said, her voice strained but soft with honesty.

Jason tried to rein himself in; he didn't want her frightened. And he no longer tried to kid himself that it was because it would make it harder to get what he wanted out of her. But he couldn't, couldn't slow down, not when she was so close, so soft, so sweet. He leaned in, closer to her.

"Don't be frightened," he said, his voice even lower, hoarser now. "I'll take care of you."

Kendall made a tiny, negating motion with her head. "It's you I'm frightened of," she said, "and what you do to me."

He groaned. "Don't you think I am, too? Don't you think how fast you do this to me scares the hell out of me?"

He pressed closer, until she couldn't help but know how aroused he was. And he knew in the instant his erection brushed against her that every last word of it was the truth.

"I didn't want this, Kendall. I've never wanted to feel this way. But there doesn't seem to be a damn thing I can do about it. I can't stop it, and I can't change it. It just ... is."

And the fact that every word of that was true as well jolted him to the core, shook his every perception of himself and his purpose in life. He made a last effort to regain command of this. If he'd ever had it in the first place.

"I know you don't trust me, you don't even know me—"

"You decided to trust me," she interrupted, sounding a little breathless. "And you don't know me."

"Don't I?" he said, his voice down to a mere rasp of sound. "Don't I know you, Kendall Chase? Everything that matters?"

And God help him, he meant that, too.

She stared up at him, lips parted for breaths that were coming quickly enough that the rapid rise and fall of her breasts beneath the pale blue silk of her blouse tightened the vise of need another notch. He couldn't take much more of this. He shifted his hips, rubbing himself against her as she had once done to him, making it clear that they were at the point of no return.

"Now, Kendall," he repeated. Although he didn't know what he'd do if she said no. But he had to do this. It had to be her choice. He didn't want her to ever be able to say it wasn't. He didn't want her to be able to blame him. And most of all he didn't know why it even mattered to him. He just knew it did. "If you don't want this, tell me now."

"I'm frightened of wanting anything this much," Kendall whispered. "But I do."

He shuddered, half in sheer relief, half in violent arousal. When he reached to flip the switch on the elevator panel once more, his hand was shaking.

"You really . . . expected this," Kendall said, staring down at the small foil packets that had slid out of the bag Jason had tossed on the bed. It seemed so . . . cold somehow. So planned.

Jason's hands came down on her shoulders and turned her around to face him. "Hoped," he corrected. "Or I wouldn't have given you the option to say no in the elevator."

"I . . ."

Words failed her for a moment; he'd unbuttoned his shirt, and she couldn't help thinking of that morning at the motel, when he'd come to the door looking so sleepily sexy.

He had only bought the condoms tonight, she thought. It wasn't like he'd been carrying them around, just in case she . . . weakened.

"Would you rather I didn't plan at all, Kendall?" he said at last, when she didn't go on. "What did you want? To be able to say you didn't know what you were doing, that it just happened, so you don't have to take the responsibility for a choice?"

God, had she wanted that? Had she wanted him to simply take over, to be swept up in the passion he created in her, so she could later say it hadn't been her fault, she just hadn't been able to resist? Where was all her fine nerve and backbone and self-sufficiency now?

"Is that what you wanted?" he repeated. "To take a chance on ending up like my mother, alone, with a child to raise? Or to have to decide about an abortion?"

She bit her lower lip, staring up at him with eyes she was sure reflected her inner confusion. "Are you saying you . . . that you are like Aaron? You'd walk way?"

She saw something flicker in his eyes, something dark

and pained in the piercing blue. "I'm saying," he began, then stopped, swallowed, and tried again. "I'm saying that you can't trust anyone to always be there for you. You should know that as well as anyone. Everyone left you, just like they did me."

And that, she thought with a shivering little sigh, was the difference between them. His faith had died, probably along with his mother, while she had clung stubbornly to hers, clung to that belief that there were people in this life you could trust. As she had trusted Aaron. As Aaron had trusted her.

Aaron. God, she wished he were here, he'd make sense out of this for her, with his acerbic bluntness, he'd—

She nearly laughed at herself. At the idea of asking Aaron whether she should go to bed with his son. Not because she loved him, or even trusted him, but simply because he seared her senses into ash. She could just imagine Aaron's answer.

She didn't have to imagine it, she thought suddenly. He'd already given it to her.

You ever find the one who sets you on fire, girl, you don't ever let go. Don't be the fool I was. Don't give up without a hell of a fight.

Sets you on fire.

Well, that certainly was exactly what Jason did to her. And no one else ever had, in all her thirty-three years. And she found she wasn't willing to take the chance that anyone else ever would.

She took a step forward, shortening the distance between them, until she could feel the heat radiating from him. Steeling her nerve, she lifted one hand and slipped it between the edges of his open shirt, pressing her palm against his chest. She felt the leap of his heart beneath her fingers. Or perhaps it was the sudden acceleration of her own pulse; she couldn't tell.

He closed his eyes, and she felt as well as heard him take a deep breath. And suddenly something else hit her about Jason's purchase tonight; he hadn't assumed she would handle it, nor had he assumed no precautions were necessary on his part. He'd simply taken care of it.

He moved then, his hands coming up to cup her face, to tilt her head back.

"No more chances, Kendall. It's too late to run."

"I don't want to run."

"Remember you said that."

Before she could wonder what he'd meant by that, his mouth was on hers, igniting that fire once more, so quickly she wondered if it had ever really gone out or simply been banked, waiting for his touch to roar to life again.

There was no subtlety in this kiss, no gentle coaxing, nothing but pure, raw need unleased. And it unleashed an answering need in her, a need she had never felt, never thought to feel. A need she hadn't, until Jason, thought she was capable of feeling.

Her hands slid up over his chest, freezing when she heard him make a low sound when her fingertips brushed over his nipples. Tentatively she flexed her fingers, rubbing, feeling the flat nubs tighten. Never breaking the kiss, he slid one hand down her back and pulled her hard against him. Inadvertently her fingers curled, dragging her nails slightly over his nipples, and this time the sound he made was louder, harsher.

She barely stifled a sound of loss when he released her, but it turned into a sigh when he yanked his shirt free of his jeans and shrugged it off his shoulders. His fingers went to the button on his jeans, releasing it, but then he stopped, watching her. Her fingers curled tighter as she looked at the expanse of his chest, lightly sprinkled with dark hair that she wanted to touch again, to savor the slightly rough texture it gave his skin.

His belly was as flat as she remembered, ridged with muscle, marked on one side by a faint, curving scar that went down his right side, curved in toward his navel, then down below the low-slung waistband of his jeans; it looked like the scar on his hand, and she wondered if he'd gotten it in the same fight. Wondered just how well he'd learned to fight back afterward, on those mean streets.

Her eyes naturally followed the direction of the scar, but when she reached the band of faded black denim, her gaze shifted to the path of silky hair that arrowed down from his navel and disappeared into the slight vee of his unfastened jeans.

She saw the muscles of his stomach contract, then he took her by the shoulders again and pulled her close. He bent his head once more, this time to press a trail of soft kisses from her forehead to her cheek, then around to her ear, making her shiver. As he had before, he traced the curve of her ear with his tongue, so delicately she was only sure he'd done it by the fiery tingle that raced along her nerves. Her hands came up between them again, to flatten against his belly, to savor and trace the ridged muscles there. They rippled beneath her touch, and the quickness of his response to her touch made her quiver inside.

She moaned softly, but the sound broke off when he moved again, reaching to take her hand and pull it gently downward. He placed her palm over the swell of his erection, holding it there for a moment. The low, hoarse sound of pleasure he made at even this slight touch from her, even guided by him, thrilled her. Somewhat hesitantly, she flexed her hand in a tentative caress.

"Yesss."

He seemed to breathe it against her ear, sending another shiver along nerves that were newly alive, nerves that she hadn't known could feel so intensely. She flexed her hand again, and he moved against her, shifting his hips so that the pressure was stronger. Then he slid his hands around her back and pulled her against him again. She continued her caress of his rigid flesh, savoring each movement that told her he liked what she was doing, each low sound that sent those little frissons of heat through her.

She felt his hands move again, this time to pluck at the buttons of her blouse. The delicate silk seemed to float away, baring the swell of her breasts above her pale blue bra. She heard him take in a quick, harsh breath, then his hands slipped up and over her shoulders, skimming the blouse away easily. He was good at this, she thought dimly, wondering why it didn't bother her to know that. His hands slid down her back to the catch of her bra, and he had it undone in moments. Her simple blue cotton bra fell away before she really had time to feel shy about her lack of sexy lace and satin underwear.

"Peach," he murmured, low and husky, staring at her breasts as if he'd uncovered an unexpected treasure. "They are peach."

She had no idea what he meant, and didn't have time to think about it; his hands came up to cup her breasts, his palms cradling her, his thumbs slipping up to rub her nipples into tight, tingling awareness. She moaned at the tiny darts of fire that leapt straight to that place low and deep within her that seemed to awaken only for this man.

Yes, he was very good at this. But it still didn't bother her. And now she knew why. Nothing like that mattered, not now, not when she could make him groan with a mere increase in the pressure of her hand, not when her hand slipped a little lower to cup him somewhat uncertainly and he gasped aloud with pleasure.

I wanted you to unzip me . . . I was so hard, just from kissing you, and I wanted your hands on me so badly . . .

Those hot, erotic words, which he'd spoken in that husky voice that sent ripples of heat through her, echoed in her mind now. Her gaze flew to his face, and she nearly gasped; he was looking at her, lips parted, his eyes hot and intense, as if he knew exactly what she'd been thinking. And then, when he spoke, she knew he did know.

"Do it," he said in a voice so ragged the sharpness of the command was negated utterly. "God, do it."

She felt herself tremble, but she couldn't resist the urgency of his plea. Not when she'd been living with the images he'd planted, the need that had grown from them, for what seemed like forever now. She fumbled with the tab of his zipper, unable to make her hands obey. She tugged, then tugged again, and at last the fastener seemed to give way easily, seemingly driven by the insistent swell of his flesh behind it.

He let out a small breath, as if at the release of pressure. She glanced up at him. His eyes were closed, his face taut with a look of anticipation. His hands, still at her breasts, shook. But he didn't move, didn't even look at her. She wondered if he was somehow afraid if he did she would stop.

Her gaze lowered, to the sight of his hands cradling her breasts, his fingers tan and strong against the pale, soft veined curves, his thumbs resting atop her tight, aching nipples. She wanted him to resume that rubbing caress more than she'd ever wanted anything. And then she knew why his face had that strained, wanting look. And knew that she wanted to touch him as much as he wanted her to.

She hadn't had much practice at this, and wasn't nearly as efficient with his clothing as he had been with hers, but he didn't seem to care. And when at last he was free of interfering cloth, when the hot, satin-smooth column of rigid flesh was in her hands, she heard his breath leave him in a throttled groan.

"Ah, God . . ."

She touched him, curiously, and with more than a touch of awe at the solid, hard smoothness. She traced his length with a delicate, questing touch, outlining with her fingers what her eyes were watching hungrily. She'd never really explored an aroused male before; in her few sexual encounters she had never felt the need for this, the need to touch, to explore, to learn. But she wanted this, wanted it as much as she wanted him to touch her in the same way.

"Yes," he said again, fervently, as her fingers instinctively curled around him. She felt a growing, spreading heat go through her in a wave, driven by her wonder at the heat and thickness of him. She thought of what was to come, and her fingers clenched around him slightly at the image of this hot male flesh filling that hollow place inside her, that place she'd been unaware of until this man set it on fire.

His breath hissed out of him again when her grasp tightened. Encouraged by his response, she stroked his hard length, varying the pressure until she heard him groan once more. She felt him shudder. It seemed to ripple upward through him from beneath her fingers, until his hands moved convulsively, flexing on her breasts, sending an answering ripple of sensation through her.

She moved, helplessly, pressing her breasts against his palms, wanting him to begin that caress of her nipples again so badly she didn't care if she was silently begging for it. As if he'd understood, his thumbs moved, flicking over the tight crests, making her cry out at the sudden flare of pleasure.

"Just don't ... stop." His voice was thick, hoarse. "God, Kendall, don't stop."

She didn't. She couldn't. She wanted to know every hot, aroused inch of him. She continued to stroke him, to caress him as she shivered at the idea of taking him inside her. Jason's mouth came down on hers again, urgently, demandingly, and she surrendered the depths of hers to his probing tongue willingly. And when he withdrew, she followed, unable to resist the lure, and surprised at the sensual delight she found in tasting him so deeply. And she found it amazingly arousing to be teasing his tongue with hers while her hand still stroked the hard, impossibly smooth contours of his flesh, wringing low sounds of pleasure from him.

When he at last broke the kiss, she was breathing in pants, quick and shallow, but unable to slow them. Then he moved, lowering his head, without warning taking one of her achingly aroused nipples into his mouth and suckling deeply, suddenly.

Her entire body seemed to ripple, and she cried out in shock and astonishment. Her back arched, thrusting her breasts upward, as if offering them. He took the gift without question, his lips holding a nipple while his tongue flicked at it, his fingers catching her other nipple and tugging at it, squeezing with just enough pressure to make her cry out again.

"Oh, God," she moaned, her hands coming up to his shoulders, her fingers digging in as her body rippled once more.

Jason lifted his head to look at her. His eyes were burning hotter than she'd ever seen them, and his breath was coming as quickly as her own. Without a word, his hands went to her waist, to yank at the fastening of her jeans. He tugged them down and away, sweeping her panties along with them.

For a moment he just stood there, staring at her, so intensely she was gripped by a tremor of shyness at standing naked before him when he was still half dressed. But then he spoke, and the shyness faded.

"God, you're beautiful," he said softly, reverently. "I knew, but . . ."

He trailed off, shaking his head slowly, as if he were feeling the same kind of wonder she had felt when she'd first freed his naked arousal from his jeans. His tone filled her with a quiet pleasure, as did the sight of the shiver that tightened his belly as he reached for her.

His hands slid back up her legs to the top of her thighs, and then she felt him touching her, probing, as if testing. She supposed she should have felt violated by the sudden, intimate incursion, but how could she when his seeking fingers found her hot and wet and ready? She felt as if she'd been that way forever, for this man.

And as his finger found and caressed a tiny knot of nerve endings that nearly made her scream, she knew that the shortness of their time together meant nothing. Nothing at all, not before the tide of emotion and feeling and sensation that swelled between them.

"No more waiting," he said, his voice rough and tight. And tinged with relief, she realized dimly through the haze of pleasure he was building with that tiny, circling caress. A relief that told her that even now he would have waited, if she hadn't been ready.

But she was. God, she was. She wanted him, wanted everything with him, in a way she'd never even imagined. She wanted him naked along with her, wanted to see his rangy, muscled body, all of it, wanted to know him more intimately than anyone ever had, and more than anything she wanted him to want her to know him.

"Jason," she whispered, unable to say anything more.

But he looked at her as if she'd said it all, and with a strangled sound of urgency, he peeled off the rest of his clothes. For a moment that was far too brief for her he stood beside her, and she drank in the sight of him, naked, tall and lean, solid-chested and flat-bellied, the aroused flesh she'd been exploring so avidly jutting out from the tangle of thick, dark curls that surrounded it.

Then, with a swiftness that left her reeling, he swept her up in his arms and went down with her to the bed, his hands sliding over her, his mouth laying down a path of kisses that left a fiery trail along her skin. In moments she was moaning, writhing beneath him in her need to get closer.

"You want it?"

His voice came low and rough in her ear, barely above a whisper, but he was so close she could feel the hot rush of his breath on that ultra-sensitive skin, making her heart hammer as it blazed anew along nerves that were alive as they had never been.

"I want you," she said, not caring that there was a difference, or how foolish she was no doubt being for ignoring that difference.

He drew back from her, and for a moment she was afraid he was going to explain the difference to her. But he only reached for one of the foil packets that lay tossed behind him on the bed. She watched as he opened it and began to sheath himself, yet another thing she'd never cared to watch before. But now, with Jason, it had become one of the most erotic, sensual things she'd ever seen.

When he glanced up and saw her eyes on him, something bright and hot flared in his eyes. And then he was moving swiftly, finishing with the condom and coming back to her. She reached for him and he came down on top of her. She welcomed his weight, his heat, and the sheer force of his need. His head bent to her breasts once more, and she welcomed with a joyous cry the hot, wet caress of his mouth as he took first one nipple, then the other, raking them gently with his teeth, flicking them with his tongue, and then sucking them long and hard and deep until her body undulated in hot, eager response.

He kept on, until her moans were coming quickly, blending together in one continuous sound of wondrous pleasure. It was suddenly too much, the vision of his dark head at her breast, his mouth on her body, and the incredible sensations that were stabbing through her. Her head lolled back, her eyes closing.

She felt him move, felt him nudge her legs apart. Her breath caught in anticipation, and she stifled a quiver of apprehension. My God, what was she doing? She barely knew this man.

Don't I know you, Kendall Chase? Everything that matters?

His words came back to her vividly. Perhaps he did. And perhaps she did, too, knew everything that mattered. Like that he was the only man who had ever made her feel so much, want so much, need so much.

You ever find the one who sets you on fire . . .

Her eyes came open then, as Aaron's words rang in her head. *Your son,* she thought, a little wildly. *God, Aaron, did you know it would be your son?*

And then Jason was moving, lowering himself, and she felt the blunt prod of his body as he probed for entry. She felt a sudden cramping, as if her own body were already grasping for him, as if it somehow knew that aching hollowness would soon be filled.

Lifting himself above her slightly, Jason moved a hand down between them, sliding it over her body, making the movement a caress in itself as he reached to guide himself home. He tilted his head, to shift his gaze downward between their bodies, and Kendall looked at the thick, dark silk of his hair, tousled now by her hands. Then she followed the direction of his gaze and felt a sudden jolt of scorching sensation when she saw his rigid flesh delving forward between her thighs.

She felt him start to slide into her, knew how truly ready she was by the easy glide of his flesh over hers, and she shivered with the thrill of the contact. Then she realized he, too, was still looking downward, watching as he entered her, and wondered if it was making him as crazy as it was her.

And then she had her answer; with a low, gruff sound of surrender, Jason moved again, driving forward, burying himself to the hilt, wringing a cry of shock from her. God, she'd been wrong, she couldn't take him, it was too much, it had been too long . . .

Jason froze, holding himself there above her, his face a mask of tension and need and forced restraint.

"Kendall?"

"I ... give me a moment, I ..." She needed that moment, to adjust, for her body to accept the fact that this time it wasn't being denied, that the aching hollowness was indeed filled to bursting. "It's been ... a very long time," she said, a little shakily.

"I can tell that." His voice was harsh, matching the strained look on his face and the beads of sweat that had broken out on his forehead.

The shock of his sudden invasion began to ebb, leaving her only with a wonderful awareness of his presence, and a need to intensify that awareness. She shifted slightly, just enough so that she could feel how deeply he was inside her. A shudder swept her and she looked up at him, not even trying to hide the wonder and pleasure and need she was feeling.

His expression changed, became one of desire barely leashed. "Damn," he said, his voice a rough, frayed thing, "I hope to God you're in a hurry."

"Yes," she said, sounding more than a little breathless. "Oh, yes, please, hurry."

She punctuated her plea with an urgent upward thrust of her hips, and had the satisfaction of hearing him try to choke back a cry as his head went back and his body bowed forward, grinding his hips against hers.

And then he was moving again, thrusting fiercely, his hands slipping beneath her and then curling back over her shoulders to hold her steady for his driving movements. Kendall savored every motion, wrapping her arms around him, wanting more even as her body, reveling in the amazing feel of him inside her, told her she could take no more. She didn't care, and raised her knees so she could take him even deeper. He was stretching her to the edge of pain, but there was no pain, only an incredible sensation of fullness, of completion, of hollowness at last filled.

His body grew even tenser in her arms, and his pace increased. He stroked her from within, each sliding thrust driving her higher. She was clutching at him now, nearly mindless from the relentless jolts of pleasure he was hammering into her. Nothing in her limited experience, or in her most vivid imaginings, had ever come close to this. She was beyond caring about anything except an unfocused hope that he was feeling what she was feeling, more than a little wild and out of control.

"God," he muttered, as if involuntarily, "what are you doing to me?"

Kendall heard it, although it was so low she wasn't sure he'd meant her to. But it gave her the answer that was the only thing she cared about right now beyond her own pleasure. And that answer was enough to send her soaring.

She felt a rising, unbearable tightness, a tension that had only one end, and she held her breath as it closed in on her. She wrapped her legs around his hips, straining, arching, striving against him. And then it exploded through her in billowing waves, making her cry out his name as she clutched at him wildly. Her body clenched around his in a squeezing, grasping rhythm that went on and on.

She heard him gasp, a sound of shock and disbelief. His body went rigid, then he arched against her in turn, a guttural shout breaking from him as his arms tightened around her until she could barely breathe. She didn't care, she couldn't breathe anyway, not when he was poised above her, his face a mask of wonder as she felt him pulsing inside her. Not when she knew with as much certainty as she'd ever had about anything in her life that Jason was as awed as she was by what had happened between them. And that he hadn't expected it. Despite all his talk about what it would be like between them, he hadn't expected this.

Neither had she. She hadn't known enough to expect this. And she wasn't at all sure where that left them.

Chapter Nineteen

~

"What else did the old—Aaron say about the book?"

Things had really gone haywire, Jason thought as he lay staring up into the darkness, when that damned book was the safest topic he could think of.

Kendall was curled up at his side, her head resting on his shoulder. He felt the soft silken brush of her hair on his skin, and suppressed a shiver. He was fighting the lassitude of a body that felt utterly satiated, yet was still tingling, a combination of release and rapidly returning need he'd never experienced before.

Yes, things were really haywire when that damn book was the safest thing to talk about. But there was no way in hell he was ready to talk about what he was sure was uppermost in Kendall's mind. He was fighting hard enough to keep it from being the only thing in his own mind. Nothing in his life had ever prepared him for what had happened here tonight.

It was a moment before she answered his question about the book.

"He said there were different legends about it, but the basics were always the same. That it ... appears to the last Hawk. And that Hawk is usually aware, but doesn't care much that he's the last."

"Like me," Jason said, more glad than he should be that she had acquiesced to the relatively safe topic of magic rather than the dynamite of what had happened between them.

"Yes," she agreed, "like you. It appears, and refuses to disappear, be left behind, or even be destroyed."

"I haven't tried burning it yet," Jason said dryly, "but give me time." He felt rather than saw her smile. "Let's say for the moment I buy into this. That it's for real, this book. What's the purpose? Why does it appear to the last Hawk?"

He felt her go very still. "I'm not sure you really want to know that. And I'm not sure I want to tell you. Especially right now."

"Right now?"

"Considering . . . what happened here tonight. After all, it wasn't very long ago you were accusing me of using the book to trick you into marrying me."

Jason went still in turn. He knew what she meant, that she was afraid he would think this was part of the plan to lure him into the net, making the book's prophecy come true. The irony of that possibility didn't escape him; each of them, for their own reasons, rigging a trap that had landed them both here in this bed, setting each other ablaze until the inferno had nearly consumed them both.

He hadn't let himself think about that part of the book's story, not since the moment when he'd realized it had been right about her being in danger. Even in this conversation, based on an acceptance of the book that was, he told himself, purely hypothetical, he wasn't ready to deal with it. And especially after the unexpectedly explosive passion they had shared tonight. He recognized the dichotomy in accepting the book's explanation of his mother's death while rejecting its predictions for himself, but had postponed dealing with that as well; what he had to do now was more important.

"And you told me I was condescending and insulting, as I recall," he said, keeping his tone purposely light.

"You were."

"Yes, I suppose I was. I'm sorry."

He could give her that much; it was most likely true. Besides, he needed to keep her in this soft, expansive mood. He'd been blown off course—hell, he'd been blasted halfway back to Seattle—but that didn't mean he had to stay there. He still had a job to do, and she was the one who could help him do it. And the sooner he got back to it, the better.

He pulled her closer, liking the feel of her naked body against his. Not that that's why he'd done it; he just wanted her to feel . . . comfortable. Enough to keep talking. And not worry too much about what he was asking.

"If you're worried that I'll think you used . . . this to help things along, don't."

She gave a little sigh. "Two days ago, that's exactly what I would have expected you would think."

Good, Jason thought; he'd gotten to her exactly when he'd begun trying to. And he'd come a long way with her in two days. But somehow it wasn't quite as satisfying as it should be, to know everything was going as planned. And he couldn't deny it was partly because he had a sneaking suspicion he might have fallen into his own trap.

"It's safe, Kendall," he said, pressing a kiss to her forehead for no more reason than that he wanted to. "Tell me about the book."

"You're not going to like it."

"Why?"

"Because you're too much like Aaron."

He supposed it was a measure of how successful his enacted "turnaround" had been that she felt she could say that to him now.

"But you said he came to believe it."

"Yes. But not being the last Hawk, he didn't have to deal with it. You do."

"So tell me what I'm dealing with."

He heard another small sigh. "All right. But remember, you asked for it."

"I promise," he said with a chuckle. It sounded satisfyingly genuine. Because it was, he realized with a little sense of shock. He liked lying here with her, talking in the darkness, liked the sound of her voice coming from so close, liked the fact that she seemed so comfortable with him, her head pillowed on his shoulder, her body pressed against his side. Before he could deal with that amazing revelation, she was beginning the story, in words he'd come to recognize as coming straight from his father's belief and pride in the Hawk family legends.

"The book appears to the last Hawk to make sure that he isn't just that. It chronicles his story, and when necessary, nudges him in the direction he's supposed to go."

She paused, and he heard her draw in a deep breath. When she went on, he knew why she'd hesitated.

"It also tells him of the woman he is destined for, the woman who will change his life forever, whether he likes it or not, and no matter how much he might protest, or how far he might run. The rest of his world may be in chaos, teetering on the edge of disaster, but in this, the book is never wrong."

She stopped, as if trying to gauge his reaction to her practiced words, words that had no doubt been repeated exactly as Aaron had spoken them; he'd probably ordered her to memorize them. If he really did believe in it, he'd be running scared by now, he thought. True, the book hadn't actually named Kendall as the supposed women in his future, but it was obvious nevertheless. Or it seemed that way to him.

It was a good thing he didn't really believe that part, he told himself ruefully, or he'd be half convinced it had been the book's magic that had made sex with her so . . . amazing. Incredible. Astonishing. Whatever it had been.

On second thought, maybe it was safer to believe it *had* been magic. Because if it hadn't been . . .

"If the book appears," he said hastily, diverting himself from that line of thinking, "then it has to disappear, right? So when does that happen? When do I get rid of the thing?"

He felt Kendall's slight movement, felt the flexing of the fingers of her left hand where it rested against his chest. He had placed her hand there a while ago, moving it from where she had let it come to rest when he'd first rolled off of her, low on his belly. Too low; he hadn't wanted her discovering just yet that he was hard again, despite the violence of his climax just minutes before. He didn't like discovering it himself. It made him feel too needy, and that was a feeling he'd left behind him years ago. Forever.

"Wait," he said, when she didn't answer right away, "don't tell me, let me guess. It goes away when I marry the woman it's picked out for me, right?" A touch of derision crept into his voice despite his efforts to keep his tone even. "Sort of a wedding present?"

She didn't react to his tone. "Not exactly. That's when the picture of the new couple appears in the book, along with a new beginning for the Hawk family tree."

"What, then? What do I have to do to get rid of it?"

"It disappears on its own when you're not the last Hawk anymore."

He went very still. "What exactly does that mean?"

"When the first child assures the continuation of the Hawk bloodline," she said, sounding like a student reciting a memorized lesson, "the family tree records the birth, and the book vanishes. Until the next time there is only one Hawk left alive in the world."

A sardonic retort about fairy tales and fools who believed in them leapt to his lips, but he bit it back. He'd come too far with her to risk alienating her again.

"So," he said neutrally, "we get married, you get pregnant, and the book leaves me alone, is that it? Goes away until our . . . what, maybe great times seven grandchild is unfortunate enough to be the last Hawk?"

Kendall sat up abruptly, clutching the bedspread in front of her, as if she wanted to hide her breasts, as if he hadn't already seen every soft, sweet bit of them. He felt the tug on the bedspread; they had never actually made it into the bed, were still on top of the covers, but he'd pulled the edges up over them when the room had become chilly. Or perhaps it had always been cold, he thought, and they just hadn't noticed it before because they were going up in flames themselves.

"I am not the woman in the book," she said, with a barely perceptible shake in her voice.

"In that case," Jason drawled, "I'd better get myself back to that coffee shop and propose to that waitress, hadn't I?"

He could see her eyes widen even in the darkness,

could sense her withdrawing from him. Quickly he reached out to touch her, to take her hand and draw her back down to him. She resisted the tug.

"It was a joke, Kendall," he said softly. "I was only kidding. I have no interest in what she was offering."

"Why should you?" she retorted, the quaver a little more obvious this time. "You already got it from me."

Uh-oh, Jason thought. Second thoughts already. She hadn't even waited until the morning after. He sat up, trying to think of how to soothe her ruffled feathers. The only thing he could think of was the truth he'd been unwilling to confront. Slowly he reached out and touched her cheek.

"If you think," he said quietly, "that there's any similarity between what she was offering and what happened here tonight, you're a fool, Kendall Chase. And I don't think you're a fool."

She ducked her head, a motion he could barely see in the darkness. But he sensed the tension ebbing, sensed the softening in her. No, Kendall wasn't a fool. But it was very much beginning to look like she had a blind spot for Hawks in general, not just Aaron.

He had hauled her into his arms and pulled her down beside him again before he realized what he'd done. He'd thought of himself as a Hawk, as naturally as if he'd considered himself one all his life. He turned it over in his mind, waiting for the surge of anger, waiting for the self-disgust he expected to feel. It didn't come. He didn't understand it. He wasn't a Hawk. Not in his mind. He wouldn't have it, wouldn't claim or accept any connection to Aaron Hawk.

But when the denial formed in his mind, it wasn't Aaron he saw. It was Joshua. The man who could be his twin. The man who had fought harder than any other Hawk the battle Jason was fighting now. He could see him, as clearly as if he'd met him face-to-face, could see those eyes, identical to his own, looking back at him, full of understanding and commiseration. And while he might find it easy to deny any connection to the man who had fathered him, denying Joshua Hawk was somehow altogether different.

"Jason?"

Kendall's soft, inquiring whisper brought him out of his odd reverie.

"It's crazy," he said. "You know that don't you? A magic book, handed down from some ancient wizard, predicting events that haven't happened yet, appearing and disappearing."

"Yes. I know."

"But you believe it."

"I believe . . . the Hawks are unusual. Different. And that most legends have some kernel of truth at their core."

He couldn't think of anything to say, so he settled for cuddling Kendall closer to him, telling himself it was for her sake, to keep her compliant, not because he simply liked her there. But he was having more and more trouble making himself believe his own disclaimers. She snuggled up willingly, and he thought once more about strong, bright women with blind spots.

She seemed to be waiting for him to speak, but there really was no more he could say, not until he'd confronted and dealt with his ambivalence about the book. He either believed in it, or he didn't. He couldn't believe in part of it and reject part of it, because one was convenient and one wasn't. And that was not a decision he was ready to make. So instead, he tried to nudge the talk in the direction he needed it to go.

"I wonder how Aaron would have dealt with all this."

"You mean, if he'd been the last Hawk?"

He didn't bother to quibble this time over the appellation. "Yes."

"I think he would have fought it as hard as you have."

"Even though he believed in the legend?"

"He *wanted* to believe in it. And at the end, I think he had to believe it, had to believe the book would do what he hadn't been able to. That it would bring you home. He couldn't bear to doubt it, because it would mean his blindness had not only cost him his son, but had brought about the end of centuries of unbroken history."

"And I can just bet which one bothered him the

most." It slipped out before he could stop it, but Kendall seemed to understand.

"I know it must seem that way. Aaron was nothing if not hard-nosed about Hawk history."

"From what I've heard, he was hard-nosed about just about everything."

Kendall sighed. "He could be, yes."

"Especially in his business?"

"Yes. It's why he was so successful."

This was the opening he'd been waiting for, and he wondered why he had to force himself to take it. Finally the words came. "I'll bet he hated having to go public with any of his companies."

He heard the smile in her voice. "He hated it," she confirmed. "That's why he rarely did. He kept everything privately held, as much as he could."

"And when he couldn't?"

"When he couldn't keep it personally, he made a private offering, to people he checked out himself."

He wasn't even having to push her for it, he thought numbly. She was handing it to him on that silver platter, just like they'd talked about. Naked. He fought back a memory of that first moment when he'd driven himself into her body, when the unexpected tightness and heat of her had nearly made him come instantly. He'd known then he was the first man for her in a long time. And he didn't like the way that made him feel, proud, and possessive.

"A . . . private offering?" He barely managed to get the words out.

"That's when an investment is offered privately to a small group of investors. Aaron would help them form a private limited partnership, and then in turn they invested in his companies."

He made a show of tugging the covers out from under them, then up over them while he turned words over in his mind. Finally, still unable to understand his own reluctance, he went on, trying to sound appropriately uninformed.

"Isn't that . . . controlled? By some federal commission or something?"

"Yes, the SEC. Securities and Exchange Commission," she added in explanation; he didn't tell her that he knew perfectly well what it was. "That's why the private limited partnership. It allows them to take advantage of exemptions to registration allowed by the SEC."

"Loopholes?"

"Sort of," Kendall admitted, "but legal ones. Let's just say Aaron knew their Regulation D by heart, and pushed it to the limit."

He knew that regulation, too, the one that set the conditions necessary for the SEC to okay a private offering. Knew it, he thought with an inward smile of grim satisfaction, probably as well as the old man had.

"So, he trusted those investors, at least," he said.

"To a point, yes."

"A point?"

"No one partnership owns a controlling interesting in any of the Hawk Industries. Aaron made sure of that."

"Is there more than one partnership with holdings in any one of the companies?"

"Yes, but that's not a problem. They're all different investors. Some of them have owned the stock for years. And they always turned their proxies over to Aaron to vote. He was careful, and it never backfired on him. And, of course, they've made a lot of money on that stock, over the years."

He took a deep breath, not understanding why the closer they got to what he needed, the twitchier he was getting. "What if they don't . . . want to turn those proxies over to Aaron's widow? What if they all decided to . . . combine and rebel, now that he's dead?"

He heard her chuckle, a small sound touched with her lingering grief for Aaron. But her words were light enough, as if she quite enjoyed the prospect. "Then Alice would have her hands full."

"What about Alice? Won't she be as much in control as Aaron was?"

He felt her shrug. "She'll inherit most of his stock. But Aaron wasn't a fool. He left some of it to people who had been loyal to him over the years."

This was something he hadn't thought of. "Including you?"

"Some," she admitted. "I'm sure Alice would fight it, if it were enough to cause her any trouble. But it's not."

But it might be enough to give him an extra margin of safety, Jason thought, just a little more maneuvering room, in case somebody was unhappy with the debt being called in after all these years.

"There's enough stock spread around elsewhere to keep her from assuming complete control without the cooperation of the other stockholders, but she'll probably get that. And I'm sure she's already been thinking of ways around it. She's probably been working on this from the moment Aaron was diagnosed," Kendall said, for the first time sounding bitter.

And I've been working on it for twenty years, Jason thought to himself grimly. But he knew Kendall was right; he'd learned that in his phone calls this afternoon. Alice was on the move, all right.

"You wouldn't like to see her in charge, would you?" he asked softly.

"No. No, I wouldn't. But there's nothing I can do about that." *Maybe,* Jason thought. *Or maybe not.* "But that's something that will take her some time," Kendall added. "Right now I'm sure she's more worried about you."

Which was exactly what he wanted her to worry about, Jason thought, all his determination flooding back. This was his chance, to get what he hadn't been able to find out. Aaron's holdings were almost all public record; Alice's were not. But Kendall knew what they were. With an effort he managed a tone of merely mild curiosity.

"Will she have the same amount of control in every company?"

There was the briefest of pauses before she asked, "Why so curious?"

Jason knew he was walking on thin ice now. Kendall was smart, too smart, and if she got suspicious, it could all fall apart. While she obviously had no love for Alice, she had loved Aaron, and her unwavering loyalty could be dangerous. Especially if she decided her loyalty to Aaron meant loyalty to Hawk Industries.

He schooled himself to an unruffled tone, and gave a half shrug he knew she would feel.

"If we're going to fight her over the will, I'd like to know everything I can about her. You never know what might be useful."

"Oh." The mention of the will seemed to decide her, as he'd hoped it would. Then she was answering him. "Her control varies. The only company she'll have a clear majority in is the original Hawk Manufacturing. But it's a small part of Hawk Industries now, so it doesn't mean that much."

"Where's her weakest position?"

She hesitated, and Jason held his breath, not knowing if she was merely considering or still suspicious of the kind of questions he was asking. He hated not being able to see her face, but he didn't dare flip on the light. It was hard enough to stay focused when he could feel every luscious curve of her naked body; being able to see her would destroy his concentration altogether.

"Hawk Propulsion, I suppose," she said after a moment. "When they made the switch, they were dealing a lot with public agencies. That took a lot of changes to meet different standards, and permit fees, a lot of expenditure. Aaron wasn't able to hang on to quite as much of it as he wanted to."

It was enough. He knew Alice's stronghold and her weak spot now, it would be enough. It had to be. If he pushed for any more, he ran the risk of Kendall backing away. Anyway, she'd already given him more than he'd expected so early on. All he had to do now was keep her from discovering what he was really up to. And he could do that easily enough, keep her distracted. The fact that she was here with him, like this, proved that.

What it proved about him, he wasn't sure.

Chapter Twenty

~

"**D**amn. I knew something was wrong."

"I'm fine, George," Kendall said into the phone receiver. While Jason had gone down to use the hotel's copy machine, she'd called the investigator, after calling the motel to see if anyone had been trying to reach her and being told Alton had tried three times.

"I got worried when I couldn't reach you. I called Martin at the desk to make sure you were still registered, and he mentioned that a cop had brought you back Saturday."

"Yes. He was very sweet."

"I called a buddy of mine at the department. He talked to the investigator that handled the accident, who said you were lucky to be alive, that you came within inches of going over the drop. Are you sure you're all right?"

"Yes." Except for the renewed soreness of her body. And a new, vaguely erotic soreness in some places she hadn't been aware of for a long time. "Except ..."

She hesitated, sinking down to sit on the foot of the bed. The spread was thicker, almost a quilt, the carpet richer, the entire room considerably more plush than the modest Sunridge Motel had been.

"Except what?" Alton prompted.

"It wasn't an accident, George."

There was a moment of silence, then, "I see. It would seem the ante's been upped."

No questions, no "Are you sure?" just immediate acceptance. Kendall breathed a sigh of relief; she was very

tired of spending all her time and energy convincing people. She briefly told him what had happened, including
her trip to the bank and her suspicions about Alice's
involvement.

"I wouldn't be surprised," Alton said. "That was a
smart move with the money."

"Thank you, but that may have been what brought
Alice down on us. She had us followed last night."

"Followed?"

She told him that story, too, eliciting a low whistle.
"Sounds like the boy can handle himself."

The boy. Kendall nearly smiled at the term, remembering how Aaron had always called Jason that. But it
hadn't been a boy who had made love to her on this bed
last night. It hadn't been a boy who had driven her to
heights she'd never known possible. And it hadn't been
a boy who had turned to her again this morning, arousing
her while she was still half asleep, awakening her in more
ways than one, so that by the time she was fully aware
of what was happening, by the time he rolled over and
pulled her on top of him, she was so hot, so hungry for
him, that she could do nothing less than take him inside
her and ride him as he asked, until they'd both erupted
into quaking spasms of pleasure.

Yes, the boy could handle himself, all right. And her
as well. And too well. She shook her head, battling the
rising heat the sweet memories had begun in her. Had
George asked her something?

"Uh . . . I'm sorry, what did you ask, George?"

"What are you going to do now? Do you want me
to talk to the police, now? I can have somebody start
digging, unofficially."

Kendall wavered before answering. Aaron had always
taught her to handle her own problems, but she doubted
he'd ever expected anything quite like this. But still . . .

"No," she said at last. "Let's wait awhile longer. We're
going to talk to Aaron's lawyer today. His office has a
number to reach him at in Germany."

"*We're* going to talk?" Alton asked. "So the son's
going to fight, after all?"

Kendall felt an odd little pang at Alton's words. The

son. Once, that had been all Jason had been to her, the
son Aaron had been trying so desperately to find. And
now . . . now he was so much more. She very much feared
too much more.

"Yes," she said. "He's going to fight."

"What changed his mind?"

That was something she couldn't explain even to him.
So she settled on part of the truth. A part she guessed
Alton would understand.

"He . . . met with Alice."

Alton let out a low, amused chuckle. "Well, that'd
change my mind."

"Yes. It would change most anyone's, I imagine."

"Where are you?"

"We're at the airport. The hotel across the street."
She explained Jason's ruse of abandoning the rental car
near the bus stop, and the two separate plane tickets to
two different locations, checking themselves in, and then
walking right back out again.

Alton chuckled again. "He's good. You'd think he's
done this before."

"In a way," Kendall said, thinking of a young Jason
on the run, "he has."

"Oh?"

"I'll explain later."

"All right. You have the addendum to the will with
you?"

"Yes. I took it out of the safe deposit box when I
moved the money, and I've kept it with me. It's only a
copy, not the original, which will make things more difficult, but it's all we have."

"I presume you've made more copies?"

"That's what Jason's doing right now." And he must
have had to wait for the machine, Kendall thought; he'd
been gone a long time.

"Get one to me. Make that two. I'll keep one, and
give one to that buddy of mine on the department, just
in case. I trust him. He won't do a thing unless something happens."

"All right. Oh," she added, having almost forgotten,
"what were you trying to reach me about?"

Alton cleared his throat audibly. "Just a couple of things I found out about Jason."

For some reason she felt a twinge of apprehension. "What?"

"Not much, really. Yet. I confirmed what we already knew, that he flew to L.A. late Thursday night, on the red eye from Seattle. Caught the first shuttle flight at five A.M., got to the airport here at six, and had a rental car waiting. Checked in at the motel at six-thirty. Martin in the office said he left just before eleven, which jives with what you said about when he got to the service."

Kendall's brow furrowed. She didn't see why any of that information was important; she'd already figured most of that out. But neither did she believe that Alton didn't have a point.

"And?" she prompted.

"Martin remembered the name of the major airline from the folder he had in his pocket when he checked in. I called a friend of mine over there, who called somebody in Seattle, and found out a couple of interesting things."

So this was what he'd been getting to, she thought. She glanced at her watch again, wondering what was keeping Jason, wondering what would happen if he were to walk in and hear her on the phone, talking about him.

"I'm sort of in a hurry, George," she said.

"He flew first class," the man said.

Kendall's brows lifted. She thought of what Alton had said about the racy gray coupe. As Alton had said, not a bottom of the rental scale vehicle.

"And," Alton added, "he paid for it with a credit card. A platinum corporate card."

She straightened. "What?"

"I thought it was interesting, too," Alton said. "Same kind of card Martin said he paid his motel bill with. I'm making some further inquiries up there, but I thought you should know that much."

It had been a silver card she'd seen at the airport, too, she thought. She just hadn't thought much about it. She caught her lower lip between her teeth for a moment before she asked, "What do you think it means?"

"I'm not sure. At first I thought the fancy car might be a front, you know, to prove something, coming back from Aaron's funeral. But now . . ." Alton's voice trailed away.

"Now it's starting to look like perhaps he doesn't have anything to prove?" Kendall suggested.

"Perhaps," Alton agreed. "I'll stay on it."

She'd been ready to call him off, to tell him she knew all she needed to know about Jason, which was that he was going to help her in her fight to carry out Aaron's last wishes. But Alton had hung up and the words had never come.

She glanced at her watch again. Jason had been gone for over an hour. A long time to simply go to the hotel business center and make a few copies. Her stomach knotted. Her gaze was caught by the glitter of foil on the floor near her feet. She leaned over and picked up the unopened packet. One of the condoms he'd bought, kicked onto the floor in their frenzy.

Moving mechanically, she gathered the others, the few that were left after last night, and tossed them into the drawer of the nightstand. She slammed the drawer shut and then stood there staring at it. Wondering if there would be any need for them.

Had he gone? Taken off, left her here? He had the copy of the codicil, he could fight Alice himself, what did he need her for? Sex? He could get that anywhere, with one look from those soft-lashed eyes, one flash of that crooked grin.

But what had happened between them last night hadn't been just sex, she thought. It hadn't been. No matter what he said or thought, it had been more than just a coupling of bodies, more than just an easing of need. And no matter how he might deny it, she'd seen that knowledge in his eyes this morning, when he'd nearly given up the trek down to the lobby in favor of dragging her back to bed yet again.

She shivered as the sudden heating of her body made the room seem cold. She'd had enough of this. She shoved her feet into her shoes and tucked her shirt into her jeans. She didn't bother with her purse, just scooped up her room key card, making sure the door latched behind her as she left.

A long, sighing breath of relief escaped her when she reached the lobby and saw Jason on the pay telephone at the end of the registration desk, just outside the business center. He'd apparently already made the copies; a small sheaf of papers lay on the phone's narrow counter. He was intent on his conversation, making an occasional gesture like someone more used to giving orders in person.

Giving orders? Where had that idea come from? Kendall wondered as she crossed the carpeted lobby silently. She paused a few feet behind him, not wanting to intrude, but wondering who he was talking to. He *sounded* like he was giving orders, too, she thought, unable to help hearing his brusque tone.

". . . deal with that when I get back . . . more important right now . . . I've called it all in . . . Alexander has the largest block . . . get the papers."

She took a step closer. Jason stiffened, as if he'd sensed her presence. But he didn't turn, didn't even look over his shoulder.

"I'll let you know as soon as I can. I don't know when I'll be back. This is getting . . . complicated. Right."

He hung up without saying good-bye to whoever it was. He picked up what appeared to be a telephone company calling card from atop the papers and shoved it into his back pocket. He gathered up the papers from the counter. Only then did he turn around. If he was surprised to see her, it didn't show in his face.

But she hadn't expected it to; he was too practiced in concealing himself. Even she, with the perception Aaron had touted as her greatest asset, could only read him erratically. And the fact that when she could, far too often what she glimpsed was a coldness, a harshness that surpassed even his father's, did nothing to ease her nerves this morning. Only the memory of last night, the warmth with which he'd looked at her, the passion with which he'd taken her and let her take him, and the tenderness with which he'd held her this morning could do that. And if her brain told her she was a fool for believing in that kind of flimsy, superficial reassurance, then so be it; she was a fool.

"You were gone a long time," she began.

"I had another call I had to make," he said, his voice no longer brusque, but hardly the warm, tender thing it had been in the night.

"Is . . . something wrong?"

"No. Not really. Just some . . . details." His mouth quirked. "I do have a job, you know."

"No. I didn't know."

She felt her cheeks heat. My God, she'd slept with the man and didn't even know that much about him. What was wrong with her? She couldn't have done anything more out of character if she'd tried. She lowered her gaze, unable to meet his eyes. She had little experience with these kinds of doubts, because she never did the kind of thing she'd done last night. She was out of her depth, and she knew it.

"Your investigator didn't get that far?"

Her gaze shot back to his face. She knew there was no way he could know she'd just been talking to the man, but she had to stifle a guilty start anyway.

"No," she said, agreeing in what she hoped was a casual tone, since there didn't seem to be any point in denying what he already knew. "So what do you do?"

He looked at her for a silent moment. "Maybe I'll just wait and let George tell you."

Kendall's breath caught. George?

"He's in the phone book, honey."

He said it gently, for all the world sounding like he meant the endearment. So why did it make her shiver, and not in a pleasant way? She drew herself up straight, not that it mattered; he still towered over her.

"He's the detective who was trying to find you for Aaron."

"I presumed that." His voice was inflectionless. "And he kept investigating me, didn't he? After I showed up here?"

She didn't know what to say. Except that she couldn't lie to him. She finally just said it. "Yes, I didn't think you were going to help me fight Alice. I needed to know who you were. So I could convince you."

"At least you're honest." He looked at her for a long, silent moment, as if he were thinking about what he'd just said. Then, slowly, one corner of his mouth lifted. "Don't worry about it, Kendall. It's exactly what I would do."

Relief that he wasn't angry filled her, followed quickly by a stab of consternation; this was something that hadn't occurred to her. "Did you?"

"No. I didn't plan on getting that . . . involved. I didn't think it mattered . . . who you really were."

Again her breath seemed to lodge in her throat. "And . . . now?"

He grinned. Or started to; the expression faded almost as soon as it had begun. It was as if he'd meant to give her that crooked grin, but couldn't quite pull it off.

"Now," he said, his voice oddly strained, as if he were fighting saying the words, "it matters."

"Charles is going to start back right away," Kendall said as she hung up the phone.

Jason looked up from the copy of the codicil he'd been reading. All his casual dismissal of the figure aside, he'd been more than a little stunned to read in black and white the extent of what Aaron had left him. And one stark, painful phrase, personal amid all the legalese, kept spinning in his mind. "Although there is no excuse for my years of neglect, this is the best I can do to give my son what he should have had long ago." He hated his own reaction, hated that he could even think of his father without the fierce burst of loathing he'd always felt.

"Jason?"

Her voice was soft, her eyes wide with a concern that told him what must be showing in his face. His jaw tightened at the uncharacteristic lack of control he seemed to be cursed with of late, and he schooled his expression to neutrality.

"What did you say? I was reading."

She glanced down at the papers he held, and at those lying in front of where he sat cross-legged on the bed.

"You hadn't really looked at it before, had you?"

"No."

"And now that you have?"

"He sounds like an old man trying to ease a guilty conscience."

"Oh, he was that, all right," Kendall agreed. "But he was much more, too. I think you know that now."

"Still hoping I'll forgive him?"

"No. Aaron knew that was too much to ask. He just hoped you might ... understand."

Jason grimaced. He did understand, a little, now that he'd seen and dealt with the woman who had run Aaron's life. He might not agree with what his father's priorities had been, since he hadn't been one of them, but once he accepted them, it was easy to see why Aaron Hawk had become the man he'd been. And Jason wasn't sure he didn't resent that understanding; he didn't want to feel anything for his father but the driving hatred that had fueled his entire life.

"I tried to get Aaron to write you," Kendall said.

"What?"

"To write you. Before he died. A letter ... explaining everything. Why he did what he did. Or didn't do. I knew there was more to why he'd quit looking for you than he'd told me, but he would never explain. He refused to explain to you, either. He said he'd never given excuses in his life, he wasn't about to do it now that he was dying."

Although there is no excuse for my years of neglect ...

"And besides, he said if you'd turned into any kind of a Hawk, you wouldn't accept excuses anyway. I think he was right about that."

He looked up at that, but saw only amusement in her eyes. Amusement, and something that looked almost like tenderness. That disconcerted him; he didn't want her looking at him like that. All he wanted from her was ... was what? He needed her, yes, to help keep Alice occupied, and distracted enough not to pay too close attention to what was going on. And he needed her handy, in case she had some other bits of information that he might want later. Her kind of knowledge could be very useful.

And, he thought, heat knifing through him, he needed her like he'd had her last night, naked and panting for him to take her. And this morning when, to drive home the point that this was her choice, he had made her take him, had made her be the aggressor, the leader, using his body to assure the pleasure of her own. That she had driven him to the brink of madness in the process didn't matter, he told himself. Nor did the fact that while he held her, he'd never once thought of anything but her. Or the fact that Kendall made him wonder about things he'd never wondered about before.

What mattered was that Kendall would never be able to look back and say she hadn't really wanted this, that she hadn't known what she was doing. Why it mattered to him he wasn't certain; such things had certainly never bothered him in the past.

He saw her eyes widen, and guessed that once again his usual poker face had failed him. Her lips parted, and the tip of her tongue crept out to moisten her lips. Need slammed through him, hot, hard, and relentless, and it was all he could do not to grab her and throw her down on the bed amid the copies of Aaron's will. It seemed appropriate, somehow, but he knew if he gave in to the temptation, he would embarrass himself with his haste; he didn't think he could even wait long enough to get either of them undressed.

Even that image, both of them still dressed, jeans merely unzipped and shoved out of the way enough that he could drive home into her body, nearly made the decision for him. It took all his considerable discipline to fight back the compulsion.

He made himself look back at the set of copies he held, only now realizing he'd crumpled them with the sudden tightness of his grip. "What—" He broke off when he heard how he sounded, swallowed, and tried again. "What were you saying about Wellford?"

For a moment there was silence. When at last she spoke, Kendall's voice sounded much like his had, as if she'd known exactly what kind of battle he'd just fought.

"He's cutting his trip short and starting back tomorrow night. He has a meeting he can't miss tomorrow, but he's going to take a late flight immediately afterward."

"He . . . believes you, then." Jason was back in control now. Or he would be, he thought, as soon as his body realized it wasn't going to get what it wanted right now.

"Some people do," she said.

He looked up at her again; the amusement was back. And this time he managed to smile back at her. "And some of us are more stubborn, is that it?"

"But worth convincing," she said softly. And suddenly it was there again, the memory of last night, alive and blistering between them. And seeing it in her eyes had him nearly as aroused as he'd been moments before.

"Damn," Jason muttered. "Don't look at me like that."

Kendall sighed. "I know. We have work to do."

No one had ever looked at him like that before, with such an expression of honest yearning. It struck a chord in him he'd never known was there before, not sexual but something buried even deeper, something that he couldn't name but that felt far too softhearted and yielding. He fought it, trying to bury it deep again, back in whatever hiding place it had sprung from. It didn't want to go.

"Go on," he said, unable to control the gruffness of his voice. Kendall seemed to hesitate, then acceded to the necessity of moving on.

"He wants us both to write out statements about what's happened. Including Alice's threats, and the money she put in my account. He'll start the challenge proceedings with the probate court as soon as he gets here."

"Not fast enough," Jason said, his brain starting to work again.

"What?" She seemed startled.

"Alice will be moving already. To solidify her position as head of Hawk Industries."

Kendall looked puzzled. "Well, yes, I'm sure she will. In fact, I imagine she's already called an emergency meeting of the board of directors."

You bet she has, Jason thought. And he wasn't the least bit surprised that Kendall had guessed it; he'd at last come to realize she was every bit as smart and knowledgeable as Aaron's executive assistant would have had to have been.

"But that doesn't matter to us right now," Kendall said. "It doesn't affect Aaron's bequest to you, which is purely cash and bearer bonds."

Uh-oh, Jason thought. That had been a mistake. He'd lost his focus for a moment there. As far as Kendall knew, he had no reason to be interested in what Alice was doing to assure her position at Hawk.

"He originally wanted to leave you a large interest in Hawk Industries," Kendall said gently, as if she thought he'd been hurt by what she'd said. "But he was afraid Alice would fight that even harder, and that she might get backing for that fight from the board, since you were an unknown quantity and it could possibly be shown to be against the best interests of the rest of the stockholders to have you hold a controlling interest."

"And fight she would," Jason murmured, almost under his breath. He barely managed to repress a mocking smile at the fact that his father had, unintentionally, provided his son with the final piece he needed to carry out what he'd been planning for two decades. He'd make the old man roll over in his grave yet.

"Yes," Kendall said. "But she couldn't legally fight a cash bequest, given strictly out of Aaron's personal assets."

"Nice assets," Jason said wryly. "A cool five million, without even touching the business."

"But Alice will still be in no hurry to give that away," Kendall said warningly. "There's always a shortage of ready cash in businesses the size of Hawk."

Time to recover from that little miscue, Jason thought. "I know she won't. That's why I think we'd better start the ball rolling now, instead of waiting for Wellford to get back here. The sooner we present this"—he gestured to the copies of the codicil—"to the court, the further along we'll be when he gets here."

Kendall looked at him for a moment. "You know once

we do that, once she knows absolutely for sure that we're going to fight her, she'll . . . throw everything into stopping us."

Exactly, Jason thought. And an old feeling he hadn't had in a long time poured through him, a feeling of challenge, of rising to the fight, of scenting victory and chasing it with all that was in him. It roused predatory instincts in him that he hadn't used in a long while, and it sent his pulse racing. His blood was up, and he was closing in.

"I'm counting on it," he said.

Chapter Twenty-one

❧

"I don't get it," Darren Whitewood said, sounding genuinely puzzled. "There's nothing in this for her but trouble, why is she doing it?"

"Because she's a naive, idealistic little fool." Alice snapped out the words, her rage making it difficult for her to keep from screeching.

"Don't know whether she's a fool or not," the other man in the room put in as he plucked two blond hairs from the sleeve of his brown jacket, scowled at them, then let them drift to the floor. "But that guy isn't. That was a very slick maneuver he pulled last night. And they disappeared afterward like pros. The bus, the airline tickets ... yeah, real slick."

"Oh, really?" Alice turned on the man, glaring. "Or were you just caught with your pants down?"

The man appeared completely unmoved by her insult. "I appreciate a real challenge now and then," he said. "This guy just might be one."

His calm scraped on Alice's already raw nerves. "Do you know how much time we wasted, after you lost them? We spent all night and most of the day trying to track them down in San Francisco and L.A., when they actually never went more than twenty miles from Sunridge!"

"I said he was slick," the pale blond said calmly.

"That's what you're supposed to be," Whitewood said derisively, patting his own waves of blond hair, as if in reaction to the other man's shedding. Then he froze in midmotion as a pair of cold, lifeless eyes focused on him. He slowly lowered his hand.

Whitewood looked, Alice thought, not without some enjoyment, like a man who had just seen a ghost. His own. And perhaps he wasn't far off the mark; she'd considered the possibility of having to rid herself of the pompous young attorney permanently when this was over. She wasn't at all sure she trusted him to keep his mouth shut. Like so many others, he was all talk, and turned a little green when faced with reality.

Seemingly unable to speak while pinned by those dead eyes, Whitewood just stared as if paralyzed, until the man finally looked away, studying his sleeve as if looking for more escaping strands of hair.

"I found them again, didn't I?" the man said. "It was easy, once we found out neither one of them got on those flights."

"Lucky, you mean, that they were still in that airport hotel," Alice said.

The man shrugged unconcernedly. "One man's luck is another man's skill."

"Well you should have gotten skillful sooner," Alice said sharply. "Before they had the time to obstruct my plans."

"You're the one who wouldn't let me do the job properly," the man in the brown jacket retorted, still without heat, in that calm, almost bored voice.

"I didn't want to draw that kind of attention," Alice said.

Whitewood finally found his voice again; clearing his throat audibly and looking a little bewildered by this turn in the conversation.

"Yes, well ... Let's consider our position, here," he said. "Presuming we don't wish to accept the codicil as—"

"Accept it?" Alice felt her heart begin to pound far too hard and far too fast. "Give that bastard five million dollars that is rightfully mine?"

"I'm merely trying to clarify our options," Whitewood said, recovering some of his unctuous polish.

"Options? What options? There's only one reason

Kendall Chase went to the Superior Court Building, and that's because that's where the Probate Court is."

Whitewood shook his head. "Why the hell does she care?" he repeated. "I still don't get it."

A pair of barren eyes flicked to Whitewood again. "You wouldn't."

"Oh, and I suppose you're a believer in noble ideals?" the lawyer said, apparently having recovered enough to let sarcasm creep into his voice.

"No. But I've removed a few people who were," he said, then, looking Whitewood up and down, added, "as well as rid the world of some scum."

Whitewood turned the color of his name, and Alice nearly laughed. The pretentious fool thought he could play in the muck without getting any of the dirt on him. It was about time he learned it wasn't possible.

"We have only one option right now," she said. "We proceed as planned. We have the evidence we need to prove everything. If they think I won't go through with this, they're fools. They can rot in jail for all I care." She turned to face Whitewood. "You make sure everything's in place. Including that witness you promised. I don't want to have any delays."

Looking relieved to be escaping, Whitewood nodded. "I'll make some calls," he said.

"It's your choice, of course," the man in the brown jacket said mildly after the lawyer had gone, "but there is still another option."

Alice turned to look at him. She knew what he meant. And she knew that he knew she understood him perfectly well. But she let him say it anyway.

"They could rot in their own graves, instead."

So the tiger wanted off the leash, Alice thought. She savored the idea for a moment, setting loose a tiger that already knew the taste of human flesh.

"Yes," Alice said softly, "they could."

She meant it; she had little enough time, and she resented having to waste any of it to keep her money out of the hands of Aaron's bastard. But she would do it. No matter what it took.

But now, since Kendall and that bastard had taken this

irrevocable step, it would be more difficult than ever if she had to resort to such a final option; suspicion would naturally fall on her if the heir to such a large chunk of Aaron's fortune were to turn up dead. But if she had to, she would do it. She would do anything to foil Aaron's final insult.

And she couldn't deny that the thought of Aaron's son dead and buried gave her a great deal of pleasure.

Jason had never felt more alive. Kendall was taking him deep and hard and home, and he wanted this to go on forever. He'd worried at first, she seemed so small, and he was so incredibly aroused, but the fit was perfect, tight, sweet. His pulse was hammering, his body throbbing, gathering itself for flight. He drew back, then thrust deeper, harder, again and again, savoring Kendall's cry of pleasure every time he did it. He heard his own breathing, coming in heavy, rapid pants, felt the burgeoning heat building low inside him as the luscious friction of her body around his ripped a harsh groan from deep in his chest.

She clutched at him then, her fingers digging into his shoulders as she lifted her hips to meet his next thrust, urging him more eloquently than with any words to drive harder, faster, deeper. With a strangled growl of sound he did it, slamming into her repeatedly, so hard he wondered again that he didn't hurt her. But she slid her hands down his back, beyond his waist to his hips, fingers curving around the muscles of his buttocks as she cried out his name.

That intimate touch, and the sound of his name murmuring sweetly from her throat, drove him to the edge, and for a long moment he clung there, desperately, trying to hold back, to wait, to prolong the exquisite torture that was teaching him things he'd never known about his body and his capacity for pure, hot, voluptuous sensation.

But then Kendall cried out, her body undulating beneath him, her hips twisting as she ground herself against him. He felt it begin for her in the instant he heard her cry out his name again, felt the clenching of deep, strong muscles around him, milking him, demanding he give himself to her. And in that instant he wanted to give himself to her, all of him, not just the explosion of seed that was boiling up in this last moment. He wanted to give her so much of himself that she was never completely without him again, that no matter where she went for the rest of her life, he would be there.

He heard someone say her name in a prayerful voice, low and deep with wonder; he knew it had to be him, even though he'd never sounded like that in his life. And then thinking was beyond him as his body gave up to the coaxing, relentless demand of hers. Her body clenched around him again, and he exploded in a burst of light and heat and a pure, pulsing pleasure that seared him to the boundaries of his body and back again, until he was straining in her arms, grasping at her frantically, not able to get close enough, knowing that even if he could get so deep inside her he could never really leave, it still wouldn't be close enough.

He collapsed atop her, barely aware of anything except the aftershock of that wild eruption and the feel of Kendall's arms around him. Intermittently a little shudder seized him, tightening all his muscles in an echo of the explosion that had rocked him. And he could feel it happening to her, too, felt the tiny convulsions as she clenched around his ebbing flesh.

"My God," she whispered.

"Yeah," Jason said. It took every bit of energy he had left just to get the word out.

He supposed it should make him feel better to know that it was as explosive for her as for him, but somehow it didn't at all. He didn't know if anything could allay this sense of unease. He didn't feel like this. He just didn't. Ever. He didn't get hot just glancing at a woman. He didn't get thoroughly aroused just thinking about her. He didn't practically come just kissing her. And he sure as hell didn't let a woman know he was so out of control that he couldn't even sit across a table in a restaurant from her without wanting her beyond his power to resist.

But tonight he'd done just that.

They'd gotten back to the hotel and stopped in the restaurant, pleased that they had gotten their tasks done today without being stopped by Alice or whoever she had hired. They had felt a sense of relief that they'd taken some action, had even laughed about spending so much time on the bus in the past two days. They'd been pleased by the simple fact that the healing cut on Kendall's temple was beginning to itch, and Kendall had even laughed a little over Alice's certain consternation when she found out what they'd done.

They had even kidded about the likelihood of winding up in adjoining jail cells if Alice went through with her threats, although he wasn't sure Kendall's heart was truly in it.

But when they'd gotten back to the hotel, the mood had shifted. And Jason had lasted about five minutes, watching her across the table, her eyes lowered as she read the menu, her soft lower lip caught between her teeth, before he'd utterly lost it. He'd yanked the menu away, then taken her hands and pulled her to her feet.

"We'll order room service," he'd said, his voice already thick and husky. "Later."

She'd understood with one glance at his face, so he could only imagine what he must have looked like. But she hadn't resisted, had, in fact, gone eagerly. So eagerly that he'd damn near had their clothes off in the elevator, ready to take her up against the wall and be damned to anyone who came along and discovered them.

As it was, they hadn't made it to the bed the first time; the minute he'd had the room door closed she was up against it and he was tugging at her jeans. The fact that she'd been yanking at his as well, and ripping his shirt away, had only aroused him more, and by the time she'd unzipped him and he felt her hands on him, he'd been in a frenzy. He'd clawed her panties away and lifted her, and her legs came around him as if they'd been lovers for years. And they'd both climaxed so quickly after he was inside her that when they slid shakily to the floor, she was still clutching in one hand the key she'd opened the door with.

And despite the fury of it, it had been bare minutes before they'd begun again. And again, it had been ...

He didn't know what it had been. Now, still panting

slightly, he drew in a deep gulp of air, trying to slow his breathing. And the spinning of his mind. He didn't understand this. Sex was pleasant, at times necessary, sometimes self-indulgent ... but it was never, ever the kind of cataclysmic thing that happened between him and Kendall. Each time, he'd expected it to ease, to be less than it had been. But each time it had been, impossibly, more.

When he could move, he shifted himself off of her to one side. But he couldn't quite let go of her, and was glad when she turned on her side and snuggled close to him. He closed his eyes and waited, a little tensely, expecting her to speak, to say something about the extraordinary fire that burned between them. He remembered what he'd thought, that Kendall was the kind of woman who would have to dress it up and call it love. And that had been before he'd had any idea what it would be like; now she'd probably be even more convinced this was something more than just unbelievable sex. He wasn't sure he wasn't convinced it was more.

God, you're losing it, he told himself acidly.

"You know we probably won't be able to prove Alice killed your mother."

His eyes snapped open. "What?"

She gave him a smile of understanding that told him she knew perfectly well what he didn't want to talk about. He supposed she must have sensed the tension in him, and made one of her uncannily accurate guesses as to its cause. He let out a breath he hadn't really been aware of holding. And he tightened his arm around her, the only thing he could think of to let her know he understood what she'd done and was . . . grateful, he supposed.

"It was so long ago, how could we find the man who did it? And prove it? You said he was a pro, so he surely isn't going to confess all, not after twenty years, even if we could find him."

"Unless he's here, now."

Kendall stared at him. "You were serious? About her using the same man?"

"Why not use him, if he's still around? He obviously did a nice tidy job the first time."

He kept his voice carefully even, but Kendall was looking at him as if she knew exactly how much effort it was taking. She probably did, he thought sourly. She read him better than anyone ever had.

"Well, I suppose, if he is still around ... But if it is the same man, he's even less likely to confess."

"I know. I didn't say we could prove it."

"Especially since we can't exactly use the book as evidence," she said.

"We could," he said dryly, "but it would land us in a mental hospital somewhere."

She sighed. "Probably. But we may wind up in that jail cell anyway."

"You think she'll go through with it?"

"Do you think she'd have the slightest qualm, after what she's already done?"

"No. I just wasn't sure you knew that."

"I don't have many illusions left about how ruthless Alice can be, just as I didn't have many about Aaron. Hawks are a ferocious bunch."

He went very still. "Yes. They are. You should remember that."

She raised herself up on one elbow to look at him. She clearly hadn't mistaken his meaning, but he hadn't expected her to.

"Was that a warning? Are you thinking of yourself as one now?"

"Maybe," he said, not really clarifying which question he was answering.

Instead of looking wary—as she should have if she had any sense at all, Jason thought—she looked very satisfied.

"Good," she said, taking it as an answer to her second question. "A Hawk just might be able to take Alice on."

"Oh, I'll take her on," he promised softly. "And I'll bring her down."

He turned to her then, before she could ask him anything he didn't want to answer. He kissed her, gently at first, then with more heat as she sighed and threaded her fingers through his hair. He trailed kisses over her jaw,

then down the side of her throat, lingered in the hollow
at the base to taste her skin with his tongue. Then he
lowered his head farther, tracing the full, soft swell of
her breasts, drawing each nipple in turn to rigid attention
with the careful rake of his teeth and teasing flicks of his
tongue. She responded, moaning softly, with the swiftness that stoked an answering blaze in him, and he was
achingly hard again so fast it almost scared him.

"Damn," he muttered, "how do you do this to me?"

"I think that's my question," Kendall whispered. "I've
never felt the way you make me feel. I think I understand what Aaron meant, now. How he felt about ..."

Jason froze as her words trailed away. He didn't want
to hear this. He didn't want to hear her say what he
thought was coming. He'd had women tell him they
loved him before, and he'd turned it aside with a laugh
and a joke about not being fool enough to fall in love,
or sometimes a callous reminder of the purely physical
basis of the relationship. But he couldn't bring himself
to be quite so cold with her. And that worried him as
much as anything else. Still, he warned her.

"You're heading for thin ice, Kendall."

She sighed, as if she'd expected it. Then her hand slid
down his back past his waist, lingered for a brief, squeezing caress of his buttock, then around his hip. He moved
without thinking, automatically, giving her the access she
had silently asked for. Her fingers stroked through the
thicket of hair at his groin, then curled around his erection in a caress that made him suck in his breath as his
stomach muscles rippled.

"Actually," she said, her light tone putting things back
on the level he wanted them, "I was heading for this.
And there's nothing thin or icy about it."

"And you," he said through clenched teeth as she
began to stroke him, applying exactly the right amount of
pressure to drive him mad, "learn awfully damned fast."

"Sometimes," she said, rather wistfully.

But then she leaned forward to place a kiss in the
center of his chest, moved to circle his nipples with her
tongue, all the while stroking and squeezing him, and
he forgot everything except how incredibly, unbelievably

good it was going to feel to be inside her again, and how much he wanted to be there when she hit the peak, wanted to feel the exquisite gripping embrace of her body, telling him undeniably that she was with him.

Before, it had been simply a matter of male pride, the need to know he'd pleased his partner. But with Kendall it was, as were so many things, different. It wasn't just pride, it was necessity; he had to know he wasn't alone in this craziness, wasn't alone in being swept up into this inferno they'd turned loose. And if that only added to his uneasiness, he couldn't think about it now. He couldn't think of anything now, except that she was touching him, caressing him, as if she found every part of him wondrous.

And he was far too close to the edge. He seized her busy hand and gently but firmly drew it up to the relative safety of his waist.

"Slow," he said, not caring anymore that his voice betrayed his need by coming out as nearly a growl. "We're going to go very, very slow this time."

"We . . . are?"

The throaty sound of her voice made him both more determined to do exactly what he'd said, and more doubtful that he could. He reined himself in, setting his jaw as he fought down the conflagration her touch engendered in him.

"Yes," he said, lowering his head once more to her breasts as he slid a hand down her body to probe the delta of dark curls. He punctuated each phrase with a flick of his tongue over her nipple, or a circling of that tiny knot of aroused nerves his questing finger had found. "We're going . . . to go . . . slow. Very . . . very . . . slow. Then we'll stop . . . and start again . . . and stop . . . and start. Until you're so damn close . . . you come the instant . . . I slide into you."

She moaned, low and husky. "Oh, God, Jason."

He caught a nipple once more, this time sucking hard and deep at the same moment he stroked her wet, slick flesh hard and deep. She cried out, and her body arched against him. He held her tightly, never letting up in his caresses, and proceeded to keep every promise he'd just made to her.

"I'll let you know if you need to come bail me out," Jason was saying jokingly into the phone when Kendall stepped out of the bathroom, toweling her hair, lifting the wet strands so they didn't soak her shirt. She wondered who he was talking to. Someone he knew well enough to kid about winding up in jail, obviously. She wished she felt as lighthearted about it as he apparently did.

She had to get some fresh clothes, she thought. Buy some, if Jason still didn't want to go back to the motel. But George had said it was probably safe enough now that they'd filed the challenge; he'd met them yesterday at the courthouse, to pick up copies of the codicil and the statements she and Jason had written out. It had been almost funny, seeing the two men eye each other so warily, but Jason had never spoken, never said he knew who George was, had merely nodded in answer to Alton's watchful greeting and stood silently as Kendall handed over the papers.

When he sensed her presence in the room Jason turned his head to look at her, rather intently, as if he were trying to judge how much she might have heard. Then whoever was on the phone said something that drew his attention. After a moment he laughed.

"Yeah, I know. But they don't. I'll play it along for a while longer. Until everything's in place."

Kendall watched as he hung up. "Problem?"

He got up and started toward her. He'd already been up and taken a shower before she'd even awakened this morning; his hair was still wet and slicked back.

"No. Just thought I'd get my one phone call in ahead of time, before Alice sics the cops on us," he said, grinning as if there wasn't every likelihood that exactly that could happen.

He'd reached her then, settled his hands lightly on her shoulders, and bent to kiss her thoroughly. Instinctively her hands came up to rest on his chest. He hadn't put on a shirt yet, and the feel of his skin, satin smooth over hard, fit muscle, distracted her nearly as much as the feel of his lips on hers again did.

It shouldn't have this effect, the thought dazedly when at last he broke away from the kiss. Not after last night, not after the hours they'd spent proving that it wasn't a fluke, this lightning that flashed between them. Not after they'd been so wild her body still ached from the unfamiliar use, and his bore the marks of her fervent response in more than one reddened line left by her nails. And they both had a few other marks to show for the night's work as well. And in some very interesting places.

No, it shouldn't have this effect on her, just a simple good morning kiss and the fact that he had no shirt on. Not when he'd kissed every inch of her, and she'd explored every inch of him, repeatedly. Yet it did. And when he at last released her, she wondered vaguely if he knew that. If perhaps that was why he'd done it, so that she would be distracted from what he'd been saying on the phone. Not that there had been anything curious about it, except for that remark about playing it along for a while longer. But at the moment, even if he had done it to distract her, she couldn't manage to care.

She set down the towel she'd been using on her hair and picked up the big, blunt-toothed comb she had bought at a drugstore they'd stopped at after their trip to court yesterday. Jason hadn't wanted to go back to the motel for their things yet, although he'd admitted that by now Alice probably knew where they were; he'd only expected his ruse with the airline tickets to give them a day. But it had been the day they'd needed, Kendall thought, to begin to stop Alice.

"So," Jason said, to Kendall's disappointment pulling on his shirt, and then leaning a hip against the sink counter as she began the somewhat laborious task of untangling her hair, "how long do you think it will take the old bat to rally the troops?"

Kendall considered that for a moment. "Aaron was once able to hold an emergency board meeting within twelve hours. But that was before things were quite so scattered. There are a couple of people on the board who are some distance away, now. It will take time for them to get here."

"And they may not be willing to jump quite so fast for Alice?"

She hadn't come out and said it, but he didn't miss a thing, Kendall thought. He rarely did. "Not right away. But she won't waste any time making sure they see things her way when they get here."

"From where?"

She paused in her combing. She wasn't sure why it mattered to him, but she answered anyway. "John Corelli's in St. Louis, he's the farthest. The rest are fairly close."

"But not all in California?"

"No."

She glanced at him in the mirror, wondering why he wanted to know, since it had no bearing on their problem. She tugged at a stubborn knot at the back of her head, then moved the comb to work at the tangle from beneath.

"Here," he said, moving to stand behind her, "let me do that."

Before she could protest he'd taken the comb and was working with a surprising gentleness at the tangle, barely causing a tug at her sensitive scalp.

"So the BOD is scattered all over? Even those here on the coast?"

BOD? Odd that he would use the abbreviation for board of directors, Kendall thought. She looked at him in the mirror again, but he appeared to be concentrating solely on her hair.

"Besides Corelli, Paul Barker is in Seattle," she said after a moment. "Martin Burr is in Phoenix. Two are original investors, still in California. The sixth seat has never been taken, Aaron always voted a proxy."

"Hmm."

It was a sound of neutral acknowledgment, as if he hadn't really cared about the answer, but had just been making conversation. And there really was no reason for him to care where the board members were. Perhaps, she thought wryly, he was just making sure the conversation didn't drift to something he didn't want to talk about. Like them.

He'd sorted out the tangle now, but rather than turning the comb back to her, he began on another section of her hair. She could feel his heat, knew if she leaned

back it would sear her. And they would most likely wind
up back in bed. She resisted the urge.

He moved unhurriedly, as if he had nothing better to
do than deal with the mass of her hair. He never pulled
too hard, just worked through the strands until he was
able to comb through them in one long, smooth motion.
Slowly. As if he was enjoying it. As she certainly was;
she was a little surprised at how good it felt to have him
lavish so much care on such a mundane task for her. He
kept on long after the tangles were gone.

"So that's it," she said teasingly when at last he
stopped, "you're a hairdresser."

She heard him chuckle. "Hardly."

She turned and took the comb from him, and walked
across the room to where her purse sat on the small desk, to
pull out the scarf she planned to use to control her wet locks.

"No? What, then?"

She looked back at him in time to glimpse a look of caution
on his face before he said, "I ... still work with marine
diesels, sometimes, but I work with boats, mostly."

She began to pull her hair back and tie the scarf
around it. It would dry into a flyaway mass, but without
a hair dryer she couldn't do much else. She could ask if
the hotel had a spare she could borrow, but it hardly
seemed worth the trouble.

"Like the fishing boat you worked on as a kid?" she
asked as she looped the scarf into a small bow.

"Sometimes. Sometimes bigger ones, sometimes
smaller ones." He lifted one shoulder in a half shrug.
"Half the population in Seattle is connected with boats
somehow, I think."

"Makes for job security, I imagine," she said.

He smiled at her, and she decided to take advantage
of the fact that he had at least answered her this time.
Besides, she wanted to know what he did with boats that
had netted him a platinum credit card. A corporate one.
Perhaps he had an exceptionally generous boss, who'd
loaned it to him to come to his father's funeral.

"So what do you do with these boats? Work on—"

The ringing of the phone right beside her made her

jump, startled. George, she thought. He was the only one she'd given the number here to.

Jason took a step toward her as she reached for the receiver, then stopped as she picked it up and said hello. He didn't look very happy, and she wondered if perhaps he'd given the number to someone and had been expecting a call back.

"Kendall?"

Alton's voice told her she'd been right in her guess, but he sounded tentative, cautious.

"I thought it must be you. What—"

"Is West there with you?"

"Yes, right—"

"Then don't say who you're talking to. I don't know what his game is, but he's up to something."

"What do you mean?"

"I'll tell you the rest later, but have you ever heard of North Pacific Marine Services?"

"No."

"Well, if you were anywhere near Seattle, you would have," Alton said, sounding a bit morose. "They're one of the biggest marine supply, repair, and salvage operations in Puget Sound. They supply parts, repair everything from engines to sails, and salvage what can't be repaired."

Kendall forced herself not to look at Jason. Was this where he had gotten the corporate card? Oh, God, was he in trouble? Had he taken it without authorization or something?

"The owner started out with just a small diesel repair shop," George said, "then added the salvage operation, and built it up from there over the last fifteen years."

"So?" Kendall said carefully.

"So, it seems that the owner of the company is also worth a mint because a couple of years ago he came up with some new desalinization process that makes small-scale conversion of salt water to fresh twice as efficient and four times as fast."

Kendall took a deep breath. "And?"

"And that owner who's worth millions just happens to be Jason West."

She hung up without another word, and turned to stare at Jason.

Chapter Twenty-two

~

"No wonder you weren't worried about going to jail."

"Kendall—"

She ignored him. "Nobody would believe you'd perpetrate a fraud for five million dollars when you're worth ten times that."

"Not quite." He smiled, although he looked a little wary. "But not bad for a kid with a GED, huh?"

She ignored that, too, except for vaguely registering that somewhere along the line he'd gotten his diploma after all. She ignored everything, except the gnawing pain that had settled somewhere between her heart and her stomach. She wrapped her arms around herself, as if that could ease the distress. It had no effect at all. She sank down on the edge of the bed. Jason took a step toward her, but halted when she drew away from him.

"But you just let me blunder along," she said. "Did you enjoy watching me worry myself sick about seeing that you got Aaron's bequest? Did it amuse you to hear that Aaron worried about how you were living, whether you were in need? Did you—"

"Kendall, stop."

"Stop? All right, I'll stop. As soon as you tell me what the *hell* is going on."

"Exactly what I told you," Jason said. "I'm going to take Alice down."

She stared up at him, seeing in his face more implacability and ruthlessness than she had ever seen in Aaron's. It made her shiver. Had she been blind?

No. She'd seen it in him before. She just hadn't wanted to believe that's all there was in him. For her own foolish reasons. But right now, she would swear there was nothing in him but determination and single-mindedness. She'd known the desire for revenge against Alice for his mother's death was part of what was driving him. She had accepted that, could even understand it. She just hadn't understood it was his sole motive. But now, looking at his eyes, fierce with hatred, she couldn't doubt that it was.

"Losing what Aaron left you will hardly ruin her."

"I know."

Her stomach knotted even tighter. She stared at him. It was impossible to believe this was the same man who had made such sweet, passionate love to her, who had held her so tenderly, the man who had laughed with her just yesterday. There was nothing of sweetness or tenderness or laughter in this man, and the only passion she saw was a passion for vengeance.

"But you're going to . . . take her down."

"Yes."

"How?"

"It doesn't matter. But rest assured I will do it." He turned and walked away from her then, to stop and stare out the window of the room. "I've been planning this for years."

Kendall got to her feet. "Years? You only just found out she killed your mother."

"It's a small matter of . . . adjusting my sights."

She looked at his back; even from here she could see the rigidity there. "You've been planning for years," she repeated slowly. "Whatever it is, it was originally for Aaron, wasn't it? What is it, Jason? What are you going to do?"

He looked over his shoulder at her. "And if I tell you? What will you do?"

She stared at him. "You think I'd help Alice?"

"No. But what would you do for Aaron?"

"Aaron?"

"Leave it alone, Kendall. You did your job. You're out of it now. Stay that way."

She surged to her feet. "That's it? 'You're out of it'? I'm supposed to walk away?"

"You'll be better off. Trust me."

"Trust you?" She stared at him. "How can I trust you, when I don't even know who you are?"

"You know all you need to know. Stay out of it," he repeated. "And don't worry about Alice's threats. I'll take care of that. I won't let her do anything to you."

"No side-by-side jail cells after all?" She hated how bitter she sounded, but she couldn't help it. "There go all my foolish, romantic notions."

Jason's eyes narrowed. "I warned you."

"Yes. Yes you did, didn't you?" She took a deep breath, trying to steady herself. "What are you going to do, Jason?"

He shook his head. "There's too much riding on this."

"So I'm supposed to trust you, but you won't even trust me enough to tell me what's happening?"

His jaw tightened. "I've already trusted you more than I've trusted anybody since I was sixteen."

"And you barely trust me at all," Kendall whispered. "My God, you really are Aaron's son. In mind as well as blood." She gestured, a little wildly, at the bed. "And what was this for, Jason? Did you enjoy . . . taking me to bed, knowing I had no idea who you really were? Or was this some kind of twisted way to strike at Aaron? You couldn't hurt him, but—"

"It wasn't like that—"

"Wasn't it?"

"Let it be, Kendall. If you push anymore, you may not like what you find."

She was sure she wouldn't. She wanted to run. Somewhere. Anywhere. To get away from this pain. A pain she somehow sensed was only beginning. Whatever he wasn't telling her, it was going to hurt her even more. But there was nowhere to run to.

I don't want to run.

Remember you said that.

Her promise and his reply echoed in her mind. He'd known they would come to this. He'd never believed anything else.

"Stay out of it, Kendall," he said for a third time.

He glanced at his watch, then back at her face. For a moment she thought he was going to say something else, but then he turned and walked away from her. Kendall stared after him, shaken, watching the door swing shut behind him as he strode out of the room. She stood there for a long time.

She supposed everyone had to be a fool at least once in their life. And she was feeling like a pretty sizable one right now, after serving as a no doubt continuous source of amusement for Jason for four days. She couldn't bear to think of it, not here in this room, where she'd lain in his arms and let him do anything he wanted to her, and done things she'd never imagined to him.

Hastily she finished dressing. She stuffed the few items she'd acquired into her purse, slung it over her shoulder, then picked up the box that still held Aaron's letters and the extra copies of the codicil. And the book.

Stay out of it, Kendall.

She set the box down.

All right. Stay out of it she would. She'd put up with Aaron Hawk, and Alice Hawk, for ten years. She'd put up with—and fallen for—Jason Hawk for four days that seemed liked ten years. She'd had a bellyful of Hawk arrogance, of all kinds. And she was through. Jason could do whatever it was he was so set on doing to Alice, and he could do it alone.

Leaving the box behind her, she left the room without a backward glance.

She would have to rent a car, she thought as she rode down, trying not to remember the moment when she and Jason had come perilously close to making love in this very same elevator.

Having sex, she corrected herself brutally. That's obviously all he thought it was. Not that he'd promised anything more; as he said, he'd warned her. It was her own fault for thinking it was more, her own fault for deceiving herself into believing he thought so, too. Her own fault for believing that the gentle, tender man had been the real one, and the ruthlessness a facade he'd adopted for self-protection.

Why? Why on earth had she gone against the practices of a lifetime, acting totally against character, falling into bed with a man she barely knew, a man she knew so little about? Was it simply because he'd affected her in a way she'd never known? Was that all it took, a man whose touch set her aflame?

The elevator door slid open. She stepped out, glad to be out of the confined space that was full of memories. She'd been safer, she thought, when she'd thought of him simply as Aaron's son.

Aaron's son.

God, was that what had happened to her? Had she been primed to fall for him? Had she had an instinctive soft spot for this man who so resembled his father? Had she never really had a chance?

The door slid shut behind her with an audible thump, snapping her out of that particular useless pit of speculation. She would get a car and get out of here, she repeated to herself as she walked across the lobby with precise and determined strides. Then maybe she could think. She had to think, to decide what she was going to do next.

When she nearly ran over an elderly lady in the lobby, she realized she'd better do a little more thinking about what she was doing now. She apologized profusely, then started for the doors again, this time watching where she was going. And this time, seeing the man who stood by the end of the registration counter, enthusiastically shaking hands with someone with his back to her.

Paul Barker, she realized with a little shock. She hadn't seen him since the annual board of directors' meeting last year, Aaron's last. Alice must really have called for that emergency meeting, if he was here already. Although why he was here at this hotel instead of at the house, where the directors usually stayed in the guest wing—an old-world style courtesy Aaron had always said cost him little and gained him much—she couldn't imagine.

She started toward him; she'd always liked Paul, and they had gotten along well in the seven years since his

investment group had acquired enough stock to warrant
that seat on the board.

"Kendall?"

She smiled as Paul looked up and saw her coming
toward him. He seemed startled, then, oddly, nervous.
His gaze flicked to the man he'd shaken hands so familiarly with, the man Kendall had barely looked at in her
surprise at seeing Paul. But she looked now. And he half
turned to look at her as well.

It was Jason.

Her steps faltered, her smile vanished, but she steadied
herself and kept going.

"Paul," she said with a nod.

"Kendall, it's good to see you. I'm sorry about Aaron.
I know you were close."

"Yes," Kendall said, "we were." She nodded toward
Jason without looking at him. "You two . . . know each
other? From Seattle?"

Paul glanced at Jason. "Er . . . yes, you could say that."

She looked at Jason then, expecting to see nothing but
that cool, distant expression he'd worn when he'd left
her. It was there, his features a mask of detachment, but
the effect was marred by his eyes; they were watching
her intently, almost warily. And in them she sensed a
touch of reluctance, as if he were facing some task he
found distasteful somehow. Or perhaps it was her he
found distasteful now.

She looked back at Paul. "Why are you here instead
of the house?"

"I . . . That is, because . . ."

His voice trailed off, and he looked at Jason again.
One of the reasons she'd always liked Paul was because
she'd sensed he was an honest man. He wasn't acting
like one now.

"He's here," Jason said, "to meet with me."

Her gaze flew back to Jason's face, startled. "You?
Why?"

"Let it be, Kendall," he said again, as he had upstairs.
If you push any more, you may not like what you find.

The rest of what he'd said came back to her; as it
replayed in her head it sounded even more ominous. The

implication, that she might learn a truth she wouldn't welcome, was clear. But she'd faced unpleasant truths before in her life. She'd always thought it better than foolishly believing a lie. And she'd already played the fool enough in this little charade of Jason's.

Her head came up determinedly. Jason sighed, as if he'd read her intent in just that movement.

"Go ahead and get settled, Paul," he said. "I'll see you and the others as planned, before the meeting tonight."

Seeming grateful to escape, Paul gave Kendall an apologetic look and walked hastily away. She was vaguely aware of him dodging someone who had just walked in through the front doors of the hotel, but her attention was already returning to Jason.

"Why would Paul Barker be here to meet with you? What's your connection with him?"

"Business."

"What business do you have with a member of the Hawk board of directors? It's part of what you're planning to do, isn't it? What, Jason?"

He shook his head. "No, Kendall."

She knew it wasn't an answer to her question but merely a reiteration of his refusal to tell her. She suppressed a shiver. Or tried to; she knew she was trembling, but couldn't seem to help it. Nor could she help the plaintive note in her voice.

"You really don't trust me, do you. Even after—"

She bit back the rest of the words, unwilling to humiliate herself quite that far.

"I can't," Jason said. He didn't sound particularly happy, but he did sound utterly determined. "I'm sorry, Kendall. I trust you as much as I've ever trusted anyone, but I can't risk you messing up out of some misguided sense of loyalty to Aaron. I've worked too long and too hard."

"Aaron's dead!" she exclaimed.

"But his company isn't." Kendall whirled, startled, as George Alton spoke from behind her, clearly the man Paul had nearly bumped into in his haste to escape the awkward situation. "At least not yet. But you're going to do your best to see that changes, aren't you, Mr. West?"

Kendall's gaze flicked to Jason; he had gone rigid. She looked back at Alton.

"What do you mean?"

"What you wouldn't let me finish on the phone. I've only been able to confirm it in two cases, but I'm willing to bet on the rest."

"Confirm what?" Kendall asked, her voice taking on a sharp edge as both her anger and her apprehension grew.

"How many seats are there on the Hawk board?"

"Seven, counting Aaron ... Alice, now."

She started to ask why, but stopped when a possibility hit her. A possibility that, she realized, she should have seen the moment she had found out how much Jason was worth. Alton's next words confirmed her hunch.

"Then I'd say your friend here controls four of them."

Kendall stared at Jason, searching for any sign of the truth of this in his face. He was closed off to her as he'd never been before, utterly unreadable.

"Paul Barker is here already, I see. He and Mr. West go way back." Alton's gaze shifted to Jason. "You helped his son out of a bad spot, about ten years ago, didn't you? Rumor has it the kid was on drugs and in big trouble with the law. You gave him a job and kept him straight until he could do it on his own. And in return, Paul fronted for you in your first buy into Hawk Industries."

"Oh, God." Kendall knew where this was going. She sensed it like a weary fox sensed the hounds closing in. *You may not like what you find.*

"And then there's Marty Burr, in Phoenix. You floated him a loan five years ago, when no one else would, because he was on the verge of his second bankruptcy. And in return, he's been holding another chunk of Hawk Industries for you, hasn't he?"

Kendall held up a hand to ward Alton off when he would have gone on. The hounds had caught her, and she wasn't the least surprised to see that these particular hounds had originated in a very unique kind of hell. A hell she had only now tumbled into, and had little hope of escaping.

"Enough," she said, her voice devoid of any emotion now.

Alton shook his head. "It's my fault. That buddy of mine in Tacoma knew about this Jason West early on, but I told him it wasn't likely, and to concentrate on the others. I'm sorry about that, Kendall."

"It doesn't matter now," she said. "Thank you, George."

"Are you all right?" the investigator asked.

"I will be," she answered, hoping to God it was true. "Will you wait for me outside, please? I'll need a ride."

He hesitated, but when Kendall turned back to face Jason, who stood unmoving, his face registering nothing, he nodded and left them.

"How much do you hold?"

"Kendall—"

"Paul has been on the board for seven years, Martin for five, and we never suspected. I suppose Corelli is yours, too? Or did you somehow manage to subvert Hartfield or Boldt?"

"Don't do this."

"No, I doubt you managed that. Why should you waste time convincing a couple of stubborn old men when you could find an easier way?"

Before he could answer, something else registered, a fragment of his conversation that day on the phone a few yards behind her. *Alexander has the largest block.* The Alexander investment group. The group that held the closest thing to an outside controlling interest in any Hawk company.

"The Alexander group," she said. "The untaken seat on the board is yours?" His jaw tightened, and he didn't speak, but she knew the answer. "Very ... patient of you, to let Aaron just vote it all these years. And the others ... they never fought with Aaron, not really. But then, as long as he made good decisions, why should they?"

"Damn," he muttered. She ignored it.

"Who got the profits, all those years? Did Aaron help build North Pacific Marine Services?"

"No," Jason said sharply, prodded by that to speak at last. "Not a cent came from Hawk. Ever."

She lifted a brow at him, thankful for the blessed numbness that had descended on her, allowing her to

talk about this as if it were of no personal concern to
her at all.

"So that was part of their payment? They just sat there
and collected all those dividends over the years, while
they waited for you to call in the debt? I presume you
did bankroll their buy-in?"

"This is pointless—"

"What were you going to do? Just stroll into a board
meeting one year and take over? Was that to be your
revenge on Aaron?"

Something flickered in his eyes then, and she knew
she'd struck a chord.

"It was, wasn't it? That's what you've been planning,
all these years. And then he died, and ruined it. But you
couldn't give it up, could you? So you switched to another target. Alice."

"You defending her now?" His tone was biting. "After
what she did to my mother, and tried to do to you?"

"She deserves what she gets," Kendall said, meaning
it. "But don't try to convince me your mother has much
to do with this, Jason. Revenge was not her way. What
she did when Aaron wouldn't marry her and when Alice
threatened her proves that. No, this isn't for your
mother. This is for you."

"What the hell do you know—"

"I know you hated your father. That you felt betrayed
by him, until you came to hate the very name Hawk,
and anything it stood for. And I know that your reaction
to betrayal is to destroy the source. In that, you are very
much Aaron's son."

He didn't deny it. "What are you going to do?"

She looked up at him, at his face, at his set, determined
expression. She tried to remember how he'd looked in
those moments of extreme, explosive pleasure, when he'd
looked down at her with wonder in his eyes. She wondered if that man had ever really existed, or if she'd
made him up somehow, woven him out of the threads
of childhood dreams and wishful thinking.

"How much do you hold?" she repeated, even though
she knew the answer, or close enough; like his father, he

would never make this move unless he was very, very certain of winning.

"Enough," he said, in the tone of one surrendering to the inevitable. "As long as you don't side against me."

She felt something shift inside her, as if something had broken or crumbled. She prayed the numbness would hold, because she knew, deep in her soul, the answer to the question that was coming. But she had to ask it anyway. She had to hear him say it.

"And that's what this was all about, wasn't it? You and me? To make sure I wouldn't ... side against you?"

"Kendall, don't. It wasn't like that. It might have started out that way, but—"

She cut him off as another realization came to her. "You decided after you saw Alice that night, didn't you? That it was time to make your move? Only stupid little Kendall was in the way. So you turned on the charm. And she fell for it. You must have been proud that it worked so well. And so fast."

"I had no choice," he said. "But I didn't mean to—"

She went on as if he hadn't spoken. "And all those questions you asked. About Aaron's work, and the company, and the board ... you were pumping me, weren't you? It was all part of the plan."

"I had to be sure of my position before I moved. You were the only one who could tell me that."

A tiny burning sensation had begun somewhere inside her, and she knew it was the beginning of the pain. And she knew it was going to get much, much worse.

"Why didn't you just ... ask?"

"You were loyal to Aaron. Everything you've done has been because you were loyal to Aaron."

"Not everything," she said, remembering the moments of pure rapture she'd found in his arms. Regret flashed across Jason's face. She looked away, willing herself not to be a fool yet again and believe he was feeling any remorse. The pain was expanding, and she knew it wouldn't be long before it overwhelmed her.

"You don't understand, do you?" she said, hearing that pain in her voice. "You'll never understand. What Alice did removed any obligation I ever had to her. And

Aaron ... Aaron would have wanted me to help you in whatever way I could."

"To take down his company? I doubt that."

"It's not his anymore. And I think he'd rather see it destroyed than in Alice's hands." She bit her lip, trying to fight back the oncoming tide of anguish. "So you see, you didn't have to ... seduce me for whatever information I had. I would have given it to you. Freely."

Jason was shaking his head. "Why should you help me? The only thing you had to gain out of this was trouble."

She shook her head in turn, sadly. "And that's the bottom line for you, isn't it? Nobody helps anybody unless there's something in it for them."

"That's the bottom line for most of the world," Jason retorted, sounding a bit angry.

"Maybe. But not for me. I would have helped you, Jason. But you didn't trust me. So you had to ... make sure of me. And you did, didn't you? Very sure. I guess I'm the naive little fool you thought I was after all. Because I believed you. I saw in you what you wanted me to see. What I wanted to see. And I'll pay for that for the rest of my life."

"Kendall, it wasn't—"

"You know what's really sad?" she said, fighting off the pain for one more moment. "You've hurt me. Badly. But I'll heal. Someday I'll be over it. And I'll look back and remember what I learned. What I learned about trusting and not trusting, what I learned about myself. And"—she took a quick breath and bit her lip for a moment, needing the sharp physical pain to enable her to go on—"what I learned about need and love and sex and how incredible it can be."

He moved then, just slightly, as if his muscles had gone suddenly tight on him. He didn't speak, but for one brief moment he looked like a man to whom her every word was a lash across his bare skin.

"But you'll never learn," she said. "Vengeance has been your motivating force all your life, hasn't it? I'll even bet, in his way, Aaron is responsible for where you are today. Because you had to succeed, to get into a position to where you could have your revenge. Well, you're going to get it, and then it will be over, and what will you have? What will drive you then, Jason?''

She turned away then, unable to bear this any longer. The pain was crushing her now, and she would die before she would weep in front of this man. But she glanced back at him one more time.

"I'll heal," she repeated. "But you never will. And I feel sorry for you for that."

She turned away again, and began to walk, her eyes fastened on George's familiar car, waiting just outside the doors. It took every bit of self-discipline she possessed to keep from running.

Jason stared after her. He concentrated on her, because not to would leave him open to whatever that was welling up inside him that felt so much like pain. He noted the straightness of her spine as she walked, and thought of her nerve and courage. He noted the quickness of her step, and thought of the tears that had been brimming in her eyes in those last seconds.

I'll heal, but you never will. And I feel sorry for you for that.

Yes, she would heal. She was strong, and had more nerve than anyone he'd ever known, including himself, he thought as the pain he was denying began to hammer at him, demanding he acknowledge it. He should be thankful for her strength; he hadn't really wanted to hurt her. He'd only meant to—

To what? Coldly seduce her, getting what he needed? And then what? Walk away? Leave her here, with the ruins of Hawk Industries settling into the dust around her?

He'd warned her, he told himself. More than once. He'd warned her it was nothing but sex, warned her never to think it was anything more. He had no reason to feel guilty. No reason to feel this agony that had suddenly engulfed him despite his efforts to fend it off.

And he had absolutely no reason to feel like it was his own world crumbling into dust around him.

Chapter Twenty-three

∿

This was ridiculous. Why was he sitting here in a damned hotel room, staring at the walls, feeling like a boat whose mooring lines had all been cut? What he was here for hadn't changed. And it was going to happen; he'd met with everyone, and everything was in place and ready. He would see retribution made. He'd worked for it all his life, and the fact that it would now take Alice Hawk down instead of his father didn't bother him. Aaron was beyond his reach, but the woman who had killed his mother wasn't.

This isn't for your mother. This is for you.

He got abruptly to his feet, slamming the chair back against the wall. He needed to move, to ease the pressure building inside him.

She was wrong. It was for his mother. He owed her that much, to see that the woman who had arranged her murder would pay, in one way or another. It wasn't for him. It wasn't all he had. When he finished here, his life would go on. Only he'd have the satisfaction of knowing Aaron Hawk was dead, and his murderous widow had paid by losing what was most important to her. He couldn't think of a more fitting ending.

He wasn't doing this for himself, he insisted silently.

He took a deep breath. Then another. Then he laughed out loud at himself for thinking some faint, sweet scent lingered in this anonymous hotel room, for thinking there was some trace of Kendall left behind to taunt him.

She'd had no right to look at him like that, he thought

as he wheeled and strode across the room. He'd told her from the beginning, it was nothing more than sex. And damn it, that's all it had been, just like it had always been in his life.

He whirled again and came knee to edge with the bed. The bed where he and Kendall had spent long, fervent hours trying to slake a need that seemed to grow instead of ease with every encounter, a need that was so far beyond anything he'd ever known, it had shaken his belief in that very concept he'd just been touting to himself. A need that had almost convinced him he was wrong, had always been wrong about need and love and sex.

I learned about need and love and sex and how incredible it can be . . .

Love. He'd been right, he thought with a determined effort at his old cynicism. She'd had to dress it up as love to accept the fact that she'd gone to bed with him. And she was trying to hang the guilt on him. Well, he wasn't buying. He just wasn't. He'd come here to accomplish one thing, the one goal that had driven him all his life. She'd been part of that, a tool he'd had to use, like others he'd used before.

But they had known they were being used. Yes, he'd charmed a woman or two for a purpose before; he hadn't seen any other reason to exert himself. It had been part of the game, a piece of information dropped here, a name there. And he was good at it. He was generous and amusing and made sure they had a good time. But those women had always known who he was, and had a good idea of what he was after.

Kendall hadn't. Even though he'd warned her, he knew she hadn't.

"I had no choice, damn it!"

He spun on his heel, unable to stand there any longer, just staring at the bed where it seemed he'd lost himself, lost his certainty of what life was, what it held and withheld, and his assurance that trust was a fool's game and love worse than that. He spotted the box that sat on the desk, and with a vicious, sweeping motion of his arm he shoved it, sending it flying.

It hit the dresser and spun to one side, falling open

on the floor, spilling papers and the envelopes marked with his father's bold scrawl.

And the book. It skidded across the carpet to stop nearly at his feet. He stood there, staring at it.

I haven't tried burning it yet, but give me time.

His own words came back to him. Maybe now was the time. He'd hold a match to this pile of dreams, and watch them burn. As all his mother's dreams had burned. He bent to pick it up, seriously wondering where he might find a match. But the moment he touched the leather of the binding he knew he wouldn't; that same feeling pumped through him, that feeling of comfort and understanding, as if an old, trusted friend had put an arm around his shoulders.

Something slipped from the pages as he lifted it. One of Aaron's letters, he supposed, caught between the pages. But he realized even as he was reaching for it that it wasn't; this wasn't an envelope but a folded piece of paper, and it was quite different-looking, heavy and yellowed, as if it were as old as the pages of the book itself.

But it hadn't been there before. He knew it hadn't. He'd looked at every page of this book before, and there had been no loose paper, nothing folded between the pages.

But the minute he touched it, he knew it belonged with the book. He got the same crazy sensation, only this time multiplied a hundredfold. It was so powerful he caught himself nearly looking around to see if there was some physical manifestation of that gentle, welcoming sensation. Slowly he sat down on the edge of the bed. When he put the book down, the sensation eased slightly, as if it had been the combination that had been so overwhelming. Whatever it was, it radiated from the letter he held—he could see now that's what it was— much more strongly than it ever had from the book.

It shook him, this vivid reminder. He'd been ignoring the book, had shoved it so far back into the recesses of his mind that he'd been able to forget about it for long stretches. He'd been so consumed with pulling all the strings that would make his plan come together, so wrapped up in dealing with the real world, the world he knew and lived in, that he'd been able to discount for the moment the book and its inexplicability.

But he couldn't discount the strange feeling of connection that came over him when he touched it. Or the fact that it had led him to the truth about his mother's death. And that put him back to wrestling with the real dilemma of the book; did he believe in it or not?

He was no more ready to deal with that than he'd ever been. With a wry grimace he unfolded the letter. With any luck it would be something even more confusing, enough to distract him from the book.

The writing looked as old-fashioned as the paper, long, sloping letters, but the few lines were bold and easily readable. But before he could begin to read, the even bolder signature at the bottom caught his eyes. He looked, and his breath caught.

Joshua Hawk.

That it would be this man seemed at first impossible, then inevitable. Of all the Hawks in the book, it had been this man who had called to him more than any other, this man who had made him feel part of something bigger than himself. Not Aaron, for no matter how much more he now understood about the man who had been his father, he could never forgive what loving him had cost his mother, and wanted no connection to him. But Joshua made him feel an unexpected and odd sense of guilt that he planned to put an end to the Hawk legend.

He dragged his gaze back to the top of the page. It didn't take long to read.

> *I don't know who or where or even when you are, or if this will ever reach you, but if I can spare you some of what I went through, I must try. If you are reading this, you are the last Hawk. If you are like me, you are fighting as all the last Hawks have fought. Don't. The legend is true. The book is real.*
>
> *Jenna and Kane Hawk are forebears to be proud of. I hope that, whoever you are, you might even find something in me to be proud of, little though there is. Don't let it end. It does matter. Jenna and Kane and the others deserve to live on in you.*
>
> *I wish you luck, and Godspeed.*
>
> *Joshua Hawk*

Jason sat staring for a long time, feeling a tightness in his throat he couldn't explain away. These simple yet formal words got to him in a way nothing in the book ever had, and he couldn't find it in him to deny it.

Moving slowly, as if the fog he was feeling was physically thick as well as mentally, he reached for the book. As if it knew, and at this point he wasn't sure he could deny it did, it opened to the page he'd wanted to see. Not his own story, at the end, but Joshua's, from well over a hundred years ago. He knew it would be the same, it wouldn't have changed, not this, there was too much of that sense of inevitability to it.

It hadn't changed. It was still there, in that lovely script, the entry of the name of the child who had assured the continuation of that bloodline, who had guaranteed Jenna Hawk and her warrior would live on in yet another generation.

Joshua's son.

Jason Hawk.

He shuddered involuntarily, and moved to close the book. If his own story had changed, he didn't want to read it. He didn't want to read some crazy tale about how he'd become the first Hawk to blow it, the first one ever to drive away the woman the book said was meant for him. But, unable to stop himself, he found himself looking anyway. Braced, ready to see Kendall's name and today's date, the day she had walked away.

The date was there, all right. But Kendall wasn't. What was there was the ludicrous claim that on this day Jason Hawk made peace with his father.

He'd only meant to pick up his car and bring it back to the hotel. On a whim he didn't quite understand, he'd taken the bus back the way they had come. It had been a mistake; all he could think about was how he and Kendall had sat there and laughed, and how he'd told her things he'd never told anyone about his life. At the time, he'd told himself it was to win her sympathy and trust, all part of his effort to charm her, but now he wondered if perhaps there hadn't been more to it. But he'd been thinking that about a lot of things lately. Since the day he'd looked into Kendall's grief-stricken gray eyes the day of his father's funeral.

And now, here he was, on that damned road to the cemetery. And he wasn't sure why. There would be no peace with Aaron, not for him. And he couldn't believe that he was being somehow compelled by the book. Or didn't want to believe it. Perhaps he just wanted to prove the book once and for all a lie.

. . . you are fighting as all the last Hawks have fought. Don't. The legend is true. The book is real.

He shook his head. The words had rung in his ears as if spoken, in a deep, gravelly voice tinged with a wry, amused recognition. A voice he'd never heard before, even in his imagination. But a voice that matched the image that had once formed in his mind, of Joshua Hawk, blue eyes identical to his own gleaming with commiseration and understanding.

Maybe that was why he was going, he thought. He could never make peace with his father, but Joshua . . .

By the time he reached he big curve, it had begun to rain in earnest. He slowed, shivering as he glanced to one side and saw the crumpled guardrail where Kendall had nearly gone over. Now, here where he could see how vicious the drop was, he knew how perilously close he'd come to losing her that day.

And then he'd thrown her away.

I saw in you what . . . I wanted to see. And I'll pay for that for the rest of my life.

What had she seen? What had she thought was there in him? He shook his head, trying to stop the fruitless speculation. Just because she'd found something in his father to love didn't mean—

Love? Was that what he was thinking, even hoping? That he hadn't just charmed her out of the information he'd needed, but that Kendall had somehow fallen in love with him?

You, Jason told himself firmly as he slowed even more as the pelting rain continued, *are going out of your mind. You don't need the book to drive you crazy, you're doing it on your own.* Even if it was true, what the hell did it mean? Love was a crippling thing, it made you weak, made you do things you would normally never do.

Like Kendall had done. By going to bed with him.

He knew it was true, and not simply because of physical reasons, or the shocked wonder in her response. He knew it because he knew, at last, Kendall, knew that she was exactly what she'd appeared to be from the beginning.

And what does that make you? he thought, fighting a wave of unexpected nausea. Kendall was who she was, playing by her own set of straight, honest rules, not the corrupted, distorted ones he'd used to his advantage so often. The fact that he didn't run his own business that way did little to salve a conscience that wasn't used to being pricked. His rationalization that people who played by those rules deserved to go down by those rules wasn't working well this afternoon, either.

He pulled off the road into the parking lot of the small cemetery, and into an empty space. He wondered yet again why he was here, what he hoped to accomplish. He sat there for a while, staring at the rain, telling himself this was pointless, he had the board meeting of his life to prepare for.

But he was prepared. He was as ready as he'd ever been in his life. He knew that, knew that there was nothing more to do. Nothing more he had to do, except wait for it to all come together, the work of a lifetime.

He yanked open the car door, and was hit with a barrage of raindrops, the kind of heavy, harsh downpour he'd only ever seen here in California. They might not have the rain totals Seattle did, he thought wryly, but they sure got a lot of it at once.

He reached over and grabbed the book off the passenger seat, braced this time for that odd sensation of comfort, of connection. He wasn't sure why he'd brought it along. Except maybe to leave it here. Now that would be an offering the old man would appreciate, he thought. Maybe he'd just bury the damn thing right beside the old man. Maybe that would get rid of it. He'd been the one to believe in the Hawk legend, after all.

The legend is true. The book is real.

Joshua's words came to him again. They seemed to be haunting him, as the image of the man had ever since he'd seen it in the book. Between his words and Kendall's, every one of which seemed etched permanently into his mind, his head seemed to be ringing with remembered phrases that seemed mostly designed to convince him he was either crazy or as heartless as his father had been.

He hadn't gone ten feet before he was soaked, water running down the back of his neck, the turned-up collar of his jacket—he'd left his coat behind, never having intended on this little expedition—useless against this kind of deluge. He told himself to abandon this ridiculous idea, but he kept walking. He found himself instinctively trying to protect the book under his jacket, and managed a laugh; he could probably throw the thing into the Arctic Ocean and it would be back the next day, dry as a bone and with his attempt at destruction neatly chronicled.

When he reached Aaron's grave, he knew he'd made a big mistake. The sensation from the book, that unexplainable sense of peace and reassurance, seemed to strengthen. But again, it wasn't his father he thought of but Joshua, and again he could almost see the man, nodding in encouragement, a small half smile curving his lips. It was as if here, at his father's grave, his connection to this man who was his ancestor was even stronger. So strong that he wasn't sure he could fight it. He wasn't sure he wanted to.

He looked at the book he held. He'd pulled out the letter from Joshua; it was neatly folded in his inside jacket pocket, a spot that was oddly warm against the wet chill of the storm. He wasn't sure why he wanted to keep it, only that it seemed very important somehow.

His gaze went to the gravestone, cold and dark and running wet with rain. To be angry at his father now was a useless, impotent thing. As, perhaps, it had always been. But if he gave that up, what did he have left?

"Damn you," he whispered. "Damn you for dying before I had the chance to break you myself."

With a fierce, arcing motion, he flung the book at the

stone. It hit the second "a" in Aaron, then settled atop the first three letters, covering them. Jason stared down at the stone, a chill that went far beyond the storm whipping through him.

---on Hawk.

Three letters. The only difference between a gravestone that read Aaron Hawk and one that read Jason Hawk.

Appropriate weather, Kendall thought. Befitting what she had to do. Not that sunshine would make admitting how badly she'd bungled things—and what a fool she'd been—any easier. She wasn't sure why she felt compelled to do this, except that she'd always been utterly honest with Aaron, and it seemed that she owed him this now.

She drove carefully in the driving rain, keeping her eyes steadfastly straight ahead as she passed the section of the guardrail she'd nearly gone over. She'd been driving with her eye more on the rearview mirrors than the road, it seemed like, but there was no sign she could see of anyone following her.

She decided to forgo the main entrance, and parked on a side road that would make the walk much shorter. Still, she was drenched from the knees down well before she got to the quiet place on the hill that Aaron had chosen; "So I can keep an eye on things," he'd said; the spot had a view straight down the valley to Sunridge.

The heaviness of the rain made her think she was seeing things when she saw the huddled shape at the side of Aaron's grave. But as she got closer, having to step carefully over the slick ground, she knew she wasn't.

Jason sat cross-legged in the short grass beside the headstone, seemingly heedless of the fact that he was obviously soaked to the skin. He was shivering; Kendall could see the little tremors that swept him every few moments. His arms were wrapped around himself, as if that could warm him.

He didn't seem to realize she was there. He was staring downward, but didn't seem to be focused on anything. His hair was as wet as it had been from the shower this morning, but now clung to his neck and forehead in dripping strands.

"Jason?"

He looked up at her, startled. And in that moment of surprise, before any of his formidable defenses could snap into place, Kendall saw something she'd never thought to see. She saw the living image of the lonely, frightened boy he had once been. The boy who had once stood beside another grave, facing the death of his mother and the fact that he was now more alone than any child should ever have to be.

And in that moment Kendall knew how much of Jason's toughness stemmed from that time, and from his determination never to be scared again. No matter what it took, no matter what he had to do. She hadn't been wrong, not about this. It *was* self-protection that had made him develop the ruthless facade. The question was, had the facade become the man?

Another shiver made his teeth chatter. She saw him clench his jaw, and wondered how many nights sixteen-year-old Jason had spent being this cold, when he hadn't had the money for the bus or the ferry, or to get to the airport where he could get warm and scrounge through other people's leavings for food scraps.

As difficult as her life had been, she'd lived through nothing as grim as Jason had. It made what he'd done, what he'd become, even more impressive. Something clawed at her, some mixture of love, compassion, and bitter longing that dug into her with talons as strong and merciless as those of his namesake.

She loved him. Fool that she was, she loved him. She loved that part of him that was Aaron, that part of him that was Hawk, and most of all that part of him that was Jason, the part he never let anyone see, but that he had revealed to her in bits and pieces, as the Hawk story had been revealed in the book. She knew how cold, how harsh he could be, but she also knew he was capable of tenderness, of laughter. And somewhere, deep beneath the shell that protected his heart from the world, she knew there was still that scared, lonely boy, who could love if only he could be sure he wouldn't be hurt, if he could be sure the one he loved wouldn't abandon him, as everyone else had. The heart of this Hawk would not be easily won.

As if he'd suddenly realized what his face was showing, or as if he'd recognized the look in her eyes, he quickly looked away from her.

She knelt beside him. As if he'd asked, she said, "I came to apologize to Aaron for failing so miserably."

His head snapped around, and he stared at her. "You didn't fail. You carried out his last wishes."

She shook her head, ignoring the water that was now streaming down her face. "It was never his wish that Hawk be destroyed." He looked away again. "That is what you're going to do, isn't it?"

"Yes." It came out harshly, as cold as the rain, as dark as the sky producing it. "I've been buying Hawk stock for years. A little bit here, a little bit there, but never so much that I had to register it with the SEC. More than half those private investment groups are mine."

"And you really have control of the board? Four votes out of the seven?"

"Paul was more than willing to front for me, after I helped his son. I loaned Martin that money, and in turn he agreed to vote as instructed. I own a controlling interest in Corelli's business, so he has no choice but to cooperate. And I funded the Alexander group myself, as a silent partner."

"Very slick, Jason," she said quietly. "Aaron would be proud."

"I'm going to take over and then dismantle Hawk Industries, piece by piece. I've spent my life planning this day." He looked at her again then, steadily. He looked more than ever like his father now. Predatory. Ruthless. "Are you going to try and stop me, Kendall?"

"No. I suppose I could try, out of loyalty to Aaron, but somehow I don't think he'd want that. He wouldn't want me to fight you, Jason. I think he would have handed Hawk over to you, if he could have, and if you'd wanted it."

"And you?" The words came out of him as if forced,

as if he'd fought very hard to hold it back. "What do you want?"

She looked at him for a long, silent moment, knowing what she felt was clearly readable on her face, and not caring. "What I can't have." She shrugged, as if it meant nothing, as, someday, she prayed it would. "I'll get over it. Maybe next time I'll approach it a little more like you. Like a business deal. Value given for value received. Nothing more, nothing less."

"Kendall—" He blinked rapidly. Rainwater in his eyes, she was certain. "I don't want to hurt you. But I have to do this."

"I know." She did know. She knew that nothing mattered more to him than his revenge. Nothing. And no one. Including her.

"I . . . care about you. I didn't like . . . keeping things from you."

He said it with some surprise, as if he'd never expected to feel that way. But it didn't matter, Kendall thought. Nothing could sway him from the course he'd set. Nothing could take the Hawk's eyes off his prey.

"Just remember something, Jason," she said. "The Hawks aren't just a company, or even just a name. And if you don't understand that by now, then you've missed the whole point of this." She gestured at the book that lay, sodden now, atop Aaron's headstone. "And Jenna and Joshua and all the others . . . it was all for nothing."

He shivered again, violently. But he said nothing, and after a moment she stood up.

"Don't you see, Jason? If you keep on, never feeling, never trusting, always just moving on, eventually it's too late to ever go home. You're going to wind up just like your father did. Dying cold and alone and full of regrets."

He shivered again, but didn't break his silence. Kendall felt tears brimming, and although she knew they wouldn't show amid the streaks of rain, she wiped at her eyes. Then she looked at the grave marker.

"I'm sorry, Aaron," she said softly. Jason flinched as if she'd struck him.

She walked away through the rain, leaving him huddled there by his father's grave.

Chapter Twenty-four

~

There was no reason for him to be this edgy, Jason thought as he paced the anteroom outside the main conference room. Everything was going like clockwork. The security guard at Hawk Manufacturing, where the board meetings were traditionally held, had gaped at him when he'd walked in, and had surreptitiously glanced at the portrait of Aaron that hung on the wall in the entry, then back at Jason's face in shock, but he hadn't tried to stop him.

Probably because of that shock, Jason thought. Or perhaps the paperwork he'd shown him from the Alexander group, listing him as their voting representative for this meeting.

He'd waited outside the gates, watching, as the others arrived. Corelli was first, then moments later Alice's limo had appeared. She was accompanied by a too well-dressed blond man who, judging from Kendall's description, was Whitewood, the attorney Alice had bought.

Kendall.

He jerked his thoughts out of that worn avenue; if he started thinking about her, he'd lose his concentration, and he couldn't risk that. He couldn't let anything distract him from the goal, not now that it was finally within reach. But the memory of the last time he'd seen her, walking away from him in the rain, was indelibly carved into his mind, and he couldn't seem to shake it.

He turned and began to cross the room in the other direction. Alice would be making her pitch about now, he thought, making her assurances to all the board members that things would continue as before, that she would step into her late husband's shoes so smoothly that they needn't bother themselves about his death at all. She would no doubt attempt to take credit for whatever profitable decisions had been made in the past. She would also, if he had predicted accurately, make some grandiose promises about future earnings, if only they would give her a free hand.

It was then, if all went as planned, that Paul would signal him. And the victory he'd been planning for, waiting for, all his life would finally be his.

Even as he thought it, he saw the door open slightly. He could hear Alice's querulous voice as Paul glanced out, found him, and nodded. The man retreated back into the room, and Jason took a deep breath.

Let the retribution begin, he thought.

When he walked into the room, Alice gasped, surging to her feet. Whitewood looked shocked. The two older men, the original investors, gaped at him and then muttered to each other. But no one else in the room was surprised; in fact, they were busy studying their hands, the table before them, or their coffee cups, looking at anything but him. He hadn't bothered to dress for this meeting; he'd thought taking Alice down while wearing the very jeans and boots she'd sniffed at would be much more appropriate.

"Gentlemen," Jason said affably.

"How dare you!"

Alice was the picture of righteous indignation. Jason smiled. This was going to be sweet. Very, very sweet. That image of Kendall flitted through his mind, but he refused to let it distract him.

"I believe we've been through this before," he said.

"Get out, or I'll have you thrown out!"

"I think not. I might, however, consider having you thrown out."

"Call security." She snapped out the order at no one in particular. No one moved.

Jason glanced around the table. "Gentlemen, I think your business here has come to a conclusion. Thank you very much for coming."

"You arrogant—"

Alice's words broke off when three of the men at the table, looking more than a little grateful at the opportunity to escape, rose and began to head for the door.

"What do you think you're doing?" she exclaimed at their retreating backs.

"There's no need for them to be here," Jason explained, his tone as gentle as if he were explaining to a child. He glanced at the two older men, who were still seated and gaping at him. "Feel free to leave as well, if you wish. Your presence is, I'm afraid, irrelevant."

"That's ridiculous. We're holding a board meeting here. Get out."

The men who had reached the door glanced back at Alice's exclamation, but Jason nodded, and they filed out without speaking.

"This is outrageous!" She came around the end of the table. "I demand—"

"You're in no position to demand anything, Alice. Not anymore."

Slowly, with great flair, he pulled a notarized document from his pocket and tossed it down on the table in front of her. "I presume you're familiar with the Alexander group?"

She brushed the papers aside with a regal gesture, not even glancing at them. "Of course I am. I run this business now, and I know every facet of it. What has that got to do—"

"They're mine."

She glanced at the papers then. "What are you talking—"

"And here," he said, tossing another folded document on the table, "is Barker's proxy. It's mine."

"This is—"

"And Burr's. It's mine."

"You—"

"And Corelli's. It's mine."

Alice appeared shocked into silence at last. She sank down into the chair Corelli had vacated.

"That's four. Out of seven." He glanced at the two men who had remained seated, and who were now staring at him, realization in their eyes. "As I said, your presence here is irrelevant. As," he added, looking back at Alice, "is yours."

"You bastard." She spat it out with all the venom of the deadly black widow spider she made him think of.

"Exactly," Jason agreed. He glanced at the two astounded men who sat as if transfixed. "Allow me to introduce myself. I'm Jason Hawk."

He'd intended to say it, for the sheer enjoyment of watching Alice's reaction, but now that he had, the strangest feeling came over him. A feeling of connection stronger than any he'd felt when holding the book, stronger even than when he'd read Joshua's letter.

He tried to ignore it, telling himself it meant nothing. Even the book seemed to have gone dormant on him since he'd tossed it at Aaron's grave; when he'd picked it up again, and opened it rather defiantly to the last page of writing, only one line had been added. And one that made no sense, talking about how all of Jason Hawk's plans, from his life to his revenge, would change. He wasn't about to change anything, not when he was so close.

But the sensation persisted now, and it rattled him; he was glad he'd been looking at the men instead of Alice.

The two men noticed nothing; they scrambled out of their chairs and beat a hasty retreat. Whitewood withdrew to a far corner, keeping the large conference table between them as if he feared Jason would physically come after him. Jason looked back at Alice.

"And just in case you're thinking of some kind of counter move, Alice dear, I think you should know that I hold a larger percentage of stock than you do in every Hawk operation except this one."

"What?" She rose swiftly again. "That's impossible!"

He grinned at her.

"It's that little bitch, isn't it?" Alice exclaimed. "She helped you. Did she turn what Aaron left her over to you? Or just agree not to side with me?"

"Kendall has nothing to do with this." He saw her eyes narrow, and swore silently at himself for what the swiftness and urgency of his response had betrayed to this vicious woman. "I've been planning this since I was sixteen." His mouth twisted. "Since you had my mother killed."

That distracted her from Kendall, and Jason felt a spurt of relief. He had no time to dwell on what his reaction meant, what it had betrayed to he himself. He had to concentrate on Alice. She looked suddenly wary, even glancing over to the corner of the room where Whitewood was staring at her.

"The Northwest Limited Partnership?" Jason said, drawing her attention again. "Mine. Maxlight? Mine. The Ulysses group? Mine. Want to hear more? I have quite a list."

Jason folded his arms across his chest and stared down at his father's widow. She was red-faced and sputtering, looking for all the world like a caricature of herself. Victory was in his hands.

"It's over, Alice," he said. "I'm going to take apart your world the way you once took mine apart."

She glared at him, but it was bluster, an impotent gesture. Jason waited for the feeling of triumph, the flood of satisfaction that he'd done it, the rush he'd been waiting for for twenty years.

But as he looked into her eyes, those dark, vicious eyes that were nearly the color of that aptly named spider, he saw only the anger and bitterness of an old woman. And a hatred for him that should have chilled him, had it not been radiating from this woman who seemed somehow to have shrunk in stature in the past few moments.

She's as bitter as you are. Aaron never loved her ... she loved him as much as she could ever love anyone, and he never loved her back.

Kendall's words, he thought, coming back to him as they did so often.

It hit him again, this time full force and with devastating clarity. Kendall, walking away from him. Walking away, after as much as admitting she loved him. Or had:

"You bastard," Alice said, so furiously spittle flew from her lips with the words. "I'll see you dead before I let you lay a finger on what's mine!"

You're a symbol to her ... of what she never had from her husband.

Kendall, who had done nothing but try to fight for him, for what she thought he should have, for what she thought was fair. Kendall, who had more nerve, more raw, pure courage than he'd ever thought of having. Kendall who had never given up, who had absorbed every setback and come back fighting. Kendall, who had given herself to him so completely, and had made him feel things he'd never felt before, made him wish he believed in things he'd never believed in before.

Kendall, who understood far better than he what it meant to be a Hawk.

The Hawks aren't just a company, or even just a name. And if you don't understand that by now, then you've missed the whole point ... and Jenna and Joshua and all the others ... it was all for nothing.

Kendall, who had been foolish enough to fall in love with him.

"Damn you!" Alice shouted. "I'll see every single piece of Hawk Industries burned to the ground before I'll see *you* take it!"

Alice, who hated him more than she loved Hawk Industries, and probably more than she had loved Aaron. Aaron, who had been the true target of his revenge, but who was now beyond his reach. Aaron, the one his vengeance had been precisely tailored for.

It hit him then, what was wrong. He had planned this, all these years, for Aaron. Specifically for Aaron, striking where it would hurt his father the most. But this wasn't Aaron, it was Alice.

The book had said his plans would change. Even his plans for revenge. He'd dismissed it, but it had been so right, all along ...

No, damn it. He wasn't going to let such craziness affect him. Wasn't going to let it change his course. To let the book tell him what to do would be crazy. And yet ...

This wasn't Aaron, it was Alice. And while dismantling Hawk Industries, which would have affected Aaron like nothing else, would hurt Alice as well, he suddenly realized there was something else that would hurt her even more. He should have seen it before. He considered it, but only for a split second; it was so right there was no question in his mind. He didn't even care that he was falling in line with the book's predictions. Maybe the thing was even causing this; he didn't know anymore. He only knew this felt right.

He sat on the edge of the table, leaning forward to say to her almost gently, "Would you like to hear the timetable? Would you like to know how long it will be until Hawk Propulsion goes under, how long before CeramHawk is broken up into bits and sold to the highest bidder?"

"You bastard," she whispered. He saw then what he'd wanted to see in her face: the sure and certain knowledge that he had done it, and that Alice Hawk knew it.

"Yes," he said. "We've already established that, haven't we? I'm Aaron's bastard. His only child. The son of the woman he had a passionate affair with for seven years, the only woman he ever loved."

Her hand came up swiftly. He caught her wrist and held it, blocking the slap.

"You know it's true, don't you? He loved her, he always loved her. You know it. It's why you tossed a yellow rose into his grave."

He stared down into her face, seeing the malevolence there, the pure, raging hatred.

"It's why you killed her, isn't it? You weren't afraid she'd come back, you had no reason to be, she'd done everything you asked. For me. But you killed her anyway. You murdered her, because you couldn't stand the fact that Aaron had loved her so much, and he'd never loved you at all."

"Yes," she said, her voice a low, venomous hiss. "And I'll kill you, too, if I have to to stop you, and that bitch along with you. And I don't give a damn about the price."

Jason drew back. He *was* right. There was nothing he could do that would hurt Alice Hawk more.

He stood up.

"It's mine, Alice. All of it. I've taken it all, everything you value, value so much that you killed for it."

She swore, low and vicious.

His voice dropped to nearly a whisper. "But do you know what I'm going to do?"

He gathered up the papers on the table. And with a motion very like washing his hands, he dropped them all in her lap. She instinctively grasped at them, then turned startled, suspicious eyes on his face.

"That's right, Alice. I'm giving it back to you. You can go on playing your little games. But every minute of every hour of every day, you're going to remember one thing. You owe it all to me. Aaron's bastard son, by the woman he loved. You're going to go through the rest of your miserable life knowing you're living on charity. Jason Hawk's charity."

The woman went pale. Then she flushed, her face turning furiously red. A pulse throbbed at her temple as she shook with her rage, and Jason guessed that the rest of her life might not be as long as she'd hoped.

"Remember it, Alice. You're a charity case now. And everybody on that board is going to know it."

He heard the crackle of paper, and saw that her thin, diamond-ringed hands had crushed the papers in her lap. He turned on his heel and walked out of the room.

He'd never felt so free.

Jason nearly broke into a run as he headed for his car. He felt light, as if he'd put down a burden long carried. He found himself grinning rather stupidly, even tilting his head back to let the rain, which had diminished to a drizzle, wash over his face.

When he reached the gray coupe he stopped, turned to look back at the utilitarian buildings of his father's first business. He'd started with less, Jason thought, remembering the much more modest, run-down building that had housed McKenna's Diesel Repair. He'd worked his tail off, for six years, and when old man McKenna had wanted to retire, Jason had bought him out. That had been the beginning. Maybe he hadn't gone quite as far as Aaron had, but he'd done damned well.

In his way, Aaron is responsible for where you are today.

Kendall had been right. About that, as well as so much else. In a tangled sort of way, his father had made him what he was today.

Kendall.

He had to find her. Tell her. He knew it wouldn't make much difference to her, not after what he'd done to her, but he wanted her to know he'd walked away from it. He wanted her to know the empire Aaron had built wouldn't die by his son's hand. That, at least, would mean something to her. And maybe, just maybe . . .

The book had been right. His plans had changed. He'd found the perfect fate for Alice. It had been right, no matter the source. Perhaps because of the source. So why couldn't that source be right about him and Kendall as well? Did he dare hope that it was, that she would see it that way, in spite of everything? He didn't care anymore that logic was telling him that he never would have thought of it on his own, that the thought of them together forever had been planted in his mind by the book, he only knew it was just as right as what he'd just done.

He only hoped he wasn't too late in seeing it. In believing. In following the plan that now seemed inevitable.

He unlocked the coupe's door and pulled it open.

"Hawk!"

He looked up at the call, suppressing a rueful surprise that it seemed so natural to respond to the once hated name. But that surprise was quickly overtaken by wariness as he saw Whitewood hurrying toward him, casting furtive glances back over his shoulder.

"I'm not looking to buy an attorney," Jason said when the man came to a halt before him.

Whitewood seemed to make an effort to appear offended, but it failed miserably. He glanced once more over his shoulder, and when he faced front again, Jason saw a flicker of genuine fear in the man's eyes. Apprehension spiked through Jason.

"What's wrong?"

"I wanted to warn you, Mr. Hawk—"

"You mean you've decided to switch sides, now that Alice doesn't hold all the cards anymore?"

The man didn't seem at all insulted. "Let's just say I'm a man who knows a stronger hand when he sees ones."

"Perceptive. Warn me about what?"

"Alice."

Jason chuckled. "That's hardly necessary. I know she'll be out for my blood."

"She won't settle for just that. She went crazy after you left. She's always been a little . . . fixated, but she went completely berserk. Ranting, screaming for your head . . ."

I'll bet, Jason thought, allowing himself a small spurt of satisfaction. He'd been right; nothing he could have done would have hurt Alice more.

"Maybe you should be a little more careful who you sell yourself to," he said.

"Look, I'm no saint," Whitewood said. "I've done a few things that are . . . out there, ethically, but I draw the line at murder."

"How . . . principled of you," Jason said dryly. "But you're a little late for my mother's sake."

"Your mother? I'm not talking about that, I'm talking about you. She's still up there swearing she'll see you cut into pieces before she's through."

"That's been tried before," Jason said.

Whitewood looked at him for a moment. "You are pure Hawk, aren't you?"

"Hawks do breed true, it seems."

"Well, maybe you can take care of yourself, but you'd better watch your back. She called the guy she's had following Kendall, and he's nobody to trifle with. He's even crazier than she is. Cold as ice. She said he'd done something for her before, and I think maybe it was—"

Jason grabbed the blond's shoulders, barely restraining himself from shaking him like a recalcitrant child. "She called him and . . . what?"

"She said they were down to the last option. And that she didn't care how he did it, as long as he did it fast."

The last option. It didn't take much guessing to figure out what that was. And if he'd been following Kendall,

it was only logical that he'd deal with her first. Jason
released the lawyer, the apprehension inside him shifting
to full-blown fear. Whitewood backed away, looking at
Jason as if he thought he was as crazy as Alice. Without
another word, he turned and hurried away, leaving
Jason reeling.

Kendall. God, what had he done?

He'd meant it to be a distraction, a diversion, he'd
wanted Alice so concerned about what he and Kendall
were doing about Aaron's will that she wouldn't notice
in time the moves he was making at Hawk. That she
wouldn't have time to talk to the board members before
the meeting, so she would have no hint something was
up. That she wouldn't have time to go over Aaron's records in depth, and make some connection that might
have led her to him. He'd wanted Alice's attention di-
vided, and he'd gotten exactly that. And he'd used Kendall to do it, just as he'd used her for the last bits of
information he'd needed to verify he could indeed take
Alice down.

He'd used her. Coldly. Cruelly. More cruelly even than
he'd realized. Perhaps even more cruelly than she realized. And it had worked. Too well.

So well that Kendall's life could be in danger.

So well that she could die.

Revulsion welled up inside him, and he staggered back
against the car. God, he was just like his father. Cold,
manipulative, using whoever came to hand as if they
were no more than tools to serve a purpose and then
be discarded.

A vivid, stark image formed in his mind, of himself on
some distant day in the future. Dying cold and alone and
full of regrets, just as Kendall had said. Just like his
father, who had died speaking the name of the one
woman he'd loved but hadn't had the courage to keep.
He was no better; afraid to admit what his gut had been
telling him, that he loved Kendall. That somewhere along
the line, the planned seduction he'd engaged in had become real. That the real reason it had been so easy was
that he'd meant every word, every move. That instead
of her knowledge being the reason for the seduction, it

had in fact been merely an excuse to do what he wanted to do anyway. Because he wanted Kendall. All of her, heart, mind, and soul. And he wanted her forever.

And it was too late. He wasn't as bad as his father, he was worse. When they laid him down, Kendall wouldn't be there to say good-bye.

And if he didn't do something, Kendall wouldn't be anywhere. He'd thrown away the most valuable thing he'd ever been offered, he'd destroyed her love with his blind need for revenge, but he could at least see that she lived to go on hating him for it. He had to; he couldn't endure knowing he'd caused her death.

He couldn't endure knowing she was dead.

Shaking off the self-loathing that was a luxury he—and Kendall—couldn't afford right now, he began to move.

Chapter Twenty-five

∽

"You are the same man, aren't you?"

The man with the thinning, unnaturally pale hair looked at Kendall curiously. "The same?"

"The one who killed Jason's mother."

Equally pale brows rose. "He told you about that, did he? He knows?"

"He knows."

Pale blond brows lowered. "I suppose the old bat told him," he said, then seemed to dismiss it. Then he smiled, and she felt a chill at the sheer callousness of it. "I'm still rather proud of that one. My first job."

The images that had haunted her, of a younger, desperate Jason, prodded her into exclaiming, "Proud? Of killing an innocent woman and orphaning a sixteen-year-old boy?"

The man looked at her assessingly, lightly tapping the barrel of the deadly looking, stainless-steel pistol he held familiarly against his chin. "Orphaning? His father was alive until last week."

"Aaron was never a father to him. Jason never even knew him. After you murdered his mother, he was alone. He had to fight just to survive." Her forehead creased. "And if you're working for Alice you know that."

His expression changed to one of satisfaction. "Yes. You're going to make my job very easy, aren't you?"

"Don't count on it."

"But you are. Because he'll come here. He'll come here for you, now that he thinks he's won."

Kendall bit back a gasp. "No. He won't."

"I suspected as much," he went on, as if she hadn't spoken, "when I watched you together. But you've just confirmed it."

"You . . . watched us?"

"Of course. Oh, don't blush, Ms. Chase. I'm not a voyeur, I get no particular enjoyment out of watching people in love. I left you your private moments. But I am grateful that your . . . attachment will make my job so much easier. We'll just wait right here."

"It won't do you any good. Jason and I didn't part on . . . good terms."

"Nice try. Very noble of you. But pointless, I assure you."

Kendall knew it was useless, had known it the moment the armed man had burst into the motel room where she'd been packing up her things, but she also knew she had to try.

"However much she's paying you—"

"Don't waste your breath," he said, cutting her off. "I wouldn't last long in this business if targets could so easily bribe me." He smiled again, a hollow parody of appreciation. "Thanks for asking, though."

"This is crazy. She can't go through with this. She has to know she'll be suspected immediately. I've told people, you know, and so has Jason."

"That is her problem, not mine."

"What makes you think she won't turn you in, to save herself?"

"She would be very foolish to do that, and she knows it. Two have tried it before. They missed the next sunrise."

She stared at him, stunned by such brutality expressed in almost poetic words.

"Wondering about me, are you, Ms. Chase? People do, I've discovered. Women, especially, seem to want to know why I am who—and what—I am. But I'm afraid I have no grim tale of childhood abuse to invoke your sympathy or understanding. I quite simply don't care. I'm very good at what I do. That's all that matters to me."

Kendall gave up then, knowing there was no way to subvert this man. If she was to get out of this, she'd have to find another way. At least she would have time, she thought. As long as he was wrongly convinced Jason would show up here, he would wait. And since she knew better—

The ringing of the phone cut off her thoughts. It had to be George, she thought. He was the only one who knew she was back here; she'd told him she was going to pack up her things and leave in the morning. Sunridge had lost its appeal for her.

The man crossed the room in two long strides, grabbing her arm and pulling her along with him. He came to a halt beside the table that held the phone, just as it rang again.

"Answer it. And hold it so I can hear."

Reluctantly, with her eyes fastened on the weapon that was now aimed at her with undeniably lethal intent, she picked up the receiver.

"Hello," she managed to get out.

"Kendall?"

Oh, God. Jason. Instinctively she tried to hang up. Only the painful tightening of the man's grip on her arm stopped her. Jason's voice echoed out of the receiver.

"Kendall? Is he there?"

The man shook his head at her, clearly wanting her to say no. She couldn't say anything at all.

"He is, isn't he? Put him on, Kendall."

"I . . ." She was shaking, but she made herself do it. "Jason, get away, he's armed—"

"Very stupid," the man said, and tried to wrest the phone away from her. She hung on, fighting him with all her strength. She heard Jason shouting through the receiver.

"Listen, you coward, it's me you're really after, not her. Leave her alone. It's my head the old bitch wants. So come and get it. I'm right across the street."

She heard the loud click as the connection was broken before the man could answer. He hung the phone up with surprising gentleness, then looked at Kendall.

"Well, well. Isn't that gallant of him?" He lifted her chin with a finger that was also surprisingly gentle. "You look surprised. You didn't really expect him to come,

did you? I thought you were smarter than that." He
shook his head. "But I suppose even the smartest women
can be blind when it comes to seeing a man is in love
with them. You have to have it in so many words, all
spelled out, don't you?"

In fact, Kendall was stunned. She barely protested as
the man dragged her across the room to the window. He
pulled back the heavy blackout drape just far enough to
look out and across the street. Kendall, jammed against
his side, couldn't help but look as well.

He was there, in the parking lot of the convenience
store, in almost the exact spot where she'd talked to
George that first night. Dressed in his usual dark sweater
and jeans, he was leaning against the fender of his rental
car, his arms folded across his chest, his ankles casually
crossed, as nonchalantly as if he hadn't a care in the
world.

Jason, in love with her? Jason didn't love anyone.
Didn't trust anyone.

And then something else caught her eye. Next to Jason's gray coupe was a small white pickup truck. With a
red and white camper shell. It was the only other car in
the lot.

George? Had he really gone to George for help?
Trusted him?

The man let the curtain drop and stood silently for a
moment, looking thoughtful.

"Very clever," he said, as if thinking out loud. "I can't
be sure of my shot from here. I could wait him out, I
suppose. You're very tempting bait, he'd come for you
eventually . . . but by then he might also be able to rally
some uniformed help I would just as soon avoid. And
besides, I'm tired of this. It's gone on far too long." Then
he looked at Kendall. "It appears your usefulness—and
our collaboration—is over."

Kendall shivered despite her efforts to stop it. "So you
just kill me?"

"Why, no, dear. I don't believe in gratuitous violence.
My last orders were to merely scare you. But I'm afraid
my employer very much wants that man out there dead."
He glanced back at the window, as if he could see

through the heavy curtain. "And I'm sure he's guessed that. He's no fool. Which would lead me to believe he has some sort of a plan."

"No, he isn't a fool," Kendall said, fighting to keep from exclaiming in pain as the man wrenched her arm around to force her toward the chair beside the table beneath the window. "He did something no one else could have done, he brought down Alice Hawk. You might want to think about that."

"Yes, he did, didn't he?" There was admiration in his tone as he forced her into the chair. "I do love a challenge."

With movements so swift and smooth Kendall had little chance to fight, he pulled her arms back around the back of the chair, yanked the phone cord free of the phone and the wall, and used it to tie her wrists behind her. She bit back a yelp of pain as the position pulled at muscles just now recovering from her last encounter with this man. He kept the weapon trained on her while he dug into the suitcase she'd been packing, coming up with a scarf and a couple of pairs of panty hose. With swift efficiency he bound her elbows to the uprights of the chair with the scarf, and her ankles to the chair legs with the panty hose.

"You should be able to get free, eventually," he said kindly.

Kendall stared at him. He was going to walk out of here and kill Jason. She shouldn't care, not like this, not after what Jason had done . . .

But I suppose even the smartest women can be blind when it comes to seeing a man is in love with them. You have to have it in so many words, all spelled out, don't you?

Jason? She shook her head; it would be just too ironic if this cold, heartless killer was right, that he'd seen what she hadn't, that Jason, despite what he'd done, loved her. He was wrong. She knew he was. She loved Jason, but he didn't love anyone, not even, she suspected, himself.

The man moved toward the back of the room, toward the bathroom. He was still going to leave here, and he was going to kill Jason. Unless she did something to stop him.

"You can't be serious. You're just going to walk out of here? I can identify you!"

He looked back over his shoulder at her. "Foolish girl, to point that out. Fortunately, I'm not worried. The police will never find me. But just to be sure, let me point out that if you go to them, I will find you, and you will wish I had killed you here by the time I'm finished."

Kendall fought letting him see the shudder that gripped her.

"But I'm afraid I can't have you alerting the neighbors, now can I?"

He yanked open a drawer and lifted out the gray scarf she'd tied her hair with the other day. He grabbed her chin and pressed a hand on her forehead, forcing her mouth open. He stuffed the scarf he'd wadded up into her mouth, effectively gagging her. She tried to spit it out, but the cloth clung, drying her mouth. She watched helplessly as he shoved the weapon into a holster under his left arm, then turned and walked into the bathroom. She could see a small slice of his reflection in the wall mirror. His movements puzzled her for a moment until she remembered the small, louvered window there, at the back of the building. Then she heard the faint clink of glass, and knew he was going to go out that way, instead of the front, where Jason could see him.

Jason.

With a jerky, squirming effort, she edged the chair around until she could nudge at the curtain with her head. It took her a couple of tries, but finally she got beneath it enough to look out through the darkness and across the street, to where the gray coupe sat in the light cast from the store windows.

Jason was gone.

She heard a scrambling sound, and realized the killer was climbing up onto the counter, ready to make his exit. She saw his leg, from the knee down, in the mirror as he lifted it over the sill.

In the same instant that she heard an earsplitting shout from behind the building, she saw a sudden flurry of legs and arms in the mirror, followed by a loud thud and a piercing curse as a heavy weight hit the floor. In the same instant the outside door slammed open once more, and a man hurtled into the room.

Jason.

He spotted her and took a step toward her.

"Nmph!"

She shook her head, then jerked it toward the back of the room. There was the sound of a step on the tile floor as the killer regained his feet.

Jason never hesitated. He spun and headed that way. Kendall tried to shout a warning above the gun. The scarf muffled her voice beyond understanding. She would have to pray he'd heard her say it on the phone.

If he had, he wasn't acting like it. He went straight for the blond man, who had just appeared in the doorway, looking a little dazed from his fall. Jason tackled him low and hard. They bounced off the doorjamb with a thud that made Kendall wince. They went down. The blond wasn't holding the weapon, and Kendall prayed he wouldn't be able to get to it.

Desperately she began to claw at her bonds. The phone cord was tight, far too tight, but surely there was enough give in the panty hose that bound her legs ...

She heard another muffled thud. Someone grunted in pain. She saw Jason jab, fast and hard, with his right hand. The blow took the blond in the belly. She heard another grunt. They rolled out of her line of sight. She could only hear the flurry of thuds and blows. She heard someone curse. She thought it was Jason. Then he was on his feet. But the blond came at him, driving his head hard into Jason. Jason staggered back.

Kendall squirmed, twisting her feet, pulling with every bit of strength she had. The nylon rubbed her skin raw, but she never stopped.

She heard a sickening sound of flesh striking flesh, again and again and again. It went on and on, brutal, dirty, and ugly, and she knew she was seeing just how well Jason had learned to fight on those mean streets.

She continued to struggle with her bonds, until the sound of blows stopped. She looked up to see Jason beneath the killer now, the blond's hands at his throat. Jason's hands came up to grab at the blond's arms, but his grip seemed unshakable. She heard an awful, rasping sound. Jason, trying to breathe. She pulled harder at her bonds.

Jason bucked beneath the deadly pressure. His body contorted, twisted, trying to free itself of its killer. Tears brimmed in Kendall's eyes as she watched him fight. She heard a choking sound. Jason's hands seemed to flail uselessly at the blond's. Then they fell limply to his chest, as if he'd lost consciousness.

"No!" She screamed it, but it was muffled by the scarf. On a surge of terror-driven strength, her left foot came free of the makeshift rope.

The killer glanced at her. For only a split second. It was enough; Jason had been feigning unconsciousness. He locked his hands together and drove straight up at the blond's chin. Kendall heard the blow as the man's head snapped back. Jason hit him again. Then again, this time from the side, still with the hammering force of both hands. The killer reeled to one side, off balance. In an instant Jason was out from under him.

Jason was on his knees, looking dazed as he gasped for air. Blood ran down the side of his face. The blond, barely three feet in front of her now, was weaving slightly, stunned by Jason's blows. But Kendall saw his right hand move, rather unsteadily, toward his left side.

The gun.

Kendall struggled and managed to free her right foot as well. It cost her; the chair slid up against the wall, pinning her still bound arms and hands in a painful trap. And the table was in front of her, too close, cramping her so that she couldn't maneuver her body to stand even if she could get free.

The blond reached under his jacket. She tried to scream a warning, but the gag nearly choked her. But as if he'd understood, Jason moved. He got his feet under him, and she could see that he was going to launch himself at the killer.

There was no time. Jason would die. Trying to rescue her.

She saw the glint of silver metal in the killer's hand. Desperately she leaned back in the chair and brought her feet up. With a strength driven by her terror for Jason, she shoved the table as hard as she could with both her feet. It caught the blond square in the back. He yelled, falling forward.

In the same instant Jason lunged at him. The gun went off. Kendall screamed as the shot echoed in the room. Both men went to the floor.

There was a shout from the open front door, but Kendall couldn't look away from the two men on the floor. Jason moved, rolling clear of the blond, and Kendall breathed again. Then he brought his knee down, hard, on the wrist of the hand that held the gun. Kendall could have sworn she heard the snapping of bone. The killer cursed, fervently. Then Jason had the gun in his hand.

"Son of a bitch."

George Alton's breathless voice rang with an odd reverence, and more than a touch of disappointment, apparently at having missed the fight. Kendall stared at him, realizing it must have been him she'd heard shout from behind the bathroom. He'd probably shoved the killer back through the window, she thought. And then had to run all the way back around the building, which would account for his breathlessness.

"My sentiments exactly," Jason said, his voice still sounding raspy. He stood up, slowly, then handed the gun rather gingerly to George, who took it with an easy familiarity. "Take him somewhere, will you?"

George nodded. "With pleasure," he said, training the weapon on the man with deadly efficiency. Kendall watched them go, trying to stop shaking. Then, stepping over the table she'd used as a weapon, Jason came to her, gently prying the scarf out of her mouth.

"God, Jason," she said.

"It's okay, honey," he said as he moved the chair out from the wall and began to untie her. "Thanks to you."

"I didn't know what else to do, I knew he had the gun, and I couldn't warn you, and he—"

"Sshhh," he said as he released the last bond and helped her stand. "It's all right. You did fine. You did great. I would have been dead if you hadn't hit him with that table. He would have had me dead center."

His arms came around her and she sagged against him. He held her close, and for the moment, just for the moment, she let him, and let herself believe.

"He was going to kill you," she said shakily.

"I know."

"Alice called him, and told him to—"

"I know."

She tilted her head back. "How . . . ?"

"Whitewood, believe it or not."

She stared at him. "Darren?"

"He decided to switch sides when he saw which way the wind was blowing."

"Oh."

She sighed. Her brief moment of illusion was over. She drew herself up, relieving him of any of her weight. It was time she got back to reality.

"Congratulations, Jason. It seems you got what you wanted."

He didn't let go of her. "I hope so. I hope it's not too late."

She drew back, giving him a puzzled look. "But he said you'd won—"

"I did. But not how you think."

"What do you mean?"

"I . . . gave it back to her."

Kendall's eyes widened. "What?"

Jason's mouth twisted, as if he were embarrassed. "I told her . . . what my position was. What I could do to Hawk. And her. And then . . . I didn't do it."

She stared at him. "You gave it back? To Alice?"

"I figured there's nothing on earth she'd hate more than being obligated . . . to me."

Kendall drew in a quick breath. She would never have expected Jason to see that. "You're right. She would hate that more than anything."

"So much she couldn't stand it. So she turned the beast loose. I'm sorry, Kendall. I should have realized she wouldn't take it and give up."

"That doesn't matter," Kendall said. "But . . . why? You worked all your life for this."

"I . . . couldn't do it. You were right. You were right about everything. There's so much more to the Hawks than just Aaron, and Hawk Industries. There's Joshua, and Jenna, and Matthew . . . all of them. They're the reason the Hawk line should go on."

Kendall went very still. "Go on?"

"I'm going to take the name, Kendall. Not for Aaron. But for Joshua. And all the others who fought for it, all those centuries."

"Jason—"

"Wait. Please. Let me get this out. I don't think I . . . have much longer."

So he was leaving. So much for her silly hopes. She lowered her gaze, unable to look at him. But it didn't seem to stop him from speaking.

"You were right about . . . me, too. It didn't matter that I'd never known my father, I was still just like him. I saw myself, winding up just like him. Like you said . . . dying cold and alone and full of regrets."

She did look at him then. And what she saw in his eyes stunned her; she'd never seen such raw emotional pain before.

"Jason," she began.

He shook his head. "Don't. Please. Let me . . ." He took a deep, shuddering breath. He swayed slightly, then steadied himself. "Tonight . . . at that board meeting . . . I just stood there, thinking about you, remembering you walking away from me . . . and how much I'd hurt you. I used you, and told myself I could walk away. I denied everything you made me feel, because . . . because I was too damned scared to admit it was real. I felt like that kid again, lost, in way over my head. God, I'm so sorry, Kendall."

She didn't want to hear this. Didn't want to hear him apologize and then walk away. But he wouldn't let her look away this time. This time he held her chin up with one hand, gently but inexorably. He'd apparently brushed at the cut on his cheek; his fingers were bloody.

"I think I understand my father a little now. I don't

think I can ever forgive him, but ... perhaps someday I'll thank him. If I learned the lesson he taught me in time."

"Lesson?"

"He lost the only woman he ever loved, because he didn't have the guts to do what it took to keep her. Well I do. What will it take, Kendall? I'd offer to give you Hawk, but I already gave it away. And you wouldn't take it anyway, would you? I've learned that much, at least."

"Jason," she said, her mind reeling at what he seemed to be saying.

"So what will it take? You want the chance to hurt me like I hurt you? I'll give it to you. You want me to tell you every day what a damned stupid fool I am? I'll do it. You want me to crawl? Beg? I'll do that, too. For years, if that's what it takes. I know I have a hell of a lot to make up for."

He swayed again, rather severely, and Kendall's brows lowered.

"Jason? What—"

"I think I'd better get this said," he muttered. "I love you."

Kendall gasped. Joy leapt in her, but it was a wary joy, uncertain; there had been far too many emotional ups and downs packed into the past few days for her to assume anything.

"I know you probably don't believe it," he said, his words seeming to come in a hurry now, "and I don't blame you ... but I do. And I have ... I think since that first time you faced me down." His mouth twisted. "Or since you made that awful Grimm joke, I'm not sure."

Despite herself, Kendall smiled.

"George ..." He faltered, and Kendall's smile faded as she noticed sweat beading up on his face. Was it that hard, to tell her this? "George seems to think you ... love me. I told him he was crazy, you couldn't. Not anymore. Not after I ... almost got you killed."

"After ... what? You didn't do this. Alice did."

He shook his head. "She wouldn't have even tried, if I hadn't ... used the will to distract her from what I was really doing."

"She would have," Kendall corrected him, "because I would have pursued the will whether you did or not."

For a long moment he just looked at her. That raw pain still showed in his eyes, but he was looking very strained as well, and almost frighteningly pale.

"Was he crazy, Kendall? When I called him for help, he said he would, but only for your sake . . . and because you'd be . . . unhappy if I ended up dead. I told him . . . you'd probably celebrate instead."

"Oh, Jason . . ."

He closed his eyes for a moment and seemed to wince. He wobbled on his feet, and Kendall at last began to realize that something was very wrong.

"Jason!"

His eyes snapped open. "I love you," he said again, urgently. And then he slid slowly down to the floor. And Kendall realized that the blood on his hand wasn't from his face at all, but from the spreading stain on his left side. And only then did she remember the shot.

"Yeah, he was pretty rough on you, girl. But no rougher than Aaron was, I don't think. And with a lot more justification. I believe he loves you. You're just going to have to teach him what that means. I don't think he's ever really known. Of course, I'm not telling you what to believe, just what I think."

Kendall looked at George and sighed. In an outpouring that had amazed her, she'd told the kindly man everything. Well, almost everything. She'd held back some of the more intimate details, but she got the feeling the man had guessed most of those, too.

"Besides," the man added, "he took that bullet because he thought it was your life that was in danger. And he wouldn't go down until he told you he loved you. That's a pretty explicit declaration, I'd say."

"I know."

"And if you'd heard him, when he called me . . . I tried to get him to wait until I got some help rounded up from the department, but he wasn't having any. He said it would take too damned long to convince them, and you could be dead by then. And that he wanted you alive to hate him."

Kendall blinked. "What?"

"You heard me. He said he loved you, but you hated him, but that was all right, as long as you were alive to do it."

God, that sounded so like Jason. She could almost hear it. She sank back in the hospital waiting-room chair, feeling like she'd been here for days. Charles Wellford had, thankfully, arrived from Berlin and taken all the loose ends out of her weary hands. They hadn't identified the killer yet, but they would, and Alice hadn't been arrested, but Wellford promised he'd see to it. George had put in a word with some friends to make sure Alice was watched, in case she tried to leave.

And Jason lay in that hospital room, with a bullet wound in his side, because he'd been afraid she'd be killed if he waited for help. Could there be, as George had said, a more explicit declaration of love?

She'd wondered if Jason could ever change, could ever learn to trust, to love. But he'd turned his back on what he'd planned for over half his life, because he'd come to believe she was right. He'd trusted in what she'd said. And changed because of it.

And he'd told her he loved her.

"Ms. Chase?" She looked up as the harried emergency-room nurse leaned into the room. "You can see him now," the young man said, pointing behind him. "He's in cubicle three."

"Thank you."

She followed the nurse's direction. The bed Jason was in was slightly raised, he was attached to a couple of monitors, and an IV ran down to his left arm. His eyes were closed, and she stood there for a moment, just looking at him. They'd told her the damage was relatively minor, all soft tissue, that it had been blood loss that had caused his collapse. And when the doctor had found out how long he'd been on his feet after he'd been shot, he had shaken his head, saying he hoped whatever he'd been doing was worth it.

Kendall very much hoped it had been.

His eyes fluttered open. The moment he focused on her face, hope flared in his eyes. She saw him fight to mask it, to hide it, and she reached out to touch his face as if she could stop him from trying to hide. He seemed startled, but turned his head slightly, toward her hand.

"Hi," she said.

"Hi." He sounded a little groggy, but his voice was a beautiful thing to her.

"The doctor says you're an idiot."

"He's right."

She smiled; she couldn't help it. "I brought you something."

He grimaced. "My walking papers?"

"No walking for you for a while," she said, her smile widening. "Here."

He looked at what she was holding out to him. His gaze went to her face. "Let me guess. It just ... showed up here, right?"

Kendall laughed, patting the cover of the book. "In the ambulance, actually. Fortunately, I saw it before the attendants did."

"Impeccable timing is a Hawk trait, it seems," Jason said. "Along with a few others I could have done without inheriting."

"There are a few admirable ones, too," Kendall said. "Worth passing on."

She held the book out to him. He took it with a hand that was surprisingly steady. But his eyes never left her face.

"I'd have to find a woman crazy enough to ... want to help me with that."

"Why don't you look in the book," she said softly, reaching out to open the cover. "You just might find her in there."

He lifted his other hand and closed the book. "I don't need to look. I've found her. I just don't know if she's crazy enough."

"Why don't you ask her?"

He took a deep breath and winced. He shut his eyes. For a long moment he didn't say anything. Then he whispered, "Because I'm afraid of the answer."

"You don't trust her, then."

His eyes flew open. "No! I mean ... yes. I do. I trust her. As much as I ... love her."

"That's all she needed to hear," Kendall whispered.

His eyes searched her face, as if he were still afraid to believe. "You ... mean it?"

"I love you, Jason. You're stubborn, you have a lot to learn about love and trust, and you're going to make my life crazy ... but I always hated being bored."

Jason swallowed heavily. "Then I'll have to make sure you never are."

"I'll hold you to that, Jason Hawk."

And this time, when she called him by the name he had once despised, Jason gave her a smile that made her melt inside. She bent to kiss him, and he lifted a hand to cup her face. And the book slipped to one side, falling open to the page chronicling the marriage of Jason Hawk and Kendall Chase.

And the not very startling observation that Hawks bred true.

EPILOGUE

~

"I think you need to look at this," Kendall said.

"Now?" Jason said in disbelief. He couldn't look at anything. He couldn't even move.

But then, he never could after his wife got through with him, and tonight had been no different than any night in the past year; the echoes of his explosive climax were still making him shudder. She'd told him he had a lot to learn, and she'd proceeded to teach him in very short order. And a lot of that teaching had been done right here, in this bed, where she'd shown him just how wrong he'd been all these years. Where she'd taught him to bare more than just his body to her; she'd taught him to bare his soul. And he'd learned that the more he gave, the more he got back; what Kendall gave him was more than he'd ever imagined possible.

"Yes, Jason," she said with a teasing laugh. "You need to look now."

He moved, paused to nuzzle her breast and press his lips to a nipple still taut from his earlier caresses, then managed to lift his head to look at her.

His eyes narrowed when he saw she was holding the book. He hadn't seen it in a while. They'd packed the book in with Kendall's belongings when she'd moved to Seattle, and he hadn't seen it again until the day they'd gotten married, when she had quietly brought it out to show him the now completed story, and that the skipped page before it was no longer empty. He hadn't been shocked at all at the picture, in the same style as all the others, that had appeared. He'd simply nodded, thinking it a perfect likeness of Kendall, who'd looked nothing short of radiantly beautiful that day, and shook his head in amazement over the image of himself, and how exactly it resembled that of Joshua Hawk.

He slowly reached to take the book from her now. It was odd, he thought, that he didn't feel that rush of warmth now when he touched it. Or perhaps not; perhaps it was that his life had changed from the cold, empty thing it had been, had become so warm, so comforting, so welcoming, that he didn't notice any difference anymore.

He ran his hand over the heavy leather binding. After the wedding, he hadn't looked at the book again until they'd moved into the island house they'd picked together, an expanse of wood and glass on the waterfront of Puget Sound, with a skyline view of the city. They'd put it on a shelf then, by itself except for their wedding photograph, not quite a shrine but close enough.

It was soon overlooked amid the joy they found in their new life together, the demands of Jason's business, and the pressure of Kendall running Hawk Industries until the board voted on a new CEO, since Alice had died of a heart attack shortly after being sentenced to prison for her attempt to purchase Jason's death. She'd tried to buy her way out of it by giving evidence against the man she'd hired, but he had already negotiated a deal that had gotten him reduced charges while sealing Alice's fate; Kendall remembered with grim acknowledgment what he'd said about what happened to employers who'd turned against him.

One thing Jason had learned early was that his wife rarely did anything without reason. So now he glanced from her face to the book, then back again.

"Why do I have to look at it now?"

"Because," she said softly, "pretty soon you won't be able to."

His forehead creased. "Won't be able—"

It hit him then, with the force of a blow. He stared at her for a long moment before he could get out a faint "Kendall?"

She smiled, a smile unlike any he'd ever seen from her before, a soft, warm, caressing smile that held all of her love and a world of promise. A smile that brought back what she'd once told him.

When the first child assures the continuation of the Hawk bloodline, the family tree records the birth, and the book vanishes. Until the next time there is only one Hawk left alive in the world.

"You ... we ... ?"

She nodded.

"Oh, God."

He'd wanted this so much he'd been afraid to admit it, afraid to even mention it. When their first anniversary had gone by, he'd almost resigned himself to the knowledge it wouldn't happen; they'd given up taking precautions months before. Kendall had merely said it would happen when he was ready, when he'd learned enough, and not before. She sounded utterly positive, as if she had some inside knowledge.

And perhaps she had, he thought now, glancing at the book.

"Better than a pregnancy test," she said cheerfully, as if she'd read his thoughts.

He found himself responding to her tone, grinning back at her. "I won't even ask if you're sure."

"It's never been wrong," she said, laying her hand atop his on the book. "Oh, and by the way, it's going to be a boy. Sorry if you wanted to be surprised."

A tiny flicker of regret nudged him, that there would be no gray-eyed little girl to watch grow up. At least, not yet. But then the joy bubbled through, and his grin widened. A son. A son who would be wanted and loved and encouraged. A son to be given what he'd never had, and what had been taken from Kendall far too soon.

"What shall we name him?" she asked.

Jason blinked. "Hey, I just found out he exists. Don't be asking me technical questions already."

Kendall giggled. He'd never imagined he would find something like that little sound so precious. But it was, as was everything about the woman who had changed his life, who had taken a man with a bitter heart and a soul of stone and shown him the way home.

"Unless," he said, turning his hands upward to capture hers, "you want to call him Aaron."

Kendall's eyes widened. "You . . . you would do that?"

He held her gaze, then nodded. "If you wanted it."

With an expression full of wonder, she reached out and brushed her fingers over the stubborn lock of hair that kicked forward over his forehead. "You have come a very long way, Mr. Hawk."

"You made me want to make the trip."

She blinked rapidly, and for a moment he thought she was going to cry. But then she smiled, a wide, loving smile that was so joyous it made him want to grab her and make long, sweet love to her all over again.

"I think I have a better name for your son," she said softly.

"What?" he asked.

"Joshua."

Jason stopped breathing for a moment. The rightness of it, the perfection of it, hit him instantly. He hauled Kendall into his arms, trying to show her with a shower of kisses and hugs what he couldn't get past the lump in his throat.

And for an instant, in some tiny corner of his mind that wasn't completely eclipsed by the feel of his wife in his arms, a vivid image of Joshua Hawk appeared. Gone was the rueful understanding in his eyes, missing was the quiet, supportive empathy.

Joshua Hawk was laughing.

BREATHTAKING ROMANCES YOU WON'T WANT TO MISS

WE NEED YOUR HELP
To continue to bring you quality romance
that meets your personal expectations,
we at TOPAZ books want to hear from you.
Help us by filling out this questionnaire, and in exchange
we will give you a **free gift** as a token of our gratitude.

- Is this the first TOPAZ book you've purchased? (circle one)

    YES   NO

    The title and author of this book is: _____

- If this was not the first TOPAZ book you've purchased, how many have you bought in the past year?

    a: 0 - 5   b 6 - 10   c: more than 10   d: more than 20

- How many romances in total did you buy in the past year?

    a: 0 - 5   b: 6 - 10   c: more than 10   d: more than 20 ____

- How would you rate your overall satisfaction with this book?

    a: Excellent   b: Good   c: Fair   d: Poor

- What was the main reason you bought this book?

    a: It is a TOPAZ novel, and I know that TOPAZ stands
       for quality romance fiction
    b: I liked the cover
    c: The story-line intrigued me
    d: I love this author
    e: I really liked the setting
    f: I love the cover models
    g: Other: _____

- Where did you buy this TOPAZ novel?

    a: Bookstore   b: Airport   c: Warehouse Club
    d: Department Store   e: Supermarket   f: Drugstore
    g: Other: _____

- Did you pay the full cover price for this TOPAZ novel? (circle one)

    YES   NO

    If you did not, what price did you pay? _____

- Who are your favorite TOPAZ authors? (Please list)

- How did you first hear about TOPAZ books?

    a: I saw the books in a bookstore
    b: I saw the TOPAZ Man on TV or at a signing
    c: A friend told me about TOPAZ
    d: I saw an advertisement in_____magazine
    e: Other: _____

- What type of romance do you generally prefer?

    a: Historical   b: Contemporary
    c: Romantic Suspense   d: Paranormal (time travel,
       futuristic, vampires, ghosts, warlocks, etc.)
    d: Regency   e: Other: _____

- What historical settings do you prefer?

    a: England   b: Regency England   c: Scotland
    e: Ireland   f: America   g: Western Americana
    h: American Indian   i: Other: _____

- What type of story do you prefer?
  - a: Very sexy
  - b: Sweet, less explicit
  - c: Light and humorous
  - d: More emotionally intense
  - e: Dealing with darker issues
  - f: Other

- What kind of covers do you prefer?
  - a: Illustrating both hero and heroine
  - b: Hero alone
  - c: No people (art only)
  - d: Other_____

- What other genres do you like to read (circle all that apply)

  Mystery Medical Thrillers Science Fiction
  Suspense Fantasy Self-help
  Classics General Fiction Legal Thrillers
  Historical Fiction

- Who is your favorite author, and why?_____
  _____

- What magazines do you like to read? (circle all that apply)
  - a: *People*
  - b: *Time/Newsweek*
  - c: *Entertainment Weekly*
  - d: *Romantic Times*
  - e: *Star*
  - f: *National Enquirer*
  - g: *Cosmopolitan*
  - h: *Woman's Day*
  - i: *Ladies' Home Journal*
  - j: *Redbook*
  - k: Other:_____

- In which region of the United States do you reside?
  - a: Northeast
  - b: Midatlantic
  - c: South
  - d: Midwest
  - e: Mountain
  - f: Southwest
  - g: Pacific Coast

- What is your age group/sex? a: Female b: Male
  - a: under 18
  - b: 19-25
  - c: 26-30
  - d: 31-35
  - e: 56-60
  - f: 41-45
  - g: 46-50
  - h: 51-55
  - i: 56-60
  - j: Over 60

- What is your marital status?
  - a: Married
  - b: Single
  - c: No longer married

- What is your current level of education?
  - a: High school
  - b: College Degree
  - c: Graduate Degree
  - d: Other:_____

- Do you receive the TOPAZ *Romantic Liaisons* newsletter, a quarterly newsletter with the latest information on Topaz books and authors?

  YES   NO

  If not, would you like to? YES NO

  Fill in the address where you would like your free gift to be sent:

  Name: _____
  Address: _____
  City:_____ Zip Code: _____

  You should receive your free gift in 6 to 8 weeks.
  Please send the completed survey to:

  Penguin USA•Mass Market
  Dept. TS
  375 Hudson St.
  New York, NY 10014